Whispering Oaks

D0872559

A Novel by Liz L. Alexander and

Date: 10/31/16

LAC FIC ALEXANDER
Alexander, Liz L.,
Whispering oaks :a novel /

Milldara, Inc.

Publisher

PALM BEACH COUNTY
LIBRARY SYSTEM
3650 SUMMIT BLVD.
WEST PALM BEACH, FL 33406

This book is entirely a work of fiction. The names, characters, places, and incidents depicted are either products of the authors' imagination or are used fictitiously. Any resemblance to actual events or locales or persons, living or dead, is entirely coincidental.

Copyright © 2012 by Elizabeth Laquidara and Jean M. Bratcher

All rights reserved, including the right to reproduce this book or portions thereof in any form whatsoever.

For information about this book go to **www.MilldaraInc.com** or write Milldara, Inc. at 7050 W Palmetto Park Rd, Suite 15-294, Boca Raton, FL 33433.

Original copyright © 2005 by Elizabeth Laquidara and Jean M. Bratcher

Digital ISBN 978-0-9838613-2-4
Paperback ISBN 978-0-9838613-3-1

The cover art has been obtained as a royalty-free license and the content does not infringe any copyright, moral right, trademark or other intellectual property right or violate any right of privacy or publicity.

ACKNOWLEDGEMENTS

We would like to thank the dear friends who read the early version of this book and offered us both criticism and encouragement. Without their help we would have been lost. In particular we owe a great deal of gratitude to Tom Laquidara. Tom, sorry we didn't rip any bodices for you, but your input has certainly earned you a lot of positive karma for your next life. We also want to thank Tom Miller for the cover art work.

Peter walked Jillian to her door. After having slow danced, it seemed natural when he took her in his arms. The kiss was slow and gentle. As Jillian closed the door, she smiled happily. There were no chills, no tingling, but a warm pleasant contentment filled her. She reflected how it might be better if there were no chills, at least for now. Her visceral responses to Drake had interfered with her judgment from the beginning. She had mistaken the chills, the tingling, and the sense of familiarity for passion when, in reality, it had only been recognition and recall. It was nice to have someone she felt comfortable with in her life again, but not taking over her life. It was pleasant to converse, knowing that her words as well as her body were appreciated.

Still smiling and humming one of the slow songs from the evening, she turned off the lights and headed to bed. She knew that she was now ready to face the future that would find her and that she would shape. She didn't need to rescue anyone any longer. At last, she was free to be herself and to grow as a person. Life looked very appealing to Jillian for the first time in many years. As she curled up in bed, snuggling against her pillows, she sighed with contentment and with a sense of happiness that had been long delayed.

Images from her past drifted through her mind, memories of the early years with Drake, while they were still in college and so full of high expectations for the future. He seemed so alive and promising then. She had been ready to tie her life to his, knowing that together they would accomplish amazing things. But that excitement had faded as Drake showed her his weaker, more vulnerable side over and over again. She saw a little boy, hurt by life; a man fearing his dreams would never come true. Jillian knew she could help him. She could rescue him from drowning in his insecurities. Refusing to heed the warnings of her family and friends, she had married Drake and then spent so many years trying futilely to save him from his path of self-destruction. It had taken quite an unexpected journey to allow her to see what she was doing to herself and why, but at last she had been freed from the wheel of repetition. She was moving on, growing, and she liked what she was learning about herself. *Yes, life is good*, she muttered as she drifted off into sleep with a smile still on her face.

CHAPTER 1

Night, after night, after night, Jillian White Harris ate chocolate chip cookies and watched whatever was on TV, drowning out her thoughts and fears. She never expected life would come to this. She had been sure that marrying Drake Harris would be wonderful, but instead she found herself lonely. She had gained thirty pounds since they'd married four years ago. She no longer tried to watch what she ate or to exercise. Her whole focus was on Drake and making him happy.

It was 10:00 PM when the phone rang. She jumped, thinking, hoping it was Drake saying he would be home soon. But it was only Anna. With disappointment in her voice, she asked her friend what she wanted. Anna stated, "John and I are having a cookout Sunday. Would you and Drake be able to come?"

"I'll have to talk to Drake when he gets home and let you know," she responded.

"He's still not home? It's a Tuesday. Jillian...is he drinking more?" Jillian heard the disapproval in Anna's voice and cringed. She hated letting anyone else suspect there might be a problem. Drake was her husband and her responsibility.

"He's working hard. This new job of his keeps him out late." Jillian was defensive, trying to hide her anger.

"When did he start this job?" Anna asked, trying to defuse Jillian's irritation.

"Last week. He really thinks it will work out this time." Jillian had her doubts, but was not about to admit them to Anna. It was the sixth job he'd had since they married.

"What's he doing? Still sales? He can talk anyone into anything when he puts on the charm." Anna continued to try to appease her friend, recognizing that she might have crossed a line earlier.

"He's doing marketing. He's sure that he'll make it big at this company. He's never done telemarketing before, but I know he'll be good at it." Jillian believed that Drake could sell anything. He just needed to "settle down." She was sure that once they had children, he would find enough reason to give up his restlessness. However, she had felt that once they were married, he would have taken more responsibility. "I hear his car. He must be hungry. I'd better go. I'll call you tomorrow." She hurried to replace the receiver before Drake came in.

Drake stumbled in with a big grin on his face. "I made a big sale this afternoon!" he announced, leaning on the doorframe.

"That's great!" Jillian smiled broadly and cocked her head, looking more closely at him. Her smile didn't reach her eyes, which reflected her anxiety and frustration. "Are you hungry?" she asked, lifting herself from the couch. She stood with her arms crossed, her hands stroking her sides, unconsciously comforting herself.

"No, we went out to celebrate and I had something." He threw his keys down on the table and moved toward her, still smiling.

Holding in her anger, she enquired, "What time did you leave the office?"

"Oh, about five; maybe it was four." He shrugged, starting to get annoyed. "You're not going to give me a hard time. Can't you just be happy for me? You always do this, and then you wonder why I stay out with the guys." He turned around and headed into the bedroom.

Jillian ran after him. "I'm sorry. I know you work hard and I really am happy for you. It's just that...I thought we could have a romantic evening." She reached out to him, putting her hand on his arm and looking up at him invitingly.

He turned to her, smiling lasciviously, "Let's go to bed." Drake reached for her, pulling her close enough that she could smell the beer on his breath.

She turned away from him, wishing he weren't drunk, but determined to make the best of it. "I'll turn off the lights, set up the coffee for morning, and be right back." She hurried out of the room to close down the house for the night, turning off the TV, setting up the coffee, starting the dishwasher, and turning out the lights. When she got back to the bedroom, she found Drake half undressed, on top of the covers, snoring loudly. She went into the bathroom; looking into the mirror as she washed her face, she started to cry.

It had been happening more and more often. Drake would come home drunk, they'd argue, and he would pass out. Jillian lay in bed trying to go to sleep. She knew if she could make him happy he wouldn't need to drink. He would want to come home and be with her. Maybe once they had children, he'd change; he was a good man and wanted a family, too. He was just getting the wildness out of his system before he had the added responsibility. After all, he was only twenty-seven.

CHAPTER 2

Jillian was up early, had read most of the business section of the Cincinnati Enquirer, and had two cups of coffee before trying to wake Drake. She knew that it wasn't going to be an easy task, nor would his mood be pleasant. After calling him every five or ten minutes for nearly an hour, he appeared in the kitchen. She silently handed him a cup of coffee. She was beginning to feel more like his mother than his wife. She wondered if her mother felt the same way when she pampered her father. She watched his six-foot frame slumping over his coffee; his straight, dirty blond hair was hiding his blood shot, brown eyes. *At least, Dad was never hung over.*

"Anna and John have invited us over on Sunday. Is it okay with you?" She tried to keep her tone light. She didn't want another fight this morning.

"Do you have to bother me with this now?" He slurped his coffee noisily and tried to focus on the sports section.

"I want to be able to give her an answer today," Jillian explained apologetically.

"Tell them we'll bring the beer. They never have enough of anything. Happy?" His sarcasm was palpable.

Jillian kissed him on the cheek, noticing he still smelled like beer. "Thank you. I need to get dressed. I have to get to work early today."

Jillian liked her job and felt she was good at it. When she graduated from the University of Cincinnati with a Bachelor's Degree in Business Administration, she would have been happy to get anything to pay the bills and student loans. But this was a great job, managing some small accounts for the bank. She really felt appreciated and everyone seemed to like her. She was able to step through the door at Midwest Bank and forget the rest of her life. Jillian was efficient and kept busy, but her social life at work was the best. She knew she did an excellent job at whatever her bosses threw at her, but it was more important to her to know that people wanted to be with her. She always took on the planning and arranging for all the birthdays, anniversaries, and showers. No one got away without a celebration, a card, and a cake in the coffee room. Jillian made sure everyone was recognized, and her co-workers had come to count on her to take care of these things. She put a lot of pressure on herself to please everyone. If someone was disappointed, she would apologize for a week.

Jillian home early that morning to pick up donut holes on the way to work. There was a 9:00 meeting and she wanted to have a treat and have the coffee made on time. It wasn't her job or responsibility, but she knew it would make everyone feel better and she reasoned that if people were happy with her, they would want to be around her. She'd been told it was an important meeting, but her supervisor, Jerry Green, had been tight lipped. She had no idea what was on the agenda. Not knowing what to expect always made her uncomfortable. She hoped she hadn't disappointed anyone.

Jillian put on her best face as she entered the conference room. She was unaware that, at twenty-six, her youth and femininity gave the room a breath of fresh air. She wore a plain, short sleeved, beige dress that went just below the knee and beige heels adding two inches to her height of 5'6". Her dark brown hair was nearly straight, falling over her shoulders, and her makeup was impeccable, enhancing her green eyes. Nonetheless, she felt self-conscious. She'd put on twenty pounds in the past year alone, and couldn't wear any of her business suits. She did not intend to buy a size fourteen; it would just be giving in to Drake's accusations that she was fat and would never take off the weight. Besides, she wasn't comfortable spending money on herself.

As Jillian watched the meeting participants enter the room, she decided that her supervisor had made a mistake. She wasn't supposed to be there. Mr. Johnson, Mr. Rhodes, Ms. Philips, and Mr. Campbell, all company Vice Presidents, were helping themselves to the coffee and donuts she'd set up. When Phil Grey, the CFO, walked in, Jillian attempted to make a quick exit. However, Jerry called her over, indicating the chair next to his. Once everyone, fifteen in all, was settled at the table, Phil Grey called the meeting to order. He announced that the company was opening two new executive offices: one in San Francisco and the other in Savannah. Mr. Rhodes would be moving to San Francisco and Mr. Johnson to Savannah. He continued announcing the changes. Jillian still couldn't understand why she was there. Then she heard that Jerry was being promoted to Vice-President of Contracts, Mergers, and Acquisitions and moving up to the CFO's floor and she would be accompanying him as his assistant. She was shocked. She couldn't believe her ears. She was being promoted to an assistant to a VP. Next Monday, she'd be moving her office to the seventh floor.

Once the meeting ended, Jillian excitedly ran to her office to call Drake and share the good news. She had already memorized his new work number. "I'd like to speak to Drake Harris, please!"

"Mr. Harris is not in today. May I take a message?" a woman's voice responded.

"Uh, no, thank you." She quickly hung up, sinking into her chair, deflated. She tried calling home, but the voice-mail picked up. She didn't bother to call his cell-phone, knowing he wouldn't answer. She wanted to run home, but she knew she couldn't. She sat there fuming until Jerry walked in smiling. Quickly hiding her feelings, she smiled broadly. "Congratulations and thank you. I'm so excited." She wore a frozen smile the rest of the day. Her peers always knew she was slated for bigger things. When her co-workers offered to take her out after work to celebrate, she turned them down. She stated, "I want to see Drake and tell him face to face." She wasn't about to tell anyone that she hadn't been able to find him.

Jillian rushed home to their Price Hill apartment, but Drake wasn't there. She called Anna to share her news and tell her they'd be there Sunday.

Anna responded as any good friend would. "That's wonderful. You deserve it. I'm so happy for you." Then she asked, "What did Drake say?"

"I didn't call him yet. I want to see his face. I'll tell him as soon as he gets home from work." As it fell out of her mouth, Jillian couldn't believe she had just deliberately lied to her best friend. She quickly cut the conversation short and hung up.

Jillian skipped dinner and sat frozen in front of the TV with a box of crackers and a cup of tea, waiting. Drake walked in at 8:00. "What's for dinner?" He plopped down on the couch and put his feet up.

"Where have you been?" Jillian demanded, the cracker she was about to bite into still half way to her mouth. She glared at her husband, knowing he had to be drunk again.

"Work! Where else?" Rising from the couch he walked to the kitchen, and then popped open a beer as he walked back to the living room.

"I called. You weren't there."

"I had a dentist appointment." He turned on her. "You shouldn't be calling my work. I haven't been there very long. That's just what I need; you'll cost me this job, too. What will they think when my own wife doesn't remember I have a doctor's appointment?" He dropped back down onto the couch, gulping down his beer and staring at the TV. His facial expression was the epitome of righteous indignation.

"I'm sorry," she apologized uncertainly, choosing to ignore the contradiction, rationalizing that maybe she had forgotten in her excitement. "What do you want for dinner?"

"You think you can give up your crackers and get off the couch to make something?" he sneered.

Jillian headed into the kitchen and opened the refrigerator. She started pulling things out, determined to make him happy with her.

When they finally sat down to eat, Jillian shared her news. Drake's only response was, "That's nice." She wasn't sure he had heard her as he continued to watch the TV through the doorway into the living room.

Jillian said nothing more about the promotion nor did she mention the raise she'd probably get. At first, she was hurt that he hadn't been happier for her. He was so selfish. But then it occurred to her that her successes might only make him feel worse. Thinking about this possibility, she felt guilty. She was the one who was being selfish. He already felt bad that she'd completed her bachelors and he'd dropped out after his third year. She'd have to remember not to talk about her work with him.

CHAPTER 3

Anna and John's house was in Western Hills, only a fifteen minute drive. Drake was in a good mood Sunday afternoon and Jillian was looking forward to time with her friends. There were three other couples, making for a pleasant group of ten, plus two infants. They had all been friends since college. The guys seemed to congregate near the barbeque, each with his own idea of the best way to cook the chicken. They were laughing and joking. As Jillian looked over, Drake seemed to be holding the men's attention. She was pleased that he was getting the attention she felt he deserved. He'd always been popular and the life of the party. It gave her a warm feeling to hear him laugh; it was what had attracted her to him when they first met, and of course, his eyes when they were laughing, too.

Jillian helped Anna carry dishes from the kitchen to the tables in the back yard, and then joined Marie, Sally, and Peggy. Marie's little girl was nine months old and sitting on a blanket playing; Sally's baby girl was only two months old and Peggy was holding her. It was late August and they hadn't been together as a group since Memorial Day. They had a lot of catching up to do. When the men joined them with the chicken, they were still involved. The conversation turned to work and Anna prompted, "Jillian, tell us about your promotion."

"It's nothing, really. It had nothing to do with me. My supervisor was promoted and I'll be moving up, too." She glanced at Drake. "It's really Jerry's promotion, not mine. But Drake has a new job. Drake, tell them about your new job." She looked at her husband who was sipping his beer and looking bored. When the group's attention returned to him, he became animated again.

"It's early to say. I've only been there two weeks, but it's looking good. I've already made some big sales. It's got a lot of potential," he stated, biting into a crispy chicken thigh.

"I know Drake's just going to dazzle them." Jillian smiled, looking around the table as she passed potato salad and ears of corn.

"What are you selling?" John asked, settling next to his wife at the table.

"Long lasting, energy saving, light bulbs. They're really a big item in large office buildings, warehouses, and manufacturing plants. They're expensive, but they'll pay for themselves and save thousands in labor and energy costs," Drake explained, adding, "We ship them all over the world."

"Sounds good, with energy costs what they are these days," George, Sally's husband, commented. "E-mail me some info at the office tomorrow."

"What do you want it for?" John asked, surprised.

"I have a friend in purchasing. I'll pass it on," George explained, licking barbeque sauce from his fingers.

"Thanks, George." Drake got up to get another beer.

Jillian was trying not to count the number of trips Drake was making to the cooler, but she couldn't help noticing that he was starting to get louder. "You guys did a great job with the chicken. Drake, don't you want some more? The potato salad is excellent." She started putting more on Drake's plate. He waved his hand at her dismissively as he reached the beer cooler and fished out another bottle.

Feeling the tension starting to rise, Anna jumped in. "Anyone else want seconds? There's plenty here."

George and Tom held up their plates. Sally stated, "I don't dare. I still have to lose the weight I gained while I was pregnant." The tension eased. However, the beers kept coming.

When Sally's baby started to cry, Jillian said, "I'll get her." She picked her up out of her seat and held her close, gently swaying from side to side. The baby quieted almost immediately. Jillian started cooing to her as she walked over, sitting down next to Drake. "Isn't she beautiful?"

Drake shot her a cold look and took another swig of his beer.

Jillian leaned in towards him and whispered, "Maybe with your new job, we'll be able to start trying for our own?"

He looked at her angrily and loudly stated, "Don't start! Aren't you getting fat enough? Or are you looking for an excuse to be a bigger pig?" He pushed himself up out of the chair and stomped off.

The baby started crying at the sound of the loud outburst. Jillian, red faced, got up, walked away with the infant trying to calm her. She was relieved for the excuse to leave the group. It gave her a chance to swallow her tears and anger before facing any of them. She murmured soothing words to the baby about how "the big man didn't mean to scare" her.

After a few minutes, Sally picked up the diaper bag and approached Jillian. "Come on. Let's go inside and change her. She must be wet by now."

Once inside, neither woman said anything as Sally set out the supplies on the bed and started to change the little girl. Finally, she couldn't hold it in any longer. "Jillian, why do you put up with him?"

Jillian shrugged, looking down so that she wouldn't have to meet Sally's eyes. "He's right. I have been putting on weight."

Picking up the freshly diapered baby, Sally reached out to her friend. "You look great. You may have put on a few pounds, but he has no right calling you a pig." Sally was getting angrier just thinking about Drake's behavior. "And in front of all of us, too."

"He didn't mean anything by it. But he's right. It seems as though I'm always stuffing something in my mouth." Jillian leaned back against the dresser to put a little distance between them. She wrapped her arms around herself protectively.

"Jillian, stop defending him! I don't understand what you see in him!" She frowned in disapproval. "I never did. Even in college he was drunk most of the time."

"Sally, he's a good man. From the first day I met him and heard him laugh and looked into his eyes, I knew we were meant for each other."

"Yes, he can be charming and he makes us all laugh, but really! What else has he done for you?" She looked up at her friend, shaking her head.

"I owe him. Don't forget, he worked while I finished school; he didn't get to finish." Jillian dropped her arms to her side, clenching her fists. Without realizing it, she was preparing to battle her friend.

"Not finishing had nothing to do with you. I was there, too. Remember? His grades weren't good. He kept skipping classes. Then you two got married so fast. He could have waited. Drake was glad for an excuse to quit school. I don't know why you were in such a rush, running off like that as soon as he asked."

"Sally, I don't want to argue with you. He's my husband and you need to respect that. You've never heard me say anything about George, have you?" Jillian was trying not to get angry with her friend, but having a hard time holding back.

Jillian walked to the bed and picked up the wet diaper. She walked into the bathroom and disposed of it.

"At least, George can keep a job and doesn't insult me in front of my friends. Yeah, he was wild in college, too. But he managed to finish and didn't become a drunk! ...I'm sorry, Jillian. ...Maybe we should change the subject."

"Maybe we should," Jillian responded coolly.

The two women returned to the group outside. It was obvious to anyone who cared to notice that neither was happy. Sally sat holding the baby. Jillian sat on the ground and played with Marie's little girl. Drake was entertaining the rest of the group. His jokes were getting louder and rowdier. However, no one seemed to mind. They just laughed the harder.

Jillian held her breath all the way home in the car. She knew he was in no condition to be driving, but she wasn't going to cause a scene in front of their friends. She played the conversation with Sally over and over in her mind. It was bad enough having Drake ruin the day, she was getting used to that, but Sally didn't have to add to it.

"What's wrong with you? You're awfully quiet." Drake asked, sounding defensive. "Usually, you're babbling at me about one thing or another." He seemed   to   be   waiting   for   her   to   start   in   on   him.
"I was thinking about Sally." Jillian wasn't sure she wanted to share that conversation with him. She knew he'd be angry and she didn't know what he might do the next time they were with Sally and George.

"What's her problem?" he questioned sourly.

"I don't know. Maybe she's not sleeping enough with the new baby. I didn't realize she could be so nasty." Jillian's lip trembled, near to tears from the betrayal.

"What did she say to you?" Drake asked, only mildly interested, thinking it involved children.

"It doesn't really matter." She turned her head and stared out the window at the dark landscape passing by. Drake let it drop, not particularly interested in any of her friends.

CHAPTER 4

Monday morning, Jillian moved her personal things from the third floor to the seventh floor. The day was filled with meetings, as was the next and the next. Each night she rushed home, wanting to be there when Drake arrived. She wanted desperately to share her excitement with him, but promised herself that she was not going to make him feel worse by her success. She dutifully prepared dinner, and then waited for him to show up. She was relieved when he arrived at a reasonable hour and hadn't been drinking. Jillian thought, *At last, he's settling down. Things are getting better for him. He's succeeding and feels better.* She allowed herself to breathe a sigh of relief. Sally was way off base. It wasn't as if he drank like his brother or father. Things were going to get better; she just knew it.

Thursday, Jillian followed her routine; only...Drake was late in coming home. When she heard the key in the door, her emotions went from worry, to relief, to anger. "Where have you been? I've been keeping dinner warm. It's dried up by now." She sat forward on the couch, ready to jump up and engage in an argument.

"I'm sure it's fine. Let's eat," he demanded, walking to the kitchen and opening the refrigerator. He emerged with his usual beer in hand. "Were you paid today? I don't get my commissions until the fifth of the month. I'm a little short." Jillian followed him into the kitchen.

"Yes, I got paid." She was trying to get the overcooked food out so they could eat. She was still irritated with him. She didn't want to hear his usual excuse for taking money from her. She had to budget their money in order to pay the bills.

"How much is your raise?" Drake asked, trying to sound casual about the question.

"I don't know yet." She put dinner plates and silverware on the table.

"You don't know?" He asked incredulously, starting to get loud. "You didn't ask?"

"Don't get angry. I don't think it will be much. I'm still really just Jerry's assistant. I don't have a lot of contracts of my own yet."

"I can't believe you didn't ask. If you don't start paying more attention to these things, we'll never get a place of our own." He sat down at the table and waited for Jillian to serve him.

"You're the one asking me for money. Where'd all your cash go? No, don't tell me. You drank it." She plopped the plate of food in front of him, glaring at him as she did so.

"I haven't had anything all week and this is the last beer in the house." Putting out his hand, he demanded, "Give me twenty bucks." He rolled his fingers, commanding.

"No! I'm going to the market tomorrow. I need that money to buy groceries."

Banging his empty beer bottle down on the table, he barked, "Where's your purse?" When she didn't respond, Drake got up from the table and went looking for it.

Breathing heavily in her anger, Jillian ignored him. She bit her lip and started dishing out her own dinner. She heard him throw her purse down, and then the front door slammed. She took her plate to the couch, turned on the TV, and swallowed her tears along with her food. It was nearly midnight when she went to bed. He still hadn't returned. Sometime during the night, she heard him stumbling around, but pretended she was still asleep.

Friday seemed like a wasted day at work. Many people had taken the day off to extend the long weekend. She wasn't looking forward to it. Labor Day signaled the end of summer. She and Drake were planning to go to Riverfest and were expected to attend her family's annual reunion at her parents' home in Springdale. Usually, she enjoyed these gatherings. Everyone had moved all over the country, but nearly all her cousins made it in for the long weekend. Drake had always been entertaining and was well liked by her cousins, but after last weekend, she wasn't so sure how things would go. There weren't any big drinkers in her family, and no one had much patience for anyone who made a fool of themselves because they were drunk. She was afraid he might embarrass her.

Jillian stopped at the market on her way home. She stared at the beer for a long time, reached for a twelve pack, and then put it back. She continued with her shopping. After waiting fifteen minutes in line, she decided to go back and get at least one six-pack. Back in line, she had another long wait. Fridays were always crowded at Kroger's, but before a holiday weekend, it was packed. She stood in line thinking, *He probably won't even appreciate that I'm standing here doing this for him.* She finally got to the register and opened her wallet, planning to pay cash. After checking on line that her pay had been electronically deposited, she had taken $200 out. She had wanted to have enough for groceries and the long weekend. There was $20 in her wallet. She couldn't use her ATM card, if she did, she wouldn't have enough for all their bills. She'd either have to leave the groceries or use a credit card. She couldn't face the clerk nor have others see her leave without the groceries. She used her credit card; it went against everything she believed about fiscal responsibility.

As she drove home, she was fuming. He took $180; she barely had enough gas to get to her parents. Tuesday was the fifth; Drake had better get his commission check. No one on the seventh floor brought their own lunch. She'd feel humiliated when she had to eat in the office. It was two weeks before she would be paid again, plus she'd need more gas. She was not dipping into savings or using the credit card again. She wanted to see him immediately; she wanted to scream. Another part of her never wanted to see him again. But then she'd be alone. *Oh, God! Not that!_* She never could stand being alone. She'd have to calm down before she saw him or he'd just leave the house. She was always afraid he wouldn't come back after they fought or that something terrible would happen to him. The thought gave her terrible feelings of guilt.

Jillian put the groceries away and sat on the couch to wait. She turned on the TV, but paid no attention to what was on. She needed the background sound to not feel alone. She was emotionally drained, having been through a wide range of emotions over the course of the week. She fell asleep on the couch before Drake returned home. She woke at 4:00 AM. The TV and the lights were still on. She turned them off and headed for the bedroom. Drake was lying across the bed half undressed. She quietly picked up his jacket and pants to hang them up. As she did, it occurred to her to check his pockets for money. There were nine dollars, some change and two lottery tickets; nothing more. She kept the five and put the rest back, counting on him not remembering. She went back to the couch, hoping to fall back to sleep. She lay there with thoughts swirling, wishing she could talk to someone, but her friends were all against him already. She wished Drake would stop drinking. She was having trouble believing what she had been telling everyone else. She feared her life would never change. The one thing she was sure of was that she would not leave him. He needed her; he'd always needed her. As long as she took good care of him, he would never leave and she'd never have to be alone.

She finally gave up on sleep and started her weekend cleaning. What else was there for her to do? She saved the vacuuming for last. She didn't want to wake him. However, a part of her wanted to vacuum under the bed. At 2:00 PM, he still wasn't up. She started feeling sorry for herself. She couldn't even rent a movie and didn't want to use her gas to go anywhere. She tried reading, but couldn't concentrate.

Finally, she heard the shower running. Her anger started to bubble up again. She sat on the couch, arms folded, waiting for him to show himself. Drake came up behind her, wrapping his arms around her and kissed the back of her neck. She did not respond. "I think we're over due on celebrating your promotion. I am really proud of you. I'm going to take you out tonight."

"And how do you expect to do that? You went through all of our money!" She was seething.

"Don't get upset. I'll put it on my credit card. I'm taking you out. You deserve it. And I have a big check coming Tuesday. I'll be able to pay it off and pay you back, too." He kissed her neck and tousled her hair. "You know I need you."

Jillian felt herself melt. She reached up and rubbed his arm. "Okay, where are we going?"

"I'll make reservations at La Petite Maison, and then we'll go dancing." He hugged her tightly, kissing the top of her head. "How does that sound?"

"La Petite Maison is too expensive!" Jillian protested.

"Nothing is too good for my little magnolia! You've worked hard and I've put you through a lot. We both need this. Besides, it's been too long since I romanced you. This is just what we both need...an incredible dinner and some waltzing with my love in my arms." Jillian's heart swelled with the joy of his words to her. He loved her and wanted her. If only her friends and family could see this Drake, they'd understand why she loved him.

Drake was able to get reservations for 8:00. He was lucky, on a holiday weekend they weren't as busy as they usually would be on a Saturday night. In fact, somehow he always seemed to pull out of bad situations at the last minute.

Jillian started going through her closet trying to find something that fit. She wanted to look enticing. She wanted Drake to be proud of her. She promised herself that after the weekend, she would go on a strict diet. She would loose the weight for Drake.

Drake opened the car door for her and bowed dramatically. Jillian smiled at him and dropped a curtsy before she climbed into the car. She couldn't get over how attractive her husband could be when he dressed up. His dark gray suit looked so good on him. She always appreciated the little things he did; he could be such a gentleman. They arrived at La Petite Maison; having no cash for valet parking, Drake looked for a parking place on the street. The maitre d' sat them at a small table along the wall and Drake immediately ordered champagne. Jillian was about to object when Drake looked at her and stated, "This is a celebration. You've worked hard for this and you deserve it."

Jillian looked around the dimly lit restaurant at the tables glistening in the candlelight, the white linen tablecloths and fine china and silver giving off an air of luxury. She sniffed the fresh flower spray on their table. Jillian sipped her champagne and looked over the menu. Drake insisted they take the seven-course Chef Tasting Menu. She had to admit that it would have been difficult choosing only three. Jillian decided she had to have the chocolate soufflé for dessert. Since each course had been accompanied by the appropriate wines, Jillian was concerned that Drake would be too drunk to go dancing after dinner. However, after he finished his Grand Marnier Soufflé, he stated that he looked forward to working off some of the food. Jillian was relieved that he was still in good spirits and gladly left the restaurant with him.

During the thirty-minute drive north on I-75 to Sharonville, Jillian and Drake joked about how they would both be waddling around the floor while dancing. Jillian reached over to stroke her husband's arm. "It's been a lovely evening so far, Drake. Thank you so much. I couldn't have asked for a better dinner. I don't care if we do waddle instead of waltzing tonight. It's all been so wonderful! I love you so much."

Smiling, Drake reached over and patted her knee. "You're my sweet magnolia and I'm your beau. You should be treated like a queen. When I bring in some more of these big accounts, we can start making plans for a house of our own. It's just around the bend for us, Sugar."

"I know it is, Drake. I have faith in you. Our future is going to be wonderful." Jillian smiled out the window, visualizing their big house overflowing with children and happiness.

As they entered the Tri-County Dance Club, they heard the strains of a waltz just beginning. There were at least twenty couples already on the floor, swirling in unison with the music. Drake took Jillian's hand and led her out onto the floor. They began the rhythmic swaying and spinning of the waltz. Jillian felt as if she were floating or flying. It had been so long since she had felt this happy. *Thank you, God, for this moment and for this man that I love so much it hurts.*

They danced several more waltzes and a polka. Between dances, Drake insisted on getting them drinks. "I'll just have a pop. I don't really need any more alcohol," Jillian stated, hoping that Drake would follow her lead in this. He returned with a beer for himself and a rum and Coke for her.

"Loosen up, Sweetheart. This is a celebration!" he ordered her jokingly. Jillian decided it was easier to go along with him than to cross him and cause a scene. After that, each break in the dancing involved another beer for Drake and another rum and Coke for her. Jillian wasn't sure whether it was the alcohol or the dancing that had her head spinning when they went out onto the floor once again.

"When we dance like this, I feel as though I've known you forever." Drake whispered in her ear.

Jillian laughed. "You always say that."

Drake spun her around several times, leaving her dizzier and breathless. Then he grabbed her at the waist and pulled her toward him, kissing her and sliding one hand up to her breast.

"Drake, not in public!" she protested, pushing his hand away and looking around to see if anyone had noticed.

Smiling lewdly, he said, "Let's go home, now." He led her off the dance floor.

Once home, they both undressed and prepared for bed. Drake grabbed both her breasts and asked, "Is this private enough?" He laughed and pushed her down on the bed.

Jillian was pleased that Drake so obviously wanted her. Lately, he'd been distant and hadn't shown any interest in having sex. She had been afraid of losing him. She didn't dare tell him that his grabbing was not arousing, but made her feel more like an object. She felt him rapidly growing against her. He moved one hand down between her legs. When he realized she was still dry, he spit saliva into his hand and used it to provide some moisture. He then pushed himself in, interpreting her soft outcry of discomfort as pleasure. He drove hard repeatedly, until he yelled out in release as he came. He collapsed on her and she lay trapped under him, unsatisfied. She held him and her silence. Jillian reminded herself that he still wanted her and that was all that was important. She told herself that he had been satisfied and she should be happy.

They both slept late the next day. Jillian couldn't believe how bad she felt. Between the champagne, the wine during dinner, and the drinks while they were dancing, her head was throbbing. She couldn't help but wonder why Drake wasn't in the same condition. Instead, he was solicitous towards her. She decided just to appreciate it and allowed him to take care of her.

CHAPTER 5

Monday, they left early for her parents. Her hesitation about the day was gone. They arrived before anyone else and both started helping with last minute preparations. When the first guest arrived, Drake started popping the beers.

Bill and Fran White did not like their daughter's husband, but they kept their counsel to themselves. They didn't understand what their daughter saw in Drake, or why she would put up with his drinking. Alcohol had never been an issue in either of their families. They noticed as he started drinking. Jillian noticed too, but convinced herself it was not a problem. After all, he didn't drink everyday, and this was a party.

Jillian's sister, Donna, wasn't going to make it this year; she had attended UCLA and, other than brief visits, she had stayed in California after graduating two years ago. However, all their cousins, aunts, and uncles were arriving. Greetings were warm and, as the patio and yard filled up, the laughter and conversation became louder. They had rented a tent, tables, and chairs, enough for forty. Coolers of soda and beer had been dragged out and platters and bowls of munchies were on the tables. The little ones quickly found each other and started in on their own games and machinations, with occasional tattling. The adolescents sat off to the side, complaining to each other about what they would prefer to be doing, but started to enjoy each other's company in spite of themselves. The adults of three generations intermingled, telling tales of family members' past antics and sharing jokes, as well as catching each other up on the latest developments in their lives. Jillian was pleased to see Drake laughing and adding to the conversation, but she worried, noticing the frequency of his trips to the coolers.

Finally, it was time for the real food. Jillian's father, Bill, yelled to the kids in the yard, "You kids better come and get it before we throw it out!" The children dropped their games and came running. For a while, the women were busy getting their offspring settled and fed. Once the younger generation was eating quietly at the children's table, the adults were able to sit down to their own meal. Occasionally, one of the mothers would have to caution a child about his or her behavior, but it generally went smoothly. Jillian wished she could say the same about Drake's behavior.

Drake was thoroughly enjoying himself. He was getting louder and drawing more attention to himself. Jillian was cringing as his monologue became more lewd and she watched him open another beer. She didn't expect anyone to say anything, until her cousin Louise pulled her aside and asked, "Are you doing okay, Jillian?"

"I'm fine. You heard I'm now working for one of the VPs?" She smiled stiffly at her cousin, fearing what was to come.

"Jillian, I meant you and Drake," Louise stated, nodding her head in Drake's direction.

"We're doing great. With my promotion and Drake's new job, we were just talking the other day that we should be able to buy a place soon."

Louise frowned and pursed her lips in disapproval at Drake's behavior. "How many jobs has he had?"

"It's taken him awhile to find himself. He's doing well now," Jillian stated defensively.

"How often does this happen?" Louise pursued.

"What are you talking about?" Jillian enquired, trying not to understand her cousin.

"Don't play dumb with me. He's drunk!" Louise grabbed her cousin's arm and shook her.

Jillian put her hand on top of her cousin's. Looking toward her husband, she said, "This is rare, Louise. He's entitled to let loose. He's working hard. And once we   have   children,   he'll   settle   down."
"Oh, God! Jillian, you're not pregnant, are you?" Louise asked, appalled at the   idea.
"No, we're not ready." A shadow of sadness passed across Jillian's face.

"If you ever need to talk or anything, you have my phone number," Louise offered, hugging her cousin.

Jillian found herself stiffening in her cousin's embrace. "Thanks, Louise, but really we're fine."

As the party started breaking up, Jillian stood by her parents and brother, Bill Jr., saying goodbye to the rest of their family. Once everyone had left, Jillian went to the kitchen to help her mother clean up. Drake stumbled along behind her brother and father to fold chairs and tables.

Fran looked at her daughter and frowned. "Jillian, I'm worried about you."

"I'm fine, Mom," she responded, tightening the lid on the mayonnaise jar.

"If you need any help, you know we'll always be here for you." Fran looked at the sadness on her daughter's face, recognizing it even though Jillian was trying to hide it.

"I know, but really I'm fine. There's nothing for you to worry about." She stayed involved with busy work so that she wouldn't have to look at her mother.

The two women heard a crash from the backyard and Bill, Jr. started yelling, "Look what you did, now! Can't you get through one family gathering without getting plastered? You're nothing but a drunk!"

"Look at you, Saint Billy! Are you trying to tell me you've never had one too many beers, college boy?" Drake yelled back.

"One too many, but not ten too many! And not every time I have a drink, either!"

"What? Were you counting?" Drake demanded, turning toward his brother-in-law and clenching his hands into fists.

Bill Sr., fearing that the two men would come to blows stepped between them, yelling, "Stop it, both of you. Let's clean up this mess."

Jillian started to go out back, but her mother stopped her, putting her hand on her arm. "No, Jillian. Stay out of it. You'll only make it worse."

Hesitantly, Jillian went back to loading the dishwasher. It was getting harder to hold back the tears.

When everything was finished, Drake announced it was time to leave. They said their goodbyes, and as they started out, Jillian turned to Drake. "I think I'd better drive."

"You, too? I'm quite capable of driving," he stated, clenching the keys in his fist and wobbling back against the car.

"Drake, let's not argue about it. You can relax and I'll drive." Jillian tried to make her voice sound both reasonable and appealing.

"No! Come on!" Drake turned to unlock the driver's door.

Jillian's father added, "Drake, I think Jillian's right."

He turned abruptly toward his father-in-law and stepped toward the older man, Drake responded belligerently, "She's my wife and I make the decisions."

Not backing down, Bill Sr. replied, "She's my daughter, and I won't have you killing her due to your macho pride. Give her the keys or I'm calling the police."

"Dad, please. I'll be fine." Jillian couldn't stand the scene in front of her. She was terrified that Drake might take a swing at her father.

"Take the damn keys. But don't expect me to come to this house ever again." Drake threw the keys on the ground and walked around to the passenger's side.

Jillian picked up the keys and hit the unlock button. As she was getting in the car, her mother yelled after her, "Call me when you get home."

CHAPTER 6

Tuesday morning, Jillian was up early still disturbed by the scene at her parents' the previous night. Not wanting to confront her husband or listen to him complain about her family, she quickly got dressed and brought coffee to Drake in bed. "I have to be at work early," she told him quietly. She kissed him on the forehead, took a cup of coffee and the business section of the paper, and took off. She drove to the office, parked, and sat in her car reading the paper and drinking her coffee until she felt she could maintain her smile and it was a reasonable time to go into her workplace.

She made it through the day and went home to fix dinner and wait for Drake to show up. Because his commission check hadn't come in, he had no cash, and since he had maxed out his credit card he came straight home, hungry. As they were finishing up dinner, Jillian said, "We have to talk."

"If it's about last night, there is nothing to talk about," Drake stated, drawing in a deep breath in preparation for a debate.

"But, Drake, they were just upset; they didn't mean anything." Jillian reached out to her husband, hoping he'd listen to her.

"Listen! I don't have anything to do with my family and I certainly don't need yours," he snapped at her, leaning toward her aggressively.

Jillian was frightened, but refused to back down. She had too much to lose, either her husband or her family. "We can't leave it like this. Please, they're my family."

"They never liked me. I've always known it. I'm never going to have anything to do with them again. And as my wife, you should support me and not go there either." He squeezed her forearm tightly, glowering at her.

Tears of physical and emotional pain began welling up in her eyes. She was afraid to try to pull away from his grip, despite the pain. She feared he'd interpret it as a rejection of him. "Drake, they're my parents. I love them."

He pushed her arm away from him, rejecting her and her family. "I thought you   loved   me.   Make   up   your   mind."
"That's not fair." She got up from the table crying and rubbing her arm and ran from the room.

Drake finished eating, cleared the table, and loaded the dishwasher. At first, he slammed things around in self-righteous indignation. Then he thought about the hurt on Jillian's face. He was beginning to wonder if he'd gone too far. He went to the bedroom to find Jillian lying on her stomach on the bed. He sat next to her and started rubbing her back. "Listen, Jilly, you can see your parents whenever you want. Just, don't ask me to go with you. OK?"

Jillian understood why Drake stayed away from his family. Whenever they did hear from them, his parents asked for money and his brother was crying and drunk. However, her parents had always been kind to him, regardless of their feelings. Her brother's outburst and father's threat were the first time anyone had said anything negative to him. She understood that he was hurt and just hoped he'd forgive them. She turned around and held her arms out to him, "I'm sorry."

Drake stretched on the bed next to her and wrapped his arms around her. Maybe it was the tears, or maybe it was guilt, but Drake was more caring and attentive to her needs in bed that night.

CHAPTER 7

The orientations were over and Jillian started the real work of her new position the next day. She would be overseeing the preparation and analysis of some of the smaller contracts to start. By the end of the week, she was tired and pleased. She was finding work more exciting than ever and Drake had been on his best behavior. He was home every night at a reasonable hour, hadn't been drinking, and they cooked dinner together. His commission check wasn't as large as he had thought it would be, but he had deposited it into their joint account. Thursday of the next week, Jillian received her first pay stub with her raise. She was shocked. It was almost double what she'd been making. In her excitement, she picked up the phone to call Drake at work, and then remembered his admonition and quickly hung up the receiver. As she did, it occurred to her that the amount of her raise might make him feel bad. She had to think about what she'd tell him.

Normally, her check was electronically deposited and she'd stop at the ATM on her way home to pick up some cash. She entered the deposit and withdrawal in her checkbook ledger, put it on the passenger seat, and drove straight home. She started to put the checkbook and pay stub in her purse, but hesitated, thinking about Drake's reaction if he saw the balance, and then locked them in the glove compartment instead. She went inside and started dinner. She still hadn't decided what to tell Drake.

Drake arrived soon after and came up behind her in the kitchen, giving her a big hug. "How's my little executive tonight?"

She turned around in his arms and gave him a kiss. "Wonderful and hungry! How was your day?"

"No big sales, but I got some good leads." He picked up the salads and carried them to the table, and then went back to get a beer out of the refrigerator. Over dinner, Drake regaled Jillian with stories of some of his peers at work and informed her he was going to a Reds game on Saturday. Eventually, he asked nonchalantly, "How much is your raise?"

Jillian felt her stomach flip with anxiety. She studied the food on her plate as if she had never seen it before, trying to avoid his gaze. "After taxes, it's not going to make any difference," she responded, shrugging. *Well, I've done it now. How am I ever going to tell him the truth? Oh, God. I lied to him.*

"They're taking advantage of you," Drake announced angrily.

"Banking is still tough for a woman. But it'll lead to better things. I'm just happy for the opportunity it's giving me." She continued defending her employer and the potential, knowing she had to cover her lie.

The next day at lunch, Jillian went to the bank. She left the amount her old check would have been in the joint account and withdrew the remainder. She took $300 in cash and opened her own savings account with the balance. She left feeling guilty, but didn't know what else to do with it after her lie. By the time she got back to work, she had rationalized that she'd save for a down payment on a house and surprise Drake with it. She called Anna and left a message on the voice mail asking her to go shopping with her on Saturday. She hated to buy clothes now, at her weight, but she knew she needed to look "corporate." She could count on Anna not to let her leave the stores without buying something. They even had an ongoing joke about it. Whenever anyone in their group needed something, if Jillian was with them, they would find all sorts of things for her. They'd load her up and practically drag her to the cashier. What she didn't realize was that her friends knew she had difficulty spending money on herself and it was their way of taking care of her.

Saturday, Anna and Jillian took off early for the Tri-County Mall, expecting to make a day of it. They found a parking place in the garage without too much difficulty and entered the mall on the second floor. Anna steered them into Dillard's first, knowing that they were having a huge sale on women's clothing. Jillian followed reluctantly. Anna arrowed directly to the women's department and found the racks of discounted clothing. While Jillian stood by chewing her lip, Anna piled suits, skirts, and jackets onto her outstretched arms, and then led her to a dressing room. Once in the dressing room, Jillian found herself getting more excited about a new wardrobe. She loved the colors Anna chose for her to try. Jillian usually went for dark or very neutral colors. As far as Anna was concerned, Jillian had been wearing the same old clothes for too long. She knew that her friend was making much more money than she had in the past and had a position that required a better wardrobe. She intended to squeeze Jillian's wallet until the dead presidents cried.

As they strolled down the mall, Anna pulled Jillian into one boutique after another. She didn't pressure her friend to buy in every store, but Jillian's purchases began to mount, a scarf here, a blouse there. According to Anna, Jillian wouldn't be properly dressed without new shoes, belts, and lingerie. Her argument whenever Jillian objected was, "You work hard for your money. You deserve to have these things. And you need them if you're going to look like an executive. Besides, this is such a bargain. You'll never find this again for less." Anna made it sound like she would be wasting food or valuable natural resources if she didn't buy these things. By the time they had made the rounds of both levels of the mall and were ready to stop for lunch, Jillian was thinking of hiring porters to carry her bags for her. "Can we please put these things in the car? I can't keep lugging them around, and we'll never fit into a restaurant with all of them," she implored her friend. Anna had to laugh at her friend's deplorable condition. Jillian looked like she was in shock over all her purchases; she'd gone through most of her cash and had been forced to use a credit card for her final purchases.

"Come on. We'll dump these then eat. Where do you want to go?" Anna asked, taking some more of Jillian's shopping bags from her.

"Some place we can get a good salad There's a good restaurant in the mall."

"Sounds good to me," Anna concurred. They found the car and deposited the bags in the trunk. Anna saw Jillian biting her lip as she looked at all the merchandise she had purchased. She quickly closed the trunk and took her friend's arm, leading her away. "Don't start worrying about all that stuff. You know you need it." Anna pushed open the door of the restaurant and held it for Jillian.

"I was just thinking about how I'm going to explain all that stuff to Drake. He's going to lose it when he finds out how much I spent." Jillian sighed and frowned with consternation.

"You're making more than enough money to afford those things now. Why should Drake object?" Anna enquired, as they were seated.

"He doesn't know how much I'm making now. I...I lied to him about my raise."

Anna listened to her friend with some sympathy. She just wanted to let Jillian know she wasn't alone.

Anna and Sally had been Jillian's roommates in college. Like Sally, Anna had seen the way Drake ruined his chances in school with drinking and cutting classes. She had watched her friend giving up more and more of herself to take care of Drake Harris, pushing him to get papers done or make it to class for quizzes and exams. There were days when Jillian had missed classes to nurse Drake through particularly nasty hangovers. When Sally and Anna had tried to talk to her about this, Jillian had told them that they didn't understand. She loved Drake and it was her duty to stand by him and take care of him, no matter what. Jillian knew that Drake needed her and that was what mattered. While Sally continued to challenge Jillian about her relationship with Drake, Anna had decided years ago that it was Jillian's life and she was old enough to make her own decisions. But Anna made sure that she was available if Jillian wanted to talk. She had a feeling that today was one of those days when her friend might need a sympathetic ear.

The waitress took their orders and returned with their drinks. Sipping her tea, Anna encouraged Jillian to continue talking.

"That's a tough one. You must have had a good reason for not telling him," she suggested to her friend, hoping that Jillian would use it as an opening to share her feelings.

"Well, you know how hard it's been for him," Jillian began.

Anna made what she hoped was a noncommittal supportive noise. She didn't share Jillian's concern for Drake's "fragile emotions."

"He isn't making as much as he did in the past at some of his jobs. I didn't want him to feel inferior because I'm making so much more than he is. Drake is so sensitive. And men put so much importance on being the breadwinners." Jillian shrugged.

"Yeah. I've heard that, but I think there's more to it than that." Anna tilted her head and raised an eyebrow. Jillian looked at her to see if her friend was being judgmental. All she could see was a supportive attitude.

Jillian took a deep breath and continued. "Drake's been taking money out of my wallet. Not just a few dollars, but large sums. Money I was going to use to buy groceries or pay bills. It seems to evaporate in a couple days and he's back asking for more. I know he's drinking it up. I don't know what to do about it. I try so hard to keep the house nice and to be supportive for him. I know I've gained a lot of weight and I'm not as attractive as I was. I don't know what's making him so unhappy that he has to drink all the time. Oh, Anna, what else can I do? I just want him to settle down and be happy. How can I make him happy?" Jillian looked devastated and close to tears. Anna reached out and stroked her friend's arm.

"Jill, you are a wonderful wife and friend to him, but you must realize that you can't make him happy. Drake has some serious problems. He has to come to grips with them and find a way to cope with them. His drinking is a problem, but it's also a symptom and an excuse. You know as well as I do that he's never been able to stick to a job for long. And it's always someone else's fault when he quits or gets fired. The boss is a jerk, the job isn't good enough for him, or the people he works with hate him because they're jealous." Seeing Jillian gearing up to defend her husband, Anna knew she had to back off a bit. "Those things might have been true to some extent, but we all face those kinds of challenges and find a way to deal with them. We don't run away from our problems or try to drink them out of existence. Drake doesn't cope with them. Maybe he can't cope with them. I don't know. But he's going to keep doing the same things until he realizes that it's not working, and he won't do that until he hits bottom." Anna stopped to see how Jillian would respond to what she had said. Anna could see there was an internal struggle going on. She waited in silence with her friend.

After several moments of silence, Jillian sighed and said, "But that means that I'm helpless to do anything for him. I can't be helpless!" The tears started running down her cheeks. Anna was startled by her friend's fear. She reached into her purse and pulled out a tissue, handing it to Jillian.

"Jill, what's happened to you? You were so bright and competent in college. You always got excellent grades. We all joked that you'd be the CEO of your own company within five years. You were our rock. Then Drake came along and somehow, somewhere you got lost." Anna looked at her friend with compassion and concern. Jillian blew her nose and wiped away the tears. She stared down at the wadded tissue in her hands and shrugged.

"I don't know. I'm still good at what I do. I love my work. But Drake needs me, and that's so much more important to me. If I'm so smart, then I can find a way to make him happy. I need him to be happy with me. From the first time I met him, I felt as if I'd known him all my life and beyond. I feel as if he'd die without me to keep him safe." Jillian laughed at her words and looked up at her friend. "Stupid, huh?"

"I wouldn't call it stupid, but it is unrealistic. No one is so powerful that he or she can keep another person alive simply by being present. Jillian, Drake has to take responsibility for his own life. He has to be the one to keep him alive, not you, just as you have to be responsible for yourself. That doesn't mean that the two of you can't be together. But it can't be all one sided. You can't keep giving everything and getting so little in return. This relationship is eating you up." Before Jillian could respond, the waitress brought their salads. The two women sat quietly, Jillian played with her romaine, pushing the croutons around. Anna chewed her Caesar salad contemplatively, not wanting to pressure her friend.

Finally, Jillian stated, "Drake doesn't just take from me, you know. He gives me a lot. I know he loves me, even if he doesn't say so all the time. Any relationship has periods when one person is needier than the other. But it all balances out. Right now Drake needs the support. But he'll settle down, and then it will be my turn. Once we have a house and children, that's when I'll need his help and understanding." She forked some salad into her mouth and chewed it with determination, as if she were chewing up any doubts she might have.

"Just do yourself and Drake a favor. Don't get pregnant until you're sure he has settled down. That might be too much pressure for him to deal with while he's getting himself ...settled," Anna recommended. She waited to see how Jillian would react to her suggestion. She was gratified that the other woman didn't take offense, but concerned that Jillian looked so sad as she pondered her friend's words.

The rest of lunch passed mostly in silence, Jillian caught up in introspection. Anna dropped her off at her apartment and Jillian carried her bags inside. She sat on the bed clipping the tags off the clothes and putting them on hangers. While she did this, she thought about her words to Anna about knowing Drake forever. When she thought about them together, it did seem that they had been together much longer than the seven years they had been dating and married. Jillian felt that their relationship was predestined. If that was true, then she had to fight to keep their marriage alive, even if she did have to give more than Drake did to maintain it. They could make it work. She could make it work.

CHAPTER 8

When she finished putting her new things away and disposed of the incriminating evidence, bags and tags, Jillian set to work making dinner. The game would be over soon and Drake might be hungry when he got back. Besides, she hadn't eaten much of her salad at lunch. She kept it simple so that he could eat whenever he got in without having to fuss over it. Then she sat down on the couch to watch TV and wait. By 8:00, Jillian decided that she wouldn't wait to eat until Drake got home. By 10:30, she got herself ready for bed, but returned to the couch. She must have dozed off, because she was startled by the sound of Drake's key in the door. When she looked up at the clock it was after midnight. Jillian could tell just by looking at him that Drake was drunk. She resolved not to have a fight with him about it.

"Hi. How was the game?" she enquired, keeping her voice quiet and light.

"Okay. Reds won. We all went out to celebrate the victory afterwards." Drake was still able to navigate through the room, but he seemed wobbly. He tried to toss his keys onto the table and they dropped onto the floor. He waved his hand at them dismissively and turned toward Jillian.

"Are you hungry? There's food in the fridge. I could fix you something quick," she offered.

"No, that's okay. I'm really not hungry. Need to get to bed." Blinking and squinting to focus, he staggered through the door into the bedroom. Jillian rose and turned off the TV, and then the lights. She followed her husband into the bedroom and watched him fighting to pull his jeans off over his shoes.

"Can I give you a hand?" she offered. She walked around to his side of the bed and knelt down to remove his shoes. As she pulled his pants off for him, he looked down at her.

"My Jilly, what would I do without you? I'd never get my pants off." He laughed at his joke and petted Jillian's hair.

Jillian helped him get his jacket off and his t-shirt. "Do you need to pee before you get into bed?" she asked him.

"No. I think I did that outside, before I came in. There was a bush that was looking a bit dry, so I watered it." He laughed again and let Jillian push him back onto the bed. She spread the covers over him and kissed him on the forehead.

"I can keep you alive," she whispered to his sleeping body. Jillian turned out the light and climbed into bed on the other side.

The following couple of weeks, there were no eruptions at home. Things continued to be exciting for Jillian at work as she learned more about her responsibilities and the expectations Jerry had for her. She felt she needed to do more than she ever had to prove herself worthy of the raise she had received. The idea of making so much was still a shock to her. She had grown up believing that she would always need a man in her life to protect and provide for her. While her mother had worked, she never let her daughters forget that their father's income from his insurance agency was what paid the bills. The concept of being financially self-sufficient was foreign. She also still feared how the news would affect Drake and influence their relationship.

Jillian had become accustomed to attending the weekly Tuesday morning department meeting. She remained quiet, listening unless called on for specific information. She was confident in her responses, but found it amazing that these powerful men and women actually listened to what she had to say. By the end of September, preparations for opening the southeast regional office in Savannah were well on their way. Phil Grey announced, "A team from the home office will be going to assist Mike Johnson. Of course, there will be people from Human Resources, but we also want representatives from each division: loans, investments, bank services, as well as ours. The team will be staying in Savannah for a couple of weeks."

Jillian sat listening, hoping the CFO would not send Jerry. She depended upon him to watch out for her and she was not fully comfortable in her new position yet.

"Jillian, you'll be going with the team," Phil announced.

Jillian's head jerked up. Without thinking she blurted out, "Are you sure? I've only been in the department five weeks."

Phil Grey laughed at her reaction, and then quickly regained his stoic façade. "Jerry assures me you're ready and from what I've seen of your work, I'm quite confident in my decision." He looked over the top of his glasses at her and sternly asked, "Do you have any other questions?"

Jillian smiled as she tried to swallow the lump in her throat. "When do we leave, sir?"

"Two weeks. The travel agency will be contacting you."

The meeting ended shortly afterwards. Jillian couldn't understand why she would be sent on this trip. She was the youngest and newest member of the department. She hoped that the recognition would not make other people upset with her. She really didn't know them yet and none of them had been particularly friendly. Even the secretaries seemed to shun her. They were efficient and did whatever she asked, but none included her in conversation at the coffee pot or asked her to join them at lunch. Even the chocolate Bundt cake had not helped to break the ice. What Jillian didn't understand was that her overtures were seen as disingenuous. The support staff was not accustomed to being included by the executives unless they wanted something from them. Jillian's promotion had moved her into a different office social level that she did not understand.

Jerry gave her a smile as they were leaving the boardroom. No one else spoke, but hurried off to their own business. As she was sitting down at her desk, Janet Shannon, Phil Grey's administrative assistant, stepped into her office. Jillian quickly stood. It was a reflex reaction out of respect for the older woman. Janet recognized Jillian's inexperience and potential. "Sit down. You're not supposed to do that. I just came to tell you, don't question Phil's decisions unless you are prepared with facts. And if you do have numbers and facts that show he's wrong, don't be afraid to confront him. He expects nothing less."

"Thank you, Janet," Jillian responded, playing with a paper clip on the desk.

As Janet turned to leave, Jillian called after her, "May I ask you something?"

Janet turned back and looked enquiringly at her, smiling.

Jillian hesitated. "Why doesn't anyone like me up here?"

Janet closed the door. Shaking her head, she said, "You really are young!" She sighed. "This is a very competitive department. All these people are going someplace. They all want to be CFOs or CEOs here or somewhere else. They haven't figured you out yet."

"But I don't want to be a CFO," Jillian protested. "I couldn't. I just want to keep this job and someday buy a house and have children."

Janet looked at the younger woman, gauging the sincerity of her words. "They won't believe it. As far as they're concerned, you're either Jerry's mistress or a rising star." The look of horror on Jillian's face made Janet laugh softly.

"I'm married. I'm not his mistress," Jillian asserted, appalled at the thought of such a situation and at the idea that others might think that of her.

"I know that. Phil doesn't play around and he never would have promoted you if you weren't competent," Janet assured her.

"Is that why the secretaries won't talk to me either?" Jillian asked, the hurt audible in her voice.

"No." She thought for a minute. "Jillian, you're an executive now. You're not one of them."

"Oh!" Jillian didn't know what to say or think.

The older woman moved to the door, and then turned back toward Jillian. "CorpTravel will call you later today. They'll have many personal questions in order to make your arrangements. They'll e-mail your itinerary to you." Janet turned again and walked out.

Jillian appreciated Janet's advice and honesty, but it did not make her feel any better. She wanted to be liked and accepted. One group thought she was a whore or after their jobs. The other group saw her as a spy and user. Then at home there was Drake. She was hiding more and more from him so that he'd feel good. Now she had to figure out how she'd tell him that she'd be going away for two weeks for business. She was afraid he'd be angry. She was afraid he'd spend the time drinking. She was afraid he'd discover he didn't need her.

She went off her diet. The next two days, she held her breath every night hoping Drake wouldn't ask her about work. He didn't. His focus was his work and the football season. Friday night, he came home excited. One of the guys from work had an extra ticket for the Bengals' game on Sunday. He informed her that he was going, but needed a couple hundred dollars. Jillian quickly agreed to the expense; it relieved her guilt. Drake had expected an argument, but didn't question her reaction.

CHAPTER 9

Jillian arrived early at work Monday morning. She was feeling pressured. After her conversation with her parents, she felt a need to get ahead on her work before leaving for Savannah. No one had arrived yet, so she started the coffee and went back to her desk to power up her computer. The quiet on the floor was both peaceful and unnerving. She double checked her schedule for the day, and then checked her e-mail. Her itinerary for the Savannah trip had been there unopened since Friday. Without reviewing it, she printed it out; she wasn't ready to think about the trip or what she'd tell Drake. She headed for the coffee.

As she approached the break room, she heard two women talking and realized the support staff must have started arriving. She stopped outside of the door when she overheard her name.

"Looks like Mrs. Harris got in early. The lights are on in her office and someone's started the coffee," Sue Ann's disembodied voice stated.

Cathy snipped, "If she thinks she's going to move up on this floor by making coffee, she has a lot to learn."

"Maybe she just wanted some," Sue Ann responded meekly.

"You are naïve. No one that young gets up here, especially a woman, unless…"

"Cathy, stop it!" Sue Ann interrupted.

"You have a friend downstairs. Find out her story," Cathy pressed her coworker.

"If it will shut you up, I will. I'll go down at lunch."

Jillian quietly backed up a few steps, and then purposely walked loudly back. "Morning! You're both here early." She noted the two women make quick eye contact with each other as if wondering if they'd been caught talking. At least Sue Ann had the good grace to blush. Cathy just pursed her lips and turned away. Jillian poured her coffee and walked out, hurrying back to her office and closing the door. She sat at her desk with her head in her hands wondering who Sue Ann's friend was. She didn't need this on top of everything else. She just hoped Sue Ann would get a good report. She hadn't been on the third floor much since her promotion. She hoped they weren't angry with her down there for ignoring them. She just hadn't had time to think about much besides her new work and Drake. And now it would be too obvious if she went down before lunch. She'd make a point of visiting later in the week. Jillian's day went by without her looking at the itinerary.

At dinner that night, she attempted to get up the courage to tell Drake about the trip. However, she rationalized that he'd have questions and she hadn't brought the schedule home.

Jillian met Anna for lunch on Tuesday. She realized she hadn't told her about the trip either.

"So what's new?" Anna asked once they had ordered. She sipped her tea and studied her friend's face where she could see an internal struggle waging.

Jillian shrugged. "I'm going out of town on business for two weeks. They're sending me and several others to Savannah to start the set up of a regional office there. It'll be great experience and will go a long way toward another promotion in the future. It's a chance to prove myself to my boss and the other execs," she explained.

"That's wonderful!" Anna exclaimed. "You deserve this chance, Jillian. It does seem to be a terrific opportunity for you. ...So why are you less than enthusiastic about it?"

"I haven't told Drake, yet. I don't know how he's going to respond when I do," Jillian clarified.

"Would he object? This is a part of the job, now that you've gotten the promotion. It's one of the reasons they're paying you more money. Surely he'll understand that," Anna stated.

"You forget, I haven't told him how big the raise was. He already thinks I'm being taken advantage of by them. If I tell him now, he'll be angry because I lied to him. And if I don't tell him, he'll be angry because I'm letting myself be used." Jillian sighed heavily, feeling the weight of her predicament.

"Oh, Jill. No wonder you're so unhappy about this. But you can't get out of going on the trip. You know it will be beneficial for you. If you can't tell Drake about the raise, the only thing to do is bite the bullet and let him think you're being a patsy. I still think you should tell him the truth, but you're the one who has to live with the consequences either way." Anna reached across the table and squeezed her friend's hand supportively.

"There's more," Jillian continued. "I'm worried about how he's going to behave while I'm gone. I'm afraid he might increase his drinking or get into trouble at work." Jillian looked as if she were about to cry.

"Jill, you've said yourself that he has a good job, one he likes. He's doing well there. Drake won't jeopardize that. And it's only going to be two weeks. He can last that long without you. Besides, when have you ever been able to keep him from drinking too much, or from screwing up a job if he's set his mind to it?" Anna tilted her head and raised an eyebrow.

Jillian nodded, accepting the truth of her friend's statement, even though she hated to accept that she was powerless in the situation. "You're right. I can't stop him when he's bent on self-destruction. But if I'm around, I can usually keep the destruction to a minimum and get him 'patched up' again quickly. If I'm out of town, I can't do anything about the problems that come up." Jillian was breathing heavily from anxiety.

"The problems will be there, whether you're there to rescue him or not, Jill. You can't keep on pulling him out of the messes he creates. He'll never learn and never change if you do." Anna knew she was taking a chance saying these things to her friend, but she also knew she couldn't just let Jillian go on hurting herself and allowing Drake to hurt her.

"Annie, he's such a child in so many ways. He needs me to be there to support him. He does better when I'm there. Really he does!" Jillian's eyes were wide with pleading. She needed to believe that she made a difference in Drake's life, and she needed her friend to confirm it for her.

"Jill, whatever is going to happen will happen, whether you're there or not. You want Drake to settle down and take on responsibility for himself. You've said so many times. If you're right, then you have to give him the chance to succeed without you, like a mother letting go of her child's hand and letting him walk on his own. This business trip will be a wonderful opportunity for Drake, too. He'll be able to show you that he can be responsible for himself, that he can settle down and be a productive adult," Anna finished.

Jillian looked at her friend thoughtfully. Anna had made some good points. She needed to give Drake a chance to prove himself, not just to her, but to her friends and family as well. And he'd do it, too. Jillian was suddenly sure that

Drake would succeed. She smiled and thanked Anna for her advice and support. She found that she actually had an appetite and finished her lunch with pleasure.

After lunch with Anna, Jillian felt she had been ridiculous not having already told Drake. She put a copy of her itinerary in her purse and stopped at the market to pick up chicken, okra, rice, and the ingredients for shoofly pie for dinner. The meal was one of Drake's favorites. She planned to get him happily fed before she sprang the news. She'd learned years ago not to bother trying his cell phone, he never answered it, but she'd leave a message about dinner just in case he checked it.

Drake arrived home while she was still fixing dinner. He gave her a hug from behind. "What's this I hear about fried chicken and rice? I do believe you're trying to fatten me up, darlin'," he stated with an exaggerated southern drawl. Jillian had almost finished frying the chicken. The rice and okra were sitting in pots waiting to be dished out. She took the baking powder biscuits out of the oven and set them on the counter to cool. Drake grabbed one out of the pan, tossing it back and forth between his hands until it cooled enough to eat. "You're going to make gravy, too, aren't you?" he asked. Jillian hadn't planned on it, thinking that there were enough carbs and fats in the meal already to blow several major arteries in both of them, but she decided it would put him in a bad mood if she refused.

"Of course. Can't have chicken and rice without gravy. What would my mama say if I left them out?" she responded, keeping up the southern drawl.

"That's my girl," Drake announced, kissing her on the cheek, and then going to the refrigerator for a beer. "How long until dinner?" he asked, wandering toward the living room couch.

"About ten minutes. Don't get too settled. We're eating like civilized people tonight, not in front of the TV," she called to him over her shoulder.

Jillian cheerfully set the table with her good china and candles. She laid the chicken out on a platter and filled her good serving bowls with all the other goodies she'd prepared. The hot biscuits were piled into a basket and wrapped with a napkin. Once everything was on the table, she called Drake. He hurried over, commenting on how he was so hungry he could "eat a horse," and how wonderful everything smelled. Drake quickly filled his plate with food and began enjoying the feast.

Jillian smiled at her husband, feeling warmly satisfied at his obvious appreciation of her work. She had to admit that she had outdone herself with this meal. When they had finished the main course, Jillian cleared away most of the dishes and brought out the shoofly pie. "Just like Grandma used to make!" she announced. Drake groaned appreciatively as he bit into the sweet dessert.

"While I've got your attention, I need to let you know that I'm going to be going on a business trip," she told him, handing him the itinerary. Drake dropped his fork onto his empty plate. His brow furrowed with emotion.

"What do you mean you're going on a business trip? Where are you going? For how long?" he demanded.

"To Savannah for two weeks. We're opening a regional office and I'm one of the people Mr. Grey wants to go to help set up things there. There are several other people going, as well," she explained, surprised by his anger.

"Why didn't you tell me about this before? These people pay you crap, and then think you should abandon your husband to run all over the country. And these other people who are going...are some of them men?" he challenged.

"Yes, of course some of them are men. There are more men than women in banking. But that has nothing to do with it. I'm an executive now. This is part of my job. It's good experience and a good way to show my boss that I deserve this promotion, to show him that I can handle added responsibility. I'm not going all over the country, just to Savannah. I know it's short notice, but that's the way things are in business," she argued.

"Just how long have you known about this trip?" he asked suspiciously.

"Not very long, really," she responded evasively.

Drake opened the itinerary and noted the date it had been sent to her. "You bitch! You've had this for several days. You've known about this for some time and didn't tell me, and then you lied to me about it. Well, this is what I think about your trip," he exclaimed, ripping up the itinerary and throwing the pieces in her face. He pushed away from the table and stormed out, grabbing his keys and slamming the door on his way.

"Oh, God!" Jillian exclaimed and burst into tears.

Jillian called Anna after Drake left the house. She turned her anger at Drake on Anna. "Some advice you gave me. Drake is very upset and it's your fault. He stormed out of here in a rage."

"Jillian, you had to tell him. Don't blame me if he's being unreasonable. This job is important for both of you. Don't get mad at me because he used it as an excuse to go out. Where did he go?" Anna asked her friend, feeling a bit hurt at the unfair attack.

"He just tore up the schedule and left. I don't know where he is." She was holding back her tears.

Anna sighed. "You know he'll be back and he'll get over it."

"I hope so." Jillian sounded desolate.

"Jill, he always comes back. Once he has some time to think things through, he'll calm down. He knows you have to go on this trip and that it's just business," Anna reassured her friend with greater conviction than she felt. Then she tried to distract Jillian. "Now, Saturday we have to go shopping again."

"What for?" Jillian asked, unenthusiastically.

"Your trip. I know you're nervous about it, but you have to look the part. I'll pick you up at ten. We'll go out to Eastgate this time."

"Drake isn't going to like it," Jillian protested uncertainly.

"Tough. You don't even have a decent carry-on. We're going." Anna was firm on the point. She knew that this was the only way to get Jillian to agree.

"Drake's back. I have to hang up," Jillian whispered, and then pushed the off button.

Jillian waited anxiously, expecting Drake to be angry still, but he walked in smiling. Jillian looked up at him sheepishly, waiting for him to berate her some more. "I'm sorry I didn't tell you earlier. I just didn't want to think about it, much less talk about it."

"It's okay, but I wish you had told me earlier. I know you have to go, but they really should be paying you more."

"They're paying all my expenses while I'm gone," she offered, hoping that would help placate him.

"Two full weeks? The weekends, too?" Drake was mollified by this information.

"Yes, but I'll call every night," she promised, hoping that he wouldn't make any further objections to the trip. He surprised her with his next statement.

"You don't have to do that as long as I can reach you. Smiling again, he led Jillian to bed and satisfied himself. She was so relieved that he was no longer upset with her, and had accepted that she would be gone for two full weeks, that she didn't mind that he fell asleep without even pretending to try to satisfy her. While she briefly wondered what brought about his change of attitude, she didn't want to consider the implications.

CHAPTER 10

The week passed quickly. Jillian went shopping with Anna on Saturday. She purchased a rolling carry-on as well as a navy blue suit and two blouses to go with it. When she returned home, Drake spotted the luggage and asked about the expense. Without thinking, she blurted out that it would be covered by her expense account for the trip. As soon as she said it, she became angry with herself for adding another lie to the mounting list of lies she'd told her husband over the last couple of months.

Early Monday morning, Drake drove Jillian to the airport. He dropped her at the curb, kissed her on the cheek, and took off. Jillian watched the car drive off, feeling empty from Drake's lack of emotion in his good-bye. It would be the first they'd been apart since they'd been married. She looked at her watch and hurried into the terminal to check-in. As she waited in line, sadness and a strong sense of loss and guilt started to take over.

When she arrived at the gate, she spotted Mike Johnson with three other men who looked familiar and Joan Fitzgerald. She had met Joan once before at Human Resources. She managed to put on a smile as she greeted the group. Mike introduced her to John Daggett from Loans, Joe Verdi from Investments, and Fred Walker from Banking Services.

Jillian and Joan were seated together on the plane for the two hour trip. As they were taking off, Jillian finally let go of her smile. Joan noticed. "Are you afraid of flying?" she asked with genuine concern.

"No. It's not something I've ever really thought about much. Why, are you?"

"No. But I noticed that you looked very uncomfortable as we started down the runway. Is everything all right?"

"Oh," Jillian shrugged. "I was just thinking about my husband. We've never been away from each other since we got married."

"Mmmm. It's hard at first. I remember my first trip away from my husband. I called him the minute the plane touched down. We spent two hours on the phone every night, while I was gone." Joan laughed softly at her own behavior. "It gets easier after a while. I still check in with him, but we both know we'll each be okay without the other one around for a few days. ...How long have you been married?"

"Five years now," Jillian replied, playing with her rings, "but we've been together for a lot longer than that. We met in college." Jillian found herself opening up to this woman and was surprised by her candor. She cautioned herself to keep the intimate details to herself. "What about you?" she asked, trying to get the focus off of herself.

"George and I have been married for almost ten years. We met after college. His sister and I worked together and she introduced us. It's amazing that we ever got together. It was far from love at first sight. But he managed to worm his way into my heart." Joan laughed quietly. "He always says he grew on me. To which I respond, 'Yeah, like warts.'" She laughed again.

Jillian shared the joke with her, and then responded with, "It was love at first sight for me. The first time Drake smiled at me, I knew I was hopelessly in love with him. He was so charming and funny. I always said he could sell snow to the Eskimos and get them to order more." It was her turn to laugh at her situation.

"Any children?" Joan asked.

"No, not yet. We've both been so busy with our careers and all. But, I'm hoping to have a baby soon. I think Drake and I would be so much happier with children in the house. They're a steadying influence." Jillian smiled confidently, even though she didn't feel very certain about it. "And you? Do you have children?"

"No. We're not ready yet. I don't know if we ever will be. George and I both have demanding careers, and we like to travel. And then there's the antiques addiction, of course," Joan stated, making a rueful face. Jillian was concerned she'd touched on a sore subject and was about to apologize when Joan laughed again.

"Oh, don't look so embarrassed. We love shopping for antiques and our house is full of them. In fact, I plan to try to work in some hunting while I'm here. George has given me permission to go moderately crazy since I'm going to be in the heart of the Old South. This should be a great place to find some antebellum items. My mouth is watering at the idea of the hunt. Maybe you'd like to come along?" she asked enthusiastically, turning to face Jillian.

"Uh, well...I don't know. I don't really have any money to spend on antiques," Jillian began, her guilt about spending money on herself rising.

"You won't have to buy anything, but it's great fun just looking at the old stuff. Who knows, you might find some little thing that you just can't live without, and at a reasonable price. I go to auctions rather than to shops. You always pay more at a shop, but you can out bid a dealer. They can't go too high because it decreases their profits."

"It might be nice," Jillian conceded. She'd think about it and when the time came, if she didn't feel right about it, she could always turn Joan down. "Let me know when you want to go. If I'm free, I'll come along."

The two women continued to chat about work and life in general. Jillian found herself enjoying Joan's company, and thought this might turn out to be a very pleasant trip.

CHAPTER 11

The six executives from Midwest Bank were met by a driver in the baggage claim area of the Savannah International Airport. Their luggage was packed into the trunk of the limo and they headed toward the downtown area of Savannah. They would be staying in the middle of the historic district at the Hilton. Jillian found herself caught up in the scenery and was surprised how quickly they covered the distance from the airport to town. She noticed how calm she was feeling and how easy it was for her to be distracted by the local flora. She had to shake herself to absorb what Mr. Johnson was saying as they exited the limo. Mr. Johnson instructed the driver to check the bags with the bell captain and informed the group that they would be starting with a working lunch. Afterwards, at 1:00 they would meet with the newly hired local executives. She breathed in deeply and noticed the sweet aroma of flowers mixed with horse manure. Something about the combination was strangely familiar and comforting. She looked for evidence of horses, but saw none. As she was beginning to question her perceptions, Joan made a face and blurted out, "What is that awful smell?"

John and Fred simultaneously responded, "Horse manure!"

Just then, a horse drawn tourist coach appeared, coming lazily around the corner. A knowing grin came over John's face and he pointed to the horse. Jillian smiled to herself thinking, *I need to trust my own perceptions. I've doubted myself too long.*

At lunch, Mike Johnson handed out packets to the group. Each included a schedule for the next two weeks and the resumes of the new hires. They would be meeting with the local employees that afternoon. As Jillian reviewed her packet, she saw that she would be helping to interview additional candidates for employment and begin training on the bank's policy and procedures in Contracts, Mergers, and Acquisitions. She saw it was a busy schedule including a number of dinner meetings with the Cincinnati group. However, she'd have a couple of afternoons free.

The day passed quickly. Jillian realized she'd been in the hotel since they'd arrived in Savannah, but she was too tired to explore. She called home only to leave her room number on the answering machine. She went straight to bed, sure that she would sleep soundly.

Jillian joined Joan for breakfast. The woman from HR asked, "How was your first night away from your husband? Did you sleep okay?"

"Yes, but I had the strangest dream. Drake and I were riding in a carriage on Drayton Street and there were other carriages all around us. Only Drake had red hair and long bushy sideburns. And he was my friend, not my husband. Also, there was the smell of horses and flowers, like yesterday, only stronger. It seemed so real."

"Red hair? What color is Drake's?"

"Dark blond. I can't imagine why I'd dream of him with red hair," Jillian puzzled as she nibbled a piece of toast.

"Dreams can be strange. I guess you're missing him." Joan smiled and sipped her coffee.

"Mmmm. I guess so." Jillian shook her head and shrugged.

The day went by quickly. After dinner, Joan invited Jillian to join her on a walk. Jillian accepted, stating, "I could use some exercise between all the eating and sitting today." The two women obtained a map of the historic district from the concierge, who pointed out areas that would most likely be interesting. They headed down Bull Street looking in storefront windows and at the architecture of the buildings. Occasionally, a horse drawn vehicle, looking like a cross between a surrey and a wagon, would pass. They made their way to Bay Street and headed east.

"Let's take that ramp down to the river front," Joan suggested.

Jillian felt a knot tighten in her stomach. "It's dangerous down there."

"No, that's one of the areas the concierge suggested." Joan looked at Jillian with mild surprise.

"What about the sailors and beggars and...you know?" Jillian whispered to her companion.

"What are you talking about? There are supposed to be artists, restaurants, shops, and musicians." Joan was confused by Jillian's reaction and looked at her as if she'd been out in the sun too long.

Jillian shook her head, trying to clear it of the anxieties that had flooded her thoughts. "Okay, you're right. I don't know what I was thinking." She tried to laugh off her concerns, feeling embarrassed, but still felt nervous about going down to the riverfront area.

The ramp was made of oversized cobblestones. Jillian looked back and noted a retaining wall made of the same. She guessed that it was about four stories high. The street was filled with tourists going in and out of cheap restaurants and souvenir stores. Caricaturists were sitting on the edge of the sidewalk with their easels before them. The soulful sound of a saxophone was wafting down the street. They left the street for the walkway next to the river and continued their stroll. Jillian was relieved that it was not as she had expected, but was also strangely annoyed by the scene. She was glad that Joan had no interest in the tourist shops and preferred the peace offered by the water.

By the time they made their way back to the hotel, Jillian was tired. She contemplated calling Drake, but did not want to face getting the answering machine again and decided to call him first thing in the morning.

Her dreams were of the waterfront. *It seemed to be late evening, not quite dark. Jillian was walking down the ramp, stepping carefully on the large cobblestones. She felt the presence of another person behind her, someone she knew, a male, but she didn't know whom it was. Lifting her skirts out of the dirt, she carefully maneuvered around barrels, anchors, and other ship's gear. At the foot of the ramp, she saw a dark haired woman wearing a skirt, but with her corset and camisole uncovered. The woman ran her fingers over her exposed bosom in a very sensual and suggestive manner as she smiled at passing men. Two English sailors, just into port, approached the woman, smiling and joking with her in a lewd way. Jillian halted her progress in disgust. She felt her companion tug on her elbow and she proceeded around the little group. Once on the riverside road, they were approached by a group of dirty, little, white children begging for money. The children were accompanied by an older boy who smiled boldly at Jillian and looked her over in a very crude way. Jillian found herself wishing she had her riding crop with her, or her buggy whip. She'd wipe the smile off that white trash face. As they proceeded down the road, the stench of fish and offal polluted the air. Jillian searched in her purse and pulled out a lacy handkerchief, and then pressed it to her nose and mouth. The pair hurried on. As it got darker, Jillian became more aware of dark figures lurking in doorways and alleys. She felt anxious and drew closer to her companion, wishing she hadn't insisted upon coming. A rat skittered across their path causing her to jump back a step. She made a startled cry of disgust.*

Jillian awoke with her heart beating quickly and the stench of the riverfront still in her nose. She could feel the strange, heavy clothing she had been wearing. The sensation was so real that she looked to see what she was wearing in bed. She was both confused and relieved to see that it was her own turquoise and lavender striped nightgown. "Huh. What a dream! I'm really soaking up the atmosphere of old Savannah." She flopped back onto her pillows and went back to sleep, convinced that the dream was the product of her outing with Joan. "Wait till Joan hears this one," she mumbled as she drifted back to sleep.

CHAPTER 12

Jillian woke feeling anxious. She wondered briefly about her dream, but pushed it aside and called Drake. She was relieved to hear his groggy voice on the other end of the line. He sleepily asked, "What time is it?"

"7:00."

"Why are you calling so early?" he mumbled. Jillian pictured him burrowing into his pillow.

"I wanted to catch you before you left for work. How's everything going?" She tried to keep her tone light and affectionate. She didn't want to challenge him.

"I'm fine. I hope they're not working you too hard." He yawned. Not waiting for a response, he added, "I'll call you tonight."

"What time?" she asked, hearing the neediness in her voice.

"Why? Do you have a date?" Drake asked the question facetiously, but Jillian felt as if she were about to do something wrong.

"No! Of course not! I just want to make sure I get back from dinner in time," she responded defensively.

"After nine, okay?" Drake was beginning to sound irritated.

"Fine. I love you. Have a good day." Jillian put as much warmth and affection into her voice as possible.

"Yeah. You, too," he responded without any emotion.

Jillian hung up feeling lost. She comforted herself with the thought that Drake was still sleepy. That was why he hadn't been more affectionate. She showered quickly, applied her make-up, fixed her hair, dressed, and headed out of her hotel room to face the day. By 2:00, she had completed her day's tasks. She changed into casual clothes, grabbed her city map, and started walking toward Forsyth Park.

On entering the park, she followed a pathway leading toward the center. She came to a fountain surrounded by benches. There were a few other people nearby enjoying the peace offered by the shade trees, the tinkling sound of the water from the fountain, and the aroma of flowers. After sitting for close to a half hour, she started walking again toward Montgomery Street. Inspired by the sight of some joggers and a woman power-walking with a dog in tow, she decided to take a brisk walk around the entire park. By the time Jillian started down Drayton Street, she was slowing down and was getting annoyed with herself for the flab she had put on. Not wanting to spoil the pleasant feelings she had been experiencing, Jillian distracted herself from these negative thoughts by focusing on her surroundings. She started looking more closely at the buildings across the street. She stopped, unable to take her eyes off of a white, three story, federal style building. Two stairways merging at the top led to the second floor veranda with large columns going all the way up to the top of the third floor. The double doors were off center. As she stared at the house, she found herself saying, "It's wrong. Part of the house is missing. And the veranda; the veranda is supposed to wrap around the side. What happened to it?"

Just then, an older couple in blue jeans and matching light blue polo shirts exited through the open door and started down the steep steps. Jillian waved to them and crossed the street. "Excuse me. What is this house?"

The   man   responded,   "It's   a   bed   and   breakfast." The woman added, "It's a lovely old house, built in 1838."

"Thank you," she responded with a smile and moved toward the house.

As Jillian headed up the stairs, the woman called after her. "I don't think they have any rooms available."

Jillian nodded and waved as she continued up the stairs. Once on the veranda, she looked across the street at the park. She thought, *What am I doing? Well, it's a bed and breakfast. I can ask for information.* She rang the doorbell and heard the clump of a woman's footsteps on a wooden floor, the click of a bolt, and then the door opened. A short, dark haired woman wearing a casual dress and heels asked, "How can I help you?"

The woman's expression was less than welcoming. Jillian felt nonplussed by her attitude, given that it was a business that catered to tourists. "I understand this is a bed and breakfast. I wanted to get some information." Jillian smiled at the woman, hoping to receive a smile in return.

"We have no vacancies." The woman looked hard at Jillian, who just waited. "If you come in, I'll get you a brochure."

Jillian stepped into a small foyer. The woman quickly closed the door and turned the bolt. "Go in. Have a seat." She indicated a settee facing into the room with its back to a fireplace. "I'll get you a brochure from the office."

Before the woman could exit, Jillian blurted out, "What happened to the rest of the house?"

The woman stopped and quickly pivoted, and then she seemed to relax for the first time. "You must have noticed the front door is off center. There were a couple of fires over the years. Instead of rebuilding, the previous owners tore down the damaged side and put up a new wall. There used to be a wrap around veranda as well." She headed out of the room to the office.

Jillian hesitantly sat down on a fragile looking antique chair. The room was impressive, from the parquet floors to the crystal chandeliers. As she sat relaxing, taking in the atmosphere of the room, she thought she heard the music of a string quartet. She closed her eyes briefly, trying to hear the music. When she opened them, *the room was filled with people dressed in their finest clothes. It was lit with candles; even the chandelier had been lighted for the occasion. The doors to the veranda were open to let in some cooler air. Jillian smiled as couples paraded past her in a quadrille. She could just hear the strains of "The Lancers" played by the small band of black musicians over in the corner.* A woman approached her, looking concerned. Jillian looked up at her curiously.

"Are you all right, Miss?" The woman stood before Jillian with a brochure in her hand. Jillian shook her head, snapping herself back. "Yes, I was seeing a magnificent ball." She saw the woman look at her strangely. "That is...I was just imagining this room 150 years ago."

"Yes, they must have had many parties in this room. It's very unusual for the time it was built. Most houses from this period had smaller rooms. This one room normally would have been three."

Jillian stood, reached out and took the brochure. "Thank you for the information." She smiled wanly, made her way to the door, fumbled with the lock, and let herself out. Her hands were shaking and she felt weak as she made her way down the steep stairs. The only thought that came clearly through her daze was to get back to the hotel and crawl into bed. She moved slowly up Drayton Street. At the hotel, she went straight to her room, ordered a sandwich, and waited for Drake's call. She needed more than ever to hear his voice.

When Drake called, Jillian could hear that he had been drinking, but chose not to mention it. She needed a sense of normality and hoped that Drake would provide it. He started in about the big sale he almost made, how he still hoped to close it, and the great leads he had. However, instead of feeling the relief she was looking for, she felt annoyed. He talked for nearly half an hour without asking how she was or how the trip was going. She didn't bother telling him.

After they hung up, she called Anna. She started the conversation describing the work she was assigned and the great experience she was getting. Anna let her go on for a while, and then finally interrupted. "Jillian, what's really going on? Why'd you really call?"

"You'll think I'm nuts," Jillian cautioned her friend.

"I already do, so no danger there. Come on. Tell me what's going on." Anna lapsed into silence, waiting for her friend to find the words she needed.

Sighing, Jillian began, "I went sightseeing by myself today; just wandering around. I saw this beautiful old federal style house that's now a bed and breakfast and went inside. While I was waiting for the proprietor to bring some information on the place for me, I must have dozed off or something. ..This is the crazy part. I saw the room filled with people wearing clothes from the nineteenth century. There was a ball going on and it was night time and a different season." Jillian waited for Anna to laugh at her or tell her she was indeed going insane.

"Well, it's not a total mental break down. You were probably just caught up in the atmosphere of the place. You let your imagination take over. That's all. Nothing to get so upset about, Jilly," Anna reassured her.

"Maybe, if that were all, but it seemed so real. I could hear the music. I felt that I knew some of the people there, that they were friends of mine. And I had a dream about the waterfront that was so vivid. It was more like a memory than a dream. Anna, it's as if I know this place. It's so weird!" Jillian gave a nervous little laugh.

"Well, maybe you've been there before, in the past," Anna suggested tentatively.

"What are you talking about? I've lived in Cincinnati all my life. I've never before been to Georgia." Jillian was confused by Anna's statement.

"I meant...well, maybe you lived there during the Civil War," Anna explained.

Jillian was dumbfounded. "Just how old do you think I am?" she finally managed to ask.

"No, silly. Don't be so dense. I meant in a past life; you know, reincarnation," Anna explained.

"Reincarnation? Do you believe in that stuff?" Jillian was amazed that she didn't know this about her old friend.

"Well, yes. I do. I think it makes sense. It's kind of like...cosmic recycling." Anna laughed. "It's just one possibility, Jilly. You don't have to accept it as the one and only explanation, but it fits the situation pretty well. And it's not uncommon for people to recover memories of past lives when exposed to the places they've lived before."

Jillian wanted to argue with Anna or tell her that she was the crazy one, but she remembered what she had thought when she looked at that house. She had seen it as it should have been, not as it was. Still, she was not ready to accept such an extraordinary concept as the explanation. "I don't know what it was, but it was damned strange. I just hope it's done with now. ..Listen, Anna, it's getting late. I'd better get to bed. Thanks for being there for me again, as usual."

"Sweet dreams, Jilly. Talk to you soon."

CHAPTER 13

The next day went by quickly. Jillian stayed focused on her work. She tried not to think about the strange experiences that she had been having. The group went to The Pink House for dinner. Joan sat next to Jillian, announcing that the women had to stick together for moral support. Conversation remained casual as they all ordered. Mike Johnson toasted the good work his team had been doing and told them they were definitely free for the weekend. The men decided that they wanted to go to Hilton Head for some golfing. The two women on the team were invited, but declined the offer.

"We're going antique shopping. Of course, any of you are welcome to come along with us," Joan offered facetiously. Her statement was received with cringing and noises of disgust. "You guys don't know what you're missing," Joan stated, looking at them with pity. The men agreed that they were hopelessly barbarian and were soon immersed in discussions of the course at Hilton Head and the challenges it offered. Jillian and Joan turned to a discussion of antique hunting.

"I've been doing some research on the subject. The concierge at the hotel told me there's an auction not too far away, in South Carolina on Saturday and another on Sunday. She said we could be there in about an hour. How does that sound?" Joan asked.

"Sounds like fun. What time do you want to leave?" Jillian found herself getting excited by the idea. And she really did want the chance to see some of the countryside while she was here. They agreed to leave after breakfast on Saturday morning.

Joan had rented a car for the weekend. They took Route 17 out of Savannah, over the river and into South Carolina. They drove through wooded swamp for miles. Finally, Jillian blurted out, "Are you sure you know where you're going? There's been nothing since we crossed over the river."

"We still have nearly an hour." Joan handed a map of the area to Jillian along with some hand written directions. "The auction is at an old farm in the country."

They turned toward McPhearson and Jillian started looking for signs. "Make a left at that light up there."

Joan followed Jillian's instructions. They turned right onto a narrow, tree lined road. The Spanish moss hanging off of the canopied live oak trees gave a mystical feel, as if they were traveling back in time. Joan instinctively slowed down. A couple of miles down the road, Jillian spotted an auction sign pointing to a dirt road. They turned onto it and drove through a densely wooded area for a half-mile, and then it suddenly opened up to what appeared to be an old cotton plantation. There were already a number of cars parked in a field to the left. Joan turned in and parked at the end of a row of SUVs, pick-up trucks, vans, and cars.

The two women started walking toward some tents that were pitched on the other side of the road. Joan started to explain to Jillian how the auction would most likely work. They'd have a chance to look at the items close up before the auction actually began, and then register and get a number to use for the bidding.

Jillian followed Joan around as she explored the rows of items, reading the descriptions and commentaries that had been placed by each one. Jillian stopped when she spotted a silver hand mirror with magnolia blossoms molded on the back and handle and surrounding the glass on the front. She resisted a strong urge to pick it up and stood staring at it, not even noticing that Joan had moved on. She read the description. "Molded silver hand-mirror from the antebellum period. Probably made in the 1850s and owned by a woman of a local plantation. Many such items were sold during the 1860s to pay debts or to get cash for taxes or necessities." Jillian looked in the program and saw it was one of the early items to be auctioned. She went to the registration table and obtained a bidding number.

Joan came up behind her at the desk. "I take it you spotted something of interest."

"Maybe. There's a hand-mirror that just seems like it…well, it would be just right on my dresser."

"Good for you. Let's go in. They'll be starting soon."

Jillian watched intently as the first couple of items were auctioned off. She had never been to one before and felt unsure as to how to proceed when the mirror came up. She hoped it would not go too high; she just had to have it. Finally, she heard the auctioneer call out, "Item number six is a hand held, molded, silver mirror. It has a floral pattern. It probably was part of a set owned by a woman from one of the local plantations. It dates to the 1850s. We'll start the bidding at $50. Do I have 50? I have 50. Do I have 60? 60? Do I have $55?" Jillian raised her number so that the auctioneer could see her bid.

"I have 55. Do I have 60? I have 60. Do I have 65? 65?" The auctioneer looked at Jillian. She felt the pull of the mirror and knew she really wanted it. She nodded her head at the auctioneer.

"I have 65. Do I have 70? 70? I have 65. Do I have 70? I have 70. Do I have 75?" He was looking at her again. The thoughts rushed through her head. Was it worth $75 dollars? Was she getting cheated at that price? Did she want it that badly? She bit her lip, took a deep breath, and nodded to the auctioneer.

"I have 75. Do I have 80?" Jillian knew she had gone as far as she was willing to go. If someone raised the bid, she was out of the running. She held her breath. "80? Anyone? Sold for $75 to number 36. Our next item...."

Jillian sighed in relief. It was more than she thought she should spend on such a foolish purchase, but not so much that she couldn't afford it. She smiled at Joan with satisfaction and received her congratulations. "You need to go pay for the mirror and get a receipt for it. You can collect it later if you want," Joan told her. Jillian went to the cashier and quickly collected her mirror. She felt she needed to get it back into her possession as quickly as possible. Holding the heavy mirror and tracing the beautiful pattern on the back and handle Jillian felt as if she had found a piece of her life that had been missing for too long. She returned to her seat next to Joan who admired the magnolia pattern, but was herself soon caught up in a bidding war for an old chest she wanted.

The drive into the city of Beaufort only took a half hour. Jillian hardly noticed the scenery as she examined her new possession, gently following the curving lines with her fingers. Joan hadn't noticed Jillian's distraction; she was too busy following the directions to the bed and breakfast. When she turned onto Craven Street, she said, "We're almost at the Rhett House. We were really lucky to get in there. The concierge in Savannah said it would be impossible at such short notice."

"How did you hear about the place?" Jillian asked, coming out of her daze.

"My husband and I stay at bed and breakfasts on our antique hunting sprees. It was in one of my books. It's a bit expensive, but it sounds worth it. Oh, there it is!"

Jillian looked to her right where Joan had pointed. A large white house with a curving stairway on the right led up to an attractive veranda. Joan pulled around to the back of the house and found a spot to park. They walked back to the front of the house and climbed the stairs, entering through the front door off the veranda. Inside, a young man sitting at a desk greeted them. He asked their names, and then started telling them about the house as he handed them their keys. A woman entered from the hallway behind the desk, introduced herself, and began giving them a tour of the house while describing the services available and the schedule, and then led them to their rooms. Joan and Jillian agreed to meet downstairs in the living room for wine and hors d'oeurves at 6:00.

Jillian's room had the feel of the mid-nineteenth century, but with all the modern conveniences of a four star hotel. She put the mirror on the bed and went into the bathroom to shower. It had been a long day. When she had packed a long, black skirt and long sleeve, ruffled, white blouse, it had felt right at the time as she thought of Savannah. The outfit seemed perfect for the atmosphere of the house. She laughed to herself when she thought about Anna's comments. She went downstairs and poured a glass of wine. Joan wasn't there yet so she sat on the couch and started looking at a book of local restaurants. Other guests sauntered into the living room; conversation about the house and the city seemed to be a common topic as the strangers shared their experiences of the day. Joan joined Jillian on the couch and they picked out a restaurant on Bay Street that they could walk to easily. Jillian couldn't get over the feeling that she'd come home. After dining, they headed straight back to the Rhett House. While it was the last full weekend of daylight savings time, it was already dark out. They both had saved room for dessert and sat down at the kitchen table with a couple of other guests. Jillian helped herself to a piece of chocolate cake, while a young man served Joan some apple pie. The conversation was amicable, mostly about hometowns and unusual or out of the way vacation spots.

Jillian finally excused herself and headed upstairs to her room. When she opened the door, she saw that the bed had been turned down and there were mints on the pillow. She groaned, thinking, *Any other night I would have dived at the mints.* Then she remembered the mirror and started to panic because it was no longer on the bed. She sighed in relief when she spotted it on the nightstand.

Jillian fell asleep quickly and woke at first light. She knew that she had been dreaming, but could only remember a feeling of contentment. She still had a couple of hours before meeting Joan in the dining room, so she grabbed a cup of coffee from the side table in the living room and headed out to the veranda. It was chilly, so she drank her coffee quickly and decided to go for a walk. She started down Craven Street. As she passed the museum, she thought, *The arsenal is still here.* She hurried on and didn't stop again until she reached East Street. She looked around feeling confused. Something wasn't right. The houses were different from what they should have been. She turned left onto East Street, moving more slowly, looking at the homes on both sides of the street. She knew she was looking for something, but did not know what. There was a small house set back from the street that caught her attention. She didn't know why it seemed important to her, especially when there were so many others that were certainly more impressive. She walked around the corner, trying to see more, and then walked to the end of the street. As she looked out onto the water, she felt the confusion pass. There were other houses within sight that she felt sure she knew.

Jillian wandered back through the neighborhood, and then headed back on North Street toward the inn. When she reached Newcastle Street, she saw a large wall that aroused her curiosity. It was unlike any other she'd seen in Beaufort; it appeared to be very old and it was too high to see over. Discovering that the back of the Rhett House was in view, she realized that she still had time before meeting Joan for breakfast and she was already close by. She continued on Newcastle until she came to an open entranceway. It was St. Helena's Episcopal Church and cemetery. She slipped into the back of the church. She couldn't shake the feeling that she'd sat there before many times, but that things had somehow changed. She lingered there, relaxing, wondering about the strange thoughts and feelings she was experiencing. She only looked at her watch when she heard someone else enter. She was late; she got up and hurried out to meet Joan.

"Sorry, I'm late," Jillian apologized.

"With the sea air, it's easy to over sleep," Joan smiled and shrugged, and then indicated they should go inside to breakfast.

Jillian didn't bother to explain where she had been or what she had been doing. She wasn't sure she could explain. She was having trouble explaining it to herself.

Breakfast started with fresh fruit. As they ate, Joan told Jillian about the afternoon's auction she had planned for them. Nearby, there were the ruins of the Old Sheldon Church that had been burned down once during the Revolutionary War, and then again during the Civil War. Joan suggested that they stop there first since they had plenty of time. Being Sunday, the auction would not start until 2:00.

They headed out of town, making their way to the Old Sheldon Church. The turn off to the ruins was about twenty minutes out of Beaufort and shortly before the village of Sheldon. Jillian felt overwhelmed with sadness as they drew near, but she could not identify the source of her feelings. Joan parked along the side of the road.

Jillian followed Joan into the graveyard where she walked among the headstones and above ground tombs, reading the names and dates. She came to a family plot with the name Peters carved at the top of a marker stone. Carved below were the names and dates of death: "John Augustus Peters, died March 30, 1862, beloved wife, Charlotte Maitland Peters, January 10, 1863, our courageous son, James Lucius Peters, March 23, 1862." There were other markers, but Jillian's eyes were blurring. She forced herself to move away, but stopped at a lone stone next to the family plot. It read "Daniel Proctor, died February 11, 1906." Her hand quickly moved to her throat as she choked out, "No, that's not possible."

Joan asked, "What are you talking about? You look as if you've seen a ghost."

Jillian pointed to the lone headstone.

Joan answered her own question. "I see what you mean. Why would they bury someone here over forty years after the church burned down?" She looked around. "There seems to be some even more recent ones across the way."

"What a strange, sad place!" Jillian dabbed at her eyes, surprised at her emotional response to the grave. "Let's get out of here."

Joan followed Jillian back to the car, confused by her companion's reaction. As she turned the car around, Joan said, "We're going to an old horse farm. It's only a couple of miles from here. We'll be there early, but I don't think it will be a problem." She went back to the main highway, turned right, and started looking at the street signs. She turned left at an auction sign. The road wound to the right. At a fork, another sign pointed the way to the left onto a narrow, paved, tree-lined road. A faded, white washed, three-rail fence ran along the right side. A broad opening in the fence revealed a wide, hard packed, dirt road. The fencing continued down each side of the drive. Live oaks formed a canopy above, with Spanish moss hanging down. After a couple hundred yards, the fencing made right angle turns, the rows of trees stopped, and the roadway widened, leading to an old house, with a barn and carriage house to the right and out buildings off to the left. Two horses grazed in a four-rail paddock off the barn. The buildings and paddocks all appeared freshly painted. The two-story carriage house next to the barn had been converted into an auction house, identified by large red lettering over the double doorway. It appeared that the owners of the property supported themselves and the old farm by regular auctions of artwork, antiques, and collectibles. They had even converted one of the small cabins into a snack bar and another into restrooms.

Joan followed the parking signs through a wide, open gate to what obviously had been a small pasture. There were only a couple of cars already in the lot. "It looks like the snack bar is open. I'm sure it won't compare to our breakfast, but I could use a little something," Joan stated.

Jillian followed quietly. She didn't have much of an appetite. She was still feeling confused over her sadness and reaction to the old cemetery. Going to what appeared to be an old slave house for food just didn't seem right. She looked at the main house. It didn't seem that they'd made any changes to it other than the landscaping. As she sipped her soda, she looked around the farm. She felt comfortable, but noting the big red auction sign on the carriage house, she became annoyed. The double doors under the sign opened.

Joan had been watching the doors while she ate. "Great, they're ready for us to start scouting out the goodies. Ready?" She tossed the rest of her sandwich into a nearby trashcan.

The first floor of the carriage house was filled with rows of folding chairs. To the right was the registration desk; in front was a raised platform and lectern; to the left was a wooden staircase leading to the second floor. A sign indicated that items were on display for preview on the second floor. Auction programs were being handed out by a teenage boy at the door. Jillian looked at the cover; it read, "Whispering Oaks Farm." Below was a drawing of a mare and foal. She held the program tightly and stumbled up the stairs following Joan, repeating "Whispering Oaks Farm" under her breath as a mantra. Jillian saw nothing as Joan perused her potential prizes.

"I'm so glad we arrived early. There are some real finds here. Let's go register," Joan said eagerly, the light of acquisition in her eyes.

"I think I spent my allowance yesterday. I'm going to skip the auction and enjoy the fresh air," Jillian informed her, somewhat apologetically.

"I'm sorry. Sometimes, I forget not everyone is addicted like I am," Joan stated, looking at her friend with concern. "Do you want to leave?"

"No, don't worry about it. Enjoy the auction. It really is beautiful here and when we get back to Cincinnati we won't be sitting outside enjoying warmth like this for many months." Jillian waved to her friend. "I'm going to explore." She walked out of the carriage house and took a deep breath. She needed some time alone.

More cars had pulled into the lot and people strolled by her, moving in the opposite direction. She walked over to the paddock. She hadn't been standing there long when a bay mare came over to her. She gingerly patted her head. "You're a friendly one. I've always wanted to have a horse, but I've never had a chance to really even ride one." As she spoke to the horse, the mare's ears twitched as if she were listening to Jillian's words. She kept patting her until the mare had enough and went back to grazing.

She left the paddock and walked to the front of the house. Jillian noticed the ceiling fans on the porch and mumbled, "Those would have been nice." She walked on around the side of the house, careful not to get too close. She wanted to make her way to the pond out back. She wondered if the magnolia trees were still there. She didn't even question how she knew these things.

Behind the house was a swimming pool and manicured lawn. Jillian was jolted by the sight. These modern features seemed so out of place. At the edge of the lawn, there were some magnolias planted, but they were relatively young. Jillian made her way toward the pond. Finding a bench near it, she sat and stared out over the water. She looked around at the tall grass waving in the light breeze and at the bright colors of the changing leaves. There were gentle ripples playing across the surface of the pond, and light speckled the water. She felt herself relaxing under the surprisingly warm October sun.

CHAPTER 14

Spring had arrived in Prince William Parish, the magnolias were blossoming, the air was fresh and clear, warm but not yet humid. Ellie had slipped out of the party, annoyed with everyone. She sat heavily on a bench under a magnolia tree near the pond and let out a sigh. She looked out across the fields and started to relax as she watched the foals romping around their mothers. She smiled at the enigma of their simultaneous awkwardness and grace, not realizing that she might present the same image to someone observing her. She wore a white muslin gown, trimmed in navy blue, with lace at the bodice and short, puffy lace sleeves. Her mother had traced the pattern out of a new fashion book from Paris; the style was all the rage for spring afternoon party dresses. Her seamstress made it for her and Ellie was quite pleased with it, but now she sat with her elbows on her knees and her hands holding up her head, indifferent to her appearance or what others might think of her. She was lost in thought.

"What is my little magnolia doing all by herself when there are such festivities going on at the house?" the tall, red-haired man asked, walking up behind her.

"Oh, Ted! Those people just infuriate me." She stamped her foot down on the trampled earth in front of the bench. Ted sat down beside her. "What happened, Ellie?"

"All those women can talk about is the latest fashions from Paris or who was seen talking with whom at the last party. And the men only want to hear, 'You are so right!' There is no real exchange of ideas, no give and take of debate."

Ted laughed. "You disagree with me all the time."

"You do not count," she stated, making a dismissive gesture.

He made a face and feigned being hurt.

"Oh, stop it, Ted. You know very well what I mean," she pouted.

"You mean I am not marriageable material." He smiled. "Well, we had better go back to the party or they will be announcing our engagement."

"You really are my best friend. You are the only one who listens to me." Ellie tilted her head and leaned it against his shoulder briefly, glad that her brother

James' friend had become her friend too. Even as children, he would argue with her brother to let her ride with them or play games with the boys. Sighing, she got up and started back. When Ted didn't follow, she asked, "Are you coming?"

"I'll catch up. We do not want to give them any ideas." Ted didn't let on that his family already had the idea. He liked Ellie; he liked her spirit, but he wasn't ready to marry anyone.

Ellie slipped back into the house and hoped that she had not been missed. She didn't want to listen to her mother go on about her role as a proper Southern hostess. Although her mother hadn't appeared to notice her missing, everyone else noticed her entrance. What Ellie didn't realize was that she was notable. Eloise Maitland Peters was a tall, slender eighteen year old, with dark auburn hair and green eyes, high cheekbones, and a long narrow face. Yet, her confidence gave her the appearance of maturity. Men would stare and enjoyed being seen with her and dancing with her. But it wouldn't take long for her to express her ideas. Some found them shocking; some amusing; some just plain wrong. The one thing they did agree upon was that, as a wife, she would be too difficult to manage.

The women didn't understand her either. The younger ones were jealous of the attention she received, but thought she was foolish. They either disagreed with her ideas, or, if they agreed, thought she should keep quiet about them, especially around the men. The older women couldn't understand how her proper mother, Charlotte, could produce such an outspoken, opinionated, young woman. Her cousin, Emmeline, was the only one who seemed to accept her as she was.

The drawing room was crowded with familiar faces, family and neighbors from the parish. Ellie had known these people all her life and pretty much knew exactly how each of them would respond to anything she might say. As she moved through the room, she smiled sweetly at each guest. She had to admit that she really did love them all. She just felt frustrated and stifled. Ellie felt a pang of jealousy seeing Emmeline sitting near the fireplace, surrounded by admiring young men. She wished she felt the social ease her cousin possessed in abundance. Emmy never said the wrong thing. She was the darling of every dowager in the room. Even the other girls their age had nothing bad to say about her. And Emmy was beautiful; no one could deny it. But Ellie also knew that she did not want to be just like Emmy. She was proud of her own independent and assertive nature. She just wished these people could appreciate it as much as she did.

Emmy saw her cousin come in and scooted her voluminous skirt over to make room on the loveseat for Ellie. The small group of young people was discussing the prospects for the rapidly approaching summer in Beaufort. As Ellie made an effort to join in the small talk, she saw her mother across the room raise her eyebrow and look down at the hem of Ellie's new dress. As casually as possible, she looked down and saw the dirt and dry grass collected there. She looked up at her mother embarrassed that she'd been caught, and then dropped her eyes, hoping no one else would notice. At least, no one was rude enough to comment on it, not even her thirteen year old sister, Suzanne, opened her mouth. However, Ellie sighed, knowing later on she was in for a lecture from one of her parents.

Most of the guests had left, but a few from farther away were spending the night. Ellie was informed her father wanted to speak to her in his study. Normally, she enjoyed spending time with him, but she suspected she was not going to like what he'd have to say. John Augustus Peters was sitting at his desk looking at some papers when Ellie entered his study. Evenings being still chilly, she wrapped a shawl tightly around herself and curled her legs under her as she sat down in an over-stuffed chair across the room and silently waited. Eventually, he looked up and sternly said, "What am I going to do with you, young lady?"

She tried her most innocent sounding voice, "I am sure I do not know what you are talking about, Father."

John got up and sat in the matching chair closest to his daughter. "Ellie, you are nearly nineteen years old. This party today was not just to sell horses, but also to give you the opportunity to socialize. It is important that we find a good husband for you, soon. What do you think you are going to do when I am not around anymore to take care of you?"

"Father, James will not stay here. He has no interest in our horses. He is going to become an attorney. Suzanne is going to marry someone wealthy; that is all she ever dreams or talks about. So, who will stay here and take care of you and the horses if your other children will not? Me! I'll have plenty of time to find the right man."

"What about Ted Campbell? The two of you spend a lot of time together. He likes the horses and being the third son, other than his trust, he is not in line for much of the family's rice plantation."

"That red-headed fool? He drinks too much. He gambles too much. He isn't interested in anything, but having a good time," she complained, listing only a few of his character flaws, as she perceived them.

"I know it seems that way. We all thought the same thing about his father. We were sure he would lose his family's business before he was thirty. But as soon as he married, he settled down. Ted will do the same. He just needs a strong woman to take him in hand. You are a strong woman, Ellie."

"He is not for me!" she stated vehemently, staring down at her feet, brows knitted.

"Then why do you spend so much time with him? And you have not scared him off with your nonsense." Her father drew on his cigar, blowing out a calculated ring of smoke.

"What nonsense?" Ellie's head snapped up, ready to do battle.

"All that Abolitionist talk for one thing. Our place is not so dependent upon slave labor, but the lowland planters would not be able to turn much of a profit without slaves. And this talk about women doing everything men do! You have got to stop such talk." Her father punctuated his words with bellicose thrusts of his cigar.

"You know I can do anything the men around here do, and as well as most. Besides, if I cannot talk honestly with a man, how could I live my life with him?" she huffed self-righteously.

"Since when do you think your mother has been honest with me?" he enquired, grinning. "She rarely is and we have a wonderful marriage and three wonderful children. What more could you want?"

"I do not know, but I am not like Mama. I like working with the horses. I love this farm and Beaufort. I could not care less if I ever went to Savannah or Charleston again. I want a man who wants what I want." She pounded her fist against her knee.

Leaning back in his leather chair, John Peters sighed. "I wish you would consider Ted. The two of you seem to get along and he will accept your attitudes."

"He might, but you know how I feel about the slaves. His family is involved with the Rhetts. Do you want me fighting with my in-laws?" Ellie was sure she had scored a point with her father.

"You can have your opinion, but you need to let others have theirs, too," he reasoned with his stubborn daughter.

"But they are wrong!" she exclaimed, jumping to her feet. "You should free our slaves now. It's coming eventually, anyway."

"Ellie, please be reasonable! The Rhetts and their friends are powerful. You do not need to cause trouble." John frowned with concern for his daughter's future.

"I do not want to fight with you, Father. Perhaps it would be best if I retired for the night."

"Very well." He sighed. "That might be best. Good night, dear." John kissed her cheek. Ellie accepted the kiss stiffly and turned to walk out.

As she left the room, her father yelled after her, "Remember, you are a Southerner."

Ellie didn't respond. She stormed up the stairs to her room only to find her mother sitting there waiting for her. "Mother, what do you want?" Ellie demanded, unhappy at being ambushed when she had already been castigated.

"Do not use that tone with me, little miss. Your father might put up with your insolence, but do not try it with me. I saw you out back with that Ted today, and with all those eligible men inside. What were you thinking?" Charlotte pressed her lips together in disapproval.

"Ted is my friend," Ellie defended.

"You do not need a friend. You need a husband," her mother attacked.

"Mother, I want one, too. But none of them were right for me."

"Ellie, you can have your pick if you would just do what I have told you." Charlotte rose from her seat and approached her daughter, trying to persuade her to be reasonable.

Ellie kissed her mother's cheek; she knew her mother's heart was in the right place. She just didn't agree with her perspective about marriage. "Mother, as soon as I meet the right one, I will tell you."

"Ellie, if you do not find a husband in the next year or two, your options will not be nearly as good. Do you want to marry a widower and have to raise someone else's children? If you wait too long, you may only be able to have one child of your own, if any." She waited for her daughter to respond. When she didn't, she added, "You have chased so many young men away already..." Sighing, Charlotte embraced her daughter. "Think about what I have said to you, child. Think about what your future will be and should be." She patted her daughter's cheek. "Sweet dreams, Ellie."

"Good night, Mama." Ellie breathed a sigh.

CHAPTER 15

The remaining guests departed over the next few days. It was nearly time to start preparations for the move to their Beaufort house to escape the heat and mosquitoes for the summer. Ellie sat in the shade on the front veranda contemplating her future. The days were starting to get warmer and more humid and the nights less cool; she was looking forward to leaving for their Beaufort cottage. Ellie looked up to see a tall, thin woman with ebony skin staring at her. Her coarse black hair was sticking out of her bandana; she shifted her weight back and forth as if she were anxiously waiting, but afraid to interrupt.

"Yes, Lela? What can I do for you?" Ellie enquired, concerned by the woman's expression.

"M...M...Miz Ellie," she stammered. "We need yo hep in da barn." The woman gestured toward the structure.

"In the barn?" Ellie was confused. Lela worked in the flower and vegetable gardens for the house. "What is wrong? Has someone been injured?"

Lela looked around suspiciously. "Please, Miz Ellie."

Ellie's curiosity was aroused; she stood up and started down the porch steps. Lela ran ahead of her to the barn. When she entered the barn, Lela was at the top of the ladder leading to the hayloft. "Come, Miz Ellie. Come up."

"Lela, you tell me what is going on, right now!" Ellie was beginning to get concerned. She'd heard of some incidents of slaves suddenly turning on their masters. But Lela? They'd played together as little ones and she'd always treated her well.

"Miz Ellie, please, he's hurt," she pleaded.

Lela hadn't answered Ellie's fears, but she trusted her anyway. She tucked up her skirt in her waistband and started climbing the ladder. When she reached the top, she saw Lela beckoning to her from behind a mound of hay. She approached cautiously. Behind the hay was a large man, darker than Lela; he appeared to be about thirty years old and had the muscles of someone who had worked the fields his whole life. He was sitting on the floor, rocking himself. As Ellie was about to ask who he was, she saw the blood caked on his face and upper body. In the deepest voice she'd ever heard, he hissed at Lela, "What ya bring her here fo'? Ya want me sent back an' killed?"

Ellie was startled and unsure of what to do. "Who did this to you?" As she peered more closely at him, she saw his ear was nearly hanging off. When he didn't respond, she asked, "Was it your master?"

"Yes'm, Miz. Ah couldn't take no mo', so Ah jist lef."

"Who is your owner? What did you do?" she asked, frowning at the severity of the injury. Ellie was sure he must have assaulted someone at the very least to receive such a beating. She didn't want to assist a felon.

"Marster Robert Anton over ta Honeysuckle Bower. Ah din't do nothin' wrong. He say Ah was too slow. He beat me wit his cane." The man's pain and anger showed in his dark eyes.

Ellie started pacing in the loft, trying to clear her head. "No one can know he is here." She paced some more, thinking, and talking aloud to herself, "If he gets caught, I could be arrested and you two could be sold or killed. I do not know what my father would do if he were to find out. There would be real problems." Looking at Lela's anxious, pleading face, "We will clean him up, and as soon as he is healed, he goes. No one can know! Understand?"

Lela just nodded. Ellie headed down the ladder. "Get a bucket of water, some castile soap, a sponge, and a couple of those horse towels. I'll be back and we will fix that ear and clean him up."

Her heart was pounding as she headed back into the house. She wanted to run, but she knew if she did she'd raise suspicions that she was up to something. She wasn't even sure what she needed. She thought about the times she'd watched when one of the horses had been injured. *Clean it; stitch it, then a poultice, and then bandage. How do I make a poultice without anyone questioning me? Witch hazel, needle and thread, whiskey and old linen, scissors.* She gathered up the supplies and slipped back out of the house. When she entered the barn, she looked around to make sure none of the grooms saw her and headed up the ladder. Lela was with the man, waiting. He was obviously in pain, but appeared more frightened of Ellie than anything. Ellie felt her heart in her throat. She didn't know this man, she didn't know if his story was true, but she refused to acknowledge that she was afraid.

Handing the man the bottle of whiskey, Ellie directed Lela to wash his wounds. After he had taken a couple swallows of the alcohol, Lela began wiping away some of the blood. He cringed and moaned with each touch of the wet, soapy cloth. Ellie knew the next step would hurt more and she was afraid he'd cry out. They couldn't allow anyone to hear. She sent Lela down to get a leather halter. She could see by the look on the woman's face that she didn't understand. When she came back with one, Ellie handed it to the man. "Bite on it. The next part will hurt; you can't make any noise."

The man nodded and bit down on the leather. She swabbed on the witch hazel. He bit down hard until he passed out. Ellie tried to quickly stitch the ear back onto his head. She felt her stomach churn as she pushed the needle through the cartilage of the ear and the flesh of his head. She poured more witch hazel over the surgery. The two women then struggled to wrap him in the strips of linen Ellie had cut up. She gave the bottle of whiskey to Lela. "If he wakes, you can give him more, but do not let him have the whole bottle. We do not want him getting drunk. With the spring grass in abundance, no one should be up here for hay, but be careful." Ellie listened, and then slipped down the ladder and out of the barn. As she walked back to the house feeling anxious, but satisfied with herself, she thought, *We need to find a better hiding place.*

Over the next few days, she gave Lela extra food and helped her change the bandages. She found out the man's name was George. Gradually, he became more trusting and told her about the beatings he and the other slaves endured on the cotton plantation he'd come from. He'd been born there, but some of the elders had told him about their homeland and the suffering they had endured on the horrible voyages in the holds of ships crossing the ocean. He talked about others who had escaped and those who had been caught and horribly punished. Ellie managed to ask questions and to listen without showing any emotion. But at night, alone, she cried and her anti-slavery feelings were strengthened. She resolved to do something to help these poor lost souls, not to just talk about it. However, she remembered her father's warning and the laws of South Carolina. She'd have to be careful. She'd already made one mistake. She'd left the scissors in the loft and her mother had been looking for them. Lela had managed to get them back to her and she'd covered, but it had been close.

Her first step for now was to help George to get to a Free State where he'd be safe. She'd seen the travel papers her father had made when he sent one of the slaves to Savannah. She would forge papers for him. She realized she'd have to do it soon, before he was caught on the farm and before they left for Beaufort. She penned the false documents that would get him as far as Baltimore, gave him some food and money for the trip. She told him to go to a Negro or Quaker church once he got there. Someone would help him from there. Although Maryland was a slave state, it shared borders with free states. The next day, George started his trek north and the Peters left for Beaufort.

CHAPTER 16

The trip to Beaufort was not far, but it was always a slow one. The roads were narrow and bumpy; often portions had been washed out or covered with mud, especially down in the low country. Bryan's Ferry was unusually crowded. During the late spring, many families left for breezier places during the hot, humid, summer months which frequently caused a long wait. It was always a relief to finally arrive at Beaufort.

During the summer of 1859 in Beaufort, most social gatherings started out or ended up focusing on politics. The movement for secession was growing stronger in South Carolina, and the inhabitants of Beaufort were some of the biggest supporters of secession. Edmond Rhett, the fifth son of the family, was one of the leaders of the Bluffton Boys, a group of men who had been pressing the state government to leave the Union. He was very powerful in Beaufort and stirred the planters' young sons to join the states rights and free trade movement. The only thing holding South Carolina back from secession, as far as they were concerned, was a lack of support from the other Southern states. Everyone was speculating on the presidential election to be held in the following year. Buchanan had been a compromise candidate in the last election. If a Northern candidate was elected president, the firebrands in South Carolina were convinced that other states would join them in the push for secession. Political meetings were being held almost constantly at Robert Barnwell Rhett's house.

Ellie knew that her new resolve was going to be dangerous for her to express in such a climate. It would impact her family just as much as her. She had to prepare. While Suzanne was still attending the Beaufort Female Seminary, Ellie had finished the year before and had free time. She was determined to learn more about the issues surrounding slavery. She had also heard rumors of something called the Underground Railroad from some of their slaves after they heard she had helped George. Ellie knew that there were other people, both Negro and white, who were secretly assisting runaway slaves to get to freedom in the North, and she felt she needed to learn as much as possible about it if she were going to follow through on the promise she had made to herself.

She went to the Beaufort library nearly every day as soon as it opened, not that she expected to find books or magazine articles on the topic. Ellie hoped to get some indication about how this conspiracy operated. She also wanted to learn as much as possible about the laws governing slave owners. She read the Charleston and New York newspapers looking for stories about the Abolitionists. She skimmed books from the law section, philosophy section, and political and history section. Whenever she found something relevant, she'd read passages more closely. Ellie knew that she was facing a difficult fight. She had to be prepared to debate with family, friends, neighbors, and strangers about the ethics of owning another person. It wouldn't make her popular here. But she also knew she wouldn't be a social pariah. There were other voices against slavery in Prince William Parish. There would be allies as well as foes. The real problem arose from helping the slaves to escape. It would be looked upon as equivalent to stealing someone's horse or gold. Her family could be sued and she could end up in prison.

She couldn't get the image of George's ear out of her head. Eventually, she ventured into the science section and read medical texts voraciously. She understood that summers in Beaufort would continue as they always had: a time for learning and socializing. The work she was planning for herself could only be carried out while on the farm. She was learning how to prepare for it and how to do it. But George's arrival had been a chance occurrence. She didn't know how to get started. She had learned that it had to be word of mouth. But if the wrong ears were to hear of it, she and her family could lose everything.

Ellie found herself looking forward to social events in ways she never had before. Along with education, politics had always been at the core of life in Beaufort. She wanted to listen; she needed to find out who might have similar opinions as her own.

An opportunity soon arose. The Peters family was invited to an evening social at their neighbors' home. Several families would be attending the gathering. Suzanne was excited about the party and bounced around the room while Ellie was dressing. All she could talk about was the beaus she would have attending her. Ellie dressed carefully, but gave no thought to beaus. Her concern was in finding allies.

Noah Tucker, the owner of a moderately large rice plantation, and his wife, Martha Emms Tucker, were the hosts for the evening. They and their three sons, Brent Thomas, Edwin Elliot, and Jonathan Danner Tucker, were all staunch Secessionists. Ellie knew that there would be no support from them and that she would have to be very careful about what she said in front of them in their home.

Franklin Adams, an elderly cotton planter, and his wife, Frances Johnson Adams, were Federalists. Franklin's father had been a hero of the American Revolution and Franklin persisted in believing that the Union was worth maintaining. He and his wife were in favor of compromise with the North. Their son and his wife, Thomas Wheeler Adams and Caroline Walker Adams, were also planters. They were heavily dependent upon their slave labor force to maintain their way of life and feared the abolition of slavery; however, they felt that secession was an extreme position. Their grandsons, Patrick and James, were devout states rights supporters and avid Secessionists. Ellie was certain that none of this family would be supportive of her work to aid escaping slaves.

Finally, John Henry Cunningham, another cotton planter, and his wife, Mary Margaret Drout Cunningham, who was originally from New York, were staunchly against secession. Mrs. Cunningham on occasion had voiced Abolitionist views that caused some of her neighbors to take umbrage with her. Ellie thought this woman might be willing to offer some information. The Cunningham girls, Rebecca and Johanna, were friends of Ellie and Suzanne. Their son, Michael, was more interested in playing billiards, gambling, and cockfighting than in politics.

The Tuckers had a larger house than the Peters' summer cottage. Their formal drawing room and their back parlor were separated by a pair of sliding pocket doors that opened up to create a greater space for entertaining. Several divans and numerous chairs were scattered throughout the two rooms, providing seating for most of the guests. Mr. Tucker had his butler set up a table in the midst of his company. Upon it were displayed all the ingredients for his favorite mint julep recipe. The host made a great show of preparing this beverage for all his guests, with much friendly joking about the ceremony he placed upon the production. Then several young male slaves dressed in their finest clothes passed the small silver cups out to the waiting company. Soon conversation turned to the favorite topic of the day, secession.

"The Union must be preserved! Our fathers fought too long and hard to create this great nation. To divide it now while it is still so young will open us up to attack from other nations who still turn a greedy eye to our borders. It is less than a generation since we fought for possession of the western lands. How quickly would Mexico move to reclaim Texas, California, or all the land between from us? We cannot afford to weaken ourselves in the eyes of the world by this division," Franklin Adams pronounced.

"Franklin, we can no longer abide the interference of the Federal government in our affairs. These Northerners have no understanding of our way of life. They see the South as rich and therefore able to bear the expense of this whole country by taxation. Our founding fathers were brought to revolution on this very topic...unreasonable taxation. Our livelihoods depend upon our exportation of cotton and rice. Yet, they continue to maintain the tariffs that hurt us more than any other region of the country. It is unconstitutional for the Federal Congress to pass laws that are harmful to the individual states. How can we ignore the rights of the individual states that make up the Union? Are we to be treated as the red-headed stepchild? Are we to sit by idly while our God-given rights are stripped away from us?" Noah Tucker demanded.

"Indeed, Grandfather, these Northerners want to strip us of more than our rights. If the Abolitionists have their way, we will each be out plucking cotton from the fields by ourselves while we are inundated by indolent Negroes who feel that they should be treated as our equals," Patrick Adams declared with disgust. "They would have us set these animals free and declare them to have the same rights and privileges as any white man."

"And would that be so very bad, Mr. Adams?" Mrs. Cunningham asked, raising an eyebrow and pinching her lips together in disapproval. "Are these poor Negroes not entitled to the same liberties as human beings that you and I enjoy? As any human being has a right to expect in this country, except the poor colored man?"

"Madam, it is well known that these Negroes are in the position of slaves because of their mental deficiencies. We do them a service by providing them with labor for their hands, and homes, food, and clothing. If they did not receive these things from our hands, they would soon return to the primitive conditions in which their ignorant, animalistic, savage ancestors lived. To free them would be to give up on any opportunity to improve them as a race. By nurturing and monitoring them as one would small children, we protect them from the travails of this world. We give them a safe haven in which to live and procreate. It is the white man's burden, as the British like to say," Brent Thomas Tucker stated. Ellie looked at him incredulously, realizing that he was sincere in his belief that he was saving, helping, and protecting these enslaved people by keeping them enslaved.

"But, Mr. Tucker, how can any of them learn or grow as people, 'improve' as you put it, when we refuse them the means to do so. We have established laws that prohibit them from obtaining the education that has helped us to rise to our current positions of power and prominence. If they are ignorant, is it not we who are to blame? If they are indolent, is it not the same as you or I might be in such an enforced situation? How many of us would willingly increase the wealth and power of those who enslave us? Is this not, in fact, the basic reason for our revolt against the tyranny of the British crown? We wished to benefit ourselves and our families from the products of our labor, rather than enriching those who were already rich. How can we not grant the same rights to those who have labored so long for us without reward?" Ellie interjected into the conversation.

"Miss Peters, you are assuming that these Negroes are equal to whites in their capacity to learn. How often have we all seen our overseers and drivers struggling to the point of violence to teach field hands to do the tasks assigned them and to do them properly and quickly? These are not true humans as you and I. They are an inferior race. God has placed them under our dominion as he did all the animals of the field. As good Christians, it is our duty to care for their physical and spiritual welfare. The Bible says nothing against slavery. In fact, there are multiple references to it. Even Father Abraham had slaves. Paul told Christian slaves to love their masters and to serve them well. We must see to it that they live up to the most of their potential, thus we give them the tasks that they are capable of learning and do not burden them with education which would only make them discontented with their lot in life," explained Edwin Elliot Tucker who, as the middle son and not likely to inherit, was studying to be a minister.

"But, if they are incapable of learning, why do we need laws prohibiting us from teaching them? And if the laws are necessary, does that not then contradict the argument that they are unteachable?" Ellie persisted. An uncomfortable silence followed this question.

Martha Emms Tucker, fanning herself, stated, "I do not know if they may learn or not. Certainly, some of them are very clever and quick to learn when they want. But I fear what would happen if they were all suddenly released from our control and influence. You were not born yet, so you cannot remember the unspeakable horrors of the Denmark Vesey revolt in '22, or worse still, Nat Turner's in '31. Sixty white people were killed in that uprising; cut to pieces and some burned alive! What would happen if all these slaves decided to rise up against us? And we have more slaves in this state than in any other. Even if they do not rise against us, what would become of us and our way of life if they were all suddenly freed? White men and women would find themselves a very put upon minority surrounded by resentful Negroes. I for one could not survive such a life. I get palpitations just contemplating it." She worked her fan harder, while Caroline Walker Adams, seated next to her, rubbed her hand.

"Well, Madam, we may well find ourselves in that situation if these Northerners have their way. They will take our property from us without compensation, and leave us all destitute. Mark my words! We will none of us have a penny or a crop to sell when they set our Negroes free," Noah Tucker prophesied.

"And that is why we must secede from the Union! The Federal government will not protect us or preserve our way of life. We must do it for ourselves. We must secede, even if it means war!" declared Jonathan Danner Tucker, the host's youngest son who was eager to test himself in battle. Ellie saw Mrs. Tucker look at her youngest son with both pride and fear.

"Surely, it will not come to war. They must realize that we are not compatible with them. They will let us go, won't they?" Caroline Adams pleaded in fear.

"There is still room for compromise," her husband Thomas reassured her. "There is no reason to believe that the North will push this to war. If we can work out a compromise, we will not have to secede. Some of these laws and tariffs will have to be rescinded. There are good men working on our behalf."

The conversation continued in this vein until dinner was served. Ellie found herself distracted during the meal, thinking about all of the arguments, pro and con, for secession and for abolition. She knew it was a complicated problem with at least some merit on both sides; however, she could not agree with the idea that one human should own and control another. She was more resolved than ever to do as much as she could to assist any runaway slaves who came across her path.

CHAPTER 17

As the summer progressed, Ellie started to collect things she thought she would need. The biggest difficulty that she had was coming up with excuses to get additional money out of her parents. She realized that she needed much more than she was accustomed to spending in order to purchase supplies and to have cash to give to escaping slaves. Blankets, food, and such, she knew she could gradually take from those kept at the farm. While she had never much enjoyed sewing and knitting, she told her mother that she was going to start taking up these crafts over the winter. When she noted her mother's raised eyebrow, she informed her that she wanted to get involved with the Ladies' Benevolent Society.

Charlotte announced that she was going to make a trip to Charleston. She was anxious to shop for some better materials for her wardrobe. Ellie asked her mother to be allowed to go along on the trip. The response was not at all what Ellie had expected. "Ellie, I will be glad for your company, but what is this new found interest in Charleston?"

"Mother, it's so stifling here. We see all the same people all of the time. I'd just like a change of scenery." Ellie thought that this would satisfy her mother's suspicions, but instead she received a raised eyebrow of disbelief.

"That is strange coming from one who seems to abhor society in general and would rather immure herself on the farm than be among people. Well, whatever your reason, I would enjoy your company."

Much to Ellie's relief, Ted Campbell dropped in the next day with a basket of various preserves his mother had sent along to the Peters family. Charlotte was effusive in her thanks to Mrs. Campbell and invited Ted to join her and Ellie for tea, and then began telling Ted of her plans for their trip to Charleston. "Of course, it will be a long and tedious trip to get there. I hate traveling on that ferry steamer. It seems to stop at every dock along the route and the boat becomes so very crowded. But such are the burdens of public travel." Charlotte sighed heavily, shaking her head, which caused her earrings to sway attractively, something she did consciously when interacting with men.

"Why, Mrs. Peters, ladies such as you and your lovely daughter should not have to be put through such hardship. It would be my great honor and privilege to convey you both to Charleston aboard my family's schooner. The Dragonfly is just sitting at our jetty. It would be a service to us, if you would allow me to take her out. And I would have the incredible joy of the exquisite company of the lovely

Peters women," Ted stated, bowing over Charlotte's hand and smiling into her eyes.

Charlotte smiled coyly at the charming compliment, and then suspicion entered her thoughts. Frowning, she said, "Hmmm. I am certain that you would appreciate the company of at least one of the Peters women. But I shall come along, nonetheless. I am certain that Ellie will not object too vociferously to my presence." The mother glowered at her daughter. Ellie realized that Charlotte thought she had asked to come along to Charleston because she planned to have Ted convey them there and she wanted to spend time in his company.

"Really, Mother, I am even more certain that Ted just desires to escape from the tedium of Beaufort's well known pleasures in order to taste new ones in Charleston. I do assure you his attentions have nothing to do with me at all." Ellie, blushing, tried to give her mother a solemn look of innocence, but Charlotte continued to frown and purse her lips disapprovingly. Ted did nothing to disabuse Charlotte of her notion; in fact, he decided to tease Ellie.

"Ah, Mrs. Peters, I am dazzled as always by your unfailing perspicacity. But I must confess that the charms of your daughter are as strong a draw for me as are the entertainments offered in Charleston. Indeed, having you present as well, makes the thought of the trip all the sweeter. Now, when shall we make this excursion?"

Ellie decided to let her mother delude herself about her daughter's motivation. It was better than having Charlotte question her further. The trio settled down to discuss plans for the trip.

Ellie enjoyed sailing and watching the view as they voyaged up the coast. The weather remained beautiful and she spent as much time on deck as her mother would allow. Charlotte remained below deck for most of the trip, warning her daughter that men did not want to marry women whose skin was tanned like leather and spotted all over with freckles. She frequently admonished Ellie to get in out of the bright sun, but Ellie refused to obey, preferring to feel the wind flying past her face and the wonderful fragrance of the sea. She loved watching the waves as the sun sparkled on the water. They were even joined by a school of dolphin for a while. Ellie delighted in their antics as they raced along side of and before the schooner. It was a glorious journey as far as she was concerned and ended far too soon to suit her.

The Dragonfly sailed into Charleston Harbor, past the watchful guns of Ft. Sumter and the other military installations guarding this teeming international port. Ted easily navigated the traffic of the busy harbor and found a berth for the schooner. The ladies were assisted out onto the dock and into a hired carriage. Once their luggage was loaded, they departed for the Planters Hotel. Charlotte was looking forward to getting settled in the hotel and complained profusely about the difficulties of travel. Fortunately, it did not take long to traverse the distance to the hotel. After getting their luggage stowed in their suite, they left their maids behind to unpack their things while the two women, accompanied by Ted, went to the hotel dining room for dinner. Charlotte and Ellie discussed their plans for shopping. Ted informed them of a performance of Shakespeare's *Julius Caesar* at the Dock Street Theater located in their hotel the next evening. They agreed to attend the show together. The travelers decided to retire early after their long trip and the busy day to come.

After a hearty breakfast of ham, rice and gravy, eggs, sausage and biscuits, and boiled fruit, Ted escorted Charlotte and Ellie through the shops of Charleston. Ellie focused on purchases that she hoped would rouse the least interest in her mother. She managed to separate herself from the others long enough to purchase canned foods which she arranged to have shipped to her at the farm. Ellie knew she might have to work out some explanation for them when the tins arrived, but she needed foods she could keep stored for prolonged periods; food that could travel in someone's sack. She also purchased sturdy cloth that could be made into clothing. She explained the material away as gifts for some of the slaves.

Charlotte looked askance at the bundles Mattie was carrying for Ellie when the party reunited, but she forbore asking about them in public. Ellie had also made some small purchases for herself: gloves, a lace fan, stockings, all things that her mother would approve. They returned to the hotel, dispatching the slave women upstairs to their suite with the packages, and went to the dining room to have lunch. After eating, the ladies retired to their rooms to rest before the night's entertainment.

That evening the trio, dressed in formal attire, attended the play. Ellie noted how stirred the audience was after the performance. She could hear snippets of conversations; most of them seemed to focus on the idea of overthrowing tyranny. Recognizing that these opinions reflected the growing unrest felt throughout the South, Ellie shivered with trepidation. She feared what might happen to her home, her state, and her country if no compromises could be reached.

The next day, the shopping party once again boarded the schooner and made the journey home to Beaufort. Ellie's anxious mood dampened her pleasure in being on the sea and she stayed below deck with her mother. Charlotte, pleased that her daughter was at last behaving sensibly, made no comment about the change in behavior and chatted endlessly on about what she had bought and all the entertainment they could look forward to during the rest of the summer at Beaufort.

As the summer was coming to a close, Charlotte started planning to go to Savannah before returning to Sheldon. Charlotte grew up in Savannah. Her older sister, Felicity Maitland Hamilton lived there, as well as many of her old friends. Ellie agreed to go with her. She knew that whenever her mother went shopping, money was freely spent. Also, she was looking forward to seeing her cousin, Emmeline. Again, Ted saw an excuse to get out of Beaufort and he offered to ferry them once more on the family schooner. While Charlotte was not pleased about the amount of time that her daughter was seen spending with Ted, she preferred the comforts of the Campbell's yacht to a public ferry. She agreed with her husband's position that now was not too soon for Ellie to get engaged. Reluctantly, she acknowledged that Ted might not be a bad candidate.

The Hamilton carriage was waiting for them when the schooner berthed in Savannah. Young Walker Smith Hamilton, known to friends and family as W.S., was sitting next to the family coachman, Henry, and grinning widely. At fourteen years of age, W.S. should have been in school, but had convinced his mother that he should be dispatched to wait for his aunt and cousin so that they would have "a man" to escort them from the waterfront to the Hamilton home. His mother had capitulated, feeling that it was important to encourage his sense of chivalry, although she suspected the idea of escaping school for a day was the greater motivator.

When the carriage drew up to Hamilton House, Emmeline came running down to the curb to greet the visitors, accompanied by a half dozen young Negro children, all of whom clamored for attention and the "privilege" of carrying the ladies luggage. Charlotte allotted the valises and boxes to the children, handing each a penny or two; they quickly manhandled their burdens into the house. Emmy embraced her aunt, and then her cousin. Taking their arms, she escorted them up the walk to the house, calling back over her shoulder for "Mr. Campbell" to keep up. Aunt Felicity waited decorously on the veranda for her sister and niece. She greeted her relatives with kisses and welcomed Ted warmly, thanking him for safely bringing her sister and niece to visit. W.S. rushed up the steps to the veranda, bubbling with news about all he had seen at the waterfront. Laughing, the party adjourned to the drawing room for refreshments.

That evening after dinner, Charlotte joined her sister and brother-in-law in visiting some old friends while W.S., Emmy, Ellie, and Ted remained at home. Reluctantly, W.S. went off to study. Before long, Emmy excused herself as well, pleading a headache, thus leaving Ellie and Ted to their own resources.

"I am sorry to do this to you, my dear friend, but I have some business to attend to, and I am afraid, I am going to have to abandon you as well," Ted announced shortly after Emmy retired.

"What? Where are you going?" Ellie demanded.

"I promised Michael Cunningham that I would look at some gamecocks for him. There is a man who has a warehouse down on the waterfront who imports them from Cuba. I thought I would go down there and speak to him while everyone else is busy," Ted explained.

"You are not going to abandon me here all alone! I need some divertissement and some exercise. I absolutely refuse to remain here reading. I will accompany you, if you cannot postpone this task," Ellie stated firmly.

"Ellie, you seem to have forgotten that we are not in Beaufort. The area of the waterfront to which I am going is certainly no place for a young lady. I will not be late. Surely, you have some correspondence you might work on while everyone is out," Ted returned, frowning.

"No! I am going with you or you are staying here with me. The choice is yours." Ellie was enjoying the challenge of dominating her friend on this point. She could see his hesitation over leaving her alone and his desire to go out warring in him.

"Ellie, be reasonable. What would your mother say if I allowed you to come along with me? You will just have to persevere here while I am gone." Having said this, he rose and proceeded toward the door with determination.

Ellie rose with equal determination and threw on her shawl. She picked up her reticule and followed Ted. Seeing her following him, he turned on her, frowning. "If you do not take me with you, I will simply follow you all the way there," Ellie pronounced, sensing victory.

"I am walking all the way there and back. There will be no carriage to take you," Ted tried arguing, hoping that the distance would prove daunting to her.

"I do not mind the thought of the walk at all. I am accustomed to greater distances than that at home, and there is no paved level lane to walk upon there. This will be no hardship at all. On the contrary, your argument has strengthened my resolve," she stated, walking past him out the door. Recognizing his defeat, Ted pulled the door closed and followed Ellie down the walk. Smiling graciously, Ellie took Ted's arm and they proceeded to the waterfront.

CHAPTER 18

The sun was well down in the west when they reached the ramp leading down to the riverside road. Ellie stepped carefully on the large cobblestones of the ramp, fearing she might lose her footing. Ted walked next to her or behind her when passing obstacles. Lifting her skirts out of the dirt, she carefully maneuvered around barrels, anchors, and other ship's gear. At the foot of the ramp Ellie saw a dark haired woman wearing a skirt, but with her corset and camisole uncovered. The woman ran her fingers over her exposed bosom in a very sensual and suggestive manner as she smiled at passing men. Two English sailors, just into port, approached the woman, smiling and joking with her in a lewd way. Ellie halted her progress in disgust. She felt Ted tug on her elbow and she proceeded around the little group. Once on the riverside road, they were approached by a group of dirty, little, white children begging for money. The children were accompanied by an older boy who smiled boldly at Ellie and looked her over in a very crude way. Ellie found herself wishing she had her riding crop with her, or her buggy whip. She would wipe the smile off that dirt smeared face. As they proceeded down the road, the stench of fish and offal polluted the air. Ellie searched in her reticule and pulled out a lacy handkerchief, and then pressed it to her nose and mouth. The pair hurried on. As darkness fell, Ellie became more aware of shadowy figures lurking in doorways and alleys. She felt anxious and drew closer to her companion, wishing she had not insisted upon coming. A rat skittered across their path causing her to jump back a step. She made a startled cry of disgust.

Laughing at her discomposure, Ted could not resist saying, "I told you not to come, but you would have your way." Ellie pulled her arm away from his grasp in anger and proceeded on ahead of him.

At last, they came to a small brick building with boarded up windows. There was no light or sound coming from the building. Ellie would have sworn that it was deserted, but Ted drew her around to a side door where he knocked. Several moments passed before there was a response. When the door finally opened, a very disreputable and disheveled looking old man gestured them inside. Ellie was amazed that she could be overwhelmed by a stench greater than that of the waterfront, but the odor inside the edifice was even more distressing. Pressing her handkerchief to her nose and mouth and lifting her skirts off the floor, Ellie proceeded to pick her way carefully across the filthy surface. In the dim interior light, she could see wooden crates and cages stacked, floor to ceiling along the walls. The floor was littered with dirty, damp straw coated with feathers and chicken feces. There was a constant din of cock crows. The old man led them through this chamber to another where a low walled ring was set up. There were a dozen or more men standing around the ring, some of them very well dressed, watching as two slaves faced each other inside the ring, holding two straining roosters. As Ellie took in the details of the scene, she realized that each bird had long blades attached to both feet. The slaves lifted the birds to show them off to the crowd as wagers were made on the outcome of the match. Then the two black men launched the birds at one another and quickly exited the ring. Ellie was aghast by the violence exhibited, but more so by the blood lust on the faces of the spectators. She turned her face away and moved back toward the door they had come through. Ted appeared to be thoroughly enjoying the spectacle, and cheered on the slaughter.

Once the match had ended, one of the men from the crowd detached himself from the group and approached Ted. Ellie was too far away to hear what was said, but the two men soon approached her. Ted took her arm and they went back out into the chamber where the gamecocks were housed. Ellie watched as Ted examined the stock and made some selections that he then arranged to have shipped to Beaufort. At last, their business concluded, Ted led Ellie back out into the relatively fresher air of the waterfront.

Looking at her somewhat green complexion, Ted again laughed at her discomfiture. "I guess next time, you will listen to me instead of insisting upon having your own way," he stated smugly. Ellie merely rolled her eyes and tugged his arm to get him moving back toward civilization.

Ellie was relieved that her mother did not discover her adventure. The next day, Ellie and Emmy took a carriage ride around the city together. Ellie decided to test the waters with her cousin, to see if she shared Ellie's feelings about slavery. Ellie told her cousin about the wrongs that slaves experienced on a daily basis, things she had learned about from George. She even told Emmy how she had helped George escape from the area.

Emmy was appalled and terrified for her cousin. "He might have murdered you! What if he had been caught? He might still be caught. You could go to prison! What would your father say? Oh, my gracious lord, Ellie! What were you thinking?"

"Hush, Emmy! Someone will hear you. We are out in public," Ellie cautioned, anxiously looking about to see if anyone might have observed her cousin's agitation. "Nothing happened and George is long gone. There's nothing to worry about now." She patted her cousin's arm soothingly.

Emmy fanned herself vigorously, trying to regain her composure. Ellie looked at Henry's back to see if he had overheard their conversation. The coachman sat stiffly erect, giving no sign that he had heard anything out of the ordinary. Seeing her cousin's reaction to the news of what she had already done, Ellie determined that she would not share anything more about her plans to continue to help the runaway slaves. They continued their drive and returned to the Hamilton's house without further discussion. The remainder of the visit was somewhat awkward for both Ellie and Emmy, but their long-standing affection overrode their mutual discomfort and they parted with great friendliness and promises to exchange letters soon.

CHAPTER 19

Ellie was relieved to get back to the farm. She had missed the horses and was excited about implementing her plans to help runaway slaves. Plus, the holidays would be coming soon; Christmas was her favorite time of year.

She quickly shooed her girl, Mattie, out of her bedroom once her trunks were brought up, stating that she wanted to rest after the long trip home. As soon as she was alone, she dug out the money she'd been saving, hidden in one of the trunks, and slipped it under her mattress. She realized she could not leave it there for very long and would have to find a better place. She then removed the new tin box she'd acquired and put it in her dresser under a winter shawl. She changed out of her travel clothes into an old, long sleeved, cotton blouse and skirt so that she could go down to the barn. She was anxious to see the weanlings and there wasn't much time before dark.

Twenty-four mares had foaled the previous spring, but there was one filly in which she was especially interested. The horse was a long legged chestnut, with four white socks almost to the knees and hocks, and a narrow blaze running down the middle of her face. Ellie had become attached to the filly the first she'd seen her and she was sure she'd be a beauty. She headed straight to the paddock where the weanlings were kept. Ellie spotted the filly immediately. She stood leaning on the rail watching the young horse romp with the others. She recognized that she would bring a good price, but she wanted her for herself. She decided to ask her father for the horse as a Christmas present. She knew it would be asking a lot, not only was the filly graceful, but she was of the Denmark line. She strolled back to the house thinking of names. Since childhood, she'd been told not to get attached to any one horse. They weren't pets; it was a business, but she never could stop herself.

The business of their farm was to breed, raise, and train American Saddlebreds. Most of the planters would breed a mare every couple of years or so. Many of them brought their broodmares to their farm for breeding. The Peters usually had at least five stallions standing stud and up to two hundred horses all totaled. Their stock had developed a reputation as the best riding and carriage horses, their closest real competitors being in Kentucky. Ellie's great-grandfather had started the farm with one stallion and four brood mares. The property had been all forest: pines, live oaks, and chestnuts. Over the years, the pines had built the house, barns, sheds, and fencing, leaving behind pastures and fields for planting. They grew and harvested their own hay, oats, and corn for sweet feed. There was a vegetable garden and orchard, including a few citrus trees, and they kept their own chickens, sheep, cows, and pigs. The pond out back drew wild ducks and geese and was stocked with bass. Ellie loved her home and the way of life. She identified with her father and felt she had horses in her blood.

As Ellie walked in the front door, she heard, "Eloise!" It was her mother's voice coming from the sewing room in the back of the house. She headed down the hall and turned right to find her mother sitting at her desk.

"Yes, Mother? Were you looking for me?" Ellie asked.

"What is all this material for?" She turned to look at her daughter and saw her attire. Before Ellie could respond, she asked, "Were you at the barn already? Get out of those clothes and get ready for dinner."

"Yes, ma'am!" Ellie quickly exited and ran down the hall and up the stairs, relieved that she didn't have to answer her mother's first question.

Mattie was still unpacking Ellie's things when she walked back into her room. "Miz Ellie, where'd ya go? Ah thought ya was goin' ta rest."

"I just could not wait to see the weanlings. Oh good, Mattie. I see you already have a dress out for dinner. I do not know why mother insists we dress up when it is just the family at the table."

"Yo mama lacks thins done right." With a knowing smile, she added, "Yo papa has company."

Startled, Ellie exclaimed, "We have not even unpacked. Oh no, I better talk to him before he sells that weanling."

"Ah doan think da gentleman is here jist ta buy hosses, Miz Ellie," she grinned.

Ellie saw her face. "A suitor? Who is it?" She was surprised herself by the mix of feelings she was experiencing. She was curious whom it might be, intrigued by the mystery, and annoyed that her father seemed so desperate to get her married off.

"How'd Ah know? Ah'm jist a stupid girl," Mattie stated, affecting a vacant expression.

"Do not say that!" Mattie's self-deprecation angered Ellie. "You are as smart as I am and you know it!"

"Miz Ellie, Ah cain't even read," the slave woman responded, her frustration and embarrassment showing on her face.

Ellie looked at Mattie, beginning to realize just a little what it meant to be a slave. "Tomorrow you start learning," she stated.

Mattie just nodded. She had no reason to trust this statement. She knew how the white folk felt about slaves learning to read. She feared to get her hopes up.

"I mean it, Mattie. If you want to learn, I shall teach you. I swear it." She looked earnestly at her maid.

Mattie studied her mistress' face. She saw the sincerity there. "What would yo mama say ef she foun' out?" the young woman asked.

"Then I guess it will be our secret. My old books are in the attic; we will find them in the morning." Ellie thought that maybe she could teach Lela to read, too.

"Ef dat's what ya want, Miz." She tried to hide her smile.

Both women were satisfied with the deal they had struck. Once Mattie helped Ellie dress, she hurried downstairs to find her father and stake her claim on the chestnut filly. Initially, he pointed out that she would make a smart, stylish carriage horse and bring a good price. After all, this was business. Eventually, he gave in to her pleas. Together, they walked to the parlor where Charlotte and Suzanne were entertaining a guest.

Ellie was surprised to see Matthew Gibbes Fuller. She had met him last summer in Beaufort. She thought he was a good looking, likeable man; his family was one of the Sea Island cotton planters and she remembered that he had seemed knowledgeable of his family's business and not frightened by responsibility. She wondered how he would handle the end of slavery; they probably owned hundreds of slaves. The subject hadn't come up when she met him a couple of months ago.

Charlotte was extolling the benefits of her home town, Savannah, over Charleston and Beaufort, not letting Matthew get in more than one word responses. John interrupted, changing the topic. Shortly after, dinner was announced and the group adjourned to the dining room.

"I am sorry not to have had the opportunity to see James here. We were at school together at Beaufort College. How is he?" Matthew enquired of the party in general.

"We miss having him here as well, Mr. Fuller, but as you know, he is studying law in Columbia. We are expecting him home for Christmas next month," John explained. "How is your family? I have not spoken with your father for several months. I hope he and your lovely mother are well."

"Thank you, sir, they are both very well. Father has been very busy on the plantation. We have been trying some new crops. Father thinks it wise to diversify, to get away from being so reliant upon cotton for our income. Unfortunately, we have had some difficulty keeping overseers. It is so difficult to find reliable men to fill that position. The best overseers are Northerners, but with the political unrest down here, most of them are reluctant to come to the South. Those who do rarely stay long. Father had to oversee all the work himself this past summer. It kept him from coming into Beaufort," he explained, and then smiling, he turned to Ellie and said, "Which I am sure he would regret even more had he had the privilege of making your acquaintance, Miss Peters."

Ellie smiled graciously at the compliment, but made no reply. Charlotte, sitting nearest to Matthew, smiled broadly at his attention to her daughter and did her best to encourage his pursuit. "Mr. Fuller, I believe you are the eldest child and the only son in your family. That must lay a great deal of responsibility upon your shoulders. I hope you have time to disport yourself on occasion."

"Indeed, I do, madam. I have an amazing matched team of bays for my carriage. I make it a point to exercise them as often as possible. I also have a handsome hunter and the gamest pair of blue tick hounds to be found anywhere. I very much enjoy hunting on the plantation. Of course, the family has a schooner, but I do not get out on her as often as I would like." Matthew had directed much of this speech toward Ellie. Her interest was piqued initially by his obvious interest in horses. She thought this could be a point of commonality.

"You will have to inspect our stock, Mr. Fuller. We have some of the finest saddle horses obtainable in this country," Ellie bragged.

"I would be delighted to see them, if I might have the pleasure of your company on the tour." Matthew smiled invitingly at Ellie who blushed. Charlotte tried to signal her daughter to respond, but Ellie avoided looking at her.

"Why, Mr. Fuller, I am certain my daughter would love to escort you while you look over our herd tomorrow," her mother volunteered.

"Uh...of course, Mr. Fuller. I would be delighted," Ellie stated, smiling uncomfortably.

"Wonderful! I look forward to it," Matthew beamed, bowing his head toward Ellie.

"So, Mr. Fuller, what have you heard from the Bluffton Boys? How are things going in the capitol? I hope there is a movement away from secession there," John interjected, seeing his daughter's discomfort with the current topic.

"I fear not, Mr. Peters. After Robert Barnwell Rhett's July 4th speech stirred everyone's blood for states rights and free trade, William Yancey called for secession before the inauguration if the Republican candidate, whoever he may be, wins the election. Everyone in Beaufort is passionately in favor of both these ideas. And you know how much influence the representatives from Beaufort have in the state legislature. I doubt that a compromise is possible. And to be perfectly frank, sir, I have to agree with their proposals. We need to show the Abolitionists that they cannot dictate to us. We have a right to maintain our lifestyle and to control our property," Matthew stated vehemently.

"Surely, Mr. Fuller, you must see that slavery as an institution is doomed. So many smaller planters are already going bankrupt and having to sell off their land and slaves. Families of slaves are being split up and scattered all over the South and West. This is inhumane and cruel," Ellie protested, her face becoming flushed with emotion.

"I beg to disagree, Miss Peters. The small planters are losing their property due to poor management. And it is hardly inhumane to sell off one's livestock. Why, your very livelihood is based upon selling your animals. How is it any different selling our Negroes?" Matthew demanded, surprised at her position on the subject.

"The difference, sir, is that our Negroes are most definitely not animals. They are people who love their families and wish to stay near them just as you and I do. Thinking of them as animals may make it easier on your conscience when you treat them as such, but it does not decrease their humanity or their pain!" Ellie was twisting her napkin in her hand as if she were wishing it were Fuller's neck.

"Now, Ellie, this is no way to behave toward a guest. Mr. Fuller, please forgive my daughter. She is young and feels things most passionately. We are all aware that there are many positions concerning slavery held by the people of the South and there is plenty of room for all of us to exchange our thoughts. We are not so narrow of vision as those in the North would have the world believe," John Peters smiled ingratiatingly at his guest.

"Ellie, I think you owe our guest an apology," Charlotte stated, staring coldly at her daughter. Charlotte was more concerned that Ellie was chasing away a good candidate for marriage than she was about the politics being discussed.

"Very well, Mother. Mr. Fuller, I am most sincerely sorry that your narrow-minded, self-interested views conflict so very completely with mine as to make further conversation between us impossible." Ellie straightened her spine and glared at Matthew, her breathing rapid and shallow.

"That will be enough from you, young lady!" her mother declared.

"That is fortunate, Mother, as I have nothing further to say." Ellie continued to sit stiffly, her lips pursed, holding in any further words.

"Ellie has such a way with gentlemen, Mama. You really should have her teach me how to win a beau," Suzanne chimed in, laughing at her sister's discomfort.

"And that is entirely enough out of you, too, Suzanne Alma Peters. You may leave the table," John ordered. Suzanne rose, huffing in disgust, and marched out of the room, but not before sticking her tongue out at her sister.

"Perhaps you should retire as well, Eloise," her father stated a bit more gently.

"Yes, Father. Please excuse me, Mother. Good evening, Mr. Fuller. Have a safe trip back to your home." Ellie rose and walked from the room with as much dignity as she could dredge up. Once out of the room, she leaned against the wall and sighed. She dreaded the thought of the repercussions to come, but she had to say what she did to that impossible man.

CHAPTER 20

The next morning, Ellie and Mattie headed up to the attic. There were so many wooden crates and trunks that neither of them was sure where to start looking. Ellie discovered piles of old clothes, shoes, and boots, worn but still serviceable, especially for escaping slaves. There were several old quilts and some small rag rugs that could be used as blankets or bedding. There were even some sheets that were still in fairly good condition, though repaired. She dumped the contents of a small crate and started throwing things into it. Mattie was on the other side of the attic when she called out, "Ah foun' some books, Miz Ellie."

Ellie had forgotten Mattie's presence in her excitement. "See if there are any more. I will be there in a moment." She scurried to straighten out the mess she had made, and then went to sort through the books. She located a couple of children's books that she and Suzanne had first read and added them to the crate. "We better go downstairs before Mother notices we are not around. We can get the rest of these things later. Take the crate. I will go first and make sure no one is around." Ellie knew that her mother believed slaves should only be taught to read if their position depended upon it; Charlotte felt it made them uppity if they could read.

"What're all dese thins fo'?" Mattie questioned curiously.

"Just put the crate in the bottom of my armoire. Remember, this is our secret." Ellie quietly started down the steps feeling pleased with herself and her find. She realized that clothes would not be a problem for her plan; there were plenty.

Mattie slowly followed Ellie down the stairs, shaking her head. Her expression plainly showed that she had grave doubts about the wisdom of whatever Ellie had in mind, and feared that she would be the recipient of any disapproval that resulted. However, Mattie's doubts were soon pushed aside when she realized the purpose of the books. Miz Ellie was good to her word. She was going to teach Mattie to read.

The two women spent most of the morning on the ABCs, and then Ellie shooed Mattie out of her room. She still needed to hide the money. She got down on her hands and knees and started feeling for a loose baseboard; she had inspected half the room by the time she found a spot where she could get her fingers between the wall and the top of the board. She was relieved to see it was a short board, only about eighteen inches long. She worked at it, wiggling the nails slowly out, and then started pulling hard with both hands. It gave suddenly and she fell back on the floor with a thud. Ellie sat very still, listening for some response from the others in the house to the noise she had made. When nothing happened, she sighed with relief and returned to her task.

She went to her dresser to get the empty tin. It didn't quite fit. She slipped downstairs and stealthily took the sewing scissors. Going back to her room, she started to chip away at the plaster, stopping frequently to check if the tin would fit, yet being careful not to make the enlargement so high that the board would not cover it. Once the tin fit into the wall, she retrieved the gold and silver coins and paper money from under the mattress. She put them in the tin, and then put it into the wall. She worked the board back into place and wiped up the chips of plaster and dust.

Ellie returned the scissors and headed out to check on her new filly. She still hadn't decided on a name. She watched the young horse running, mesmerized by the flashing of her long, white legs.

It was a few days before she was able to see Lela alone. She didn't know how Lela had gotten involved with George and needed to know if she was willing to take risks for other runaways as well. She also understood that some of the other slaves were aware of her having helped the runaway last spring. She needed to know who knew, who would help, and who wanted to leave. She understood that would be the most difficult part. If she was not willing to assist any of their own slaves to leave, she'd be nothing more than a hypocrite. The slaves would know it, and worse, she would too. But if too many of them wanted their freedom, everything would fall apart. Not only would she be stopped from helping the Negroes, but she couldn't hurt her father in that way.

"Lela, did you know George before he came here?" Ellie asked as she slowly took some peaches, one at a time, out of the crate and put them in her basket.

"No, ma'am! How'd Ah know him?" Lela appeared concerned that she was being questioned by Ellie.

"Well, why did he come to you?" Ellie tried to sound casual about her questioning. She didn't want Lela to become defensive and closed mouthed.

"He din't. Ah foun' him in de woods when Ah was searchin' fo' mushrooms. Ah couldn't leave him dere like dat." Lela looked anxiously at Ellie. "Is somethin' wrong? He din't git caught, did he?"

"No, nothing's wrong." She hesitated. "I want to help."

Lela looked at her, questioning without responding.

"I have been collecting supplies," she explained.

"Miz Ellie, it's gittin' too cold up North now. No one'll be through now till da spring."

"Lela! You've been doing this all along." Ellie was surprised and pleased. "How?"

Lela looked around. "Ah jist leave packages o' food in de woods down near de stream. Ah checks dem ever couple a days an' replace dem when dey's gone."

"What about animals?"

"Ah wrap de food in burlap soaked in candle wax. It keeps de water out, too."

"How do they know where to find them?" Ellie was amazed by the cleverness and courage of this woman.

"Ah don' know. Ah put dem near de game trails. Ah know it ain't de animals what's eatin' dem 'cause de bags an' all is gone."

Ellie could tell her childhood playmate was holding something back from her, but decided not to push her for more information. They were interrupted by a hardy laugh before Ellie could ask her how many of the others knew she had helped George.

Lela's grandmother, Lottie, was the family's cook. "You two look lack you 'bout ta steal mah cakes, like when you was little."

"Mama Lottie!" Lela objected.

She looked at her granddaughter and sternly stated, "Doan you git yo'sef in trouble, girl." Under her breath she added, "You neither, Miz Ellie." Then louder, "Now, git outta mah pantry."

As the two women left, Ellie whispered to Lela, "Does she know?"

Lela shook her head and giggled. "She'd whip me hersef."

They headed in separate directions.

CHAPTER 21

It was time to begin decorating for Christmas. The bows and ornaments were brought down from the attic. Fresh pine boughs were brought in to make into new wreaths and garlands for the doors and mantles. The tree had been set up in the parlor, but would not be decorated until James came home from Columbia; it had always been a family activity, even her father joined in decorating. The wonderful scent of fresh pine filled the house. All the silver was brought out and slave hands were set to polishing it. New candles of every length were dipped so that there would be no shortage. Every inch of the house was cleaned thoroughly. Bedding was hung outside to air so that guests would have fresh quilts and sheets. Carpets were taken outside, away from the house, and beaten to get the dirt out. Party dresses were brought out and brushed up. Special foods were made, pound cakes and fruitcakes. Fresh hams were smoked and baked ahead with honey glaze, and then stored in the pantry. Fruit and nuts were brought out of the root cellar along with piles of sweet potatoes and turnips. John Peters went through his wine cellar, selecting the vintages to be served before, during, and after the dinner. A man was brought up from Beaufort to tune the pianoforte.

Ellie was also busy making gifts and wrapping them. She wanted something special for Lela and Mattie. Three days before Christmas, her brother James arrived home from Columbia with two friends. Both were from Texas and unable to get home for Christmas. Most everyone spent Christmas in their own homes with family. Ellie loved the excitement of the holidays: the decorations, the carols, the special foods and, best of all, the laughter. She enjoyed making people happy and seeing the surprise and pleasure on people's faces when they opened her gifts to them. She scrambled to come up with something for her brother's two friends. She was tempted to give one of them the book she had for Ted, thinking she probably would not see him until sometime in January, but then decided against it.

Many of the planters had parties during the weeks before and after Christmas and invited their neighbors. The Peters' party was known as the one to attend in the Sheldon area. It was the one time Ellie looked forward to working hard along side of her mother. Charlotte wanted everything just right; she felt her reputation as a hostess was at stake. Ellie wanted their friends and neighbors to enjoy themselves. Every detail was thought out down to the bundles of mint candies wrapped in lace and tied with red ribbons.

Christmas Eve morning, Suzanne finally joined Ellie and their mother to work on the finishing touches. She had been complaining of headaches every time they started working. Ellie was surprised to see her before the party was to start at six in the evening. Charlotte was concerned that Suzanne would over do and insisted that she take a rest in the afternoon so as not to miss the party. Ellie always tried to help take care of her little sister, but was a bit suspicious about the timing of her illnesses.

At three in the afternoon, Ellie and her mother were in the sitting room together, having tea and cookies. They were reviewing their list one last time to make sure they hadn't forgotten anything.

"Scuse me, Miz Charlotte, Marster Ted Campbell is here." The butler, Peter, didn't seem to know what to do with him.

"Show him in, Peter, and fetch more hot tea," Charlotte responded.

Peter turned to find Ted right behind him. "Please jine da ladies, Marster Campbell; Ah'm goin' fo' mo' tea."

"A little scotch would warm me a lot faster, Peter." Ted laughed, and then went into the sitting room.

Charlotte put out her hand from where she was sitting. "Mr. Campbell, what a pleasant surprise. You certainly are far from home on Christmas Eve."

Ted took Charlotte's hand in his and bowed over it. "I hope you do not mind my arriving so early for your famous party, but I had to catch the ferry and wanted to make the ride before dark."

"Not at all. It is always a pleasure to see you," Charlotte responded graciously.

Ellie rolled her eyes. "You certainly are full of surprises. I did not expect to see you until after the holidays."

Sitting down in the chair next to Ellie, Ted drawled, "Did you not did tell me that Whispering Oaks Farm had the best Christmas party in South Carolina and that I really should come? How could I resist an invitation like that?" He grinned broadly at her, knowing she was discomfited by his exaggerated compliments.

"Really, Ellie!" The pleasure in Charlotte's voice was palpable. She then turned to Ted, "I do not know about all of South Carolina. With all your friends on the islands, I just hope you will not be too disappointed, Mr. Campbell."

Peter entered with another pot of tea, a crystal decanter filled with scotch, a cup, and glasses. He placed it on the table and turned to Ted. Before he could ask what he'd like, Charlotte started giving orders. "Peter, see to it that a room is prepared for Mr. Campbell. Ellie, do not just sit there. Serve our guest."

Ellie poured out some scotch, filled the glass part way, hesitated, and then filled it up before handing the glass to Ted.

Charlotte tried to hide her displeasure at Ellie's choice of beverages for Ted, but knew her daughter was right, considering the young man's reputation. "How long will you be able to stay with us, Mr. Campbell?" she enquired with a tentative smile on her face.

"Throughout the holidays, Mrs. Peters." Ted flashed his winning smile at her. "That is, if you do not mind putting up with me."

"Now, Mr. Campbell, do not be foolish. You always brighten things up around here. It is so good of your family to let us have your company for Christmas," Charlotte purred. She finished her tea and stood. "No, sit down, please," she gestured as Ted rose respectfully. "Ellie can entertain you. I have some last minute details to attend to before the party."

As soon as Charlotte was safely out of earshot, Ted laughed. "You do know she hates me."

Ellie burst out laughing. "Certainly not hate, though I do not think she approves. However, she does love your effusive compliments. Oh, it is good to see you. I was so afraid things would be so dull. James brought two terribly serious Texans home with him. I do not think either has laughed in their entire lives."

"It is my pleasure to laugh for you," he offered, leaning over to play with the lace at her wrist.

Grasping his fingers, so that he would stop fussing and look at her, Ellie asked, "Now, why are you really here?"

"To attend the best Christmas party in all of South Carolina." Ted tried to put on the most innocent expression he could produce, eyes wide and surprised at her question, his smile slightly hurt at the suggestion that he might have ulterior motives.

"Ted Campbell, I know you too well. What happened?" Ellie demanded, eyebrow raised and lips pursed.

Sighing, Ted slumped back in his chair and folded his hands in his lap. His expression turned to one of disgust. "I was home for a week. I could not stand it anymore. Every time I walked into a room, someone would ask what I was going to do with my entire life. So, I finally told them I had had enough and I was going to spend the next couple of weeks with the prettiest girl in South Carolina. So, here I am."

"Oh, stop your flattery. I better go upstairs and get dressed for the party. Your room must be ready by now. Come on. Peter!" Ellie stood and led Ted to the stairway. "Take Mr. Campbell to his room and make sure he has everything he needs."

Ted bowed to Ellie with exaggerated formality and ran up the stairs ahead of Peter. Ellie had to admit to herself that Ted did make things more fun and she did enjoy his laugh. She headed up the stairs to dress.

Pine torches lined the drive and lamps and candles lit the house, making every corner bright. Each slave was dressed in a freshly washed and pressed uniform and wore a huge smile. Carrying silver trays of eggnog, they began serving guests. Silver bowls filled with nuts or candied fruits were set about the rooms on tables so that they would be at hand for the guests. The evening was cold enough to require fires to be lit in the fireplaces; the smell of burning wood added to the holiday spirit. The Christmas tree twinkled with the lights of tiny candles reflected in hand-blown imported glass ornaments. The packages of mints had been hung on the tree along with other small presents. As the rooms filled with guests, the sounds of laughter and friendly chatter floated from one chamber to another.

Dinner was to be served buffet style because the dining room could not accommodate all the guests. Behind the closed doors of the dining room, the slaves laid out the banquet. A huge turkey stuffed with oyster and chestnut dressing was the centerpiece of the buffet set out on the table. It was surrounded by roasted goose, baked ham, chilled boiled shrimp, an oyster casserole, bowls heaped with mashed turnips, candied sweet potatoes, rice with turkey gravy, boiled carrots in a honey glaze, peas, boiled okra, piping hot biscuits and fresh breads, and mounds of fresh butter and homemade preserves. The desserts were displayed on the sideboard: three kinds of pound cake, two fruitcakes, fresh apple and pecan pies, baked apples with raisins and cinnamon sauce, and a bowl of whipped cream. Checking on the display of food for her mother, Ellie found her mouth watering and had to sample a piece of turkey just to have a taste. Smiling servers stood at stations to help the guests to whatever they wanted. Ellie wondered if the sentiment was genuine, as each of them knew that the food was for the white guests and that they would be punished for filching any of it. While the crowd waited outside, Ellie promised the slaves they would be permitted to take leftover food home to their families. She would arrange it with her mother. She complimented them on the excellent work they had done, and went to find her mother to let her know that everything was ready.

Once the repast had been consumed and every guest sated, calls were made for volunteers to entertain. Several young ladies took turns playing the pianoforte or singing, or both. Charlotte finally called upon her youngest to demonstrate her skills. Suzanne pretended to demur, and the guests made a show of coaxing her to play for them. Blushing with pleasure, she allowed herself to be persuaded and rushed to the bench to begin. Ellie shook her head at the silly little game Suzanne had to play before performing, but was proud of her little sister's talent once she began. After Suzanne had played two or three pieces, her father called to her to play Christmas carols so that everyone could join in. The rest of the evening was spent in enjoying the music and camaraderie of their neighborhood set.

Immediately at 11:30, the partygoers thanked their hosts and left. The Peters and their overnight guests followed in two carriages. Someone started singing "Silent Night" and the song was picked up by others joining in. It was a two-and-one-half mile drive to the church in Sheldon. Torches lit the walkway from the entrance of the grounds to the church. Inside, candles glowed. The midnight Christmas mass was a long tradition. Some claimed that services were held on the sight even after the church had been burned down by the British and before a new one was built. After the service, the tired parishioners headed back to their own homes.

CHAPTER 22

The house was slow to rise Christmas morning. Suzanne was the youngest in the house, so the adults felt no need to rush to open presents. Ellie was the first one down for breakfast. She was excited to see her filly. Today, she would be given the ownership papers. She was anxious to see her and felt foolish, but wanted to see how the young horse would respond to the name she had chosen, Denmark Princess. She also had planned a secret gift to give her fellow conspirator, Lela, at the woman's cabin rather than in the main house with everyone else present. She ate quickly, put a piece of bread in her pocket, and went to the weanling paddock. She had been slipping small treats to the horse since her father had agreed to let her keep the filly. When the young mare heard Ellie call out, she recognized the voice and came running. As she nuzzled Ellie, trying to find whatever morsel she could, Ellie gently slipped a halter and lead on her. All the young horses were handled, rubbed, and brushed regularly so they would be accustomed to humans, but Ellie wanted Princess to know her.

As Ellie was patting and talking to the filly, Ted came down from the house and leaned on the fence to watch. Ellie was so involved she hadn't noticed his approach. When she kissed the filly, he spoke up. "What does a man have to do to get one of those?"

"Ted! How long have you been standing there?" Ellie exclaimed, turning to see her friend so close.

"Just long enough to get cold," he laughed, rubbing his arms to create heat.

"Isn't she beautiful?" Ellie asked, awe and love in her voice as she looked at the young horse.

"I see why you chose her. I am sorry to say my gift to you will not match up, but when you look at it, it will be even more beautiful," Ted said mysteriously.

"That certainly is a strange thing to say, Ted Campbell," Ellie said, quizzically.

Ted smiled, but added no details. "Are you ready to go back to the house?"

"You are cold. Go ahead. I will meet you there," she suggested

"What kind of gentleman would I be if I did not wait for you?" Ted persisted in remaining, much to Ellie's chagrin.

"Since when have you worried about being a gentleman?" she teased him, pushing him playfully away.

"I will sit here all day, and shiver and freeze if I have to, but I am not leaving without you," he affirmed, wrapping his arms tightly around himself.

Ellie knew that once Ted got something into his head, he was determined. She had to decide whether to give up her plan or trust him. It was only a book; it might serve as a good test. She slipped the halter off of the filly's head and walked over to the fence. "I have to put the halter away and make one stop before going back to the house."

Ted climbed over the fence and followed Ellie. "Where are we going?"

"It is a secret and you need to keep it a secret." She thought she certainly had kept plenty of his. Smiling, she thought about the times in Beaufort that she'd caught her brother doing Ted's homework for him or that she'd helped to hide him when he skipped school to nurse a hangover. She led him around the back of the house to the opposite side, past the vegetable garden that was empty of produce and covered with horse manure. Together they stepped up on the porch of a slave house. They could hear laughter inside; Ellie knocked.

Lela's younger brother, Samuel, opened the door. He mostly worked with the livestock. He was obviously surprised to see them. "Miz Ellie?"

"Merry Christmas, Samuel. I would like to see your sister."

Lela appeared at the door, surprised by the visit. "Miz Ellie, Marster Ted. Please come in. Kin we offer ya somethin'?"

"We have to get back to the house, but I wanted to give this to you here." Ellie pulled a small book out from inside her coat. "Merry Christmas."

Tears came to Lela's eyes as she took the book and held it to her breast. She knew she would not be able to read it yet, but she was learning. "Thank ya."

"We will see you at the house, later." Ellie turned to leave, but Ted seemed frozen. She grabbed the sleeve of his coat and pulled him away.

As they were walking back to the house, Ted stopped her; taking her by both arms he asked, "Ellie, what, in God's name, are you doing?"

Proudly Ellie responded, "I am teaching some of the slaves to read."

Ted inhaled slowly, considering what to say. He knew how a lecture on the law would be received. Shaking his head, he finally said, "Just be careful, Ellie."

"I have heard it said that Mrs. Chestnut, the Senator's wife, taught some of her slaves to read." She knew by the tone of his voice that he would keep this secret, but his concern warned her that he would try to stop her if he were to find out about her other plans.

The family and house guests met in the drawing room before afternoon dinner to exchange gifts. The gifts for the slaves had been distributed earlier. It was Suzanne's job as the youngest to distribute the gifts from under the tree. Ellie had forgotten Ted's comment until Suzanne handed her a package, saying, "This is from your beau!"

"Suzanne, stop it. You will embarrass our guest. You know better," Ellie snapped at her.

Everyone laughed, including Ted.

Ellie carefully unwrapped the package. She had no idea what it could be and was excited to find out. She slowly pulled out a silver comb molded with magnolias, and then a brush and hand-mirror set in silver with matching molded silver handles. She blushed and turned to Ted. She did not notice the quiet that had come over the room. "You really have out done yourself. It is lovely."

Ted approached her and turned the mirror so that she could see herself. "Now, there is a sight even more beautiful than Denmark Princess."

Ellie's blush grew deeper. "You stop that right now, Ted Campbell. What will everyone think?" she whispered to him. Ted merely shrugged and smiled down at her.

CHAPTER 23

The day after New Year's 1860, Ted left Whispering Oaks Farm for his family's plantation in the low country of Prince William Parish.

With the holidays behind them and James and the houseguests having left, the house became quiet. Ellie's mornings were taken up with teaching reading to Mattie and Lela. On especially cold and windy days, she sewed and did needle work. On sunny days, she disappeared from the house. Some of the time, she spent with Princess. But most of the time, she was with Lela preparing for the spring arrival of more runaway slaves. She was hoping to have things in place to help anyone heading for freedom. She wanted to make a safer hiding place than where they had hidden George last year. Others might also need a place to stay for a few days to rest or heal. She decided they should build a shelter hidden in the woods. Lela recruited Samuel to help them. It was a slow project, between finding the supplies and managing to slip away to do the work. Ellie worked alongside of the slaves, collecting supplies and carrying them into the woods, dragging boards, and patching gaps with mud. By the end of the day, she was dirty and at times had tears in her dress. After the first ripped dress, Mattie repaired it. She did not ask what had happened; she already knew, but played ignorant. After the second, she repaired it and brought both to Lela's cabin. The next day that Ellie showed up to work, Lela insisted she come inside first. She showed her the dresses and suggested she change into one of them before going into the woods. Ellie had been afraid her mother might catch her coming into the house looking a mess, and then ask questions. She hadn't thought of changing somewhere else and was relieved that Mattie had come up with the idea.

In the middle of March, the first slaves escaping to the North came through and used the shelter. Lela informed Ellie that there was a family with three children. There were two boys, about seven and nine years of age and a five year old girl. Ellie was upset with herself when she heard the news. She hadn't thought about clothing for children; she had falsely assumed the runaways would be adults traveling in ones or twos. She headed back to the house and slipped up to the attic. She rummaged through the trunks looking for children's clothes that had belonged to James, Suzanne, and herself. Ellie knew much of it had already been given away, but was sure her mother would have held on to some things. She found the trunks with their old clothing. She picked out some outfits that still looked good and she hoped would be about the right sizes. Moving quietly, she folded them tightly and wrapped a blanket around them. Before she headed downstairs, she paused to come up with a story to explain the blanket if she was spotted.

Ellie slipped out the back door without running into anyone and headed in the direction of Lela's cabin. When she arrived in front of it, she checked around to make sure no one was looking, and then went along the side, past the hog pen and into the woods. She was excited about meeting the family and hearing their story. She just hoped they were still at the shelter and that the clothing would fit.

The family heard someone approaching. The man picked up a board and prepared to defend his wife and children. The woman gathered the three young ones to her in the back of the shelter. When Ellie stepped into the opening of the shelter, the man was blocking the way with the board up in the air over his head, ready to bring it down hard. They both froze looking at each other. Ellie was able to blurt out, "I brought clothes for the little ones." Slowly the tension in the man's body seemed to melt away. She repeated to herself, *Hide the fear. Don't let them see it.* Her father had drilled that into her when she was first learning to ride. She tried to hide it, but this was different. She'd never before had a person threaten her. Ellie carefully opened the blanket to show him the contents. When he saw that she was being truthful, he lowered the board and motioned to his wife to come and take them. Ellie handed the bundle, blanket and all, to the woman. "I hope they fit. I was not sure just how big the children were."

The man laughed. "Miz Peters, Ah thought you was all talk."

"You know me?" Ellie was caught off guard by his statement.

"You was at da Tuckers' lass summa. Ah's dere doeman." Indicating his wife, "She Miz Tucker's gal."

"You were in the house?" Confused, Ellie continued. "Why did you leave?"

"Dey owned us, Miz. Dere ain't no dignity in bein owned. Mah chillen'll have dignity an' edication," the man proudly stated.

Ellie swallowed hard; until that moment her anti-slavery ideals had all been an intellectual position. This man made it real. "Where will you go?"

"It's betta you doan know, Miz."

"I suppose you are right. Good luck, and may God go with you." Ellie turned and left. As she walked slowly through the woods, she realized she didn't even know his name. She thought, *That, too, is probably better.*

The next day, Lela did not show up for her reading lesson. Ellie spent time with Mattie in her room, and then headed out after lunch. She found Lela working in the vegetable garden. "Lela, where were you this morning?"

"Ah has ta work." She continued hacking at the ground with a hoe. She appeared to be using more force than was necessary.

Ellie saw the anger. She knew Lela had always been proud of the gardens, but hadn't thought much about the other feelings she might have about working there. As she stood there trying to find her voice, not knowing what to say, a child of about five years of age came running up to her.

Softly the child said, "Miz Ellie?"

Ellie looked down at the young slave before her, making eye contact.

Deciding that Ellie wasn't frightening after all, she boldly spoke up, obviously feeling very important. "Mama Noli wants ya ta come ta her house soon as ya kin."

Concerned for the old woman, Ellie looked to Lela. But before she could ask her anything, the other woman quickly looked down, pretending not to have heard or seen anything. Ellie then understood that this had nothing to do with Mama Noli's health, but couldn't imagine for what other reason she would be summoned to a slave's quarters. She left the garden, heading toward the old woman's hut. The little girl skipped ahead.

Mama Noli was the oldest of the slaves on the farm. Unlike the others who had been born in this country, she had been brought to South Carolina from Africa. She was an elder of the slave compound and the others looked to her for guidance and wisdom despite the fact that, to any white owner, she technically held lower status, due to being a "new import" and not one of the stock bred in America.

When Ellie got to her cabin, she found the old woman sitting in a rocking chair near the fire of the primitive hearth. The cabin was rough and sparsely furnished, but clean and neat. Ellie felt guilty that this old woman, who had given her life and strength to the labors that supported the Peters family, had so little of her own to show for that labor. There was a braided rag rug on the hard dirt floor, a low rope bed just wide enough for two people with a tattered quilt covering the corn husk filled mattress, a table and bench of rough-hewn wood, and some dishes and battered pots on a shelf. A medium sized cauldron hung over the fire, and something was cooking in it, but Ellie could not identify the contents.

"Mama Noli, you asked to see me. Are you well? Is there something you need?" Ellie enquired of the old woman who had risen to take her hand. The wizened elder smiled up at her young mistress. Ellie observed how stooped the old woman was and how painful her movements seemed to be.

"Miz Ellie, it sho is good a ya ta come see me. Come in, chile. Sit down, sit down," the old woman signaled toward the chair.

"No, no, Mama Noli. You take the chair. I will be just fine sitting here on the bench. How is your rheumatism? Can I send you anything to help ease your pain?" Ellie helped the elderly slave seat herself in the chair, and then retired to the bench to sit.

"Mah rheumatism come an' go. It a bit bad taday, what wit da cold wedder we bin havin' an' all. Thank ya fo' axin', Miz Ellie. Ah wouldn' say no ta sumpin ta hep wit it ef ya gits a chance." The old woman pulled her crocheted shawl more closely around her and nodded to herself for a few moments. "Miz Ellie, ya knowed Ah come from Africa. Not like all dese udder ones what ya got here on da fahm." She looked at Ellie who nodded politely, wondering what could be on the other woman's mind. Perhaps she just wanted some company and attention.

"Yes, Mama Noli, I do know that. Do you remember what Africa was like?" Ellie asked, hoping to lead the woman into telling stories of how she came to be a slave.

"Yes, um. Ah does 'member Africa. Maybe better dan Ah 'member yistady mornin'. Ah was a gal, 'bout maybe twelve years ol'. Ah libbed wit mah mama an' daddy in ah village. Dere was tree or foe udder famblies what libbed dere b'sides us. We wasn't no rich folks or nuthin' lack dat. Jist fahmas growing corn, melons, an' sich, an' keepin' some goats, chickens, an' a cow. Da mens ud go out huntin' an' bring back some meat onest in a while. Life was hard, but we was happy bein' together. Mah mama had five chillens. Mah oldest brudder was fixin' ta git married. He had him a woman in anudder village who was gonna come an' live wit us in ah village. Da youngest chile was still at mah mama's breast.

"We lived peaceably wit ah neighbas in da udder villages aroun' us. Da old mens tole stories 'bout wars, but mostly dere weren't no troubles ta fight 'bout. Folks'd jist talk it out. Maybe somebody'd have ta give some chickens or a cow fo' doin' somethin' wrong ta somebody. We all prayed ta Allah, not Jesus, an' we tried ta live good lives.

"Den, one day while most of da mens was off huntin', strangers come. Dark mens from far away come. Dey had guns an' knifes. Dey kilt some o' da mens dat was still in da village an' den dey drove da rest o' us all tagedder. Dey kept da mens an' da womens separate, leavin' da chillens wit dey mamas. Den dey took da ol' ones, mens an' womens, an' dey kilt dem while we all watched. Next dey took da babies what was too little ta walk far or work hard an' kilt dem, too. Ah seed mah baby brudder git his head smashed lack a melon. Mah mama took ta screamin' an' cryin'. She tried ta fight da strangers what kilt da baby. One a dem mens jist club her down. She weren't never no good afta dat. She couldn' talk too good, an' she kinda walked wit one foot draggin'." Mama Noli paused in her narrative, shaking her head as if to clear away the visions of horror. Ellie rose and brought her a cup of water. The old woman took it in her gnarled hands and sipped it, and then handed the empty cup back to Ellie. "Much obliged, Miz Ellie." Ellie returned to her seat and waited for Mama Noli to continue.

The old woman sighed. "Da mens, dey tied us all tagedder by da neck, lack beads on a strang. Dey tied ah mens hands tagedder so dey couldn' fight. Den dey marched us away from da village. We walk fo' days an' days. Sometimes we stop an' wait while dey raid anudder village. Walkin' all dat way, some o' us got wore out an' fell down. Ef ya couldn' git up dey kilt ya. At night, dey mens would lay wit us womens. Ya'd hear cryin' an' screamin' in da night. Den, in da mornin', some o' da womens couldn' hardly walk an' wouldn' look at nobody else. Dey look lack dey was beat up bad. No mans touched me 'cause Ah was virgin. Dey says virgin brings mo' money.

"We finally come ta a place near da ocean. Da mens drove us inta wooden pens. Dey give us water ta drink an' some food. Said dey need ta 'fatten us up' a might. Day or two later, some white mens come. Dey talks funny. Doan nobody know what dey sayin' ta us, but da dark mens pull us out da pens, one or two at a time. Da white mens tell dem ta strip us. Da white mens touch us all over; dey looks in ah moufs at ah teef. Dey touch ah breasts an' bellies an' women places; not fo' sex, but ta see ef we strong an' good breeders. Den dey says ef we go in dis pen or dat one. After dey look it all o' us, da white mens give da odder mens money fo' us. Most dose mens go away wit da people in da udder pen. Some stay an' hep da white mens take us down ta da ocean.

"Dere was big boats dere. Da white mens drive us onta da boats an' down inside. Dere was shelfs in dere in da dark, big long shelfs, an' stacked up. Da mens took us an' put iron rings round our necks wit chains on dem. Dey pushed us inta dem shelfs, tight up again' each udder. We was naked, mens an' womens rubbin' aginst each udder, an' not thinkin' nothin' 'bout sex. Couldn' hardly breave much less turn nor sit up. Onest everone was shoved in an' chained, da white mens lef an' closed da does up top. We feel da boat movin' an' rollin' back an' forth. Folks was screamin' an' prayin', some started retchin'. Da stink got God awful in dere. Ever few days, mens would come down an' throw water around on us. Dey say it stink so much down dere dat it stink all da way up on top. People tried ta git out o' da chains, tried ta fine some way ta 'scape. But da days went on an' on. Sometimes da white mens would come down an' git some o' us. Dey take us up top an' make us dance aroun' on da deck an' git washed down wit sea wadder. Dey wanted us ta git some exercise sose we'd sell better when we got ta da new land. First time we goed up top, da mens Ah was chained wit talk 'bout how dey gonna jump off da boat an' swim ta da land. Dey say dey carry me wit dem. When we got up top, dey run ta da side o' da ship ta jump over, but dere ain't no land...no land nowheres. Da white mens laugh at dems, den whips us ta git us movin' round. Da mens Ah was wit jist give up hope den. Dey couldn' 'magine not bein' close ta da land. Dey thinks da white devils was takin' dem ta hell where Allah could never fine dem agin.

"When da white mens come down, dey look ta see ef anybody died. Dey drag da dead bodies out an' throw dem in da sea while we was up on da deck. Ya could see da sharks followin' da ship, waitin' fo' da bodies ta be throed. Sometimes, ef somebody was too sick ta live dey'd throw dem ta da sharks, too. By da time we git ta da new land, dere was maybe a bit mo' dan half o' us still alive ta git off da boat.

"We was landed at a pretty big town...bigger dan any place what we ever seed afore. Most of us was too sick an' weak ta pay much mind ta where we was. Dey drove us inta pens agin. Onest we was all out da boat an' in da pen, Ah went lookin' fo' mah fambly. Ah axed aroun' fo' dem. Mah mama was gone. Somebody tole me she die on da boat. Mah daddy an' ol'est brudder was away from da village when da mens come, so Ah hopes dey was safe. Ah find one o' mah udder brudders who was jist a bit older den me. He was terrible po'ly, couldn' hardly stan' an' had da runs no madder what he et. Ah stay by him fo' two, tree days, till da mens come fo' us agin. Dey took me away. Ah never seed my brudder agin.

"Da mens git us washed up some, den took us ta anudder place. We was pulled up onta a platfom one at a time ta be sold off. Mens come up ta examine us. Dey touches us all over an' look at us all over. Some o' dem smile evil lack at us womens what was young an' pretty, an' come an' touch us like fo' sex wit dem. Everbody was watchin' dem touchin' me, an' dey was laughin' an' winkin' at each udder. Ah feel so ashamed. Ah want ta die right dere, but Ah doan. Mah firs' marster was a young man who was one what touched me lack fo' sex. He send me down ta his daddy's plantation wit da udder slaves what he buyed. Ah slave on dat plantation fo' five years. Ah bore him tree babies...beautiful cream-colored babies...but only one o' dem lived. Ah guess dat baby all growed up now. When young marster git hissef married, he wife doan want me roun' no mo' an' he sell me off. Dat when yo' granddaddy buy me an' Ah been here ever since. Ah git me married ta a good man. No white mens come trifling wit me here. Ah have seven mo' babies an' tree o' dem lived. Now Ah got me seventeen granchillen an' great granchillen. Dey all live here on dis fahm. Yo' daddy never sole a one o' dem away. Mah man was yo' daddy's driver fo' twenty years, till he die an' git buried on da fahm. Ah git too ol' ta work no mo', but yo' daddy let me keep on in dis here cabin wit foe of mah gran'daughters. Dey takes care o' me an' Ah gits along all right, Miz. Yo' daddy been a good marster ta me an' mah fambly.

"Now, you wonderin' why Ah tells you all dis here tale. Well, Miz Ellie, Ah tell you dis so you unnerstans why slaves wants ta run away. Not me, mind. Ah'm too ol' ta go high-tailin' it off somewheres. But deres folks what ain't so ol' or tired as Ah is. Deres folks what live in pain an' hate. Womens who git driven out inta da field ta chop cotton or work da rice fields jist tree weeks afta givin' birth ta a baby, an' dat baby maybe da child of dey own marster or his son, or maybe da overseer or some visitor ta da plantation what seed da woman an' decided he wanted her. Miz Ellie, Ah seed womens tied up by dey wrists ta a tree, wit dey feet tied ta a log, danglin' wid dey toes jist touchin' da groun'. Da driver or overseer strip her down an' beat her thirty, forty, or more lashes, while de marster watch. Why dey does dat? 'Cause dat fool gal say no ta her marster when he want her ta warm his bed. An' once she give in an' sleep wit him, his wife say, "You gonna sell dat ho' off down ta Mississippi or Alabama where she ain't gonna cause me no mo' trouble." An' da marster, he sell dat po' whipped slave away from all her fambly an' friends an' everone she ever knowed.

"Ah seen mens and womens who got dey hamstrings cut through fo' runnin' away two, tree times. Ah seen slave mens hung 'cause some white man think dey jist look at his woman. Ah seen da overseer come an' take away da money what a slave done saved up from sellin' his own work done in his own time. Ah seen ol' mens an' ol' womens thrown out dey homes when dey gits too ol' ta work da fields, an' forced ta live what little time dey has lef' livin' under brush shelters till da winter come an' kill dem wit da cold. Ah seen little babies taken from dey mama's an' sold away ta white womens fo' pets, an' dey mamas glad ta see dem took dat way 'cause dat mean dey be house slaves some day, not field slaves.

"Miz Ellie, not all marsters lets dey slaves have dey own gardens or chickens or ta own nothin' o' dey own. Lack Ah said, yo' daddy has been a good marster ta me an' ta all his slaves. But, Miz Ellie, even so, Ah'd leafer be free an' starvin' in my own shack somewheres dan be a slave on yo' daddy's farm. Ah'd leafer breave da foul stench o' da swamp in freedom dan ta have da sweet smell of gardenias bloomin' next ta mah slave cabin. Kin ya unnerstan dat, Miz Ellie?"

"Yes, Mama Noli. I think I can," Ellie replied sincerely to the old woman, tears flowing freely down her cheeks.

"Ah believes ya do, Ma'am." The wrinkled face looked deeply into her young mistress' eyes and nodded. "Now...Miz Ellie, we knows what you an' Lela been doin' out in da woods. Miz Ellie, Ah kin see yo' heart's in da right place 'bout dis. Ya wants ta help. But, Miz Ellie, you an' dat girl is gonna git all o' us inta trouble. Ya needs ta be leavin' dis business ta dem what knows how ta do it, an' not be messin' about. What you been doin' is most dangerous an' needs careful plannin' sose no one gits caught. Ah hopes ya takes mah meanin', Miz Ellie." The faded brown eyes stared steadily at Ellie. At first, she thought that Mama Noli was telling her to stop helping the runaways because the slaves on the farm would be punished if she and Lela got caught. Then she realized the true import of the old woman's words.

"You have all been helping runaways, have you not, Mama Noli? I am right about that. I know I am." Ellie leaned forward, willing the old woman to confirm her beliefs.

"Now, Miz Ellie, dat's aginst da law, ain't it. Ef a slave was caught heppin' anudder runaway, dat slave would be punished somethin' terrible. We all good Negroes here on yo' daddy's farm. We wouldn' never do nothin' ta bring shame on Marster John or his fambly. We all jist happy ta be livin' here where yo' daddy take sich good care o' us. Doan you go gittin' no wild ideas in yo' head, Miz Ellie," Noli cautioned her, shaking her head and frowning as if she were talking to a wayward child.

Ellie understood that Mama Noli would never directly admit to assisting runaways. Nor would she ever again tell Ellie or anyone else the horror she had experienced in her life. Ellie rose. She took the old woman's hand gently in hers and caressed it. "I will send the medicine for your rheumatism as soon as I get back to the house. Thank you for letting me visit with you, Mama Noli. You take care now." She left the small slave cabin and walked slowly back to the house. She had a lot to think about.

CHAPTER 24

Over the next few weeks, she heard from Lela that more slaves had passed through the area and had used the shelter. She continued to provide packages of supplies for Lela to leave at the shelter. She included some money in each one, but never mentioned to Lela that there was cash in them, too.

Princess was now a yearling and Ellie wanted to spend as much time with her as possible before leaving for Beaufort. The young filly seemed to know her, or at least associate her with treats and attention. Ellie enjoyed currying and brushing Princess. She had even trained the young horse to let her pick up her feet and clean her hooves.

One day when she was down at the barns working with Princess, Samuel approached her. "Miz Ellie, kin Ah speak wit ya?"

"Is there something wrong, Samuel?"

"No, Miz." He picked up a brush and started working on the other side of the horse. "Ah wants ta go."

Perplexed, Ellie asked, "What are you talking about? You want to go where?"

"Ah wants ta be free. Ah figure Ah'd go north lack da udders."

"Oh." She hesitated. "When do you think you will leave us?"

"Ah doan know. Ah's jist thinkin' 'bout it."

"I'll miss you; so will Princess. You have always been good with our horses. I wish I had the power to free you, so you could stay."

"Will ya hep me, Miz Ellie, lack ya done da udders?"

"Of course, Samuel." Ellie knew eventually someone would leave, she just hadn't expected it to be Samuel. She'd gotten to know him much better over the winter, working on the shelter, and had come to like him. The two continued brushing Princess in silence. When they finished, Ellie led the filly back to the pasture with the other yearlings. She walked back to the barn and made a point of handing the halter and lead to Samuel. She sadly stated, "I will see you here tomorrow."

Samuel nodded in response.

Ellie walked slowly up to the house. She knew this day would come, but she hadn't wanted to think about it. She believed that all people should be free, but her father had been strict about their slaves being treated humanely. If her father lost a couple of slaves, it wouldn't hurt him. However, if they all left it would be financially devastating. If slavery was abolished or her father freed his slaves, he could then hire them to stay.

Ellie prepared another package specifically for Samuel, including extra money, and brought it to the barn the next day. She found him in the tack room, handed him the package, and took a halter and lead as she left. She didn't bring the filly back to the barn; instead, she brought her to the front lawn to graze. She didn't want to talk to anyone.

She continued to avoid being alone with any of the slaves, other than Mattie, for the next few days. She was out in the yard cutting flowers for her mother when she heard loud voices coming from her father's study. Although concerned, Ellie started to walk away, knowing that eavesdropping was rude, but stopped when she heard Samuel's name mentioned. Stealthily, she crept closer to the study windows. Inside, John Peters and his overseer, Philip Barton, were arguing with each other. Her father was seated at his desk; Mr. Barton was pacing back and forth in front of him, waving his arms in the air to punctuate his speech.

"Mr. Peters, this is a valuable piece of property we are talking about. That boy, Samuel, is young. He could work another thirty or forty years for you here. His sale price would pay for a good-sized parcel of land. I cannot believe, you would willingly ignore his running off this way," the overseer raged.

"Mr. Barton, I wish you would calm yourself. You will surely take a fit if you do not. That boy is not worth this entire storm. Besides, he may well have gone off looking for a girl. He has only been gone two days. Even if he has run off, he may not get very far before he decides he was better off here than enduring the hardships he will encounter by trying to make his way to the North. Samuel may well return on his own and contrite for his foolishness," John stated calmly.

"This is a slap in your face, Mr. Peters! You cannot afford to ignore this behavior. What message are you giving to your other Negroes? What are you saying to your neighbors if you turn a blind eye to this? Those damned slaves will get it in their heads that any of them can walk off and nothing will happen to them.

They will not even care to work because they can leave if they do not like the conditions here. And your neighbors! They will surely not thank you for putting such notions into the heads of their niggers!" he yelled, leaning across the desk.

"I will thank you not to use such language in my home or on my property, Mr. Barton. I find it offensive." He glared at his employee until the man backed down.

"I apologize, Mr. Peters. I just cannot stand here and do nothing when this boy is abusing your kindness," the man cowed.

"It seems to me, Mr. Barton, that it is your pride and 'kindness' that you feel are being abused. Samuel is my property, not yours. If I can accept what has happened calmly, I cannot see why you should be so very agitated. However, your behavior aside, I have to agree that doing nothing will send the wrong message to both the slaves and my neighbors. Therefore, I will have notices posted offering a reward for Samuel's return. I still think it is a waste of time, but I will concede that it should be done to maintain order. You may go, Mr. Barton, and thank you for your concern."

Philip Barton nodded his head and walked out of the room. Ellie could see by his expression and posture that he was not contented with the outcome of the discussion, but had no power to do otherwise than accept his boss' decision. Ellie leaned back against the house, breathing heavily from anxiety for Samuel and from holding her breath as much as she could. She quietly pushed away from the wall and hurried away with her basket of flowers, not wanting to be discovered anywhere near the study.

John was visibly upset at dinner. Charlotte, oblivious to her husband's feelings, stated, "That man is so crude. He is only an employee. Why did you allow him to raise his voice in our house?"

"One of the slaves ran away," he explained. "He was upset."

"All those Abolitionists, it's their fault. None of our slaves would even consider such a thing if they did not hear all that nonsense."

"I just do not understand it. I have always treated our slaves well. They have never been beaten; I take good care of them. And this one has family here."

"Maybe... he wanted to be free," Ellie risked.

"There you go again. It is statements like that that encourage them to do things like this." Charlotte was getting upset and directed her fears toward Ellie.

"Ellie, do you know something about this?" John looked at his daughter.

"How would I know anything about this?" She looked back and forth at her parents trying to look indignant. "Do you think he would tell me something?"

John Peters shook his head. He did not know what to think. He knew things were changing and much too fast for his liking. "Well, I am amazed by the ingratitude. Samuel and all of our people are treated like our family. I have never allowed them to be whipped nor sold them off away from their families. I have even allowed them to marry away from the farm if they so wished. I could not have treated my own children with more consideration than I have my slaves."

"Perhaps the difference is that you have always treated your children as free human beings and have always treated the slaves as dependent children, Father. No matter how kind you have been to them, you still own them and they know it." Ellie stated quietly. Charlotte raised her eyes to the heavens in despair over her daughter's hopeless behavior, but John's brows creased in deep thought. Ellie prayed she had touched something in him.

CHAPTER 25

The following week, while checking the mares in the south pasture, it was discovered that one of the horses was missing. The mare had not taken the last three breeding seasons, but was only ten years old. John still had hopes that she would conceive. She had been well broken and at the least would have made a good saddle horse even for an inexperienced rider. He was more upset about the mare than the missing slave, and had sent workers out to make sure there was no breach in the fencing. However, he suspected that Samuel had taken her.

Ellie suspected the same thing. She was angry. She felt that Samuel had betrayed her in some way. She had helped him and he had stolen from her family. She understood that some people would think that she had given her father's property away, but it was property that she believed he had no right to own. The horses were a different story; they were the family's livelihood and were rightfully theirs. She wanted to hear that he had not done it; the only one who might know was Lela. As soon as she could get away after having heard the news she went to talk to her.

It was late afternoon when Ellie found Lela in her family's cabin. Having finished her garden work earlier, Lela was sweeping the dirt floor of the cabin while one of her seven siblings was preparing the family's dinner on the hearth.

"Lela, I would like to speak with you," Ellie announced from the porch.

"Yes, Miz Ellie," she replied, leaning her broom against the wall and walking out to join her young mistress.

"Walk with me, Lela," Ellie commanded, and proceeded to move away from the cabin and prying ears. Lela followed dutifully along behind until they found a crude bench to sit on under an oak. Lela remained standing until Ellie invited her to sit down.

"Lela, did Samuel steal the mare?" Ellie demanded.

"Ah don't know, Miz Ellie, but Ah s'pose he did, more than lackly," Lela responded, looking down at the ground.

"Did you know he was going to take the horse?" Ellie continued suspiciously.

"No, 'am, Miz Ellie. Ah done told you Ah didn't know nothin' about the hawse. But Ah guess you think all us Negras is liars anyways." Lela kept her head down so Ellie couldn't see her expression.

"Lela! How can you say that to me after all we have been through together? When have I ever treated you as less than a good person and my equal?" Ellie was incensed at the other woman's attitude.

There was a significant pause while Ellie waited for Lela to respond.

"Have you nothing to say? I think that you cannot; for I am most certain that I have never acted in any way that would merit such a statement." Ellie, puffed up with indignation, stared at the slave woman.

"Ah recon Ah can't say nothin' ta that, Miz Ellie, on a count that you is mah mistress. Ah know mah place." Ellie looked at Lela, ready to berate her further, when she realized that the young woman was just as angry with her as she was with Lela. Ellie was incredulous at this turn of events. What did Lela have to be angry about?

"Lela, what do you imagine I have done to you? Why are you angry with me?" she asked, too stunned to be angry any longer.

The slave woman looked up at her mistress' face, allowing her frustration and anger to show. "You axed me what you did ta me. You axed me ef you ever treat me lack Ah is...am less than you. Miz Ellie, you allas treat me lack Ah am less than you, but you jist don't see it. Jist afore, when you come ta the cabin doe, you didn't ax could Ah come wit you or was Ah busy doin' somethin'. You jist tell me you want ta talk wit me an' Ah was s'posed ta drop everythin' an' come along with you. You wouldn't never talk that way with a white woman, even a po' one. Ah know you don't even think 'bout it, Miz Ellie. You was jist brung up that away an' you can't hep it. But that one o' the ways that you treat me lack Ah'm less than you is," the thin young woman finished. She continued to look into Ellie's eyes, challenging her to deny the accusation.

Ellie turned away from Lela, her cheeks burning with shame as she realized that the accusation was true. She didn't treat the slaves as equals. "I am sorry, Lela. I never realized.... I have been criticizing my father for treating the slaves as if they were his helpless children, but I am no better than he is. You have given me something to think about. I am sorry to have taken you away from your work, and I do believe that you did not know Samuel was going to take the mare. Please excuse me, now. I must get back to the house." Ellie rose and walked back to the house, leaving Lela to sit in amazement at her own temerity at speaking to her mistress in such an honest manner.

That evening, after dinner, John Peters had the overseer call all of the slaves to the main house. When they were assembled outside on the lawn, the Peters family came out. John commanded that chairs be brought for the three eldest slaves, who would find it difficult to stand while he addressed the group. Once this was done, he began speaking.

"I am certain that all of you are aware that Samuel has run off and has taken one of my mares. I find it difficult to comprehend how any of you would want to flee your home to face the dangers of the world outside of this place. I have always treated you as my children. Is there one among you who can complain that I have been unfair to you?" He paused to look around at the sea of dark faces before him. Many heads were shaking, others looked down at the ground.

A male voice from the crowd called out, "No, suh, Marster John. You's allas been good ta us. You lack a father ta us."

"Then how is it that one of you would treat me in this way? How could one of you steal my property? I am deeply hurt by the ingratitude shown by Samuel. I want you all to know that I will have to punish him when he is caught. Such actions cannot and will not be tolerated. Further, if I discover that any of you has aided him in this, you too will be punished. Am I understood?"

A chorus of "Yes, Marster John," arose from those assembled.

"Very well. You may all return to your cabins." John turned to go, but was stopped by another voice from the crowd.

"Please, Marster John, we want ta sing fo' you an' yo' fambly." John looked at the faces of his people. They seemed eager to perform for him and his family. He looked at Charlotte who nodded her acquiescence, and then ordered that chairs be brought for him and the family members. Once this was done, the slaves began their impromptu concert of traditional spirituals. They sang moving songs of long toil and hardship: "Lay Down Body" and "Been in the Storm So Long." They finished with "Steal Away to Jesus." As the lyrics of the song reached Ellie's ears, she suddenly realized what these people were really saying. She looked at Mama Noli who was one of the seated elders and caught the old woman's eye. Mama Noli smiled broadly at the young, white woman and continued nodding her head and beating her cane against the ground in time with the music. Ellie covered her mouth with her hand to hide her surprise. No one else in her family seemed to understand that the slaves were standing before their masters singing openly of running away.

When the concert was finished, John Peters thanked the performers and had sweets passed out to them as a reward. Ellie held back a laugh as she watched her father and mother congratulating each other on having handled the runaway problem so well.

Spring had been eventful for Ellie. She had struggled through many personal changes. It was nearly May and time to prepare for another summer in Beaufort.

CHAPTER 26

On the first of May, the Peters family made their annual trip from the farm in Sheldon to Beaufort for the summer. While politics and talk of secession had been popular topics of conversation, as the Republican Convention in Chicago was about to begin, the increasing of the possibility of secession was on everyone's mind and the talk of it was on every street corner.

Ted came to call on the second with an invitation in hand for dinner at his family's on Saturday. It would be a small dinner party: the Campbells, the Peters, the Samms, and the Means. Ellie joined Ted and Charlotte. "Ted Campbell! Where have you been keeping yourself all winter?" she enquired, teasing. Ted rose and kissed Ellie's hand in greeting.

"Ellie!" Charlotte scolded.

"Mrs. Peters, your beautiful daughter is right. I am afraid I have been woefully inattentive. I have been spending much too much time in Charleston." He shook his head regretfully, as if remorseful for such behavior, but the smile on his face belied that sentiment.

"I am sure you had important business keeping you there," Charlotte purred.

"Alas, none whatsoever." Ted smiled again and shrugged.

Ellie rolled her eyes, and then she had trouble holding back her laughter when she saw that her mother was speechless. Charlotte recovered with, "You are such a tease."

Ted started laughing. For Ellie, Ted's laugh was infectious and she joined in. Charlotte was confused by it, but pretended to laugh along with them, and then excused herself. "I must check that everything has been unpacked. You young people enjoy your visit." She heard them laughing harder as soon as she walked out of the room.

"Did you really spend the entire winter in Charleston?" Ellie asked him, amazed at his profligacy.

"I went home from Sheldon. My father and brothers decided I needed to take a more active role on the plantation. I sat in the office writing business letters for them for an entire month. Then, I left for Charleston."

"Ted, what are you going to do with yourself?" Ellie was concerned for her friend.

"Please, do not start on me, too!" Ted started to rise, his hackles raised, but sat back down and sighed when Ellie gently put her hand on his arm.

"Ted, is there anything you think you would like to do? I know you will be good at whatever you choose." She smiled gently and encouragingly.

"I just know I do not want to live in my brothers' shadows, answering to them my entire life." He slouched back on the divan, stretching his legs out and crossing his arms. The look on his face showed his unhappiness and discontentment.

Ellie was surprised by Ted's sadness; usually he was angry and contemptuous when he spoke of his family. She caressed his hand, reassuring him, "You will find something."

"How is your Princess?" Ted asked, perking up a bit. He needed to change the subject.

"Oh, Ted, she is going to be beautiful and I think she knows me already." Ellie bounced in her seat with enthusiasm.

"You mean she knows you keep sugar cubes," he chuckled.

Ellie laughed and swatted his arm. "Be quiet. That is my secret."

"And how is your other secret going?" Ted leaned in toward her, his tone conspiratorial.

She was taken off guard and leaned away from him. The first thought that came to mind was the runaway slaves. Then she realized he was talking about teaching the slaves to read. "Uh...They are doing very well and Lela has been teaching others after she learns something."

Ted always watched her closely and became suspicious that she was withholding something. "Ellie Peters, what are you keeping from me?"

"I am not keeping anything from you." Ellie tried her best to sound indignant, sitting up straighter and turning her face away from him.

Ellie's response made Ted even more certain that she was hiding something. Annoyed, he demanded, "Has someone been calling on you?"

She turned to study his face. "Why, Ted, you actually sound jealous!" Ellie smiled at him.

"Ellie, I need to know." He reached over and grasped her wrist, squeezing it firmly.

Looking at his hand, and then at the intensity in his eyes, she stated slowly, "Ted Campbell, you are jealous!" She wasn't sure if she should be upset or pleased. The one thing she knew was that she didn't want to ever hurt her friend. "I should make you worry a bit...but I have to admit that I chase them all away when I tell them to free their slaves and that I can do anything they can do." She patted his hand where it gripped hers.

Ted had shown more of his feelings than he had intended. He knew she was still hiding something, but decided he would find out another time. With a feeble laugh, he changed the subject to the upcoming events for another summer in Beaufort. Eventually, Ted excused himself, headed down to Bay Street, and spent the rest of the day putting down scotches at the Beaufort Billiards Club until some of his friends there dragged him out of the club and took him home.

As Saturday approached, Charlotte was resigning herself to the idea that Ted Campbell would probably become her son-in-law. She had heard about Ted's drunken escapade after leaving their house; he had apparently made a complete fool of himself. She only hoped that her husband was correct, that he would settle down and stop his nonsense once he was married. His father had been wild, too, but he had the added responsibility of the family plantation to temper his behavior; Ted would not.

Suzanne was looking forward to the event. Due to her age, she was not often invited to dinner parties. She was sure it had to do with Ellie and Ted and had started teasing Ellie as soon as she had heard. She was also sure that, given the right opportunity, Ellie would upset everyone with her ranting about the Negroes not being inferior and insisting they should all be freed and educated. She was determined to give Ellie the opportunity. She enjoyed seeing her sister get into trouble with her parents and didn't want her big sister to marry someone so wealthy. Suzanne dreamt of being the mistress of a large plantation where everyone would bow to her wishes. In her adolescent machinations, what she didn't understand was that the better the marriage Ellie made, the better would be her own possibilities.

James Peters had joined the family in Beaufort and hoped to spend the summer. He had his own plans and ideas about finding a wife. He had another year of studying law before he could start practicing. But he was sure it would not take long before he could afford to marry. He was methodical about plotting out his future and believed a long engagement would suit him. However, he had not yet told his father he had no intention of returning to Sheldon. He knew Ted frequented houses of ill repute, drank too much, and gambled. They had even gone out carousing together a few times. But Ted had no responsibility and his own income; he'd settle down once he had his own family. James felt a marriage between his sister and Ted would release him from assisting his father to manage the horse farm. Ted could help and eventually take things over. Besides, he knew Ellie was capable of managing it; she'd just need to have a man to enforce her decisions.

After Ted's extravagant, beautiful, and very personal Christmas gift, John Peters felt he knew the young man's intentions toward his daughter. He suspected Ellie was right that James would not want to have much to do with the farm. He would need his daughter to marry someone educated, but with no place within his own family's business. Then he would get to keep his strong-headed daughter close, too. Thomas Campbell had been as wild during his college years as his son was now. Yet, John had grown to respect Thomas; he had managed his family's rice plantation successfully and kept his philandering to his slaves. That was his only concern about Ted. He was sure the drinking and gambling would stop, but on Whispering Oaks, there would be no dallying with the slave women. He would not tolerate it. At this point, he laughed to himself; he knew his daughter would not either.

Ellie was trying hard to refuse to think about Saturday. However, Suzanne kept harassing her. One by one, each of the other family members came to her, extolling Ted's potential. When she objected to his drinking, each attempted to reassure her that he would stop getting drunk once he was married and had some responsibility. Ellie wasn't so sure. She had heard from Ted about scenes that had occurred in his home while he was growing up. There had been many fights between his parents when his father was drunk. But these were Ted's secrets; she didn't feel she could even tell her father. She believed he had potential if he would stop getting drunk; she just didn't believe he would stop drinking too much and everything that went with it. She admitted to herself that she enjoyed Ted's company and she could do worse. She even loved him as a friend. But as a husband? She couldn't answer the most important question. She wasn't going to let Ted, his family, or hers push her into having to answer that question yet.

CHAPTER 27

Saturday evening the Peters arrived promptly at the Campbell's summer home on The Point. It was one of the larger houses with water frontage. They had their own dock where The Dragonfly and a couple of smaller boats were tied up. Ellie had always admired this house. The grounds were beautifully landscaped and the view of the river from the back lawn was so peaceful. She smiled at the memories of her childhood, playing there on the lawn, fishing off the dock, and eating the cookies prepared by the Campbell's ancient, Negro cook. How simple life had been back then, she mused as she followed her family up the stairs to the broad front door of the Campbells' house.

The evening began with friendly conversation; distant family members and acquaintances were discussed, as were the past year's crops and expectations for the next harvest. Ellie watched as her sister practiced her flirting on fourteen year old Langdon Means and fifteen year old Christian Samms. They were the youngest sons of Alexander Means and Zebadiah Samms, both owners of rice plantations neighboring The Willows, the Campbell's plantation in Prince William Parish. Ellie was relieved that talk of secession did not come up during this time. She was able to relax and enjoy the society of these friendly people without experiencing any discomfort by her loathing for the slave-dependent Southern way of life. She even managed to ignore the presence of the dark skinned attendants serving the dinner. Claudia Martin Means and Martha Lee Hecht Samms were charming women and welcoming toward Ellie. Ted behaved very appropriately, for which she was grateful. She had the opportunity to get to know Anderson Marsh Campbell's young bride, Esther Burroughs Campbell. Ted's older brother and sister-in-law had only recently returned from their honeymoon in Europe. They had spent six months traveling through England, France, and Italy and regaled the company with details of their trip. For a change, Ellie felt herself relaxing and enjoying being out in society. She caught Ted staring at her across the room and smiled warmly at him, for once content and at peace. She even felt a flutter when he returned the smile.

Lost in the reverie of this moment, Ellie just barely heard Suzanne saying, "But are not all the slaves contented and better off being taken care of on the plantations?"

Ellie felt her sense of peace shatter. She turned her head toward her sister who was sitting across the room from her. Suzanne looked directly at Ellie and smiled. Only Ellie realized the wicked intent behind that smile. She was determined to keep her thoughts to herself and avoid any confrontations. She knew that Suzanne wanted her to embarrass herself and her parents in front of all these people. Narrowing her eyes, she returned her sister's smile, showing her teeth in a feral grin. Suzanne's smile quickly disappeared and she swallowed hard as she turned away to look at anything, but her sister.

"Certainly the slaves are better off being protected on a plantation, Miss Suzanne," Zeb Samms replied to her question. "They receive food and shelter and have nothing to worry about from life other than doing the work they are given. However, not all are contented; there have been an ungrateful few who ran away. Most of them end up wandering around in the swamps for a few days or weeks, and then return to their homes because they realize how inhospitable the real world can be. They come back to us sadder, but wiser, I would say. Of course, it is necessary to make an example of them for the others. We cannot have slaves running off, willy-nilly. The work would never get done. The Lord knows those darkies are lazy enough as it is," he continued, shaking his head.

Alexander Means added, "Lazy indeed, my friend. The ignorant lot of them would sooner sit about in filth than do an honest day's work for the food, shelter, and clothing they receive. You have to have a good overseer and a good driver to get a decent day's labor out of them. And they are always coming up to the big house begging for sugar or cloth or some such thing." He looked disgusted at the remembered behavior.

"You are certainly right about that, Mr. Means," Martha Lee Samms stated, fanning herself. "Every time Mr. Samms and I go down to the plantation we are inundated by our Negroes begging for favors from us. I have to set limits on when they may come to the house to make their requests. One can barely travel around the property without two or three of them running at you."

Ellie could no longer hold her tongue. "Mrs. Samms, surely these poor slaves are not asking extravagant boons from you. Sugar, cloth, and relief from illness or pain do not seem unreasonable things to provide to your people. They have little other recourse if they cannot obtain these things from you."

Martha Samms looked at Ellie with surprise. Claudia Means responded for her. "Miss Peters, our people are permitted to walk to town once a month to purchase necessaries. Most of them have some money of their own. We provide grain and rice to them. They are allowed to raise their own chickens and vegetables in their own time. We give them cloth or clothing every year, and sometimes more frequently for the growing children. They are permitted to fish or hunt for game to supplement their diets. I assure you, our people are well cared for and have no reason to complain." Claudia's tone had remained calm and reasonable throughout her speech. She seemed to expect Ellie to "see the light" and accept her words.

"I appreciate what you are saying, Mrs. Means. But most slaves have little time or energy at the end of their day to work their own gardens. If they have chickens to feed, they have to choose between feeding the fowl or themselves from their own stock of grain. When they go into town, the shopkeepers charge them double or more for the same goods that we buy and the slaves have no one to complain to about this treatment. You allow them to fish and hunt, but what weapons are they allowed for hunting? They are not permitted guns or even bows and arrows. At best, they might fashion slingshots and snares to catch a rabbit or 'possum once in a great while. Is it unreasonable that they come to those of us who benefit from their labors for some assistance in ameliorating their misery?" Ellie struggled to keep her voice as calm and reasonable as Mrs. Means' had been. She felt near to tears with frustration. She could see her mother across the room glaring at her, lips pursed in disapproval. Nearby, Suzanne was gloating at her victory.

Ted's mother, Agnes Ferguson Campbell, quickly spoke up in an attempt to calm the situation. "Miss Peters, I do assure you that our darkies are all quite contented. Many's the time I have traveled around the plantation and heard their voices raised in Christian hymn as they labored in the fields. Why, they are singing all the time at their work. Surely, they would not sing if they were so very discontented and miserable as you seem to think they are." She smiled reassuringly at her young guest.

Ellie felt it wise to cease in her arguments at this point, certain that her mother was already furious enough with her to lock her in her room for the rest of the summer. She returned her hostess' smile, stating, "Doubtless you are correct in this, Mrs. Campbell. I hope I have not distressed you or any of your guests with my questions."

"Not at all, my dear. You are young and your heart is tender. Your farm is a different world from that of the plantations. If you were to see the Negroes' lives there, you would understand how childlike and innocent they are. Now, shall we have some music? Esther, would you be good enough to play for us?" Everyone present joined in, pressing the bride to perform. The rest of the evening passed quietly enough. Ellie sat quiet and contrite, knowing a lecture would follow once they returned home. It also crossed her mind that she would have to find a way to revenge herself on Suzanne for her instigations. Ellie silently prayed that Ted's family didn't despise her too much.

As church was letting out Sunday morning, Ted was waiting at the foot of the steps at St. Helena's Episcopal Church. He rarely made it to church, but he knew Ellie would be there. Ted greeted Mr. and Mrs. Peters, and then his friend, James. He turned to Ellie, only nodding at Suzanne. Ellie smiled, "I am glad to see that at least one member of the Campbell family is still talking to me after last night."

"Actually, Mother really likes you, in spite of yourself," he laughed, widening his eyes in false alarm.

"Ted Campbell, do not say such things to me unless they are true," Ellie protested, slapping his arm playfully with her folded fan and pouting prettily.

He laughed. "Oh, she does! She just thinks you need to be educated as to the ways of our plantation. She is sure you will come to see things the way she does."

John interrupted, afraid his daughter would criticize Mrs. Campbell. Ted had been able to ignore most of Ellie's statements, but that might be too much. Ted walked with them to their carriage, and then left to join his family.

CHAPTER 28

Things seemed to be settling into the routine of another summer until the papers came out on the seventeenth of May. The Republican Party had chosen their candidate for the upcoming Presidential election, Abraham Lincoln. The Democratic Party was in turmoil and had not chosen their candidate yet. Ellie read every paper she could get hold of in Beaufort. There were newspapers from Charleston, Savannah, and New York. The Beaufort paper only came out every three weeks. She wanted to know who this man Lincoln was and why so many people seemed so upset. She learned that he had been a mediocre congressman, and then had returned to Illinois to develop a very successful law practice. The main objection to him in the South was that he was so strongly in favor of maintaining the Union. This seemed to Southerners to mean that he was against states' rights. Local gossips pointed out that he was crass, crude, and uneducated, being self-taught. Among the aristocratic Southerners, he was little better than the common, unwashed, backwoods farmers that populated much of the interior of their part of the country, hardly presidential material, and certainly no gentleman.

As spring turned into summer, Stephen Douglas was named the candidate for the Democratic Party, John Breckinridge for the National Democratic Party that split off from the Democrats, and John Bell for the Constitutional Union Party. Ellie continued reading the political sections of the newspapers. It seemed that most of the residents of Beaufort were for John Breckinridge. She was confused by their position. She was for state's rights; South Carolinians should be able to govern themselves as much as anyone else. Of the four candidates, Stephen Douglas was the only one who seemed to hold that position. Yet, everyone around her was extolling the benefits to South Carolina of the National Democrats. Slavery had come to the front of the campaigns. Ellie was disappointed that none of them voiced an Abolitionist position. Although she suspected this Mr. Lincoln was an Abolitionist at heart, even if he wasn't saying so.

The Republican Party was resolved that slavery would spread no farther. They did not demand the abolition of slavery, but they did not want it moving into any of the new territories. Their party platform spoke of "human rights" as listed in the Constitution, but avoided stating that slavery would be eliminated if they won the election.

The Democratic Party, as represented by Stephen A. Douglas, also avoided stating that slavery should be abolished. They felt that each state should decide the question of slavery for itself. While this pleased the Southern states, they were unhappy with the decision that the party would not have the federal government protect the institution of slavery. Southerners wanted guarantees that their right to own slaves would be protected.

The Constitutional Union Party had only one position, which was to support the Constitution: the union of the states and the enforcement of laws. This seemed rather vague to Ellie and there was little support for this party in Beaufort.

Finally, the National Democratic Party claimed that no power existed in the federal or local government to restrict slavery in any area while it was in territorial status. This meant that slavery would be legal in all the territories until they entered the Union as states when they could decide for themselves if they would continue the practice. Southerners were certain that slavery would be spread into the territories quickly and would take root there, thus guaranteeing the continuation of slavery.

Ellie wanted to discern the real issues from the leaders of Beaufort, which meant the Rhetts. When she heard that the Campbells were invited to tea at Robert Barnwell Rhett's, she asked Ted to take her along. She promised him that she would not say anything to embarrass or upset his family. Ted didn't care if she upset his family; he did it all the time. However, he did not want her to be disappointed or insulted. In the end, he acquiesced. Ellie kept her word to Ted, much to his surprise. She listened, kept her own comments vague, and asked questions, being careful in her wording not to expose her true feelings. It became obvious that Breckenridge would uphold their way of life by pushing through legislation that would make slavery available in those places where it did not exist or was still minimal. He would keep out legislation that abolished or abridged slavery. Besides, he would keep up the grand tradition of Southern presidents, nine out of the past fifteen having come from Southern states, and thereby continue a strong Southern influence on the federal government. By the end of the afternoon, Ellie thought she understood; the Southern politicians were only concerned about money, and power, and their way of life. These men were willing to risk everything in order to sustain it against outside forces and for that matter inside forces as well.

Ellie noted that the summer seemed to pass quickly. The talk and newspapers were filled with the upcoming election. She was aware of an irony in the air. While people claimed they wanted Lincoln to lose, they seemed excited by the idea of his election which would justify secession. She couldn't criticize her friends and neighbors regarding this, when she was seeing the same type of conflict in her own behaviors, but in a different area.

She had been trying to be aware of her behavior toward any slaves with whom she came in contact. She was purposely being as polite as possible and asking for things instead of demanding. Yet, she knew that due to their status, they needed to respond to any request as a demand. She could not find a satisfactory resolution to the problem, but was determined to change her own attitude, even if the slaves could not change their reactions. No one commented to her about what she'd been doing; however, she knew by the looks she had received from her family that they had noticed a change in her.

Toward the end of September, Mrs. Campbell invited the Peters women for afternoon tea. They were surprised when they arrived to discover they were her only guests. The visit started with the usual chatter. Eventually, Agnes came around to the purpose of the visit. "Will you be calling on your sister in Savannah again before leaving Beaufort for the winter, Mrs. Peters?"

"I am afraid not. I do love Savannah so, but Mr. Peters wants to be back in Sheldon to vote." She sighed. "Alas, we will be leaving early this year."

"Mr. Campbell is insisting that we leave for the plantation early as well. We will be leaving in two weeks."

"Oh, that is early," Charlotte commiserated.

Suzanne and Ellie exchanged looks, wondering where this was leading.

"That is a shame," Charlotte continued.

"Well, I thought that, since this is such an unusual year, maybe you and the girls could come and visit for a few days on your way back to Sheldon. The rest of the family will be returning just in time for the elections and it will be so lonely for me. It will be harvest time, so I will see little of Mr. Campbell."

"Oh, that would be wonderful. Mama, may we go? I want to see a proper plantation." Suzanne clapped her hands in excitement.

"Now, Suzanne, calm down. You have been to the Campbell's before. I suppose you were too young to remember much about it."

Ellie kept quiet. She knew that Mrs. Campbell wanted to prove to her that she was wrong about slavery.

Believing that this had something to do with Ellie and Ted, Charlotte was more than willing to accept. "We would love to come. I will speak to Mr. Peters about the arrangements."

The two older women continued talking about the details of their plan. Once satisfied with their arrangements, they went on to other subjects before ending the visit.

Ellie was sure that Mrs. Campbell's intent was to convert her to being a supporter of slavery. She believed nothing could change her mind, but she was curious about the rice plantation and the actual treatment of the slaves there. She had not been to The Willows in six years. At that time, they stayed mostly in the area of the house, and at thirteen years of age, her awareness of the degradation of the slaves was only beginning.

Suzanne had been too young last time they visited the Campbells' winter home to remember much. She was excited about the detour on their way home and continually asked Ellie about the place. Ellie did not have the heart to destroy Suzanne's fantasy about the life style of plantation living. Some plantation owners' homes were little more than a three or four-room cabin or farmhouse. Fortunately, the Campbells spent five or six months out of the year at The Willows and were not about to give up any luxuries. Ellie remembered there being a large dining room and sitting room and numerous bedrooms between the second and third floors. She shared every detail about the house she could remember. But Suzanne wanted more. It was not easy to get rid of her, especially since they had to share a room in the Beaufort house. Finally, she sent her off to ask Mattie, assuring her that Mattie would remember more.

Ellie needed time alone. While she was getting excited about visiting the plantation for her own reasons, she needed to make some special preparations. Although she still had plenty of cash left over from last year, she had been hording more again from her supposed shopping this summer. She needed to get it home safely. Some of her things were to be sent on ahead and some were to accompany her to the Campbells'. With the new plans, she would not have the same control over her things as she had last year when returning to Sheldon. Whenever she had some time alone, she opened hems and slipped in dollars, and then re-sewed them. She filled pockets with gold and silver coins and sewed them closed. Finally, she opened the lining of the bag she would keep with her and put the remaining money in, and then sewed it back up. Her only concern was that some of the items felt a little heavier than they should.

Finally, the day arrived. Ellie, Suzanne, and Charlotte went by carriage to the Campbell's dock in Beaufort. The slaves followed by wagon, accompanying the trunks. Ellie was relieved when her mother and Suzanne went below deck in the schooner. Ted's parents had left Beaufort the week before for The Willows. She and Ted would be able to talk more freely topside.

It was a warm fall day with a pleasant wind out of the east. Ted teased Ellie about his mother's plans for her and the two laughed together for much of the three hour cruise. Ellie convinced Ted to give her a complete tour of the plantation and not just what his mother had planned. She was beginning to think the visit could be more than educational. She enjoyed Ted's companionship; she found his laughter warmed her heart.

CHAPTER 29

As soon as the schooner docked at The Willows, two barefoot boys of about fifteen years of age, dressed in shabby, calico shirts and ragged, cotton trousers tied with twine, grabbed the lines and started tying up the boat. Once the vessel was secure, they jumped on board and greeted their young master. Ted gave them instructions to take the trunks to the main house. After helping Suzanne and Charlotte make their way up, the ladies' maids stayed close to the trunks.

Ted took Charlotte's arm to guide the women toward the house, but they were soon swarmed by young black faces with hands outstretched. "Marster Ted, Marster Ted. Ya home an' ya haf beaudeeful ladies wit choo."

Stopping, Ted laughed and reached into his pocket. He always made sure he had plenty of pennies when he came home. He tossed them around to the waiting slave children. "Now, give the ladies room; they've had a long ride." He continued leading the way to the house. They were trailed by a ragtag band of laughing children.

The foursome climbed the stairs, and as they were crossing the porch, the front door was opened by the Campbells' butler. "Marster Ted, you sho is lookin' mighty good. You been gone too long, Suh. Miz Agnes' waitin' fo' you an' da beautiful ladies in da parla."

"Joseph, I still think you are Irish. You are always so full of blarney." Ted laughed, and then led the way to the parlor.

Agnes Campbell put down her book and patted the seat next to her on the settee. "Charlotte, come sit down. You must be exhausted after your trip." She turned, smiling at the girls. "Ellie, Suzanne, please sit." She picked up a small silver bell. Two thin teenage girls, both dressed in grey cotton dresses, carried in trays, one with butter cookies and the other with a tea set. They set them on the table and, both trying to stifle giggles, quickly scurried to the side table to retrieve tea cups, spoons, and linen napkins embroidered with three small flowers in one corner. As the group enjoyed the refreshments, Agnes Campbell chattered on about the blessings of The Willows, the peace and happy interaction of all the residents. Ellie watched Ted roll his eyes. She wondered how much of Mrs. Campbell's monologue was for her benefit. Finally, Agnes let her audience adjourn to their rooms to rest and prepare for dinner.

Ellie was given a second floor room with two large windows, which opened out onto a veranda overlooking a garden behind the house. Her trunk was at the foot of the large four-poster bed that was high off the floor. Mattie had obviously been busy unpacking Ellie's things. She found her dresses hung in the armoire and her toiletries set up on the dresser. Ellie sat down in an overstuffed armchair and unlaced her shoes. She felt a need to wiggle and stretch her toes. She hadn't realized the stress she had felt while listening to Ted's mother until she was sitting in the quiet of the room. After a few minutes, she noticed that Mattie was nowhere to be seen. She suddenly became obsessed with where Mattie was going to sleep.

Mattie appeared shortly before dinner to help Ellie dress. "Where have you been?" Ellie questioned her maid as she sat down at the dressing table.

"Ah was puttin' mah things in da cella where da udders sleep. Did ya need me?" Mattie replied distractedly as she tried to dress Ellie's hair.

"No. I just…. I was concerned." She looked up at Mattie in the mirror over the dressing table. "You let me know if anyone is mean to you here," she earnestly told the other woman.

"Ah'll be fine, Miz Ellie," the slave woman shrugged. "But Ah won't wear one o' dem gray dresses," she stated emphatically, pursing her lips.

"What are you talking about?" Ellie asked, confused.

"All da women what works in da house has ta wear dese gray dresses." Mattie made a disgusted face at the thought of the uniforms.

"Oh!" Ellie nodded, understanding the reference. "Do not concern yourself with that, Mattie. I promise you will not have to wear 'one o' dem gray dresses.'" Ellie chuckled as she saw Mattie's expression in the mirror.

"Hmmph. No need ya go makin' fun o' da way Ah talks, Miz Ellie," she stated, irritated.

Ellie turned and looked up at her slave. Her contrition was written on her face. "I am sorry, Mattie. I only meant to tease you a bit. You cannot help that you have had no schooling in proper speech. You speak very well." She watched Mattie struggle briefly to forgive her mistress.

"Well, no hahm done, Ah guess," the maid stated, finishing her mistress' hair.

Dinner was formal, but simple fare. Servants were kept to a minimum so as not to interfere with the family atmosphere.

"How was your journey down, Mrs. Peters?" Thomas Campbell enquired of Charlotte.

"Most pleasant, thank you. It was so very gallant of your son to escort us here, and so very gracious of you to have us stay. You have a lovely home here. I know that Ellie is looking forward to seeing it again," Charlotte responded, smiling amiably at her host.

"And I look forward to showing her about tomorrow," Ted responded, smiling warmly at Ellie.

Looking into his eyes, Ellie believed she saw something there that was warmer and deeper than just their companionable relationship as it had been. She felt herself blushing as something fluttered in her stomach. She looked down at her plate, but not before a smile could steal across her face. Ellie thought this visit might become something more than just an opportunity for Mrs. Campbell to convert her to proper slaveholder attitudes.

Mattie woke Ellie the next morning, announcing, "Ya coffee gonna be cold ef ya doan wake up soon." She had brought up a silver tray with breads, butter, sliced apples, and coffee and cream. "Everbody is up an' Ah think yo Ted is gitting impatient." Mattie set the tray on a small table and helped Ellie prop herself up in the bed while they talked.

Ellie stretched. "It will be good for him." She accepted the lap tray and began sipping the coffee immediately.

Mattie smiled broadly as she watched Ellie hurriedly eat, and then helped with her toilet and dressing. Soon Ellie darted out the door of her room, nearly running down the stairs.

Ted had heard Ellie's footsteps and was waiting at the foot of the stairs. "I guess you only get up early for Princess." When he saw the expression on her face, he started laughing before she could respond. Her expression passed, and shaking her head, she smiled. "Mother insists I show you all the wonders of The Willows," he informed her, offering her his arm.

As they headed out the front door, Suzanne came running after them, "I am coming, too."

The three made their way, passing small shacks that Ted stated were some of the slave homes. The area seemed empty of all adults; it was a time of work. Small children ran about chasing the chickens or playing other games. Many were holding babies. When they came to a larger wooden structure, Suzanne asked what it was. Ted explained, "That is the infirmary."

"You have your own infirmary?" Suzanne was impressed.

"We have hundreds of slaves. It is easier caring for them in one place." Ted explained.

"May we go in?" Ellie was curious about what kind of health problems they treated.

"I do not remember when I was in there last, but certainly, if you would like. Though, I think you will find the mill much more interesting." Ted seemed in doubt of the wisdom of entering the building.

"We do not have to stay long." Ellie's voice was especially sweet as she laid her hand on his arm and smiled up at him.

He sighed. "This way then. We will have time for both before the afternoon meal." Ted slipped his arm through Ellie's, guiding her toward the entrance.

Suzanne pouted as she followed her sister and Ted, and then passed them with heavy yet quick steps when she saw the door. She opened the door herself and stepped in. Ted gave Ellie a questioning look. She shrugged in response.

Ellie nearly gagged at the stench when they walked though the doorway. The smell of feces, urine, dried blood, and rotting refuse was overwhelming. A feeble fire burned on the hearth at the far end of the room, giving off little heat and no light. There was little other lighting in the large room. Most of the windows had closed shutters on them to keep the cool drafts from coming through the broken glass in the windows. There were no beds or chairs in the place. It appeared that the floor was littered with piles of rags until Ellie realize that the piles were actually people lying on the cold, filthy floor. There were eleven women in the room; one was a heavy, tall woman who was bent over a woman lying on her stomach on a stained, ragged blanket on the dirty tabby floor. She was applying a paste-like substance to livid welts and bleeding wounds on the woman's back. Ellie didn't need to ask to know what the wounds were from; she only had to remember George. Another woman lying on a pallet was nursing a newborn. She called out, "Marster Ted! Look, Ah's had anudder baby. Ah give yo' mammy an' daddy six little brown babies now."

Ted didn't know how to respond. He didn't even know her name. Seeing his awkwardness, Ellie asked, "Is your baby a girl or a boy?"

"Oh, you is so nice ta ask, Miz. He a boy. You is Marster Ted's Miz Ellie. Ah heard 'bout you." She looked at Ted, and then back to Ellie. "Miz Ellie, will ya hep me?"

"How? What is it you need?" Ellie was afraid of what the woman might say; she did not know what the slave might have heard about her. She held her breath as she waited for the answer.

"Ask Miz Agnes ef Ah kin stay wit dis baby. Doan let 'em make me go right back ta da fields." The woman's voice was filled with pleading and misery.

"When do you go back to work?" Ellie asked the poor mother.

"Dey gives us tree weeks," the slave woman responded.

Ellie was appalled. That was little enough time to try to recover from a birth, not to mention the other problems that had to be worked out. "But who looks after your baby? How do you nurse the baby?"

"Issa, dat's mah six yeah ole, she care fo' da baby den brings him ta da field when he git hungry." Proudly, she added, "Last one, she did good work an' she only foe den."

Ted interrupted. "We should go now." He put his hand on Ellie's back and said to the woman, "I will talk to my father for you." As Ted took her arm to lead her away, Ellie looked back at the exhausted new mother suckling her infant. She couldn't help but feel concern for the woman's plight and wondered if Ted would keep his word to her.

Suzanne was already impatiently standing in the doorway. As Ellie and Ted joined her, she looked up at Ted and tried to sound mature. "I cannot believe she would talk to you like that. Why should she receive special treatment?" Ellie bit her tongue and shooed her little sister out the door. She was greatly relieved to leave the stench and filth of that building and to get out into the sweet fresh air. The trio continued their tour of the grounds.

Ted pointed out the gristmill. They walked along a narrow pathway leading in its direction. He kept up a running monologue of the sights along the way. He pointed out the raised mounds of earth that served to keep back the river water. There were sluices that could be opened to allow water to flow into the rice fields in order to flood them for planting, and others that would allow the fields to be drained. The dikes were wide enough for people to walk across. Ellie thought it would be difficult for a horse to make its way along them. The banks were covered in tall grass and weeds with patches of low brush or flowering plants. There was no shade or any place where people might sit down to rest and cool off in the heat. Ellie thought of the long, hot days of summer when the slaves would be laboring in these fields without any relief from the scorching sun.

The mill was built of tabby, a mix of sand, mud, and shells, and the grinding wheel was steam powered. The machine made a dreadful noise when steam was vented, but was a marvel to behold. Ellie was surprised by the efficiency and the level of competence of the slaves in running and maintaining such complicated machinery. She made a mental note that it was one more example of the intelligence and learning capability of the Negro people.

After completing the tour, they started walking back to the main house. Suzanne started complaining, "All this walking has made my feet hurt."

Ted attempted to placate her, "We will go by horseback after lunch. That should save your delicate little feet." Suzanne, not hearing the irony in his voice, smiled broadly and shook her curls in what she thought was a flirtatious gesture, convinced that Ted was offering horses to accommodate her.

As they neared the slave shacks, men and women sat on the ground holding bowls, eating out of them with their fingers. Children licked their fingers and their bowls. Ellie pointed out to Ted, "Those children seem terribly hungry." She had never seen anyone eat that way.

Ted stopped to watch, "You may be right. I do not remember ever walking by a group of them without being accosted. They always want something."

At lunch, Suzanne ate heartily, having worked up an appetite after all the walking. Ellie found herself playing with her food; she'd lost her appetite. She noticed that Ted didn't seem to be eating much either. Both were quiet. She was pleased that she might have had some influence on him. Misinterpreting the quietness, Agnes insisted that Suzanne stay at the house to play the pianoforte for her. She thought Ted would do better without the little girl around. There would be enough eyes watching them on the plantation. She also knew that Ellie was a proper Christian lady even if she might have some strange ideas. Suzanne was torn between being escorted around by "a beau," and showing off her talent. She decided on the latter, knowing that she wouldn't win the battle if she argued with her mother. Ellie had already turned to go out the door, so she missed Ted's very satisfied smile at this turn of events.

As Ted and Ellie started down the stairs, two saddled horses were brought up. Ellie exclaimed, "Why, they are both Whispering Oaks horses!"

Ted was surprised. "You know every horse that comes from your farm? You are amazing!"

"These two I remember." Ellie stopped at the second step from the bottom and waited for the groom to bring up the bay with the sidesaddle. "Sometimes, I just recognize the traits my father bred for or the resemblance to one of our stallions." Once securely in the saddle, she leaned forward to stroke the neck of her mount, appreciating the ripple of muscles in its neck and shoulders. She felt great pride in the animals they bred and knew that others saw the quality of their stock. She turned to watch as Ted mounted his horse. She couldn't help but realize how attractive he looked, especially when he wasn't brooding over his unhappiness with his family. *Maybe he will settle down once he gets the wildness out of his system,* she found herself thinking.

The two rode out first toward the rice paddies. Ellie was quickly aware of the warmth of the afternoon sun and was grateful for the straw bonnet she had worn. At least, the humidity of summer was over. The days were still very warm, but the evenings cooled off pleasantly. There was a light breeze blowing from the river that helped to cool them as they trotted along the paths between the fields. Near the river the land remained little better than swamp, even where it had been cultivated. Ellie was not keen on going down there, as she didn't want to encounter any of the alligators that occasionally nested along its banks. It was bad enough that they might have to cope with copperheads or water moccasins, or other poisonous predators. Most of the mosquitoes wouldn't be out until sundown, at least. The soggy earth of the harvested fields smelled sour from the water that had saturated it for so long and rotted the vegetation.

As they rode along, Ellie could see the men and women toiling in the fields, pulling up the rice plants, bent over for hours in the hot sun. Up on the dike, a white man walked along observing them. Ellie could see that he carried a whip in his hand. As she watched, he called to one of the slaves who turned quickly and ran to the man, nodding and cringing. The white man was obviously the plantation overseer. He waved the whip threateningly at the slave who nodded even more vigorously and quickly returned to his post in the field. Ellie glanced at Ted to see his reaction to the event. He appeared not to have noticed. Ellie sighed and shook her head. *How do you go about changing attitudes that are completely outside of someone's awareness?* she asked herself.

When they got closer to the fields, Ellie heard the voices of the laborers raised in song. She was amazed at first. It was true. They did sing Christian songs in the fields as they worked. It wasn't until they were close enough to hear the lyrics of the song that Ellie realized that once again the song was about escaping to freedom. It was a "Christian" topic, Moses speaking to Pharaoh, "Let my people go!" Its message was so very blatant to Ellie that she was stunned that none of the white masters of this plantation recognized it for what it was. *How could they not hear the message?* She realized that people generally heard only what they wanted to hear unless the message was forced upon them.

The pair rode on, moving westward away from the river and the rice fields. The land was higher there. Stands of pine and hard wood trees grew more frequent. Honeysuckle was still blooming in some of the more sheltered spots, perfuming the air. A hint of color was coming into the leaves of the oaks and chestnuts. As they entered a thicker stand of pines, the needles crunched under the hooves of the horses, adding another scent to the warm afternoon air. They rode on in companionable silence, enjoying the quiet, broken only by the song of birds and the muffled clop of the horses. The narrower path forced the horses closer together. Ted's knee brushed against Ellie's legs. She was startled by the sudden contact, but even more startled by the pleasant shiver that passed over her body. She hesitated to look at Ted for fear that he would see the flush spreading over her neck and face.

Heavens! I am getting as giddy as a schoolgirl! Whatever is the matter with me? she asked herself. She had to admit that her attitude toward Ted was changing. She was becoming more aware of his attractiveness. Was she being foolish? He'd been a good friend. But, would he make a good choice for a husband, if she had to marry someone? She certainly enjoyed his company more than any other man she knew. Ellie began feeling uncomfortable about this train of thought, especially with Ted riding so close to her. She needed to distract herself, and quickly. Thinking this, she kicked her horse into a trot, and then into a gallop, racing ahead of her escort.

Ted was caught by surprise by her action, and shouted at her as she sped off. Ellie turned her head to laugh at him, calling, "You had better hurry, if you plan to keep up with me!"

Not one to be bested by anyone else, especially a woman, Ted urged his gelding into a gallop and raced after Ellie. He had the advantage as he knew the trail and she didn't. Ellie had to slow up to negotiate around a turn in the trail. This gave Ted a chance to close the gap between them. Ellie could hear him drawing closer. Laughing, she urged her horse to greater speed. Ahead she could see what appeared to be an open field. Ted was gaining on her again. Her horse had her ears laid back and was running with all her heart. Ellie shared the horse's joy in their speed as they emerged from the woods into a lovely meadow sprinkled with wild flowers. At the end of the field was a pond, a good place to stop and give the horses a drink and a rest after their race. Ellie turned her horse toward the pond and glimpsed Ted rushing past her on the right side. He had missed the turn and she gained a greater lead as she neared the water. Finally, she pulled her horse up and allowed her to walk slowly around to cool down. Ted arrived, laughing and protesting that she had cheated. Once the horses had cooled enough to be watered, Ted dismounted and helped Ellie down. She was acutely aware of the strength of his hands and arms as he held her by the waist. She leaned into him as he set her on her feet. Each felt the heat of that moment of contact. Ted's hands lingered at her waist. Ellie slid her hands down his arms from his shoulders. He pulled her closer against his body and bent his head toward hers. Ellie felt her breathing quicken as his lips neared hers. She could feel his heart beating under her palm as it rested on his chest. She lifted her head for her first kiss, offering her lips to his. His kiss was gentle at first, his lips soft and inviting. Ellie felt herself melting into his embrace, moving her arms to encircle his neck as she returned his fervor. She felt his hands moving over her back, pulling her more tightly against him. The kiss seemed to last an eternity and Ellie hoped that it would go on and on; but she had heard where this could lead and she had to stop it before she was no longer able to do so. She slid her hands down to his chest once again and gently pushed him away.

Breathlessly, she said, "We have to water the horses and head back. It will be getting dark soon." She couldn't bring herself to look into his eyes or to move completely away from his embrace. Ellie was very aware that Ted's breathing was as ragged as hers. He didn't make any move to release her at first, and Ellie felt a twinge of apprehension. He was much stronger than she was. She had never been so aware of his strength before. At last, she forced herself to look up at him. His eyes seemed clouded with emotion. Ellie watched as he struggled to bring himself back under control.

"Yes. The horses need to be watered. It is getting late." He released her and took up the reins of their mounts to lead them over to the pond for a drink. Ellie wandered off a little distance to collect herself and to pick a few of the wild flowers growing in such profusion there.

By the time they were ready to return, both of them were back in control of their emotions. Ted was able to give Ellie a leg up into her saddle without either of them feeling uncomfortable. They rode back in silence, both lost in their own thoughts. Once back at the house, they had no opportunity to speak alone. Ellie wasn't sure if that was a good thing or not. She couldn't help but remember the feeling of Ted's mouth on hers, of his hands moving over her body. At dinner, she did her best to praise the plantation, knowing it would please her hosts, but it was difficult not to point out the poverty and misery of the slaves laboring there. When at last it was time to retire, Ellie went gratefully to her room. She had a lot to think about. Mattie helped Ellie change into a long white cotton nightgown, hung up her clothes and started extinguishing the oil lamps. Ellie crawled up on the bed. She told Mattie to leave the lamp by the bed on and said good night. Mattie left the room, closing the door quietly behind her.

Ellie pulled the heavy quilt up; the heft of the covers felt cozy. As she started to try to read, she found that she could not concentrate and began to feel warm. Not wanting to give up the security of the quilt, she got up and opened the window a few inches. She turned back to the bed, but the sound of a mournful, baritone voice wafting through the night air stopped her. She turned back to the window opening it all the way. The house seemed silent; the song was soft and in the distance. Ellie stepped through the open window, drawn to the sound. She looked out into the darkness, wrapping her arms around herself, trying to stave off the cold of the night. She listened intently, trying to make out the words. She recognized the melody before she caught any of the words. "...Swing low, sweet chariot, Comin' fo' ta carry me home. Ah looked over Jordan an' what did Ah see? Comin' fo' ta carry me home! A band of angels comin' after me. Comin' fo' ta carry me home!..."

Concentrating on the music, she did not hear the approaching footsteps until the squeaking of the wooden boards warned her that someone was nearly upon her. She looked in the direction of the new sound to see a dark figure approaching. The aroma of the cigar reached her before she was able to make out the movement of Ted's swagger as he walked toward her. The thought of running back through the window crossed her mind, but she knew he had already seen her since she was standing in the dim light coming from the lamp in her room. The memory of the afternoon kiss sealed her decision to stay where she was, leaning on the railing with both hands, listening to the baritone.

Ted placed his hand on hers and leaned against the rail, watching her. The music grew louder as other voices joined in harmony. The tears began to flow silently down her face as she felt the depth of the sadness and the beauty of the Negro voices in song. Having set his cigar on the rail, Ted gently reached out to her, wiping a tear from her cheek. He had never seen her vulnerable before this. She turned to him and they sought each others eyes. He put his hands on her bare arms and noticed for the first time that she was cold and shivering. He looked down to see what she was wearing, stopping at the sight of her breasts, seeing the outline of her erect nipples through her thin, cotton gown. She blushed when she realized that he was staring at her body. She started to put her arms over her chest. Before she could complete the action, he slid his hands down her arms to her hands and pulled her out of the light from her window. He moved one arm around her, pulling her close. "You're cold." Then he walked her across the veranda to the wall of the house next to her open window.

She realized, as he held her close, that in the darkness no one could see them. The voices in the distance had continued, repeating their mournful song. He lifted her chin with one hand and leaned down, meeting her mouth with his. When she did not pull away, but moved slightly in toward him, he gently parted her lips with his tongue. He explored the interior of her mouth, stimulating her tongue to respond to his in kind. With one arm still around her, he unbuttoned his jacket and moved it out from between them, wrapping one side around her and moving her even closer. He ran his hand up her back and into her hair, pushing his tongue in deeper while supporting her head. He gradually moved his other hand farther down her back drawing her into him. As the kiss deepened, his hand continued slowly moving down to her lower back. She knew she should object before he went any farther, but it felt too good to stop. As his hand went lower, he pulled her hard against him. Her heart was pounding, and when she felt him grow beneath his pants, her curiosity and desire grew with his. A voice in her head kept saying, "Stop," but she didn't want to stop. The song abruptly ended, it was followed by a cry, and then the wailing began. She pulled sharply back. Her ardor had been subdued by the knowledge that some woman had just lost someone she loved. Ted seemed to understand that the moment was gone and nothing further would happen that night. He kissed her forehead and, without a word, offered his hand to help her step back through the window to her room. He turned, retrieved the cigar that had gone out on the railing, and walked away.

Ellie stumbled into bed. She could not hold back the tears. She was sad for the slave who had lost a loved one and grateful that the same woman had saved her from her own desires. She needed to find a way to protect herself from Ted and herself. There were three more nights to get through before returning to Whispering Oaks.

CHAPTER 30

In the morning, Mattie woke her early. She had some coffee, dressed for another day on the plantation, and headed downstairs for breakfast with the rest of the family. She found herself unable to look directly at Ted and chatted with his mother. Before breakfast was over, the rain started. The day was spent inside with passive entertainments. Suzanne moped about for awhile, pestering everyone to entertain her, until Charlotte suggested that she practice the pianoforte. Ted, desperate to spend time with Ellie without others interfering, invited her to play chess.

"I fear I do not play. But, if your patience will extend to teaching me, I would enjoy learning," she smiled seductively, knowing that no one else knew what had occurred between them. Ellie was gratified by the hungry look that came into Ted's eyes at her suggestion.

"It would be my great pleasure to teach you all the moves of the game, my dear Miss Peters," he stated, licking his lips suggestively. Ellie shivered and blushed, glad that their mothers couldn't see or understand the interaction. They adjourned to the smaller drawing room, away from immediate surveillance and the noise of chatter and music. Ted demonstrated how to set up the board and the moves each piece could make.

"Of course, the queen is the most powerful piece on the board. She has the most moves and is most likely to capture the king through subtlety and planning." Ted's smile and veiled eyes implied that he was not talking about chess.

"Then it is all up to the queen?" she asked with mock innocence. "It seems she would need some help in her efforts." Ellie tilted her head and glanced up at Ted through lowered lashes.

"Oh, I have no doubt that there will be a great deal of help and encouragement provided for a bold campaign," Ted assured her, gazing into her eyes. Ellie felt another shiver pass over her.

"But a beginning player would not be able to launch a bold campaign. The queen would be more tentative in her moves, leaving her vulnerable to her opponent," she countered.

"Ah, then the queen might find herself swept off the board and taken by her opponent," Ted stated boldly. He reached out and brushed his fingers over her hand as she moved a piece on the board. Ellie drew back from the contact, feeling an unexpected tingle at his touch.

"I fear I am no match for you, Mr. Campbell. I believe your greater experience leaves me at a disadvantage," she murmured in some confusion over her physical response to Ted. She surreptitiously stroked her hand where he had caressed it.

"On the contrary, Miss Peters. I believe you will be a perfect match for me once you get over your initial doubts about your ability. I look forward to future contests," he purred. Ellie caught her breath at the reference to their meeting the night before and what might have happened. She was amazed at how easily Ted aroused her passion and somewhat disconcerted at her desire to give into it. She was grateful when his mother called them to lunch. She needed to have some space in which to calm herself and collect her thoughts.

After lunch, Ellie decided to go to see where Mattie had been sleeping. She wanted to be sure that her maid was being well cared for and had not been mistreated. She was appalled at the conditions of the basement room where Mattie was expected to sleep. The pallets on the floor were covered with dirty blankets. The walls were damp and mildewed. Ellie saw several cockroaches scurry away at her approach. When she looked more closely at the bedding, she realized that there were fleas and bedbugs crawling around there. Disgusted, Ellie hurried back up the stairs to the first floor. How could a woman as fastidious as Agnes Campbell allow such squalor to exist in her home? It would be easy to ignore it out on the plantation grounds, but right under her nose! Ellie was determined that Mattie would not spend another night sleeping in those conditions. She found Mattie in the kitchen, helping with the dinner preparations and called her.

"Mattie, why did you not tell me how hideous it is down in that basement? You cannot stay down there. No one should have to do so. I want you sleeping in my room for the rest of our stay. But, for pity sake, bathe before you move in there. I hate to think of the fleas and Lord knows what else you might have picked up down there. I do not want you taking ill because of it. And burn that dress. I will give you one of mine. There must be something in my trunk which will not draw too much attention. I am so sorry that you have had to endure that for as long as you have." Ellie was almost panting with anger.

Mattie looked at her mistress with surprise. "Yes, Miz Ellie. Ah'll do as ya say, ma'am, but ya got ta calm down. Ya gonna git everone all stirred up wit ya lookin' lack dis. Ah'll move up wit ya; an' Ah'll git me a baff an' all dat stuff. Please, Miz Ellie, doan fret yo'sef so. Ah's all right," she reassured her.

Ellie nodded and took a few deep breaths. She knew Mattie was right. She couldn't save all the slaves, and it wouldn't help them or her to upset the Campbells. Once she was in better control of her emotions, Ellie went to join the others who had returned to the sitting room. She was relieved to see that Ted had gone out somewhere and would not be there to tease her. She picked a book from the library shelf and seated herself in a quiet corner. She wasn't able to concentrate on the novel, but she made an effort to turn the pages occasionally so that no one would disturb her reflections. Maybe it would be better for her having Mattie sleeping in her room. At least, she would not be tempted to allow Ted to go further in his pursuit of her than he had already done. Mattie would be a good chaperone and Ellie would be able to relax and sleep, rather than lie in bed thinking about what might be waiting out on the veranda. *Yes, it will definitely be better that way.*

The rains continued through the next day and night. Ellie kept herself busy with reading or entertaining Suzanne. At night, she had felt restless and found it difficult to get to sleep, but the rain driving against the veranda kept her safely in her room. By the third evening the rain had finally stopped. It was too late to go out riding and the ground was too wet for walking. Ted had been gone all day, but returned for dinner. Ellie found she was acutely aware of his presence and craved some attention from him. After dinner, the family went into the drawing room and the young people congregated at the pianoforte. The older women called for songs from their children. Ted moved close to Ellie, but kept his behavior very proper. Ellie longed to feel him touch her, to feel his body against hers; it was very distracting. When they all retired for the night, Ellie found that she was still thinking about him.

It was her last night at the plantation and the rain that had kept her safely ensconced in her room with Mattie the last two nights had stopped. She had refused to let Mattie sleep under her bed. While reluctant the first night, Mattie had acquiesced to her demand and slept on top of the bed, but refused to get under the covers. Ellie laughed to herself when she watched Mattie wrap herself in a blanket and happily climb up on the soft bed the second night.

When Ellie heard the soft breathing of sleep, she lit the lamp on the dresser and opened the window enough to squeeze out onto the veranda. As she slipped on her robe, she tried telling herself that she wanted the air and the peace of listening to the sounds of the night before sleep. However, she knew she was hoping Ted would find her again; she was looking forward to the feel of him and his kiss with the safety of Mattie in her bed.

As soon as she emerged, she heard Ted's voice from the shadows, "I was beginning to fear you had decided never to be alone with me again." He was holding two long stemmed glasses in one hand and a bottle of champagne in the other. He filled both glasses, and then set the bottle down. Ellie took a glass from him. He put his arm around her and they sipped their champagne. The two normally talked so much, but no words seemed necessary. They shared the sound of the crickets and the song of the night birds.

Ted bent to pick up the bottle to refill their glasses, but became distracted by the sight of her bare feet and ankles. "You have such tiny, delicate feet." He knelt and lifted her foot. He ran his hand over her foot to her ankle, and with a gentle touch, ran his fingers down her foot and under its high arch.

She jerked her foot away. "That tickles!" she giggled, sloshing a bit of champagne out of her glass.

He laughed. "Oh my beautiful Ellie, do you not know that ticklish feet are a sign of your passion for the tickler?" He caught the hem of her nightgown with one finger and began slowly raising it as he looked up at her questioningly.

Ellie blushed, lightly slapped his hand away, and laughingly said, "Ted, stop that."

He stood with the bottle of champagne and refilled her glass, encouraging her to drink it as he tossed back his own, and then filled it again. Ellie was starting to feel as though the bubbles were going straight to her head; she giggled with the thought of them actually entering through her nose.

Ted took her empty glass from her hand and set both glasses down with the bottle. He stood and looked into her eyes, and then slowly moved in for the sweet taste of her mouth. He pulled her close with one hand and moved his other to untie her robe only to find the soft, thin cotton of her gown underneath. She moved her body up against his, feeling the strength of it against her, enjoying the pressure of his chest against her breasts. She opened her lips slightly, inviting him. His hand slid up her side and he attempted to caress her breasts, but she reached for his hand, moving it down to her waist, only to feel him push it back. The kiss was not broken. He moved her back to the wall of the house, and then eased his hands down to her buttocks pulling her hard against him. She could feel his hardness growing against her stomach with only the two layers of thin cotton between them. She felt a new tingling sensation between her legs. She wanted to touch him, but did not dare. He started kissing her all over her face and her neck. She leaned her head back, sighing in pleasure. When he reached again for her breast, she stopped him. She didn't want to stop, but she was not that type of woman. He understood that she had given him more than she had any man. He gently broke the embrace, kissed her softly on the lips, and then walked her to her window entrance. Kissing her hand, he whispered, "Good night, darlin'. Sweet dreams."

Sighing, Ellie climbed back into her room. As she blew out the lamp, Mattie spoke up, "You been teasin' dat man ever night, Miz Ellie?"

"Mattie!" Trying to sound indignant, Ellie was still flushed and glad of the darkness.

"No wonder, he been callin' fo' da slave women all times o' da night!"

The color drained from Ellie's face.

CHAPTER 31

South Carolina had previously held its general election for the state legislature on the eighth of October. It proved to be an overwhelming victory for the radical Secessionists. Even back on the farm, there was no relief from politics. Local farmers and plantation owners came to visit and to discuss what was happening in their state and their nation. Every man who was eligible made sure he voted in the national election in November. There was too much riding on the outcome to ignore it.

Ellie was down at the paddock working with Princess on the seventh of November when a rider galloped up to the house looking for her father. The man announced that Abraham Lincoln had been elected president and that there was to be a meeting at Sheldon Church to discuss what should be done next. Her father returned from that meeting looking very despondent and agitated.

"It does not seem very hopeful that the Union will be preserved," he told his family. "There is a great deal of pressure to secede. No one believes that Lincoln will accept the rights of the states to govern themselves without federal interference. Most of them are certain he will abolish slavery as soon as he can. There will be a general meeting for the local parishes in Beaufort by the end of this month or the beginning of the next. I will have to go. God help us all. It seems the best we can hope for now is that we will be allowed to secede without any struggle." He shook his head and sighed. There was little else to say, and dinner was a very quiet affair.

A few days later, Charlotte called Ellie downstairs. "Your father picked up the mail in town this morning. You have a letter from Ted Campbell!" She handed it to her daughter and watched the frown come over her face. "I thought you would be happy." She watched as Ellie stared at it, and then shoved it into her pocket. "Why, Ellie, whatever is wrong?" Charlotte asked, frowning with concern.

"Nothing, Mother!" Ellie responded, shrugging and sighing.

"That boy has been writing to you for years, and you rip those letters open, and then run to write back. Now you just put it in your pocket and frown. There is something going on here." Charlotte pushed, genuinely concerned for her daughter's happiness.

"I would rather not discuss it, Mother. He is an irresponsible boy. You have been right about him all along. I should have listened to your warnings," Ellie confessed, desperately wishing her mother would drop the subject and let her seek seclusion.

"What happened, Ellie? What did he do to you to change your mind after all these years of friendship?" Charlotte's face reflected her fear that Ellie had perhaps allowed Ted to take liberties with her.

"Nothing, Mother, honestly. I just do not want to talk about it." She turned and ran up the stairs.

Charlotte called after her. "Eloise Maitland Peters, if it were nothing, there would be nothing to not want to talk about!" The only response she received was the slamming of Ellie's bedroom door.

Ellie sat on the foot of her bed and stared at the letter, slapping it against her palm while her indignation built. *He has his nerve, caressing me and kissing me, and then going to some other woman and doing the same to her. And he thinks he can just go on writing to me as if everything were the same between us.* She wanted to tear it to shreds and throw it in the fire, but she couldn't bring herself to do it. Neither could she read it. Finally, she shoved it in a drawer unopened.

Later in the month, word came that the state legislature had established a Board of Ordnance that would employ a military engineer to begin planning defenses for the coast of the state. Militia units from Beaufort had previously been formed into a battalion in 1858. This unit began meeting and drilling more frequently. In general, there was a martial atmosphere growing everywhere in the state. In early December, John Peters left for Beaufort to participate in the meeting to discuss how the legislature should proceed.

Charlotte, Ellie, and Suzanne were in the back sitting room working on decorating the pine branches brought in to make garlands and wreaths for Christmas. Peter knocked, and then bowed to Ellie, "Miz Ellie, there's a letter fo' ya." He handed the letter to her.

Ellie took it, looked at it, frowned, and put it in her pocket. Peter raised an eyebrow, turned, and left the room.

"Are you going to open it?" Suzanne questioned eager to know Ellie's business.

"Later, right now I want to finish this wreath." Ellie worked to keep her expression as indifferent as possible and her voice emotionless.

Charlotte was sure something was wrong, but thought she would wait until Suzanne was not in the room before she tried to get her older daughter to talk to her. When Suzanne continued to pester, her mother stated firmly, "Suzanne, that will do," which left her younger daughter pouting, but silent.

John Peters returned from Beaufort on the fifteenth of December. At dinner, he told his family the results of the meetings in Beaufort. There was to be a Secession Convention to be convened in Columbia, the state capitol, on the seventeenth of December. Colonel John Edward Frampton was chosen as the delegate from Prince William Parish, William Ferguson Hutson for St. Helena Parish, Joseph Daniel Pope for St. Helena Island, and Robert W. Barnwell for Beaufort. These men were all from powerful families that had been the earliest settlers of the area and the first to import slaves. Slavery was a part of who they were; they were not prepared to lose this way of life.

"Barnwell fears that only Mississippi will follow if South Carolina leaves the Union," John reported. "It is the only thing that gives me hope that we will not secede. But they are all determined to press for secession. Barnwell has stated that he believes the Negroes will rise up and kill us all if they are freed by the federal government. Whether other states follow or not, it seems very likely that South Carolina will leave the Union in the next few months. If we do, it will surely lead to war."

Charlotte rather naïvely offered, "Surely, they will release us from the Union!"

"My dear, I fear that Lincoln will not allow us to go peacefully. His party is bent upon maintaining the nation as a whole. Only time will tell for certain, but the state is organizing for war. I suspect that they will not quietly accept federal domination. We are headed for dangerous times and we will need to be prepared." Once again, the family was moved to silent meditation during the meal.

When the third letter arrived three days later, Ellie huffed and snatched it out of her mother's hand. This time Charlotte followed Ellie to her room. "What is wrong with you? You have been moping around this house ever since we came home from The Willows. You do not even get excited when you get one of Ted Campbell's letters." Charlotte entered the room, closing the door behind her.

"Nothing is wrong with me, Mother! Please, can we not leave this in peace?" Ellie pleaded, not wanting to have this discussion with her mother again.

"Have you written to Ted?" Charlotte sat down on Ellie's bed, trying to maintain her calm. She was determined to get the truth out of her daughter.

"I have not had time," Ellie replied stiffly.

"And what have you been doing that takes so much of your time?" Charlotte demanded.

"I have been busy. Princess needs a lot of attention. She is almost a two year old and her carriage training will have to begin. I have been trying to get things ready for Christmas." Ellie waved her hands around vaguely, trying to distract her mother from the truth.

"You are not leaving this room until you tell me what is really going on with you." Charlotte crossed her arms and settled in for a long wait.

Ellie paced the room, tapping her hand with the unopened letter.

"Are you going to open it?" Charlotte pressed.

"No!" Ellie stopped pacing momentarily. "He...he really could say nothing I would be interested in reading." She waved the letter at her mother, and then threw it down on the bed.

"Eloise Maitland Peters, did that man harm you? Did he do something to you?" Charlotte asked in a very quiet voice, her hand going to her throat in fear.

"No, Mother!" Ellie exclaimed in disgust, rolling her eyes at the thought. Briefly the memory of what had passed between them, and what might have happened, returned flaming her cheeks with color.

"Then what is the problem, child?" Charlotte's concern for her daughter's obvious distress was colored by her relief that she had not been indiscreet. Charlotte truly wanted to help her daughter, if only she could determine what the problem was.

"He...he drinks too much!" she stammered, knowing she needed to give her mother something to pacify her.

"He has always drunk too much and you have always known it. Why is that so important now?" Charlotte's confusion and disbelief were apparent.

"He will never stop. I am wasting my time," Ellie responded, pressing her lips tightly shut against the truth.

"Your father says his father was like that and he stopped drinking once he was married," Charlotte parried, not accepting this excuse.

"Do you actually think I would marry Ted Campbell? He is a drunk." Ellie was becoming desperate to have her mother leave off questioning her.

Charlotte persisted. "Ellie, your father believes he will stop drinking."

Ellie found herself infuriated by her mother's defense of Ted. "Why do you suddenly care about Ted Campbell so much? You have always hated him." The disdain in Ellie's voice was palpable, as she stood in front of Charlotte, ready for battle.

"I never thought he would settle down," Charlotte conceded. She hesitated. "I am not supposed to tell you, but your father saw Ted while he was in Beaufort. Ted asked your father for your hand, if you will have him."

"How dare he! He's never even asked me if I was interested in becoming his wife. He has a lot of gall approaching Father." Ellie's eyes were wide with indignation, her hands clenched in fury.

"Ellie, your response to his proposal is totally out of proportion. This is not about his drinking; you are not telling me something." Charlotte reached out and clasped her daughter's arm. She leaned forward and looked intently into her eyes, searching for the source of this pain.

Ellie's lip began to tremble. Tears welled up in her eyes. Her breathing became more rapid. Finally, she blurted out her secret. "He takes the slave girls. Right there, under the same roof...when we were there!"

"Oh, child." Charlotte sighed and patted the bed. Ellie angrily dashed the tears from her cheeks and sat down with arms crossed. Charlotte put her arm around her daughter, pulling her close. "Ellie, all men do this sort of thing. Every Southern lady knows that her husband might take a slave into his bed from time to time. As long as that is all he does with her, we pretend we do not know and we never talk about it."

"Father never did that. I will not marry a man who does," she pledged, leaning against her mother's bosom.

"Ellie, I do not know if your father has or not. He has frequently been here when I was in Beaufort or Savannah; I do not know what he has done and I do not want to know." Charlotte stroked her daughter's head soothingly.

"Well, I know he has not!" Ellie thought of what Mama Noli had told her, that none of the female slaves were forced or encouraged to engage in sex with the master of this farm.

"I know how you idolize your father, but..."

"Mother, it is wrong! It hurts the wives and it hurts the slaves." Ellie pushed herself away from her mother, indignant at the implication that her mother even thought her father capable of such behavior.

"The slaves do not seem to mind. I have heard some are actually proud of themselves when their masters take them to bed," Charlotte offered tentatively.

"That is nonsense. They have no choice." Ellie huffed. "I will not marry Ted. I will not live at The Willows. Those people are cruel to their slaves and he is still a drunk."

"You have chased away all your suitors. You liked him before, knowing very well that he was a drunk. He will probably stop drinking, and you need a husband." Charlotte was becoming exasperated with her daughter.

"'Probably stop drinking?' I think no husband is better than a drunk husband." Ellie stated emphatically.

"You will change him. Wait and see. He is a good man, just a bit rudderless right now." Charlotte squeezed her daughter. "Now, open the letter."

Ellie reluctantly broke the seal of the letter. She opened it and started reading. "He is coming for Christmas." The tears started again. "What am I going to do?"

"Give him a chance, Ellie. Is there any one better that you have not chased away?"

"No," she admitted reluctantly through her tears.

"Read those other letters." Charlotte patted her on the leg, stood up, and left the room, closing the door behind her.

Ellie retrieved the letters from her drawer; she opened and read the first, and then the second. She couldn't help but wonder, *All those sweet words, did he say the same thing to the slaves he bedded?*

Ellie was confused and she only had a week to think before he'd arrive. Ted had been her best friend. His drinking never mattered to her because he would never be anything to her but a friend. However, over the last year, things seemed to be changing between them. It had started with the boudoir set last Christmas. Friends did not give gifts that personal. She wondered if she had been missing his intentions all along. She enjoyed being with him; no one else made her laugh the way he did. And when he laughed, his eyes seemed to express such spirit. But was that enough on which to base a marriage, a lifetime? Oh, but his kiss, the feel of him, she felt herself flushing at just the thought of it. She pulled herself out of it, reminding herself that no one else had ever kissed her that way before; she had no way of knowing if she felt that way because of Ted or the passion of the kiss. Would she feel the same way with another man?

She knew things were different for men, but it still angered her that he'd called for other woman when she was in the house. There were so many problems: The Willows, his bedding slaves, his drinking, and his wanderlust. Would he be willing to give them all up for her? And if he did, what would he do with himself? Would he become dour? Things had already gone too far; she knew if she said "no" they could no longer be friends. She did not want to lose her friend, but she did not know if she could commit her life to him.

CHAPTER 32

The next morning, Ellie was about to go out the front door to the barn to spend time with Princess when her father called her. She turned back, entering his study, dreading the conversation she expected would follow.

"I see you are dressed for the barn. Good. I will be finished in here soon. Tell Old Joe to saddle up a couple of horses. We will go riding."

"Yes, Father. It has been a long time since we have ridden together." Ellie usually enjoyed riding with her father; some of her best memories with him were on horseback. However, she suspected that he was trying to make a difficult discussion less awkward for both of them. She trudged out to the barn, less than enthusiastic.

After giving Old Joe her father's instructions, Ellie called Princess in from the paddock. The filly did well leading, and Ellie had started working her on a lunge line. She thought she'd spend some time with her before her father was ready to go riding. She became so involved with the filly that she didn't notice her father come up to the rail to watch.

"Ellie, you make me proud. It is a relief to me to know you love the horses so."

She looked up at her father and smiled. She loved his praise, but was confused by his statement. She hoped he would explain on the ride. She walked Princess in, taking the reins of a large liver chestnut, she handed the filly's lead to Old Joe. She accepted a leg up from her father. He then mounted a young stallion and trotted out toward the drive. Ellie followed his lead, catching up. The two rode side by side.

They rode on in a slow easy canter for a couple of miles. John Peters broke the rhythmic sound of hooves. "I need to talk to you." He slowed his horse to a walk.

"Do you have to ruin our ride?" she asked, sounding petulant.

"Your mother told me about your conversation with her yesterday," he began, ignoring her attitude.

"She suddenly thinks nothing matters, but that I marry Ted. I do not think it would be right for me, but I do not want to lose my friend. I do not understand how things changed so."

John laughed, "You turned into a beautiful woman, that is how things changed,"

"Oh, Father, stop it." Ellie blushed at his compliment.

"Ellie, this will be your decision, but there are some things I want to tell you. Ted will not stay at The Willows. If he marries you, I plan to ask him to come here and help me run the farm. James has not told me yet, but he is not able to look me in the eyes. Eventually, he will tell me he is not coming home. Oh, he will visit, but he does not want anything to do with the farm." Ellie could hear the disappointment in her father's voice.

"It is true about James, but what makes you think Ted would want to live here?" Ellie questioned.

"Ted needs to feel useful, needed, and respected. He is a bright man. I am confident he would learn the business quickly. He will settle down when he feels he has a place."

"I do not know." Ellie sighed. "Did Mother tell you everything?"

"Your mother never tells me everything." He laughed awkwardly. "You do not have to worry; there will be no nonsense on this farm while I am here." He was firm in his conviction.

Ellie had not noticed the direction they had been riding. They were in the center of Sheldon when John asked, "Would you like some candy?"

Ellie laughed. Riding to the general store together for candy had been their secret tradition. "Oh, Daddy, I am not a little girl who can be distracted with candy any longer," she responded, but the smile on her face belied the statement. They tethered their horses in front of the store and went inside. Ellie had always loved going into this store. Even though it was much smaller than anything similar in Charleston or Savannah, it always seemed to offer more variety because it served the day-to-day needs of the people of the parish. The store had to carry staples and some specialty items. Ellie especially enjoyed looking for the little treasures. She had found a gift for Ted last spring, before she had learned of his untoward habit of taking advantage of female slaves. She had purchased a silver cigar case for him and had left it there to be engraved. The local blacksmith enjoyed etching and engraving work as a hobby and earning some extra money. He often contracted jobs with the general store. Ellie decided she would have to pick up the cigar case after all, since Ted was coming for Christmas. She also bought some small gifts for some of the slaves with whom she had developed special relationships. Their purchases completed, Ellie and John mounted and headed back toward the farm. As they rode out, Ellie turned to her father, "Do not think I have made up my mind to marry Ted just because of the gift," she stated sternly when her father made a comment about the cigar case.

John Peters covered his laugh with a cough. "Of course not, my dear." They rode on in companionable silence for a while before he broke the stillness. "Ellie, there is something else. I want you to start learning how to keep the books and the business side of the farm."

"Whatever for?" she enquired, looking quizzically at her father.

"Your mother thinks the Union will happily let us go. I am afraid South Carolina will have to fight for her freedom. If we do, I will join the Cavalry. James will fight for our home, too. Your mother... well, you know your mother." His expression was grave.

"Let us pray it does not come to it," Ellie breathed.

"There is still hope, but we must be prepared. That means you will have to be ready to take over operating the farm. I want you to know where our capital is invested and what outstanding debts and credits we have. I have to know that you, your mother, and your sister will be all right, no matter what happens."

Ellie looked at the concern on her father's face. "Of course, Father. You know you can rely upon me to do my best."

Over the next couple of days, Ellie had little time to spend with her father. The decorating and preparations for their annual Christmas party were in full swing. The time she did spend with him was limited to learning where he kept things and their purpose. Both understood that she would not really begin until after the first of the year. Ellie hated the circumstances, dreading the thought that her father and brother might have to go off to war. Simultaneously, she was thrilled that her father believed her capable of running the farm in his absence.

There was too much going on. She put Lela and Mattie's lessons on hold; she was too distracted. Her father had relieved one fear; it was unlikely that she would have to live at The Willows. She knew this would also please Ted given that he hated living in his family's house as well. She still did not know what to do about Ted. But even if her father could stop Ted from taking slaves to bed at the farm, what about when he was away? What kind of man was he that he would abuse his power that way? If he cared so much about her, why would he want to be with another woman? How could he kiss her, and then immediately have someone else in his bed? She trusted her father, but was he right about the wanderlust and the drinking? There would be no way of knowing until it was too late. Her internal struggle continued and she was running out of time.

CHAPTER 33

On the twenty-first of December, Ellie was walking back to the house from the barn when a rider came galloping down the drive at full speed. As he neared, she realized it was James. She waited out front for him and hugged him when he jumped off his horse. He excitedly declared, "The secession declaration was unanimously signed in Charleston yesterday!"

"So soon?" Ellie's heart sank. She believed South Carolina should be able to govern itself; however, she also believed in her father's judgment.

"It is time for us to be free of the tyranny and arrogance of those damned Northerners. You will see Ellie; the rest of the South will follow."

A groom ran up, welcoming "the young marster" back home, and took James' horse. Ellie called to the house that James had arrived and other servants rushed out to greet him as well. One of them took his saddlebags. The brother and sister walked arm in arm up to the house where they were awaited by their parents. Suzanne was leaning out of her bedroom window shouting her greetings to him.

"James, I am so glad you are home. There is so much to tell you," Ellie murmured to her brother, "but I guess it will have to wait." Any chance of conversation was immediately disrupted as soon as they reached the veranda where they were engulfed by the family members and house slaves. At dinner that night, talk was about secession. The family agreed that South Carolina needed to be independent, but at what cost was another issue. Finally, James turned to Ellie, "You have been quiet. I thought you had a lot to tell me." He waited expectantly, as did the rest of the family.

Ellie looked at all the waiting faces turned toward her. She smiled weakly at James and stated, "Princess is turning out to be one of the best horses Whispering Oaks has ever produced." She had no intension of talking about Ted with the entire family present, especially Suzanne.

James looked at her strangely. He knew Ellie understood he had no interest in the horses. "I am happy for you, Ellie."

"Ted Campbell wants to marry her." Suzanne jumped in, wanting to impress her big brother with her knowledge.

"This is none of your business, Suzanne. If you open your big mouth when Ted gets here, I will lock you in your room and hide the key." Ellie jumped up and ran out of the room.

Charlotte called, "Ellie..."

John interrupted her. "Let her be, Charlotte." Then he turned to Suzanne. "You are not to talk about this with anyone outside this family, including the slaves." His glare bore into her, but she felt she was far enough away from him to have some safety.

"How do you think I found out? No one in this family tells me anything. A piece of candy, a ribbon, or a penny buys a lot of information. The slaves all know," Suzanne snippily responded.

"Suzanne, now dear," Charlotte started, but when she caught Suzanne making a face at her, the tone changed. "One word that embarrasses any member of this family or guest and I will let your sister lock you up."

James stood, "Excuse me, Mother, Father. I think I should go talk to Ellie."

Suzanne mumbled, "Ellie, Ellie, Ellie."

Both parents gave their youngest daughter scathing looks; James shook his head as he walked out of the room.

James knocked on Ellie's bedroom door. When he received no response, he called, "Ellie, it is I. May I come in?"

Ellie unlocked her door, let her brother in, and then closed it. James sat in a chair, stretched his long legs out, and waited silently for his sister to begin. Ellie paced; finally she said, "Ted is coming the day after tomorrow for the Christmas holidays, but he is really coming to ask me to marry him." She paced faster as she became more upset, gesturing dramatically. "I am not supposed to know; no one is supposed to know. However, apparently the entire house knows and I do not know what to do." She caught her breath. "Poor Ted." She shook her head and laughed without humor.

"Ellie, please settle down just a bit. I am beginning to feel seasick with your agitation." He smiled winningly at his sister. They had always been close. Even as children he had been able to calm her when she railed against the family. They confided in each other. "Now, why all this frenzy? If you do not want to marry

Ted, no one will force you to do so." He cocked his head, waiting for her to explain.

Sighing, Ellie sat on the bed. "I am not sure exactly how to explain how I feel, James. Ted is a wonderful friend. We enjoy each other's company and there really is no one else I want to marry. To be completely truthful, my suitors are not exactly lined up at the door. But Ted has some character flaws that I fear he cannot overcome and that I cannot tolerate in a husband, while I might overlook them in a friend." She paused, trying to organize her thoughts. James watched her, his hands folded in his lap, his legs crossed at the ankles.

"You know how he is. He is irresponsible and immature. Have you ever known him to do anything worthwhile with his life? He gambles and plays all the time. He has no direction in his life. And his drinking! I fear he will never change." She shook her head in despair over his condition.

"Ellie, Sugar, Ted is just sowing his wild oats. He is irresponsible because he has no need to be responsible for anything or anyone. His family does not need him to run the plantation, which is fortunate since he loathes the place. Yes, he does gamble and pursues frivolous pastimes, but he has the money to do so and a man needs to fill his time with something. And I will grant you that he does drink to excess at times, but he is not always lost in the bottle. What he needs is a good woman who will give him something to be responsible for; someone who will act as an anchor for him. You would make all the difference in the world for him. And you would have someone to love as well. ...You know I worry about your future, Ellie. I want to see you surrounded by a family of your own." James drew his legs up and leaned toward his sister, reaching out to her. She took his hand and smiled at him.

"James, I know you want the best for me, but you do not understand the whole situation. I do not know if I can explain it to you. It is a rather indelicate topic, but it is the crux of my objection to Ted as a husband." She released his hand and rose once more. She walked to the window and played with the lace on the curtains hanging there. Behind her, Ellie heard the creak of the chair as James rearranged himself to look at her.

"Ellie, we are both grown. You can talk to me about anything. Tell me what it is. What has he done?" A sudden fear came to him that Ted had violated her in some way. "Ellie, did he do something to you? Did he hurt you? Tell me what he did. If he hurt you in some way, I will call him out immediately. I will shoot him down like a rabid dog!" James was on his feet. He reached out and clasped Ellie's arm, turning her toward him.

Seeing the anger in her brother's face, Ellie became alarmed. "No, James! Oh no, no. Nothing like that," she reassured him, laying her hand on his as he squeezed her arm. She felt his grip relax.

"Then what is it? I really do not understand this blithering evasiveness on your part. These faults you have listed against him are not new. You have known him all your life and have never been bothered by them. Ted may be wild, but he is not a wastrel. Tell me what is truly at the heart of this matter!" James' anger had now become directed at Ellie. She felt her own anger rising.

"Very well. I will tell you. Ted has been carousing with the slave women on his family's plantation. He was sleeping with them while Mother, Suzanne, and I were under their roof, after leading me to believe that he was enamored of me!" Ellie was becoming livid with rage once more at the memory of what had almost occurred, at the feeling of betrayal she had experienced, and at the abuse of the power he held over the slave women there.

James laughed without humor. "Good God, Ellie! Did you think that Ted was some limp virgin saving himself for marriage? Men have certain needs. They often seek out women who are readily available to them to satisfy these needs. You cannot be so naive as to think that Ted would not avail himself of the slave women on his plantation."

Ellie glared at her brother, taking in what he had said. "And have you used the slave women on our farm? Has Father?"

"That is different. Father never did such things because he respected Mother too much. He stopped me from doing it when I was very young." James was blushing at this admission. Ellie stared at him, amazed.

"James! You never took advantage of any of our Negroes, did you? They have no choice but to submit to their masters. They could not say no to you, even if they wished to do so. Taking one of the slave women is tantamount to rape, even if she consents. Oh, James, tell me you never did this terrible thing," she pleaded, tears starting in her eyes.

"I told you, Father prevented me from doing it for the very reasons you have just stated. But believe me when I tell you, I would have done it. I was young and felt the need. The desire was very strong, Ellie, and there were women who were more than willing. Some even pursued me. Oh yes. I see your disbelief, but it is true. But I thought about what Father had told me about respecting their vulnerability and respecting myself, and I refused them. And it was not always easy. Most of my friends at school had taken a slave woman as a mistress. Some of them told me their fathers had arranged it the first time...Ellie, it is difficult for a woman to understand these things. I do see how you feel about what Ted did, but you need to understand the way he was raised. By taking a slave woman, Ted undoubtedly felt he was showing respect for you. He was treating you appropriately by not forcing his needs upon you. Once you two are married, he will no longer need to go to the slave women or to prostitutes."

"Prostitutes! Are you telling me that Ted also goes to prostitutes?" Ellie seethed.

"Please, Ellie, do not let Ted's indiscretions be the impediment to your happiness. And I think I know you well enough to say that you will not find married life...distasteful. If you think that you could be happy with Ted in other ways, give him the benefit of the doubt. He will change. He will settle down once you are married. I promise you." James looked into his sister's eyes, willing her to believe him, to feel reassured about Ted.

Ellie nodded her head and shrugged. It was apparent that her brother had taken his friend's side in this matter. "You have given me something to think about, Brother dear. I will consider your words. Thank you for talking with me so candidly." She reached up and caressed his cheek. James reached out and pulled her to him in a warm hug.

"I love you, Ellie, and want you to be happy. I think Ted will be able to bring you the life that you want and deserve." He kissed her on the forehead and released her. "Well, I am off to bed. Sweet dreams, Sugar." James crossed the room and left, closing the door behind him. Ellie turned back to the window, staring out at the evening stars, already lost in thought.

Ellie knew that while her family wanted the best for her, with the possible exception of Suzanne, each had their own reasons for wanting her to marry Ted. The one person she had always trusted to hold her confidences and give honest feedback had been Ted, but this time she was afraid of his reaction. She finally fell asleep asking herself who she could trust that had wisdom and nothing to gain by her decision.

CHAPTER 34

She woke in the morning feeling especially cold; she smiled, realizing that it was the first full day of winter. The smile faded as it occurred to her that Ted would be arriving the next day. She had made no decision. After dressing and breakfast, she went back to her room to hide from her own family. She feared someone asking for her decision. She tried unsuccessfully to read but she couldn't concentrate. She sat looking out the window, but too many confusing thoughts passed through her mind. She thought she needed some busy work and started organizing her gifts that she had accumulated for the slaves. When she got to the shawl she had for Mama Noli, the image of the worn quilt on the old woman's bed came to mind. She searched her closet and dresser, but could not find anything satisfactory. Deep in thought, she stared off. Her own bed was in her line of vision. She moved to the bed and began fingering the quilt on it. Quickly, she ripped it off the bed, folded it neatly, tucked it under her arm, and left her room. She stopped at the pantry and filled a large bowl with a variety of treats that had been prepared for the Christmas party--cookies, candies, chestnuts, candied fruits—treats which she thought the old woman would enjoy. She also grabbed some pieces of chicken from the batch Lottie had cooked for lunch and wrapped them in a napkin. Already heavily burdened, Ellie looked around the kitchen to see if there was anything else she could pilfer. Lottie caught her eye as she was about to slip out the back door. Ellie looked straight at her, said nothing, and walked out the door, heading to Mama Noli's.

When she reached the old woman's cabin, Ellie knocked and called, "Mama Noli?" The child that had summoned Ellie to Mama Noli the previous spring opened the door. Ellie looked down and, giggling, said, "Mama Noli, you have shrunk!"

The child looked at her confused, "Ah ain't Mama Noli, Miz Ellie."

"Chile, don' jist stan' dere. Let Miz Ellie in," a quiet old voice called.

"Come, sit. Jine me. What ya have dere?" She didn't wait for an answer, but ladled some broth into a wooden cup and handed it to Ellie. Still holding the bowl of treats and the chicken in her hands, with the quilt under her arm, Ellie managed to set some of her burdens on the rough wooden table, and then sipped the hot broth; it seemed thin yet unusually flavorful.

"Thank you, Mama Noli. It was so cold this morning, I thought you could use another quilt." She put down her cup and took the quilt from under her arm, handing it to the woman.

Mama Noli fingered the quilt and rubbed it against her face. "Ah ain't never had nothin' dis fine befoe. Thank ya, Miz Ellie." The old woman's face wrinkled in a huge grin as she stroked the quilt in her lap.

The two women sat together in silence, sipping their broth. Once they finished, Ellie continued to sit, playing with her empty cup. Mama Noli watched, "Would ya lack s'moe?"

"Oh, no thank you." Ellie remained quietly playing with the cup.

Mama Noli turned to the child who had been playing quietly on the bed, "Go on outside an' play, Lily. Ya need some fresh air." A gnarled, wrinkled hand waved at the girl. The child stood and, slowly dragging her feet, walked to the door. It was obvious that she was not happy about being sent away.

Mama Noli gave Ellie a few more moments. When Ellie continued to sit silently, Mama Noli finally asked, "How kin Ah hep ya, Miz Ellie?"

"I do not know Mama Noli." Ellie frowned and sighed, chewing her lip.

"Is it Marster Campbell?" Noli ventured.

"Oh yes, Mama Noli!" Ellie responded, relieved that she didn't have to open the subject. "I am so confused. Everyone wants me to marry him."

"What's ya confused about? Dat man been chasin' ya since you's a baby. Ya care fo' him?" The old slave looked attentively at her young mistress, seeing only a child in pain.

"He has been my best friend for a very long time," Ellie evaded. She thought how much simpler things had been when she was just a little girl and Ted would chase her around the gardens of the Campbell's Beaufort house threatening to make her eat worms.

"Ya care fo' him?" Noli demanded more forcefully.

"Yes..." she admitted, hesitantly.

"Is he a good man?" the slave asked, bringing a crooked finger up to her cheek.

"I used to think so, but..." she hesitated again, "I am not sure now."

"Uh-huh. What makes ya question him?" the wise woman asked.

Shrugging, Ellie stated, "He drinks."

"Yes, he do. Many white mens drink." She waited for Ellie to respond. Finally, she said, "An'?"

Ellie looked around, almost as if she were checking to see if anyone was listening, and then whispered, "He takes slaves to his bed."

"Mos' white mens does," she responded, shrugging her thin shoulders.

"It is wrong. It is no different than rape!" Ellie exclaimed indignantly.

"Does da man know dat?" Mama Noli pursued.

Ellie was surprised by the question. She hadn't considered that possibility. "I...I do not know."

"Maybe ya need ta fine out," the old woman suggested.

"How?" the young woman asked helplessly.

"How'd ya find out anythin'?" Another shrug of the thin shoulders.

Ellie sighed.

"Does ya love 'im?" Noli questioned gently. "Dat's da impotent question."

Nodding, Ellie took the old woman's hand in hers, "Yes, it is, is it not? Thank you for your wisdom, Mama Noli. May I come back to talk again?"

"Chile, Ah's here," the old slave responded, patting her mistress' hand gently.

Ellie stood to leave. "If you need anything..."

Noli held up the quilt and smiled, rubbing it against her face. "Ah know, Chile."

Ellie smiled and left. She walked back to the house with a lighter step. She still had not made a decision, but she felt she now knew what she had to do to make one. She was still nervous about Ted's arrival, but she no longer dreaded it

CHAPTER 35

The next morning, Ellie rose early after a restless sleep. Putting on a robe, she went down the back stairs to the kitchen. Lottie was there starting preparations for breakfast.

"Miz Ellie, you up early. Da coffee's 'most ready. Where'd ya wan' it?" she asked her mistress.

"Right here is fine, Lottie." Ellie sat at the kitchen table. Lottie fixed it the way she knew Ellie liked it, with plenty of cream and two sugar cubes, placed the cup on the table, and returned to the stove to stir the oatmeal. Ellie sipped the hot beverage, trying to calm her nerves. She realized that she had not sat for breakfast in the kitchen for years. She started to reminisce about when she was a little girl and up early before the rest of the household. She would come down to visit with Lottie, and Lela would come, too. They would sit together at the table, giggle, and have breakfast. She missed the simplicity of her childhood.

Just then, Lela entered. "Miz Ellie!" she exclaimed, surprised to see her young mistress sitting in the kitchen, and so early in the morning.

Ellie laughed, "I was just thinking about when we were little and used to eat breakfast together. Get some coffee for yourself and sit with me."

Lottie and Lela exchanged looks, and then Lela poured her coffee and sat down across from Ellie. "It was nice of ya givin' Mama Noli yo quilt," she stated after a quick sip from her cup.

Ellie shrugged dismissively. "She needed it more than I did."

Mattie entered the kitchen next. "Miz Ellie, Ah's sorry. Ah thought you'd be up early, but..." she hesitated. "Ah'll bring yo breakfuss up ta ya."

"No, Mattie. I want to eat it here with Lela. You probably need breakfast, too."

Everyone understood that Ellie was anxious about the day. Lottie prepared breakfast for all three women. The childhood friends sat reminiscing about the past, games they had played, and mischief they had gotten into. For a little while Ellie forgot about her anxiety, simply enjoying the companionship of these women. The class differences dropped away as they laughed and teased each other. Ellie marveled at the comfort provided by the company of other women. It wasn't until the other housemaids began collecting the morning coffee to take upstairs to the rest of the family that Ellie was pulled back to the present. She began fretting about what to wear for Ted's arrival. Her best guess was that he would arrive some time after lunch. That gave her all morning to get ready. She intended to make quite an impression on him. Whether she accepted him or not, he would pine his heart out for her if she had her way. She and Mattie hurried upstairs; there was so much to do.

Once in her room, Ellie began pulling dresses out of her armoire and throwing them on the bed. She quickly plucked up the inappropriate ones and had Mattie re-hang them. She narrowed down the choices to four gowns appropriate for the afternoon and receiving guests. Ellie was studying the effects of each one in her mirror; as she held one of the gowns up against her, Suzanne barged into the room.

"What are you doing?" Suzanne demanded.

"What does it look like I am doing?" Ellie snapped back, not inclined to put up with her sister's intrusion.

"You are getting yourself all dressed up for Ted Campbell!" Suzanne accused, laughing at her sister. "You want him to moon over you." She taunted as she plopped herself down on the bed, sitting on top of two of the dresses.

"Get off of my dresses and get off of my bed, you little beast. I do not need your help or hindrance this morning. Why don't you go bother Mother?" Ellie demanded, grabbing her sister and dragging her to her feet.

"Keep your hands off of me!" Suzanne ordered, rubbing her arm. "I think you bruised me!" She squeezed her skin, hoping to raise a bruise that she could show her mother when she went to complain of Ellie's treatment.

"I will bruise more than your arm if you do not get out of here! Mattie, help me get my corset laced up," she commanded, abandoning the dresses for the moment. Mattie quickly wrapped the corset around her mistress and began lacing it up the back.

"Grab on ta da bed post, Miz Ellie," Mattie instructed. Ellie gripped the post with both hands as Mattie tugged at the laces, pulling it as tight as she could.

"You will never get your waist as thin as you would like it to be. You are just too fat now that you've gotten so old," Suzanne taunted, keeping her distance from her sister.

Ellie glared at Suzanne, but was too busy exhaling to comment. Once she was tightly corseted, she began adding on her crinolines. "I think three layers will be enough, Mattie. We do not want to overdo it for an afternoon dress." Mattie hurried to complete this portion of the toilette. Then Ellie returned to the dresses. She picked up a long sleeved, emerald green, wool dress with black trim and studied her image once again.

"I think you should choose that one," Suzanne offered.

Ellie turned to look at her sister, skeptical of her proffered assistance. "Do you? Why?"

"Yes, I do. The green brings out the green in your face!" she laughed and pointed at her sister, whose face was rapidly grown red. "Stay that way. You look so very appropriate for Christmas, all red and green!" Suzanne rocked so hard with laughter that she nearly rolled off the chair in which she was sitting.

"You little brat! Get out of here, now! If you do not leave, I will beat you to within an inch of your life!" Ellie approached her sister in a very threatening manner.

"If you lay a finger upon me, I shall tell Mother that you are beating me!" Suzanne countered. Ellie continued moving toward her. Suzanne opened her mouth and began screaming for her mother's assistance.

Ellie grabbed her by the hair and began pulling her out of the room. "Do not bother screaming for Mother. I will be happy to escort you there myself," she stated as she continued out of the room and down the hallway, dragging the screeching Suzanne behind her. At the foot of the stairs, Ellie and Suzanne were met by Charlotte who had come from the back of the house to discover what all the screaming was about.

"Ellie, let your sister go!" Charlotte demanded. Ellie complied, pushing the tearful Suzanne toward their mother.

"Mother, this disgusting little brat has been annoying and insulting me all morning while I have been trying to get ready. Please do something with her now, before I am forced to do her some irreparable physical harm!" Ellie stood before her mother, puffing with exertion and anger, in her underwear, her hair in disarray. Suzanne clung to Charlotte, sobbing.

At that moment, one of the slaves came bursting in through the door, calling, "Marster Campbell is here! Marster Campbell is here!" Through the opened front door, Ellie glimpsed Ted climbing the steps to the veranda. At the moment she spied him, he looked up and saw her. She stood frozen to the spot as his gaze took in her appearance. Her eyes dropped to see what he was seeing. Realizing how she looked, she screamed in dismay, turned, and rushed up the stairs. Behind her, she heard Charlotte welcoming their guest and calling to James to come downstairs. James walked out into the hallway and saw Ellie dashing into her room. He followed her to make sure she was all right.

"Oh, James! Ted is here and he just saw me like this! I am nowhere near ready to go to see him. Please go down and entertain him. Suzanne is being beastly and may do something to ruin everything," she begged him.

"I will take care of him. Just get yourself dressed. Everything will be fine," he reassured her, turning to leave the room. It was fortunate Ellie could not see the grin on his face as he left.

Before she closed the door behind her brother, Ellie saw Charlotte dragging Suzanne toward her own room. "I am going to see to it that you will not sit down for a month, young lady. If you do anything to spoil this engagement, I will swear that you are a mulatto and will sell you down to Alabama to work in the fields!" Charlotte threatened her. Closing the door, Ellie felt a great wave of satisfaction before panic set in once again.

She sat down at her dressing table for Mattie to dress her hair. They had almost finished when Charlotte came in to see how things were progressing.

"You are not finished yet? Child, do not leave that man down there cooling his heels for too long. A little delay is good. It makes them more eager to see you. But too much and he may decide to go down to the barn with James. Now, what are you wearing? Ah, good, the green wool. Hurry, Mattie." Having said all of this, Charlotte left the room, and Ellie breathed a quick sigh of relief. It took another twenty minutes, but they finally finished and Ellie was satisfied with the young woman in her mirror.

Ellie paused at the top of the stairs, took a deep breath and, with head held high, she started slowly down the stairs. She heard Peter summon Ted and James to lunch; they entered the front hall as Ellie was halfway down the stairway. Their eyes met; Ellie blushed at the intensity of Ted's look and nearly looked down, but then remembered her anger.

"Mr. Campbell, you certainly arrived early. I hope your ride was pleasant and you did not overwork your horse."

Ted was confused by her formality. James stepped in, trying to dispel the awkwardness of the situation. "I am sure Ted would not harm his own horse. Come, we will be late for lunch and I imagine Ted is hungry after his long ride."

Ellie came down the stairs and took her brother's arm as they walked into the dinning room.

John was already in the dining room. He gave his daughter a look of disapproval when he saw her walk in arm in arm with her brother, ignoring their guest. He immediately stood and approached Ted, extending his hand. "Welcome, it is so good of you to share your holidays with us again."

"After last year's Christmas party, I hope to be invited back every year." He flashed John a conspiratorial smile, looking for some sign of reassurance after the greeting he had received from Ellie.

"Ted, you will always be welcome at Whispering Oaks. Sit down; you must be hungry."

Before he seated himself, Ted made a point of pulling out Ellie's chair for her. She mumbled, "Thank you," as she seated herself, but would not make eye contact.

Charlotte and Suzanne entered as Ellie was sitting. Suzanne started, "Ted, it is so good you are here." She exaggerated her own drawl. "How can you tear yourself away from your beautiful plantation? The Willows is the most magnificent place I have ever been. I have missed it so."

Ellie had all she could do to keep herself from turning on Suzanne. Charlotte jumped in before Ted could respond, "I am so sorry I was detained and could not give you a proper greeting. I do hope James kept you entertained." She sat at the end of the table across from her husband.

"James and I had a lot of catching up to do. We have not talked since last summer and there are so many things happening here so quickly."

Lunch was served and the men turned the conversation to the recent secession. They speculated about which states were likely to follow and leave the Union. Ellie had trouble concentrating on the conversation, but tried to follow along. However, she remained unusually quiet. Ted turned toward Ellie who was seated next to him. "Ellie, you have not said one word about your Princess. How is she?"

Looking across the table at James, Ellie quietly responded, "She is nearly a two year old and probably one of the best Whispering Oaks has ever produced."

"Maybe after lunch, you would show her off to me," he requested, trying to get her to make eye contact with him.

"Certainly. If you like. James has not seen her either. We can all go to the barn together." She couldn't help the small smile that crept over her lips, knowing that Ted would feel very frustrated by this maneuver.

James was about to object, but decided he would go along, and then make an escape, leaving his sister alone with Ted. He knew what she was angry about and that Ted would need time with her before he proposed, if she was ever going to say yes. If Ted and Ellie were married, it would be much easier telling his father he would be remaining in Columbia after finishing his law studies. With the hopes of a new South, he had started thinking about getting into politics.

Suzanne interrupted before her brother could respond, "I will go with you, too."

"I am afraid, Suzanne, that you will have to stay here with me. I need your help. We still have some tree decorations to finish." Charlotte turned to Ted. "I am so glad you are here to trim the tree with us. It is a Peters' family tradition."

"There is not much time left before Christmas. When will the event take place?" he enquired politely.

"Tonight, after dinner."

"I am looking forward to it with great anticipation." Ted smiled warmly at his hostess.

Charlotte smiled. "I will see you at dinner, then. I must get back to my decorations. Suzanne, come with me." She walked out of the room with Suzanne pouting behind her.

Ellie stood. "I will get my coat and join you at the door." As she left the dining room, she hoped the men in her life would not talk about her while she was gone. She did not want her brother giving Ted any hints as to why she was so upset with him.

Mattie met Ellie on the stairs with her coat and a pair of gloves. She followed her mistress down to the door and helped her with her coat. She gave her a smile and squeezed her arm in support. Ellie nervously smiled back and silently mouthed, "Thank you."

Ted and James joined her, talking and laughing together. Ellie watched them approach. She noted Ted's laugh, but wished he had her brother's strength of character. She hoped he might someday.

Ellie led the way to the barn and went through one of the stalls that opened out to the paddock. Princess looked up as soon as she heard the sound of the door and came prancing over when she heard Ellie's voice.

"Ellie, you have every reason to be proud of her." Ted was actually impressed by the filly.

"Thank you. And, James, what do you think?" Ellie turned to her brother, dismissing Ted.

"She is pretty, but I am sure you and Ted would know her worth better than I." James was slowly backing away.

Ellie shook her head at her brother and shot back, "When are you going to tell Father?"

"I have not yet decided, but right now I am supposed to go over some business with him. I will see you at dinner." He turned and abruptly left, pretending to be annoyed with his sister.

Ted started rubbing Princess' neck and shoulder. "Now, young lady, what is going on here?"

Feigning ignorance, Ellie explained, "James does not want to work at Whispering Oaks after his studies. He has not told Father yet."

"I understood that, Ellie. I meant, why are you upset with me?" He turned from the horse to look at her. Ellie remained silent. She wanted to talk about it, but did not know how to begin.

"You did not answer any of my letters. You have been formal and distant, not at all yourself. Please, Ellie, what happened? Have you met someone?"

"Have I met someone? How dare you? No, I have not." She took a deep breath, "Ted, I thought you cared for me. I thought you…"

"Ellie, I do. Whatever would make you think that I do not?" He spread his arms helplessly, shaking his head in confusion.

"I understand that things are different at the Willows, but...but you cannot kiss me the way you did. I will not allow you to...to caress me and seduce me like that, and then..."

He interrupted her, "I thought you wanted me to kiss you and caress you. As I recall, you were certainly a willing participant. You made no protest then. Are you telling me now that you did not give me your permission?"

"I would not have, if I had known that you were in the habit of taking slave girls. Did you kiss them that night and the next, the same way as you did me? Did you hold them and caress them as you did me?"

"Ellie!" Ted was shocked, not only by her words, but by her knowledge of his actions. He wanted to be allowed to explain.

"Did they kiss you back? Did they moan and swoon against you in the moonlight? They had no choice, whether you think they liked it or not! How could you? How could you, right after touching me, kissing me?" Ellie beat at his arm with her fist, punctuating each word with a blow.

Princess started getting nervous. As Ellie became louder, the mare began prancing in the stall. Ellie turned away from Ted and tried to calm the filly.

"Ellie, please. They meant nothing to me." He reached out toward her, attempting to grasp her shoulders and turn her toward him.

"That is even worse. They are women, too!" she snarled at him as she shrugged off his hands.

"I do not understand what you want from me. What did I do wrong? I did it so that I would not treat you without respect." Ted's voice carried his confusion and hurt, but Ellie could not hear these emotions through her own wall of hurt and anger.

"I want you to understand that what you did was wrong! I want you to understand they have no freedom to say no." She stood glaring at him, her chest heaving with fury.

Ted was angry now, too. He could not believe she would talk of these matters. He wanted to shock her as she had him. "I have never hurt or forced any of them. The women I choose are happy to have me. They pursue me when I am on the plantation. They whisper to me that they want light-skinned babies. And they know that I will give them gifts afterward. I take care of them. They are grateful to me. Force them? How could you think that of me?"

Ellie looked him in the eyes and saw that he believed what he was saying. "You really do not understand. You are their master's son. Every time you ask anything from any of them, you have forced them to do your wishes. They do not have the luxury of choice as you or I do. We all do it to the slaves to some degree, but...but this is..." she could not find the right words.

The anger in Ted's face drained away. He stood speechless for several moments. Finally, he lowered his arms and said, "I never thought of it that way. I hope you will believe me, Ellie. I have always tried to treat those women with kindness. But I was raised to see them as something to be used as needed. It never crossed my mind that they would want to say 'no' to me, much less feel that they could not refuse."

"Well, you had better start to think of it that way. But that still does not explain how you could kiss me, and then go to another woman."

"Ellie, I wanted you, but I knew I could not have you. A man has needs. I went to them because I wanted you so very much it was painful to me. I still want you." He reached out and gently touched her cheek.

She looked at him, much of the anger gone now. He started to move in to kiss her. Raising her hands and placing them against his chest, she stopped him. "You cannot kiss me unless you promise there will be no other women."

"Ellie, on my life, I will not touch another woman." He took her into his arms and kissed her mouth. She opened her mouth slightly, relaxing into him, returning his passion with her own. Once again, she felt his strong hands on her body. She longed to feel them against her bare flesh. Another moment and she would pull him into an empty stall where he could explore her more intimately.

Princess calmed down with the change of atmosphere. She had not received her anticipated sugar from Ellie and pushed the couple, looking for the attention she expected. The embrace and its tension were broken. Ted laughed, "Did you train her to be your chaperone?"

Ellie laughed, too, relieved and disappointed that their embrace had been broken. She reached into her pocket for the sugar and gave the cube to Princess, and then turned the filly back out into the paddock. The pair walked back to the house, holding hands and talking. Both were feeling a sense of relief. They had weeks of conversation to catch up on.

CHAPTER 36

That evening, dressing for dinner, Ellie was frantic once again. She wanted to dress to titillate Ted, but knew she had to be careful not to set her mother off on a lecture about young ladies and propriety. She pulled out all her newer dinner gowns and had Mattie inspect them to be certain they were clean and in good repair. She decided on a blue and red plaid taffeta with velvet trim on the sleeves, bodice, and skirt. The puffy sleeves came down to her elbows, where navy blue bows dangled attractively. The neckline was just low enough to show off some cleavage and a bit of shoulder. Ellie knew it was too dressy for a family dinner, but was certain that her mother would do no more than raise an eyebrow at it.

"What do you think, Mattie? Will this impress Ted?" Ellie asked anxiously.

"It gonna pop da eyes right out o' his head, Miz Ellie. Doan ya fret about dat," Mattie reassured her with a broad smile. "Dat boy doan stan' a chance wit dis here dress on ya." She laughed at the thought of how he would be affected.

"Lord, I hope you are right, Mattie. After this afternoon, I am not sure he will still be willing to ask me to marry him. I made him swear he would not be with another woman again. I do not know where I got the courage to make such a demand. I just know I could not be with him, if I thought he were still sleeping with the slave women." Ellie chewed her lip in concern.

"Now, Miz Ellie. Doan ya fret 'bout dat needer. Dat boy is love sick fo' ya. He ain't gonna be thinkin' 'bout no udder women when he sees ya lack dis," Mattie reassured her.

Ellie handed the dress to Mattie to press in the kitchen. "Take care of this please, Mattie. Then we will do my hair. And do not let my mother see the dress. She would never let me come down to dinner in it if she got wind of my plans." Mattie rushed out of the room carrying the gown. Ellie sat down at her dressing table and studied her reflection. She debated using some rouge on her lips and cheeks. She knew Charlotte would be shocked if she discovered her painting her face for a simple family dinner, but it would help enhance the mood she was trying to create. Deciding that it was worth the risk, Ellie reached for her rouge pot and dotted tiny spots of red on each cheek, and then spread them evenly until there was just a hint of color on her cheekbones. Admiring the effect, she decided to apply some to her lips as well. Next, she applied perfume to her throat and wrists, and then with a naughty smile, she ran a line of scent between her breasts and another along the part of her hair. By the time she had chosen earrings and a broach to wear on the navy blue, velvet choker she would wear around her neck, Mattie returned with the gown.

"You were quick!" Ellie exclaimed.

"It weren't so very wrinkled. Ah jist teched it up a might. Din't take no time at all," Mattie declared, hanging the dress up.

"Good. Now we have plenty of time to fix my hair. I want it pulled up in the back to show off my neck and shoulders," she instructed. The slave woman quickly arranged her mistress' hair so that a cluster of curls cascaded down her back, leaving her neck and shoulders bare. Ellie approved the coiffure, and then stood so that Mattie could help her step into her dress. Once all of the buttons had been fastened, Ellie examined her image in the mirror again and, nodding her satisfaction, left the room to join her family downstairs.

She found them all assembled in the drawing room, waiting for dinner to be announced. Ellie was gratified by the responses she received upon entering. As Ellie had predicted, Charlotte raised an eyebrow in disapproval, but withheld comment. John and James smiled appreciatively at her as they sipped their pre-dinner scotch. Suzanne made a show of being totally indifferent to Ellie's appearance. But the reaction she was most interested in was Ted's. He stood when she entered the room, his glass of scotch halfway to his opened mouth. His eyes flowed over her, taking in all the details of her appearance. When she looked into his eyes, she saw raw desire burning there and felt a similar response course through her body. She blushed with embarrassment when she recognized her own desire for Ted. She wished her family were anywhere but in this room at this moment. But, even as she was acknowledging these thoughts, she saw Ted pulling back his emotions so that he could behave appropriately. She hurriedly did the same.

"My dear, Eloise. You are incredibly more lovely tonight than you were this afternoon, if that is at all possible," he purred as he crossed the room and took her hand.

She smiled invitingly at him and responded, "Why, thank you, Edward. You are too kind." She allowed him to escort her to a seat on the divan and to sit next to her there. Conversation revolved around the workings of the farm and politics. Ellie felt a small frown forming when Ted drained his glass and accepted a refill from the butler, but decided not to allow her concern to grow.

When dinner was announced, Ted offered Ellie his arm and led her into the dining room behind her parents. He was seated next to her at the table, and she felt a thrill when his hand moved over to cover her knee under the table. She debated whether to surreptitiously remove it, or to allow it to remain there spreading warmth up her thigh. Through the conversation and compliments on the dinner, Ellie again became concerned about Ted's drinking as he consumed his first glass of wine and began on his second. Suzanne, not wanting to be left out, demanded that she be allowed to have a glass as well. Charlotte began to refuse her, but John signaled the butler to bring a glass for his youngest daughter. The slave poured about a quarter of a goblet of wine, and then thinned it with water poured from a cut crystal pitcher. Suzanne began to protest the dilution, but John told her she had the choice of that glass of wine or none at all. Rolling her eyes, Suzanne lifted the glass and sipped. The face she made when she tasted the mixture set the table to laughing. Ellie allowed her worries about Ted's drinking to fade for the moment, and dinner passed without any problems.

The atmosphere was jovial. Suzanne was giggling from the little bit of wine she had and was hanging on to her big brother. Ellie was relieved to see that she was leaving Ted alone, at least for the moment.

John and James began the decorating project by draping the tree with the strings of popcorn that Suzanne and Charlotte had completed only that very afternoon. They began at the top and passed it round, going lower with each pass until they reached the very bottom of the tree. Peter served hot brandy toddies to the adults and tea with cream and honey to Suzanne. The crate of candles was placed next to the tree. Each candle had already been wrapped securely with a length of wire. There were two strands at the bottom of each, long enough to fasten the candle to a branch. The job of attaching them to the tree belonged to the men. The placement was important, so that no flame would overheat or catch a branch above it. Ted joined in helping to firmly attach candles. Occasionally, Charlotte or Ellie would comment, vetoing a placement as being too close to another candle. The spacing and aesthetics were important to them.

When Ellie stopped James for the third time, he snapped, "If you think you can do a better job, get up here."

"I had enough of those wires on my fingers." She laughed. Nothing was going to spoil this evening for her. "It is just that, from a distance, it is easier to see how it looks."

The banter became lighter as they teased and joked with one another and sipped on the hot drinks. The candles took some time, but soon it was the women's turn. They started by using bright red and blue ribbons to tie on lace bags filled with colored candies. Ellie and Suzanne made a big point of walking away from the tree between each one they tied on to look for the perfect spot.

Charlotte held a basket of gilded fruits and nuts. She carefully began placing them gently on branches all over the tree. Ellie took the molded pastries out of another basket. They had been threaded with loops of ribbon to be easily hung. Suzanne had the stars of gilt paper similarly threaded and looked for the best spots. There was one over-sized star left. This was reserved for the top of the tree. After much debate, it was decided that Ted should have the honor. Peter brought over a step stool and Ted climbed up. He stretched and with both hands fastened the star to the very tip of the top. Applause from all followed.

Charlotte asked Suzanne to play some carols on the pianoforte. After checking that the water buckets were full and near by, the men lit the candles. Every year, they lit them briefly on the night the family decorated the tree. They wanted to enjoy the beauty that resulted from their hard work in the peace and solitude of the family. Once the candles were all lit, the lamps were turned down, except the one on the pianoforte. Suzanne began to play Oh Christmas Tree. Charlotte took John's hand to begin a semi-circle around the tree; Ellie motioned Ted to stand next to her. In the dim light of the tree, he found her hand and gently caressed it with his fingers. James stood by his father. The family sang the words along with Suzanne's playing.

Once the song was over, everyone congratulated each other on a job well done. Ellie made a point of complimenting Suzanne on her playing. She wanted to reward her sister for behaving herself during the tree ceremony. Charlotte then escorted Suzanne upstairs for bed, while James and John started putting out the candles. They never let them burn long; it was important to keep them for Christmas Eve and the party.

Ellie went to her father and kissed him goodnight on the cheek. She said goodnight to James and walked up to Ted. She took his hand in both of hers, looked him in the eyes, and thanked him for spending another Christmas with her and her family. She turned and glided out of the room and up the stairs to her room.

Mattie had put out her nightgown and turned down the bed. She had dozed off sitting in the armchair waiting for Ellie. It had been a long day for both women. Ellie, however, was still too excited to be tired. She gently woke Mattie.

"Miz Ellie." Mattie stretched. "Let's git ya ready for bed."

"No, Mattie. I am not quite ready to settle in for the night. You go to bed. I can undress myself."

"Is ya sure?" Mattie asked as she moved hesitantly toward the door.

"Thank you. I am sure. Now, go get some sleep."

Mattie gratefully left Ellie to herself. As soon as the door closed, she went to her dresser, pulled out Ted's Christmas gift, and put it on the bed. She had decided to hang it on the tree after everyone went to sleep. She had already attached a ribbon to it. She sat at her dressing table, took off her shoes and stockings, and let down her hair. She picked up the brush that Ted had given her and started running it through her long hair. She stopped and stared at the handle. It was the first time all day, that she had a few minutes alone. She closed her eyes and brought up the image of the way Ted kept looking at her all night. With all his bad behaviors in the past, he had never broken his word to her in anyway. She realized she trusted his promise not to be with any other woman again. She was also beginning to believe she could help him be a man that she could love and respect. There was still the issue of his drinking; she told herself that she needed to trust her father that it would not be a problem.

Ellie heard footsteps in the hall. Her parents' room was past hers and she listened as her father walked by. James' room and the guest room Ted was using were down the other hallway from the stairs. She decided to wait a little longer and finish brushing her hair before going downstairs with the gift. She was nearly done when she heard the creak of floorboards in the stairway. She listened and guessed it was probably the last of the slaves leaving for the night. She waited a few more minutes, and then opened the door and looked down the hallway. It was dark with no lamplight showing under any of the doors.

Ellie went back to the bed and picked up Ted's present. She took the small lamp off her nightstand, and tiptoed down the hall and stairs. The brightness of her lamp out shown the little candle on the back credenza; she didn't notice it as she placed the lamp on the first table she came to and stared at the tree. She wanted to find the perfect spot. She pulled over the stepstool, hiked her skirt up, tucking it into her waistband, and climbed to the second step. Leaning in toward the tree, she could feel the branches rubbing on her bare legs. Reaching, careful not to loose her balance, she looped the ribbon over a branch. Pleased with herself, she backed down the steps. Turning away from the tree, for the first time she noticed the candle and the sparkle reflecting off a crystal decanter. She scanned the room, not knowing if it had been forgotten or if someone was there. Then she saw a small movement in the shadows.

Ted was nursing a scotch on the divan. Curious and careful not to startle her, he had been quietly watching and admiring her. When her eyes finally reached him, he spoke up. "I was wondering how I would get you alone. Will you join me for a nightcap? I like what you've done with your dress," he grinned and indicated her exposed legs.

Taken aback and realizing he had seen every move she'd made, she blushed, quickly tugged her skirts back into place, and clearing her throat to recover her dignity responded, "Yes."

Ted stood and sauntered over to the decanter, topped off his own glass, and poured a second for Ellie. They met halfway. As he handed the glass to her, the touch of their fingers tingled. They sat together on the couch. Ellie had never had scotch, but she knew it was Ted's favorite. It smelled strong, but she took a tentative sip. "Oh Ted, how can you drink this stuff?" she questioned, screwing her face up with distaste.

He laughed at the face she made. "It is an acquired taste," he acknowledged.

"Why would you ever want to acquire it?" She shivered at the thought.

"Feel the warmth as it goes down your throat," he suggested.

She sipped some more, continuing to make faces. Looking into her glass she ventured a question, "Why do you drink so much, Ted? It worries me."

"Ellie, have you ever seen me drunk?" he asked her, tilting his head.

"No, but you know I have heard. Why do you do it?" She turned toward him, but avoided looking into his eyes.

"I do not do it when I am with you." He raised her chin with his hand so that their eyes met. "You are all I need to be happy." He placed his empty glass on the end table.

"Do I really make you happy? I know that when you are with me everything seems so much better. I miss you terribly when you are off somewhere." She had never been so honest about her feelings with herself much less with him. She wanted to tell him she loved him, but she was still not sure if he might have changed his mind. If he had, her words would be a wedge between them.

He took her half finished drink from her hand and put it next to his. "Ellie, I do not know when it happened or how, but you seem to be on my mind all the time." He saw she was about to interrupt and he put his fingers to her lips. "I tried to stay away last spring. You have always told me I was not for you. When you came to Beaufort for the summer, you were too close not to be with you. When you did not slap me at The Willows, my heart soared." She touched his cheek, but he took her hand in his and removed it, not wanting to be distracted. However, he could not let it go. "We have talked about everything in the world." Embarrassed, he smiled. "Even my, uh…personal habits. But Ellie, we have never seriously talked about us." It was getting harder for him to express himself. "When you joined me on the veranda the last night you were at the plantation, you gave me hope. With you by my side, nothing else matters. Not the pain of being ignored and regarded as worthless by my family. When you laugh with me, I know I can do anything." He took a deep breath, knowing that what he was about to say would change his life one way or another. "Ellie, I love you. If you will not marry me, my life might as well be over now. I will just drown myself in scotch." He slipped off the couch and with one knee on the floor, taking both her hands in his, asked, "Ellie, will you be my wife?"

Ellie's eyes were glistening with tears, she squeezed his hands, "Ted, I have been struggling with this for the last week and I have come to realize you have been my best friend for years, but something changed between us for the better. I do love you. Yes, I will marry you."

They slowly leaned forward and kissed, still holding hands. Ted broke the embrace. "I have something for you." He reached in his pocket and took out a small leather box. As he opened it he said, "I hope it fits." He displayed a ring with a large diamond in the center surrounded with little ones set in silver with a gold shank holding one diamond on each side. He removed it from the box and slipped it onto her finger.

Admiring it, Ellie whispered, "Oh, Ted, it is beautiful." She brushed the tears from her cheeks.

Relieved, Ted sat back on the couch next to her. He looked at her questioningly, "What did you mean, you were struggling with this all week?"

Ellie laughed. "It seems there are no secrets on this farm or, apparently, on plantations either. Let me see. Father told Mother, who told me. Suzanne bribed the slaves for information, and then told James."
In disbelief he moaned, "You knew all day and tortured me anyway!"

"Ted, I knew how I felt, but I did not know what my answer would be until after we talked in the barn."

"After our argument, you mean." He smiled. "You could have told me then and saved me hours of discomfort."

"I was afraid you might not want to marry me after finding out I was not like other Southern women and was not willing to put up with your…"

"If you were like other Southern women, my sweet magnolia, I would not want you as my wife." He leaned over to kiss her briefly, and then lightly touched her bare shoulder with his fingertips, following the line of her dress down to her chest and across the front, nearly touching her breasts. He wrapped his other arm around her, pulling her close, kissing her on the side of the neck, and then continued kissing along the trail his fingers had blazed. Ellie sighed in contentment and desire. She wanted to let him go on, but they were not married yet. She took his head in her hands and pulled him up. Their lips met. He held her so hard to him, she thought she'd never breathe again. She had allowed him more intimacy than he had hoped for and he realized that, after his promise, he would have no relief. He broke the embrace, pushing himself back on the couch next to her. They held hands in silence until Ellie started to giggle.

"What is so funny?" he enquired, a bit disconcerted.

"Everyone in this house has been singing your praises all week."

Pretending to be indignant, he huffed, "And what is funny about that?"

"I have told no one my answer. I would not tell them before you. Can we wait to tell them until just before the party?" She smiled mischievously at him.

Laughing, Ted responded, "You want to torture them, too."

Ellie laughed and nodded. "Just a little. They truly have been harassing me for days."

"If we can announce our engagement to the world at the Christmas party, I will agree." He laughed with her. "You better put the ring back in the box."

"I will put it back on when I dress for the party." She smiled and snuggled under his arm with her head on his chest. "We are going to have a life filled with love and laughter." They cuddled, sitting together on the couch, dozing on and off half the night. Finally, Ellie stretched and said, "I had better go upstairs before someone finds us."

As she started to walk away, Ted said, "You have beautiful legs."

She blushed and ran up the stairs, lamp in hand.

CHAPTER 37

Both were slow to rise the next morning. However, no one in the family thought much of it, considering the time Ellie was up the day before and the amount Ted had drunk at night. Ellie arrived at the table as the rest of her family was finishing breakfast. She was still sleepy and nursed her coffee. Ted came sauntering in shortly afterward and sat next to her. They avoided looking at each other and attempted to focus solely on the food in front of them. When Ted rubbed his leg against Ellie's, she froze, trying not to notice.

John excused himself, stating that he had gifts he needed to distribute to the slaves and wanted to get started. He asked James to join him, but the offer was quickly rejected.

As soon as John left, Charlotte spoke up. "It is a beautiful day for this time of year. A little cold, but the sun is bright. If I did not have my last minute preparations, I would take a long walk."

Ellie and James exchanged looks, both thinking that their mother never took long walks. They knew she was up to something.

Charlotte continued, "Ellie, I am counting on you to entertain our guest today. You and Ted should enjoy the weather. You just do not know, this time of year, how long it will last. Why, you should take a walk."

"I have things to finish too, Mother," Ellie demurred.

Charlotte quickly responded, "You will still have the afternoon."

"Ellie, it might be nice." Ted stated. Ellie kicked him under the table. He quickly added, "James, you look as if you could use some fresh air and exercise. Come with us."

James was unsure what had happened after he left them in the barn the day before. For some reason, his sister and his friend seemed to be uncomfortable about going alone. "I guess I could use the air."

Charlotte frowned. Before Suzanne could say anything, she interjected, "Good. Suzanne, I need your help. Let us get started." She stood and started to leave, "Suzanne, now!"

Ellie and Ted were still eating. Without the rest of the family present James asked, "Do you really want me to accompany you?" He seemed to be directing his question at Ted.

"Oh yes! You must!" Ellie quickly responded. She did not want James to figure out what was going on. "Peter, we are nearly finished. Would you have our coats brought to the front door?" She hesitated. "At least Ted's and James', I need to get something upstairs; I will get my own." Ellie excused herself and went to her room. She put on her coat and took Mama Noli's Christmas present with her. The two men were waiting at the front door for her, looking uncomfortable.

The threesome headed out the door and toward the front drive. It was colder than any of them had anticipated. As they neared the drive, Ellie stated, "I am going to deliver this gift. You two go ahead without me." She veered off to Mama Noli's cabin. She hid a smile when she caught the look of confusion on James' face.

Ellie walked to the hut and knocked on the door. When the door opened, she pulled a candy out of her pocket and handed it to Lily.

"Come in, Miz Ellie. Lily close dat doe, ya lettin' in all da wind."

Ellie handed the shawl to Mama Noli. "Merry Christmas!"

"Ah, thank ya. Ah kin use it taday. Dese bones are cold. Ya wan' some tea."

"No, thank you." Ellie sat down and smiled at the old woman.

"Lily, go git some firewood from Ol' Joe," the old woman directed the child.

The child put on a sweater with a number of small holes and ran out the door. Ellie took note and decided to go to the attic to see what she could find as soon as she got back to the house. "Mama Noli, he asked last night and I said yes. Thank you for your help. You were right, he had no idea what he was doing."

"Ah's happy fo' ya chile." The old, wrinkled face crinkled in a broad smile.

"We have not told anyone, yet. We will tell them tonight just before the party."

Mama Noli started laughing. "Ya teasin' da whole place. Well, God bless ya both." She reached out and patted Ellie's knee.

"Thank you. Please keep the secret." Ellie knew how swift the slave grapevine was with any news.

"Ah will. Ya better git goin'. Ah specs yo man is waitin' fo' ya. Ya doan need ta be settin' wit an ole woman when ya gots a warm young man." Mama Noli laughed knowingly.

Ellie left and went in the back door and up the servants' stairs. She threw her coat on her bed and went up to the attic. She made no effort to hide her actions this time. She knew exactly where the children's clothes were stored. She found four coats of various sizes. She decided to take all of them. If Lily was without a warm coat, others probably were too. As she was walking back toward the exit, she heard someone on the attic steps. She found Ted at the top of the stairs. "Did you tell James?" she demanded, surprised to see him inside already.

"Ellie!" He sounded hurt.

She smiled, kissed him quickly, and ran down the steps with her bundle of clothing. She went back to her room. She was happy about her decision, but she realized she did not trust him completely. Her heart sank at the thought. She'd need to feel differently by the time they were married. She'd asked a lot from him. They had not yet talked about when they would marry; she'd insist on a long engagement. She needed to be positive. She also realized she needed to avoid everyone except, of course, Mattie, until just before the party when she and Ted would tell the family.

Mattie was in her room, hanging up her coat. "What ya got dere, Miz Ellie?"

"Coats. Will you take this one to little Lily? You and Lela may decide which other children most need the other three coats."

"Wit winds lack taday, dey can use dem."

"When you get back to the house, will you please bring my lunch up here? I need to rest this afternoon for tonight." Ellie snickered to herself, thinking how that would frustrate her mother. She also felt a bit guilty, having accepted Ted's proposal when she had some doubts at a time when she believed she should be nothing but excited and in love.

Mattie brought her lunch, and then disappeared until it was time to help Ellie prepare for the party. Ellie had already picked her dress for the evening, a maroon velvet gown with an almost scandalously low cut neckline that would show off her shoulders and bosom to their best. It was really a ball gown, but this night merited the most alluring outfit she owned. After Mattie finished arranging her hair so that her curls cascaded down the back, she instructed Mattie to cinch in her corset as tightly as possible, and then blew all the air out of her lungs. When she felt the whale bones bite into her flesh, she nodded and Mattie tied off the laces. Ellie had to sit down for a minute afterward, feeling her head swim.

"Ah ya sure ya wan' it dat tight, Miz Ellie? Ya gonna swoon away wit it dis way," Mattie cautioned.

"I will be fine in a moment, Mattie. Besides, look how it pushes my bosom up," she giggled, catching a glimpse of her image in the mirror.

"God done blessed ya, dat fo' sho. Dat man gonna fo'git how ta breathe hissef," the maid laughed, tugging the lace on Ellie's shift up just a bit. "Can't have ya popping out o' yo dress in front o' all dem people tanight."

"Now the crinolines, Mattie. I want at least seven of them. This skirt will sweep away all my competition for belle of the ball." She stepped into them one at a time, struggling to get the stiff material stuffed inside the next layer. Finally, Mattie spread the skirt of the gown on the floor and Ellie stepped over it into the center, and then Mattie gathered the material up and pulled the dress up while Ellie held all the crinolines in place. Once the gown was in place at her waist, Ellie slipped her arms into the short sleeves and Mattie pulled the dress up into place. They spent the next several minutes with Mattie buttoning all the small velvet covered buttons on the back of the gown. Ellie admired the effect in her mirror, thinking about how Ted would respond. A wicked little smile perked up the corners of her mouth.

"Oh, Miz Ellie, ya sure is lovely tonight. Ya never looked mo' beautiful. Marster Ted gonna come crawlin' on his knees ta ya, beggin' fo' ya ta marry him." She smiled broadly at her mistress.

While Ellie brushed off invisible lint and nonexistent wrinkles, Mattie went to get her jewelry box. "What ya gonna wear wit dis? How 'bout da onyx beads an' earbobs?" She offered them to Ellie to try on. Ellie quickly rejected them. They went through almost everything in the box. Mattie was getting very frustrated, but Ellie knew it had to be just right. She didn't want her jewelry to distract from or clash with her wonderful ring.

"Miz Ellie," Mattie finally exclaimed, at the end of her patience, "ya ain't got no mo' jewelry what's fit ta wear wit dat dress, 'cept maybe dis here gold chain what was ya granmama's." She held up the old fashioned gold necklace with disdain.

"No, Mattie. That will not do. It has to be special tonight." She finally put on the ring and showed it to Mattie. "My necklace has to go with this."

"Miz Ellie! Where'd ya...Marster Ted?" A big smile came over her face.

"Mattie, if you say one word to anyone..." She trailed off, not being willing to threaten her.

"Ah won' tell nobody, no how." Her smile went from ear to ear.

"Then wipe that silly grin off your face. You will give it away if you go out there grinning like that." Ellie smiled back and hugged her maid. Once she was satisfied with her appearance, she picked up her black lace fan and left the room, calling back to Mattie to bring down her full-length black velvet cloak later for the midnight service at the church.

Ted was waiting at the bottom of the stairs. When he saw Ellie appear on the landing, his eyes grew wide and his mouth dropped open just a bit. Seeing his expression, Ellie smiled broadly and tossed her head, setting her curls swaying. She straightened her back and began her decent. Ted moved up the staircase to take her hand and escort her down.

"My God, you look lovely. You take my breath away. Is there no way we could just run off somewhere tonight and avoid this whole crowd? I want to spend the night just admiring you." He kissed her hand, but she noticed he was staring at her cleavage.

"The whole night? And just admiring me?" She laughed at him.

"Hmm. Well, certainly the whole night, although I might not just admire you," he returned wickedly, stroking a finger along the neckline of her dress.

Ellie shivered at the touch, but slapped his hand with her fan. "Do not start that now! We still have to face the family and I will not be able to do that if you get me all riled up." She tried to frown at him sternly, but couldn't help smiling at his affected contrition.

Ted sighed dramatically and turned to proceed down the stairs once more. "What a waste of such a dress," he mourned. "You will let me know if you have difficulty getting out of it later, won't you?" He widened his eyes hopefully. Ellie giggled, but did not encourage further intimacies.

The couple joined the family in the parlor, trying to hide their smiles. Peter was serving eggnogs. Within moments, Ellie spotted Lela, Lottie, and Mattie peeking around the corner, listening to every word. She tried to send a disapproving glare at Mattie for breaking her promise of silence, but all Ellie could manage was a poorly suppressed smile.

Charlotte approached the couple first, ready to be sharp with her daughter for hiding herself away all day in her room where her suitor couldn't reach her. As she opened her mouth to speak, Ellie put her left hand on her mother's arm and leaned in to kiss her. It took Charlotte a moment to notice the ring. When she did, she almost collapsed with surprise and relief. Her exclamation of surprise drew the others over. Everyone was delighted for the couple, even Suzanne. Ellie showed off her ring and the couple received warm hugs and congratulations from all. Once the family had settled down from the surprise, the three women waiting in the doorway and Peter, the butler, came in asking to be allowed to add their good wishes as well. John ordered that a bottle of champagne be opened immediately so that they could toast the couple before the guests arrived. Peter quickly returned with the bottle and glasses.

"Father, will you make the announcement at the party?" Ellie requested.

"I will be delighted," John promised. They didn't have long to wait before the first guests arrived. Within an hour, everyone who was expected had joined the party. The tree was lighted and Peter was instructed to pass champagne to all.

Tapping his glass with his ring, John called for the attention of everyone. "I have a very happy announcement to make tonight. Mr. Edward Campbell has asked my daughter, Eloise, to marry him, and she has accepted his offer. Please join me in welcoming Ted to our family and in wishing the new couple health, happiness, and a long life together."

The crowd echoed, "The new couple!" and then sipped their champagne. Old friends moved quickly to congratulate them. The evening passed in conviviality, with good company, good food, dancing, and entertainment. Once again, at 11:30 the guests took their leave and headed for their carriages to ride to midnight mass at Sheldon Church. Ted held Ellie's cloak, wrapping it around her as an excuse to put his arms around her. Outside, he handed her into the carriage, jumping in after her, the party then departed for the church together.

CHAPTER 38

Ted and Ellie's engagement was just the beginning of the changes leading into the new year of 1861. Although everyone knew it was coming, John Peters announced to the family that James had informed him of his plans after completing his studies in Columbia. He would not be returning to assist his father at the farm, but would remain in Columbia. He would stay in the state capital to practice law, and later enter politics.

Ellie knew that Ted was not happy with his family, but she did not want to upset or hurt him by telling him she did not want to live with the rest of the Campbells at The Willows. After her father's announcement about James, Ellie asked her father to offer Ted a career and home at Whispering Oaks before he returned to the Willows.

Ellie and Ted had been together nearly every waking minute, walking, working Princess, horseback riding on the farm, playing board games, and eating meals with the rest of the Peters and, of course, having private conversations. But they had not yet broached the topic of their future. Ellie was in no rush to be pressured for a wedding date. The holidays and New Year's Day had passed; it was the second of January when Ted opened the subject.

"Ellie, I need to leave for The Willows tomorrow." He reached for her hand. "I am sure my family has heard by now, but it is important that I tell them myself that you have accepted my proposal."

"I wish you could stay longer," she stated, smiling a bit sadly. "However, I know you are right." She squeezed his hand. "How long will you be gone? Surely, not as long as last year." She laughed.

"Nothing could keep me away so long again." He kissed her hand. "My little magnolia, my mother will want to know when we will be married and where it will happen. My father will want to know how I am going to take care of you and where we are going to live."

"Do we have to make all these decisions now?" Ellie was feeling pressured and getting worried.

"No, but I think we should start talking about it." He did not want to pressure her. He brought her hand to his mouth, kissing it, and holding it close.

"Your father and I had a long talk this morning." He kissed her hand again. "I suspect you know what it was about."

"Maybe... He wants you to...run the farm," she offered tentatively.

"Not exactly. However, he asked if I would consider moving here once we are married. He said he would be willing to teach me the business. I think he just does not want to let you go." He smiled ruefully at the thought.

Ellie laughed, but when she saw the look on Ted's face, she stopped laughing. "He understates everything. My father has known for a long time that James was not coming back. He had always thought that someday he would turn the reins over to James. He needs a son." She turned to face him, her expression showing her earnestness. "Ted, he believes in you."

"Why? Your mother certainly does not," he responded, looking away from her.

"Ted, how can I say this? ...They both know you're...uh ...reputation, but Father says your father was the same way until he married your mother." She reached up to stroke his cheek affectionately, hoping to take the sting out of her statement.

"I am not my father!" He pulled away from her caress, angry about the comparison.

"No, you are not. You are a much better man. I trust my father to know men, as well as he knows horses."

"Ellie, are you sure he is not trying to make me...respectable?" Ted looked into her eyes, seeking the truth.

"Oh, Ted! You have no confidence in yourself. I do not understand it. He believes you are bright and can do anything you want once you decide to do it." She laughed, trying to lighten the conversation. "Besides, with your charm you could sell the oldest of our horses for the price of a two year old." She looked around quickly and kissed him on the lips.

After returning her kiss, Ted paused thoughtfully. "I would like to discuss it with James before giving your father an answer. I do not want to offend him."

"I believe he will be relieved. He has felt terrible about disappointing Father." She snuggled closer to her fiancé.

Ted put his arm around her. "Then, we agree. We will live here and I will work with your father. Ellie, I will still have my trust fund. We will not be dependent on your father." Ellie heard stubborn pride in his voice.

"I had not even thought about that. I only thought about where we would live. I hope you know I am not marrying you for your money." She tilted her head up to look at him.

"I have no fear of that, Sugar. I still want to talk to James before I tell your father," he stated, squeezing her reassuringly.

"I will leave that to you," she promised.

"Thank you. I will talk to them both before I leave." He raised her hand and brushed his lips over it. "How soon can we get married?" He flashed a suggestive smile. "I do not know how long I can wait; nor do I want to give you a chance to change your mind." He proceeded to kiss her fingers and palm, his lips moving softly over her flesh.

Ellie shivered with pleasure, but pulled her hand away, not wanting to give him the opportunity to persuade her against her will. "Ted! There is so much to do. Mother will want me to have a dress from Paris. Plans for the wedding and celebration will have to be made. We will have to plan a honeymoon, as well."

"So, you will not marry me before I leave tomorrow?" He smiled.

"Ted!" She swatted his arm.

"I guess we do not have to decide now," he stated, sighing.

"It is important to me that we are married at the church here in Sheldon. I have always worshipped there and it will be our church once we are married," she stated definitively, brushing unseen dust from her skirt in an attempt to brush away the pressure she was feeling.

"Not St. Helena's?" Ted was surprised by her choice.

"No, here!" she repeated, lifting her chin defiantly.

Ted reached for her hand, kissing it again. "If it is important to you, we will be married in Sheldon."

"Thank you. It is important to me." She allowed him to continue holding her hand.

"Ellie, we do not have to decide today, but I do want it to be soon. Maybe, if I take you to Paris for our honeymoon, your mother will let you have a dress made here."

"Paris? Are you serious?" Ellie bounced with excitement at the thought.

"Yes. We can travel all through Europe if you would like." Ted seemed pleased that he had found something that excited her.

"Oh, yes!" She laughed. "May I tell...."

Ted interrupted her. "You can tell anyone you want." Her childlike excitement pleased him. He was sure they would be happy together. Her passion would make it easy to give up other women.

"I am going to tell Mother now." She kissed him quickly without even looking for watching eyes in her excitement, jumped up, and ran out of the room looking for Charlotte.

Ted laughed as he watched her run out. He decided it was as good a time as any to talk to James.

Ellie excitedly told her mother about Ted offering to take her to Europe for their honeymoon. She did not even mind answering Suzanne's questions. She heard Charlotte laughing at her exhilaration as she went bounding out of the room in search of James.

When she could not find him downstairs, she went up the back stairway thinking to check his room. As she approached her brother's room, she heard two masculine voices. She stopped short of the opened door and leaned against the wall. She told herself it was not proper to eavesdrop, but she couldn't resist.

"...you can learn new tricks? Remember, I have known you for a lot of years, Ted. Marrying my sister may be more of a challenge to you than you think. She can be quite stubborn, especially about issues that she deems critical. She will not put up with your old boozing and wenching ways. How are you going to feel about settling down?" James asked him.

"James, you were often a party to my exploits. How will you settle down?" Ted responded.

"I was never as wild and free as you have been, my friend. And I am not the one planning to marry. In all honesty, Ted, you have been a bit of a roué for some time now. That will not work with my sister. Ellie will not tolerate your gambling and womanizing." James' voice carried a burden of concern for both his sister and his friend. Ellie leaned closer to the door to hear Ted's response.

"James, I have had more than my share of pleasures of the flesh. The things I did were to fill an empty life. With Ellie as my wife, I will not have to seek out other women. I cannot imagine wanting anyone else. Believe me when I tell you that I love her," Ted assured his friend.

"But how will you fill your days? Can you really give up the excitement of Charleston and Savannah and settle down here on this farm?" James' disbelief was apparent in his voice.

"The farm will keep me busy enough. And I do not believe that there will be no time away from here. Your family, even your father, goes to Beaufort for almost half the year. Ellie and I will have time to go to Charleston or Savannah. And your father will be the one running the farm for a long time yet. There will be plenty of time for diversions. I do not have to grow up tomorrow," he laughed. Hearing his words, Ellie cringed. She couldn't help wondering if he would ever "grow up." Could he really settle down in the country and fill his life with work?

"I only worry how you will feel about me filling your place here. Are you certain that you have no interest in returning here?" Ellie was relieved to hear Ted's genuine concern for her brother's feelings; however, she still felt disturbed that he had not expressed disinterest in the pleasures of the big cities and believed that she would join him in his adolescent pursuits.

"Have no concern about that. Father understands that I want to pursue the law. I am no horse breeder and never have been. Besides, we will be going to war soon. The political climate down here is becoming explosive. It cannot be much longer before something sets off a conflict that cannot be handled by diplomacy. What do you think? Will the North let us leave peacefully?" James asked.

As the conversation turned to politics, she tiptoed away. She needed to consider what she had heard; it certainly gave her more reason to delay the wedding. By the time she reached her own room, she had decided she would talk about what she'd heard with James later. For now, she would pretend she had not heard anything. She turned around and walked down the hall, walking more loudly than before. As she reached James' open door, she mustered up her excitement, knocked, smiled with as much enthusiasm as she could, and said, "Ted, did you tell James about Paris?"

Ted was warmed by her enthusiasm and pleased that he was able to tempt her with his own desire not to settle down immediately.

"Paris? Ted, what is this about?" James initial reaction was concern.

Before Ted could answer, Ellie explained. "Our honeymoon! Ted and I will go to Europe for our honeymoon."

James laughed. Ellie watched as his expression changed to excitement and happiness for his sister. He teased, "Ellie, I hope you will not be one of those wives who never let their husbands talk."

Blushing and flustered, Ellie quickly apologized. "Oh, Ted, I am sorry."

Both men laughed at her reaction. She joined in with their laughter, not knowing which one she wanted to hit.

"Let's tell Father now." She grabbed Ted's hand and began tugging him out of the room.

"Ellie, maybe Ted wants to talk to his family first," James suggested.

"Did you talk to your father before making your decision?" Ellie shot back at James.

Ted laughed. "I can see one of my tasks will be to maintain peace between the Peters. My family will be relieved I will not be making trouble on the plantation."

"Ted, that is not true." She thought it probably was true, but she hurt for him because of the way his family treated him. She could see him fighting off the sadness.

"My mother will be disappointed. She is hoping you will take an active part at the plantation." He forced a laugh. "She does not understand how you would be active; active helping our slaves to revolt or run away."

"Ted!" She was afraid he would say too much. James did not know about the reading lessons. The attorney in him would not approve.

Realizing her concern, he laughed and turned to James. "You are right. She is fun to tease." Taking Ellie's hand, he kissed it. "Come; let us find your father."

James smiled and shook his head as the two left the room.

They found John in his study, reviewing the anticipated foaling schedule. He looked up when Ellie knocked, smiling to see the couple there. "Come in, children. What can I do for you? You look as if you have something on your mind." He indicated chairs for them to sit in.

"Sir, we wanted to talk to you about our plans. Ellie and I would like to go to Europe, especially Paris, for our honeymoon. I want to show Ellie all the splendors of the Old World, the art and architecture, the culture. I know Ellie would like to see it as well. We are concerned what you might think about our being away for several months. After all, you have said that you would like me to move here with Ellie, but we have not discussed your expectations of me if I do come to live under your roof." Ted looked at Ellie to see if she had anything to add. She smiled encouragingly and took his hand, but added nothing, understanding Ted's pride and masculinity were at stake.

"Well...it sounds like quite the Grand Tour. I am certain that Ellie would enjoy such a trip, but it would be quite expensive. Will you be able to manage the costs or would you expect me to contribute to it?" John questioned. His expression was closed, giving nothing away, but Ellie suspected that her father was concerned that Ted might turn out to be a burden rather than a boon to the family. She watched her father's face for some indication of his thoughts.

"Oh, no, Sir. My trust will be more than sufficient for our expenses. Besides, I suspect that Ellie will already have a completely new trousseau by then. She could hardly bankrupt me buying Paris gowns or Italian boots if she already has an entirely new wardrobe." He chuckled as Ellie scowled at his teasing. John joined in the laughter.

"You are lucky you are marrying her and not her sister. I suspect that Suzanne could run through your trust before you even got onto the boat; however, I am certain that we could facilitate things for you. As to your time away, I must express some concern about a lengthy honeymoon given the political climate here at this time. Perhaps it will be more settled by the time you wed. We can only hope for a speedy positive outcome." The young couple nodded their agreement to that sentiment.

"Father, it would be helpful if you could give Ted some idea of what you will expect of him here on the farm," Ellie suggested, not wanting her father to become lost in his concerns about the possibility of war.

"Ah...yes. You both know that James has decided not to return to the farm once he finishes his studies. I have to admit that I have long suspected he felt this way. He was never very invested in horse breeding. He preferred riding for pleasure to training a mount to be a good saddle horse. I have waited to be certain of his mind in this matter. Now, we are all certain; therefore, I will need someone to take his place, someone who can oversee the slaves while they do their jobs, someone who has the social skills to sell our stock to worthy buyers, and someone who has good social connections so that he will have access to a large market. I think, Ted, you are that man. I want to train you in all aspects of the work here. That will mean learning the pedigrees of the horses, learning to decide which mares to breed with which stallions, which foals to keep for training and which young stock has breeding prospects. You would have to work with the horses to learn how they are trained. It would not be a position of leisure, I can assure you. The work is year round and does not leave much time for play or for roaming about the country seeking diversions. Do you think you would be interested in such a position? Answer me honestly on this, Ted. I would not stop you from marrying my daughter, but I would have to make other plans for running the farm." He peered intently at Ted, waiting for the young man's answer. Ellie held her breath, but knew she could not interfere in his response. What he would say next was too important to her, as well.

Ted looked down to where his hand held Ellie's, and then up at her waiting face and smiled. "I have been waiting all of my life for something worthwhile in which to invest my life. I find your home and family both comfortable and accepting. The work here will be interesting and involving." He turned to look at John. "I would be delighted to have this responsibility along with that of my new wife and the family we will create. Yes, Sir, I would like the position very much."

Ellie smiled and squeezed his hand. Not all of her fears had been quelled, but his statement of commitment to her father helped her to feel more comfortable with her decision to marry Ted. John rose from his seat behind the desk and extended his hand to his future son-in-law.

"Excellent!" was John's only comment.

When the plans for Ted and Ellie's future were discussed at dinner, Suzanne was the only one who seemed less than happy. She had expected to be rid of Ellie, yet have an excuse to spend time at The Willows and to socialize with interesting people. Instead, Ellie would be getting a trip to Europe and later would remain the center of Charlotte and John's attention.

CHAPTER 39

The next morning, Ted left for The Willows; James left for Columbia. In little more than a week, news arrived that the South Carolina artillery at the entrance to Charleston Harbor had fired on an unarmed merchant vessel, the *Star of the West*, which was secretly carrying federal troops and supplies to Fort Sumter. Then the lower southern states joined South Carolina in secession. On January 29, Kansas was admitted to the Union as a state with a constitution prohibiting slavery.

Letters between Ted and Ellie, Agnes and Charlotte, and Thomas and John went back and forth. Plans were made for the Peters family to visit The Willows at the end of February. Agnes had sent a guest list to Charlotte for an engagement party to take place during the visit. She asked Charlotte to add to the list. Ellie reviewed it and wondered if there was anyone of importance left in all of South Carolina to add; many of the names she had only read of in the newspapers, but had never met.

The Peters women traveled by coach to The Willows. It was apparent to Ellie that her mother was extremely nervous. It was important to Charlotte that they make a good impression on the notable guests, not only for Ellie's sake, but also for Suzanne's future prospects. Although Suzanne had just turned fifteen years old, it wasn't too soon to start making a memorable appearance. Suzanne was excited, expecting to outshine her sister with her charm. She had already been warned not to make Ellie look bad, as it would only detract from her own prospects. Ellie was excited about seeing Ted, but dreaded the party. She'd had enough of the high society pro-slavers she'd met in Beaufort and their ideas, which she considered antiquated.

Charlotte was not pleased that John was not accompanying them; she had wanted his support. However, he had refused to be away from the farm any longer than he had to with so many mares due to foal. James planned on riding down to Whispering Oaks from the capitol; the day before the party, he and John would then ride to The Willows together.

As the main house came into view from their coach, Ellie could see Ted pacing on the first floor veranda. It had been seven weeks since they'd seen one another. It was difficult to contain herself and not tell their driver to put the matched pair of bays into a full gallop. When they pulled into the front circle, Ted came running down the front stairs. Ellie was ready to fling open the door when Charlotte grabbed her arm. "You will have a lifetime together, darling."

Ellie regained her poise and pushed Suzanne toward the door when Ted opened it. He graciously offered his hand to assist her, "Suzanne, you are looking lovely after your trip." She smiled at him and fluttered her eyelashes. She didn't see that he was holding back a laugh at her attempted flirtation.

He then offered his hand to Charlotte. She took her time, seeing his anticipation. "Why thank you, Ted."

Ted smiled, thinking it was the first time she had not called him "Mr. Campbell." He bowed graciously to her, and then turned back to the coach door. When Ellie appeared in the doorway, he grabbed her by the waist and swung her out of the coach, spinning her around before gently setting her down on the ground. She laughed in surprise, and then quickly glanced toward her mother, afraid she would be upset. Charlotte was pretending not to have seen. Ted saw her glance toward Charlotte and realized she might see his action as too forward. He let go of her waist and took both her hands in his, squeezing them. He seemed unable to find the right words. Simultaneously, they both started to say, "I missed..." and then they started laughing together.

Slaves came running up and assisted the three ladies' maids in unloading the coach. Ellie had already instructed Mattie that she would be staying in her room with her again. After the greeting she had received, she realized she had made the proper decision. In a moment of great personal honesty, she admitted to herself that she needed protection from her own desires as well.

As soon as they entered the house, Agnes took Charlotte by the arm as if they were long lost friends. It was a cold day for so late in February. The warmth of the drawing room was welcome after the long trip, as well as the hot toddies and imported Scottish shortbread. To Ellie's relief Agnes was too much the gracious hostess to bring up the reason for the visit or any of the plans that needed to be made, at least, not until her company had a chance to rest and refresh themselves after the trip.

However, at dinner she started to extol the benefits of St. Helena's and a summer wedding in Beaufort. The women all understood the impossibility of a spring wedding in Sheldon. There simply would not be enough time to make the proper preparations. Ted wanted the wedding to be as soon as possible and believed Ellie was willing to begin their life together immediately, but that she was determined to be married in Sheldon.

As she quietly listened to everyone else discuss the place and date of her wedding, Ellie realized she did not need to make her feelings known about wanting a long engagement. She did not want to risk hurting Ted. She only needed to be stubborn about where to have the wedding. Agnes and Charlotte would never be prepared for a spring wedding and summer in Sheldon would be out of the question due to the heat. The earliest they could be married would be late in November. She continued to refuse a Beaufort wedding and allowed the rest of them to fight it out. To Ted's disappointment, the mothers agreed on the first of December. Ellie tried her best to muster up a sad look to give Ted. Inside she was feeling relieved; December would be perfect as far as she was concerned.

Ellie crawled into bed exhausted and fell asleep before Mattie finished turning down the lamps. By afternoon the next day, Agnes had received three letters by messenger. The first was from the Barnwells, they were sorry for the last minute change in plans, but Robert Woodward Barnwell was leading the South Carolina delegation at the convention in Montgomery, Alabama and would be unable to attend. The other two letters were also from participants of the convention. By dinner, Agnes was agitated. She felt slighted that even the wives would go to Montgomery, rather than attend one of her parties. Not one of them, Thomas, William, Anderson, nor Ted could convince her that the Confederate Convention was history in the making.

That night before bed, Ellie looked out her window. The wind was blowing a light drizzle onto the veranda. Mattie looked at her, shaking her head, "Miz Ellie, not tonight, ya'll catch yo death." Ellie knew she was right and sadly crawled into bed.

The next day, Agnes received two more letters. One was from Mrs. Barnwell Rhett, the other from Mrs. John Chestnut. Both were apologies for last minute changes in plans. Agnes was very upset. Ellie was surprised by her own disappointment. She had been looking forward to the opportunity to meet Mary Chestnut. Fortunately, no one had much time to dwell on it. Charlotte's sister and her family arrived from Savannah. Ellie was excited to see her cousin, Emmy. The house became filled with laughter from the young people.

Ted and his brothers and sisters-in-law, and Ellie and her cousin all stayed up well beyond the older adults. As the alcohol flowed, the laughter got louder. Ellie enjoyed the attention Ted received as he entertained the group with jokes and wild tales. She couldn't help but notice that his brothers drank as much if not more than he did; they were just quieter about it. Ellie stumbled upstairs, giggling the entire time as Mattie struggled to help her to strip off her clothes and put on her nightgown. At last, she collapsed into bed.

The next morning, John and James arrived at The Willows to find Ellie had not emerged from her bedroom yet. Mattie reported that her mistress had a headache, but would be down in time for lunch. When she did come downstairs, James gave his sister a hug and whispered in her ear, "You look like you have been practicing to become a Campbell."

She wanted to hit him but refrained, only whispering back, "I will get you back later." The day passed quietly. Ted disappeared into his father's study with both John and Thomas for most of the afternoon. Ellie spent a quiet time visiting with Emmy. The cousins were sharing a room.

By dinner, she was feeling like herself again. The two families seemed to have relaxed with one another and were intermingling well. Ellie observed them contentedly. She felt it was a good sign for the success of the party and the life she anticipated with Ted. The entire house decided to turn in early. After the previous late night, most felt a need for extra rest before the party, which was scheduled to begin at two in the afternoon. As they were on their way upstairs, Ted whispered to Ellie, "The stars should be beautiful tonight."

In frustration, Ellie replied, "Emmy is staying in the room with me, remember?"

He stopped her on the staircase, leaning in to whisper to her, "I need to know you want me, too."

Looking into his eyes, she squeezed his hand in response, a sensual smile playing over her lips.

CHAPTER 40

The day of the engagement soirée arrived. Ellie was surprised at how nervous she was feeling as she got ready for the party. Emmy attempted to reassure her that she would be a huge success. After all, Emmy reminded her, almost everyone at the party already knew the couple and had for most of their lives. It wasn't as if she were going to be a surprise for any of them. Emmy suggested a new hairstyle for Ellie to try. Getting Mattie to get it right distracted both of the young women for quite some time. Ellie had a new, ashes-of-roses watered silk afternoon gown with puffy, mutton chop sleeves and cream-colored lace at the collar and cuffs. She selected a gold pendant studded with seed pearls and pearl drop earrings. The pearls picked up the color of the dress. Emmy told her how lovely she looked several times before she stopped asking if she looked presentable. Emmy's celery and dark green dress complimented Ellie's, as if she were the bower for Ellie's rose. When they were both finished dressing, Ellie continued to fuss until Emmy took her by the arm and pulled her out of the room.

"You are absolutely stunning. Everyone will be awed by you. Is that not true, Mattie?" Emmy asked, turning to the maid.

"Yes'm, Miz Emmy. She is gonna be da belle o' da party taday. Ya ain't never looked so good, Miz Ellie, an' dat's goin' some," Mattie reassured her mistress with a wide smile.

Ellie looked doubtfully at both of them, but allowed herself to be led into the hallway. Once downstairs, they were greeted by all the family. Both women received compliments on their appearance. Ted, who had been across the parlor pouring a drink, turned when he heard the women arrive. A huge grin spread across his face and he toasted Ellie with his glass of scotch before approaching her. Ellie felt a frown cross her face when she saw him drinking so early in the day, but quickly suppressed it, replacing it with a warm smile.

Guests began to arrive, greeting the couple with their best wishes. Before long, the rooms were filled with laughter and the buzz of conversation from dozens of people. Ellie was introduced to so many people, she was certain she would never remember all of them. Much of the time Ted was at her side. Occasionally, he would wander away to speak with someone, leaving her to converse with whomever was near. The entire afternoon, Ellie noted, Ted was never without a glass in his hand, except when dancing. Ellie commented on this to James, knowing that she could confide in him, but he dismissed her concerns, stating that it was a party. He pointed out that Ted seemed to be enjoying himself and that he was not causing a scene. Feeling that she was being too critical, Ellie decided to ignore her concerns and try to enjoy herself. After all, Ted was being his usual social self. Everyone around him was enjoying his joking and conversation. And whenever he returned to her side, he was attentive and affectionate. She was warmed by the happiness she saw in him. It wasn't often that Ted was happy at The Willows. By the end of the day, she had to acknowledge that the party had been a great success and that she had had a wonderful time.

As Ellie went to bed that night, she wondered if Ted was as frustrated as she was about not being able to meet on the veranda. She had never thought a time would come that she would be anxious for Emmy to leave for Savannah.

The day after the party, Ellie's father and brother left right after breakfast by horseback. Anderson Campbell volunteered to take the Hamiltons back to Savannah on the family schooner. He had some business to follow up on; his wife stayed behind. Ellie, Suzanne, and Charlotte were to stay a couple more days. Agnes was insistent that she and Charlotte still had considerable planning to do. Ellie was pleased with the arrangements; it would give her an opportunity to get to know her future sisters-in-law better, and of course, spend some private time with Ted.

Ellie and Ted walked Anderson and the Hamiltons down to the dock. As soon as the schooner was out of sight, Ted took Ellie into his arms. "Ted, the slaves will talk," she protested, shocked and titillated.

He laughed, giving her a squeeze, and then letting go. "They will not dare tell our mothers. Besides, they expect to see affection between us. You are to be my wife."

"May we walk for a little while before going back to the house?" she asked, wanting to be alone with him and away from the interference of family.

"Certainly. We can walk more of the dikes. We did not do much of that when you were here last. It will give you a different view of the place." He took her arm and directed her toward the fields. She liked the feel of his body so close to her. Soon she slid her hand into his.

The couple walked holding hands. They were trailed by an entourage of children. Ellie was relieved by their presence when she realized that some of the areas were rather isolated this time of year. She tried to keep her giggle to herself, thinking Ted had probably expected to have her alone.

"What is so funny, my little magnolia?" he asked, raising an eyebrow quizzically.

"It seems we will be chaperoned one way or another," Ellie explained, nodding in the direction of the children.

Ted turned to look at them, and then leaned close to Ellie's ear and whispered, "Get rid of Mattie tonight."

"Will I see you on the veranda?" Ellie asked, a shiver of anticipation passing through her.

"If you wish. You realize it will be colder." Ted blew on her neck, tickling the small loose hairs that curled there.

She shivered again, and purred, "I do not think I will be cold if you are there."

Ted leered. "No, I promise to warm you."

She blushed almost hearing his thoughts by his tone. They continued their walk companionably, with Ted pointing out landmarks of interest. After strolling for over an hour, they headed back to the house. If anyone had noticed they had been missing, no one mentioned it nor did they receive any disapproving looks. Ellie's reputation for proper behavior protected them from anyone questioning their absence.

After lunch, Ellie was dragged off by the women to discuss plans for the wedding. When she objected that they had plenty of time, she was informed that not only would her dress be ordered from Paris, but they might be deciding to order other things from Europe. They would need the time. As far as Ellie was concerned, the important decisions had been made. She and Ted would be married in Sheldon on the first of December. The rest did not matter to her and she trusted her mother to make sure everything was pleasant for their guests. The only planning she wanted to do was her wardrobe for the trip to Europe. Since no one else was ready to talk about it, she sat quietly daydreaming about her wedding night.

At dinner, Ellie made a show of being tired, "probably from all the excitement." Ted kept giving her looks as if he were unsure whether she truly meant it or not. Her yawns seemed to be contagious. She said her goodnights and headed up to her room. She laced up the front of her nightgown tightly so that it pushed her breasts up more, while Mattie hung her clothes. She took her hair down and started brushing it out slowly, thoroughly. Mattie watched, and then finally blurted out, "Ya gonna tease Marster Ted agin?"

"I hope so," she muttered as she practiced smiling seductively in front of her mirror.

"It's mighty cold out dere. Ya gonna take sick, Miz Ellie," Mattie cautioned.

"I will be fine. Where is my robe?" She turned, looking around for the garment.

Sighing and shaking her head, Mattie handed it to her, turned down the lamps, and crawled into bed, pulling the covers up over her head. "Ah doan want ta know nuthin'."

Ellie wrapped the heavy, dark blue robe around her, tying the cloth belt tightly. She opened the window enough to look out and check if there were any lights shining through the windows. While she was watching one light went out, leaving only one remaining. She wasn't sure, but she thought it belonged to Ted's oldest brother. She sat back down at the dressing table and started brushing her hair again. She stopped to listen to two sets of men's footsteps walking down the hall, and then the sound of two doors opening and closing. She waited a little longer before looking out the window again, this time there was no light; she opened the window further and climbed out. It was cold, especially with the wind off the water. She waited for what seemed like forever. She was just beginning to wonder if he was disappointed that she had refused to send Mattie away and was not going to meet her when she heard someone coming around the corner of the veranda.

The moon provided enough light that, as he approached, she could see that Ted was wearing a dark, quilted robe and what appeared to be a flannel nightshirt. Although she was in her nightwear, their first encounter on the veranda had not been planned and it seemed normal after that time. She had never seen him like this; she blushed as she felt a strange tingling between her legs. She moved toward him, stopping short of the next window.

Ted walked up to her and, without greeting or hesitation, untied her robe and reached in under it, wrapping his arms around her, pulling her in tight and kissing her firmly on the mouth. She pushed him away, breaking the embrace.

Frustrated and a bit annoyed with her behavior, he stated, "You are mine now,   Ellie."
"Not yet, my love." She laughed softly.

"Your presence has kept me on edge all week. I need you." He sighed when she did not respond. He untied his robe, parting it, and then wrapping it around both of them as he moved her back against the wall. When he saw a look of discomfort in her eyes, he said, "I am just trying to keep us out of the wind." He then kissed the side of her neck, tickling it with his tongue. Ellie began to relax, enjoying the attention. He moved one hand, gently tracing her collarbones and around the edge of the neckline of her nightgown. He worked his tongue back up to her lips and slid his hand down to her breast. When he squeezed the left one firmly, she flinched at the pain, but did not try to stop him.

Ellie realized that now that they were engaged, he would expect more. She wanted more of him too, but she didn't know what to expect or how much would be too much. There was a part of her that wanted to excite him, wanted to test him, and another part that felt guilty tempting him. She thought of her brother talking about men's needs and was about to stop him when he gently started rubbing her nipple. The sensation was distracting and stimulating; she leaned her head back against the wall, thrusting her breast toward his hand. She moaned quietly. He started to untie the string at the top of her nightgown. Startled, she quickly reached up, gripping his hand.

He whispered, "Ellie, let me see you." It was both a command and a plea.

She removed her hand from his, putting hers gently on his chest and stared into his eyes; she wanted to see him, too. She wanted to touch his skin, feel his muscles. He slowly unlaced the front of her gown to the waist, and then pulled the gown to the sides. Once her breasts were fully exposed, he broke the eye contact and looked down. "They are more beautiful than I have ever dreamed."

She felt his hands move on to her bare breasts and start to rub her nipples with the side of his thumbs. She moaned, throwing her head back. She slid one hand under his robe, feeling his side through the flannel; her other hand moved down to his waist. He kissed the side of her neck, and then her throat. His tongue tickled its way down to her cleavage. She thought she should stop him, but it felt too good; she couldn't bring herself to say "no." He held her breast firmly, pushing up the nipple, and ran his tongue over it. She felt heat between her legs. Then he bit down. The pain shooting through her, she tried pushing him away. He didn't let go.

"Ted, you are hurting me," she protested, pushing harder at him.

He released her breast from between his teeth. "You will get used to it and it will excite you. A little pain can be very erotic."

She had no experience to know if he was right and no one to ask. "Please, just hold me."

Her hand that had been on his waist had moved down to his hip, when he pulled her close it slipped over his buttocks. Her curiosity kept it there, exploring. His response was to kiss her on the lips passionately and grab her bottom. He pushed her hard against him. She felt his engorged penis pressing hard against her stomach through their nightclothes. He moved himself up and down against her. It was intriguing, exciting; she felt the moisture build between her legs. The head of his penis pushed against the cloth of her gown that was pressed against the moist flesh between her thighs. Suddenly, she was frightened. "Ted, stop," she protested.

"Not yet, Ellie." He pushed further into her. She could feel his penis sliding between her legs.

"We are not married," she pleaded.

He kept moving against her. "We will be," he groaned.

"Ted, we have to stop." She tried pushing him away.

Finally, he stopped, moaning in frustration; he was breathing heavily when he rested his head on her shoulder.

"I am sorry. I want you, but not this way, not before we are married." She reached up to stroke his face.

"I do not know if I can wait until December," he warned her, beginning to rub against her again.

"Please, Ted." She was insistent this time. Ted stepped back from her, pulling his robe closed. Ellie quickly pulled her gown and robe closed to cover her nakedness.

Ted looked away from her, licking his lips and rubbing his face with his hand. "You had better go inside now," he told her.

"Please, do not be angry with me." Ellie reached out to him, not quite touching him.

"I am not angry. But I am too worked up to trust myself with you." He kissed her gently on the mouth and walked her to her window. As she climbed in, he caressed her bottom.

Back inside the room, Ellie closed the window, noting that Ted had already disappeared from view. She slipped out of her robe and laced her nightgown closed. She crawled into bed, but had trouble falling asleep. She found herself wanting to touch herself in a way she never had even thought of before. She could still feel Ted's hands on her breasts and her skin tingled where his penis had rubbed against her. If Mattie had not been there, she knew she would have pulled her gown off and explored her body as Ted had done. She tossed and turned, unable to fall asleep and unwilling to give in to this strange urge. At last, sleep carried her off to disturbing, sensual dreams.

CHAPTER 41

The next morning, Mattie woke Ellie. She had brought coffee up to the room. "Ya'd best git up. Dey's worryin' bout ya down dere an' wanna know why ya's sleepin' so much."

Ellie stretched, sat up in bed, and then took the coffee cup from Mattie. "Would you do a favor for me?"

"Favor?" The slave woman was confused by the idea. "What ya mean?"

"Mattie, could you…could you find out if Master Ted is still calling for slave women?"

"Ya mean after las' night?" she smirked.

"No…Yes…Well, since he came home from Christmas."

Mattie giggled, "Ah'll try." Then she became serious, "What ya gonna do, ef he's called dem?"

"I do not know." She thought about what James had said about once they were married and she would be meeting Ted's needs. "But I need to know if he has kept his promise."

"Ah'll try. Now git up befoe dey think ya sick o' pregnant."

"Pregnant!" Ellie was horrified. The thought had never crossed her mind; she had said "no" to Ted because it was not proper, not because she might get pregnant.

Ellie dressed quickly and ran downstairs. Everyone had already finished breakfast. Ted was the only one sitting at the table still drinking coffee. "Good morning, my little magnolia."

She was relieved by the affection in his voice. "Did you sleep well last night?" she asked, sitting down next to him.

"I could have slept better." He put his hand on hers. "You do not know what you do to me?"

Before she could reply, Anderson's wife Esther walked in. "You two look as though you have been married for years."

Ellie blushed.

"Ellie, you blush too easily." She was enjoying teasing Ellie.

"Esther, what do you want?" Ted was annoyed at the disruption.

She laughed, "Did I interrupt your sweet nothings, Ted?"

"Yes. Go away!" He frowned at her and waved toward the door.

"Ted!" Embarrassed, Ellie added, "Ignore him, Esther."

"When you are finished eating, Ellie, Mother Campbell wants you to join us in the sewing room. You need to be measured so that your dress can be ordered." Laughing she added, "Do not rush or your fiancé will be grumpy all day." She made a face at Ted and left.

He kissed Ellie's hand, "She is right. I am grumpy when you are not with me."

Ellie frowned. "You will have to try harder than that at your sweet nothings."

He smiled, "I love you."

"That is much better." She smiled and leaned toward him, offering him a kiss.

Ted reached up and brushed a finger over her breast as he brushed his lips over hers. "Now that is much better."

Ellie felt her nipple harden and blushed at her quick response to his caress. "I have to go or your mother will be in here looking for me," she stated, needing to get away from him as quickly as possible. She heard Ted chuckle as she left the room.

The day passed quickly. When Mattie met Ellie in her room to help her prepare for dinner, she was grinning. "Well, dey thinks you's a witch."

"What?" Ellie demanded, looking at Mattie.

"Dey thinks ya cast a spell on Marster Ted. Dey cain't figure any udder reason why he ain't callin' fo' dem." She laughed. "Dey think ya must a made him imp'tent."

Ellie laughed, thoroughly pleased with this news. She happily prepared for dinner and was early for the first time. Dinner was a pleasant affair. She was able to laugh at the teasing, but then started to get nervous about what Ted might expect from her later that night. It would be her last night on the plantation. When she heard thunder in the distance followed by a cloudburst, she felt disappointment and a great sense of relief. She noticed Ted's frown.

Ellie was relaxed and content as she was preparing for bed. The rain was blowing against the window. She was about to get into bed when she heard a different sound at the window. She thought it might be a tree branch, but when it got louder, she decided that she needed to check. She was startled to see Ted's face in the window, water dripping off his chin. She opened it up. "Ted! What are you doing?"

"Let me in!" he demanded urgently.

"Doan ya do it, Miz Ellie. Dat man's crazy!" Mattie cried from the bed, pulling the covers up under her chin.

Ellie opened the window further and stepped back. "Ted, you cannot stay here."

He grabbed her and kissed her hard, getting her all wet. "I know, but you are leaving tomorrow. I had to get at least one more decent kiss before you left."

"Come to Whispering Oaks, soon. I will miss you. Now, leave." She kissed him and shoved him back toward the window and the rain.

The Peters women left in their coach right after breakfast the next morning.

CHAPTER 42

Abraham Lincoln had been sworn in as the sixteenth President of the United States on March 4, 1861. His inaugural speech was printed in all the papers. Ellie read it, as did the rest of her family. She was struck by many of his arguments in favor of preserving the Union. She was relieved to see that he promised not to interfere with slavery where it already existed. She still wanted to end slavery, but she hoped this would pacify those who feared the Abolitionists. Lincoln went on to promise that states' rights would be preserved and that the Fugitive Slave Act would continue to be enforced, although he didn't say the federal government would be the one to enforce it. Ellie had to agree that it was vital to protect free men from being enslaved, something which had been known to occur where slavery and free Negroes coexisted. She also agreed that "Nothing valuable can be lost by taking time."

She was deeply moved by his statement that "In your hands, my dissatisfied fellow-countrymen, and not in mine, is the momentous issue of civil war. The Government will not assail you. You can have no conflict without being yourselves the aggressors. You have no oath registered in heaven to destroy the Government, while I shall have the most solemn one to 'preserve, protect, and defend it.'" Certainly, the South could have no argument with that statement. Lincoln had even stated that he would support a Constitutional amendment making it illegal for the federal government to interfere with any domestic institutions of the states, including slavery. How much greater a guarantee would the South need to avoid this threatened conflict?

Still, there were some troublesome passages in the speech. Lincoln stated that he would not move against any of the states, but would "hold, occupy, and possess the property and places belonging to the Government...." This worried many people in the South, as it seemed to imply that he would not withdraw any troops from the forts along the coast or inland. And many people feared that, because the Constitution did not promise that escaped slaves would be returned or that slavery would be protected in the Territories, these things might not be carried out by the Federal government. Tensions continued, and the South continued down the road of secession. In February, the Confederate States of America had convened in Montgomery, Alabama to elect a president and other government officials. Robert W. Barnwell led the delegation from South Carolina to the convention. His vote was the one that swung the election of the president of the Confederacy to Jefferson Davis. This choice was not universally popular in the South, but Davis was only appointed temporarily until a popular election could be held. The Northern papers carried stories that suggested that the North did not believe the South was serious about secession. Most Southerners were coming to believe that war was inevitable. On the fifth of March, the new Confederate flag was raised at the site of the convention in Montgomery, Alabama.

Ellie had arrived home to discover she had missed two foals being born. Late winter and early spring were an exciting time on the farm from Ellie's perspective. She only wished Ted was there to enjoy it with her. She consoled herself that he would share it with her the next year.

March was passing by quickly for Ellie, between the news, arriving letters, talk at the store, and neighbors stopping by. But none of it seemed real to Ellie. Her thoughts were all of Ted and Princess. As soon as she arrived back from The Willows, she had decided that she would train Princess herself.

It was the thirtieth of March, the last Saturday of the month. Princess had accepted the harness and was responding to the directions of the long reins. Ellie was cooling the young mare out behind the barn. She entered the back door of that building with Princess to find her brother's horse on cross ties being unsaddled.

"Marster James rod in hard. Dis po' hoss look lack it been runnin' fo' hours," the groom complained, wiping down the animal.

"When did he arrive?" Ellie demanded. She hadn't known he was coming.

"'Bout ten minutes ago. He wearin' a uniform or somethin'. Never seed 'im dress lack dat befoe."

"Take Princess, please." Ellie handed over the lead and ran out of the barn and up to the house. As she opened the front door, she yelled, "James!" and continued running through the house looking for him. She heard his laughter coming from her father's study and barged in.

"It did not take long for you to hear I was home," he laughed, standing and opening   his   arms   to   greet   her.
Ellie stopped dead when she saw her brother. "James, what have you done?" She looked at him in his blue-gray, double breasted frock coat with blue trim on the collar and cuffs, white pants, and at the gray forage cap, with a large 1 and CSA on it, that was lying on their father's desk.

"I have joined the First Infantry of South Carolina." Proudly he added, "I am a Second Lieutenant."

"Why, James?" Ellie cried out, unable to stop herself.

"Because it is the right thing to do," he responded, frowning and stepping back from her, hurt by her attitude.

"But, James, we are not at war. Surely, you could have waited. You might be injured... or worse." She appeared close to tears at the thought of what her brother had committed to do. The sound of the other family members crowding into the room quickly distracted them.

"Oh, my good Lord! James, look at you," Charlotte exclaimed when she saw him. Beyond that, she could say nothing. She was in shock and could only plop down in a chair and stare at him.

"Oh, James! How handsome you look. You must have your photograph taken. All my friends will be so taken with you when they see you like this!" Suzanne gushed, hugging her brother and demanding his attention.

"Father, talk to him. Tell him he should wait. There is no reason to rush into this business," Ellie pleaded, hoping that her father would be reasonable.

"I will do no such thing, Ellie. James is following his conscience. He feels strongly about defending the South, especially South Carolina. I am very proud of him," her father stated, turning to smile at his son.

"Thank you for understanding, Sir. I will do my best to fulfill your belief in me." He reached out to offer his hand to his father in promise.

"How long can you stay, James?" Charlotte managed to ask.

"Only through the weekend," he explained. A brief silence fell on the room as each person realized how little time they had with him, and then each made an effort to be supportive and cheerful. James attended church in uniform with the family on Sunday, ate dinner, and then left to return to his regiment. With a profound sense of sadness, Ellie watched him ride off. She had prayed in church for a peaceful division of the Union. Things were changing, and seeing her brother in uniform frightened her that war would come soon to the South.

CHAPTER 43

The month of April 1861 saw tensions escalating rapidly. President Lincoln sent notice to the South Carolina state legislature that he would be sending supplies to Fort Sumter, which was located in Charleston harbor. He had notified them in advance in the hope of avoiding conflict. On the eighth of April, six man-of-war ships from the United States Navy were stationed outside of Charleston harbor. Residents there were certain that hostilities were about to begin. A delegation from Charleston rowed out to Fort Sumter on the eleventh to negotiate the surrender of the fort with the commander, Colonel Robert Anderson. He was given until four the next morning to evacuate peacefully. Anderson agreed to surrender, but only after his supplies were used up. His offer was rejected. On the twelfth of April, thirty minutes after the deadline, Confederate troops under General Pierre Beauregard opened fire on the fort with fifty cannons. The shelling lasted for two days before the fort surrendered. The South was at war with the North. President Lincoln issued a proclamation calling for 75,000 militiamen and summoning a special session of Congress for the fourth of July.

Robert E. Lee, a twenty-five-year, distinguished veteran of the United States Army, and a former superintendent of West Point, was offered the command of the Union Army. He declined the offer.

The attack on Fort Sumter prompted four more states to join the Confederacy: Virginia, Arkansas, Tennessee, and North Carolina. With Virginia's secession, Richmond, Virginia was made the capital of the Confederacy. The Confederacy now consisted of eleven states with a population of nine million people, including four million slaves. They would soon face the twenty-one states of the Union and its twenty million people. Still, the people of the South believed they could win the war.

On the nineteenth of April, Lincoln ordered the blockade of the Southern ports. Although the blockades were slow to be arranged, people feared that they would not be able to sell their crops to their European markets and would not be able to get the imported goods to which they were so accustomed. It was argued that there would be plenty of ships that would willingly run the blockades to continue trade with foreign markets. Those who lacked faith in the South were accused of being traitors by their neighbors. Still, there were those who voiced their doubts about the possibility of a Southern victory, but they were few in number. The general public was wild with the desire to trounce the North and get on with their new lives.

On the twentieth of April, Robert E. Lee resigned his commission in the Union Army, stating, "I cannot raise my hand against my birthplace, my home, and my children." He traveled at once to Richmond, where he was offered command of the military and naval forces of the Confederacy. He accepted the command. Most Southerners were delighted. Lee was from an old and heroic Southern family. He was considered by many to be the epitome of the Southern gentleman.

It was also about this time that Wade Hampton, a wealthy son of South Carolina approached President Davis for permission to form his own legion of infantry, cavalry, and artillery. Men from all over the South began flocking to join him.

By the third week of April, John Peters understood that there was no turning back. When Lincoln made his proclamation of the blockade of the Southern ports, John decided he would have to join up. He knew he would seek a commission in the cavalry. However, he first needed to make preparations so that the farm responsibilities would not be overwhelming for Ellie; he felt it was best to reduce the stock.

John sold off all twenty-five three year olds; all had been broken to cart and some were already saddle broken. He selected ten mares that had either been difficult to breed or had histories of difficult deliveries. He gelded five four year olds that he'd been debating whether to keep for breeding stock or not and sold them, too. Five more old mares were sold, bringing the total sale to forty-five horses. John loved his horses, but he was a keen businessman and, taking full advantage of the high hopes and spirits of the Southern men, he negotiated top prices. He hoped these men were right that the new Confederacy would win its independence. Although he kept his doubts to himself, Ellie could see them on his face. He needed Ellie to manage the farm as if the worst were coming. He had never been to war himself, but he knew enough to no longer trust the banks, and believed that the only safe currency would be precious metals: gold, silver, platinum. He conveyed all this to Ellie.

"Listen carefully, Ellie," he instructed his daughter. "As the war progresses, paper money will undoubtedly become inflated. It will cost more and more in paper to buy less and less. Any gold or silver, no matter what form it is in, will be far more valuable than paper money. I have gone over the books with you, so you know what we owe and to whom, and who owes money to us. I want you to pay our debts in paper when you can. And try to collect the debts in coin, even if you have to give them some advantage in doing so. Do not spend any money you do not absolutely have to spend. Do you understand why I want you to do all of this?" He waited for her answer.

"Yes, Sir. That way I will be reducing the amount of expensive or worthless paper money we have and will be increasing the amount of more valuable metal money we possess." She nodded at the wisdom of this advice.

"I wish Ted were here for this planning session, but we will have to get things in place quickly. I know you will explain the plans to him. Now, with the reduction in the herd, our people will have more time for their own pursuits. Encourage them to plant their gardens and harvest as much food as they can. They will need to store most of it. Times will be hard, especially with the blockades on the ports. And there will be demands made by the Army for supplies. Do not neglect our obligation to them. Give as much as you can and allow them to pay with paper. If the war goes well, we will recoup our losses. If not... well, it will not matter. Your mother will not be of much help in this, but she can oversee the kitchen help in canning and preserving vegetables and fruits. You may want to butcher more of the pigs than usual and get the meat smoked. It will keep longer that way. I hate to suggest this, but you will have to hide some of the food stores. Be very careful when you do this. If things get difficult, hoarders will be prosecuted. However, I do not want my family or my people starving." John leaned back in his chair, rubbing his face as if trying to wipe away his fears.

"Father, do you think things will get that bad? Surely, some of these things will not be necessary. How long can this war go on?" Ellie felt her stomach knotting with tension. She doubted she would be able to handle all these things on her own and felt grateful that Ted would be there to help her.

Not wanting to face her questions himself, he ignored them, continuing with more instructions. "I am leaving behind several hunting rifles and two sets of pistols. There should be enough ammunition for all of them if you should have to drive off pillagers or thieves. Consider carefully before arming any of the slaves. And God forbid you find yourself confronted by any large group of troops. If that happens, you must hide the house silver and other valuables, but do not hide everything. If soldiers come here looking for plunder, they will not be willing to leave empty handed. Make sure they get something that convinces them that it is worth taking. You can tell them that you had to sell everything else to support the farm." He watched as Ellie twisted her engagement ring in anxiety. "You had better hide that ring as well. Think about where you might hide things in advance, so that you will be able to dispose of them quickly in case of necessity."

"Yes, Sir," Ellie replied, biting her lip.

"I know this is a heavy burden for you, Ellie. We can only hope the war will be short. I promise I will return as often as possible to check on how things are going and to help out here. I wish I did not have to leave you women here on your own. But I would not be able to live with myself if I did not go. I hope you can understand that." He looked intently at his daughter, willing her to understand why he was going.

"I wish you and James did not have to go, Father. But I do understand why you are doing this. I just pray that all these terrible troubles will end quickly, so that we can all go back to the way things were." Ellie felt a tear start to roll down her cheek and moved to quickly wipe it away.

"My brave girl!" John praised her, reaching across the desk to her. "The North is lucky you were born a woman. They would not stand a chance if you had been a man." He smiled proudly at her. Ellie tried to return a brave smile for him as well.

CHAPTER 44

Letters had been flying back and forth between Ted and Ellie. He came to the farm as soon as he heard from her about John's plans. She was relieved to have his strong arms to support her. He only brought up once that it might be better if they married immediately due to the circumstances. Ellie saw it as taking advantage of her difficulties and a lack of trust in her abilities. She was furious. After her tirade, he recognized he would get farther with her if he waited at least until the next time. This trip he would only hold her hand, cuddle her, and keep the kisses brief. It did not seem as if she could stand still long enough for anything more anyway. John left as a captain in the Seventh South Carolina Cavalry by the middle of May, taking five horses with him.

Ted escorted the Peters women to Beaufort for the usual summer hiatus. He maintained proper decorum and made certain that the women were safely ensconced in their Beaufort home before returning to his parents' house. After he left, Ellie felt badly that she had been so hard on him at the farm. He seemed to have become more mature and certainly more responsible when it had become apparent to him that he was needed. She hoped he wasn't too angry with her; he had barely touched her after she had become so upset. She reluctantly admitted to herself that she was disappointed, now that they were in Beaufort, that he had given up so easily. Maybe she should have trusted him and agreed to a speedy marriage.

Ted visited daily. Ellie realized that, without him there, the house would have been terribly dreary. Charlotte was not happy about both her son and her husband being off fighting a war. When a day passed without a letter from one or the other she obsessed that something had happened to them. Ted attempted to reassure her that she would have heard if either of them had been injured. He brought them newspapers and regaled them with the news of Southern victories. The women rejoiced at the news when the first land battle to take place in Virginia on June 10, 1861--Big Bethel--proved to be a Confederate victory. Ted assured them that it would be only the first of many.

Ellie noticed that Charlotte's attitude had changed from relief that Ellie had found a man of wealth and connections, to genuine acceptance of Ted as a man of the family. It bothered her to see her mother's weakness and dependence upon having a man around.

Ted offered to take them to Charleston, but Charlotte was too afraid to travel. Ellie wondered why he really wanted to go. However, he had been so kind and helpful that she felt guilty questioning his motives.

Agnes Campbell frequently invited the Peters to join her. Ellie enjoyed these visits; they generally provided more time for her and Ted to be alone with the two mothers entertaining each other. Agnes had also been upset about Anderson joining the militia. Her husband and William had gone to Richmond, trying for a political appointment for William. Ted made one brief trip in the middle of June to Whispering Oaks at Ellie's request. She would have liked to have gone herself, but she knew Charlotte would not let her go alone with Ted. The idea of going alone with Ted was both exciting and frightening.

By the end of June, Agnes and Charlotte were in a panic. They were afraid their orders from Europe would not get through the blockade. When a letter came from Felicity Hamilton inviting the Peters to Savannah, after much debate with Agnes, Charlotte decided to accept her sister's invitation. They had determined that it would be prudent to buy another wedding dress for Ellie. Ted escorted them to Savannah. Ellie was disappointed and surprised when he informed her that he would not be staying. However, he promised to be back by the end of July.

Ellie fought with her mother about shopping. She insisted that it was not necessary to buy another gown or travel clothes. She remembered her father's admonition. She told her mother if the war was still going on, she and Ted would not be able to leave for Europe. She did not want to waste the money. Other than buying a dress for her wedding, she refused to accompany her mother shopping. The one other expenditure she did make was to sit for a photograph to surprise Ted when he returned to Savannah. She spent most of her time reading every newspaper she could get her hands on to find out news of the war. She was especially looking for news of her father's and brother's units. She found herself annoyed with everyone, except perhaps Emmy.

The Hamiltons lived just off of Forsthyth Park. Emmy and Ellie frequently walked there to get out of the house. At times, Suzanne would tag along. However, on the far end of the park, they had converted the pastures to drilling areas for the military. Emmy and Suzanne would insist they watch the men train. When Ellie objected, she was told she already had a man; they did not. Watching the men drilling gave Ellie a bad feeling; she was not able to share their enthusiasm. She was fearful that the war was going to bring pain without victory. She didn't dare express her feelings. She attributed her mood to not hearing from Ted since he had brought them to Savannah.

At the end of July, the Hamiltons and their houseguests were invited to a ball to send off the Savannah troops. It was to be held at one of the houses overlooking the drilling area on Forsyth Park. Ellie did not want to attend, especially without Ted. Charlotte was insistent, stating she needed a diversion and that the festivities might get Ellie out of her vile mood.

Ellie was in her room, wearing a petticoat, refusing every gown Mattie presented to her. When the two women heard a commotion downstairs, Ellie sent Mattie down to find out what was happening. She really didn't care what was going on, but it would give her time without Mattie pushing dresses at her. She was afraid she was going to take her frustration out on her maid. The woman had been nothing but kind and patient; she did not want to lose her temper with her.

Mattie came back in the room short of breath. "Miz Ellie, Marster Ted is here!"

Ellie headed toward the door.

"Ya's not dressed. He's not goin' nowhere wit' out ya."

"You are right. I will wear the midnight blue satin gown with the black, lace trim. It shows off my shoulders and is cut low enough to be almost scandalous! Mother may object a bit, but I do not think she will make me change." Ellie suddenly was looking forward to the ball with her handsome redheaded fiancé. She loved the way he would show up unexpectedly. But, she hated it when he disappeared just as suddenly.

Ellie wanted to make an eye-popping entrance as she came down the stairs. She could hear Ted's voice in the parlor regaling the group with some tale of his adventures. She realized that everyone was waiting for her. When she turned the corner, seeing Ted leaning against the mantel in a naval uniform, she went pale.

He stopped talking and crossed the room when he saw Ellie frozen in the doorway. She looked at him in shock as he walked toward her, taking her hand, and bringing it to his mouth to kiss. She wanted to scream, "NO!" but couldn't find her voice. He led her to a chair among her family. Ellie still had not spoken when the Hamiltons' butler announced that the carriages were ready. However, Ellie's shock was turning into anger. She could not believe he was running off to war when he knew he was needed at home. When he offered a hand to assist her into the carriage, she refused it, turning away from him and lifting her skirts to step up. She didn't see the look of confusion and hurt on his face. She was furious as she thought about him making such a commitment without even discussing it with her. She wondered if this would be how he would handle all the important decisions in their life once they were married.

It was a short ride to the party. Ellie had noticed the house the carriage stopped at during a previous viewing of the troops drilling. It was a three story, white building with double stairs leading up to a veranda and the main entrance on the second floor. Each story appeared to be at least twenty feet high, with large columns going up to the top of the third floor. Ellie stiffened when she felt Ted's hand on her back as they walked up the stairs. As they proceeded through the double doors side by side, Ted whispered, "Ellie, please give me a chance to explain."

Not wanting all of Savannah to know of her anger, she forced a smile, "You had better explain."

"Try to enjoy the party until we can slip out and talk." He looked at her frown. Before either of them could say anything more, they were being greeted and introduced. Ellie had never seen such an expansive room; rather than three or four large rooms separated by double, sliding doors, it was one gigantic room with parquet floors and crystal chandeliers. Small chairs had been set up along the walls. The string quartet was set up in one corner of the room, and the black musicians were tuning up their instruments. Couples were milling about in small groups, chatting gaily. The doors to the veranda were open to let in some cooler air. The room, large as it was, was filled with color and noise. Before long, the first dance was announced and couples formed up for the Grand March. This was followed by a Virginia reel, a quadrille, a gallop, and a schottische. Ellie danced with a number of the young men there, some of them also in uniform. Ted waited to dance with her, wanting to have a waltz with her so that he could hold her intimately in his arms. They had made several sweeping turns around the dance floor when Ted danced Ellie out the double French doors onto the south side of the veranda and off to the right, out of sight of all within the ballroom.

"How could you do this without telling me first?" she snapped at him once they were out of earshot of the others.

"Ellie, this has become bigger than us. I was afraid I would change my mind if I talked with you first." He backed her into the shadows against the wall.

"I was counting on you. My father was counting on you." She tried to shrug off his hands, too angry to allow him to touch her.

"The blockade has become too effective. If the tide does not turn, we will be strangled. If we do not win this war, there will be no trip to Europe for us. My trust will be worth nothing and our lives will be turned upside down," he reasoned, lifting his hands from her, but not moving away.

"Your brother is fighting, my brother and father joined up. Why do you have to go, too?" She felt her anxiety feeding her ire.

"They need men with experience on the water. I know Port Royal Sound. I have to protect our homes, our livelihood. Ellie, I will be close by the entire time. I will be in the Sound. I will be able to come to Beaufort often." He reached out to stroke her cheek soothingly.

Ellie reached up to clasp his hand. "But, Ted, you will be in danger. If anything were to happen to you…" Her voice trailed off in fear. Her lips trembled.

"Nothing will happen to me." He laughed, "You know I always manage to get out of tight spots."

"It is not funny!" she hissed at him, pushing him away from her.

"Ellie, we now have new ships. They are faster than anything ever made. We can out maneuver any Union vessel. I have been assigned to one of them."

"Is that what this is about? The excitement of these new ships? You will never settle down. I do not know what I was thinking." She turned away from him, shaking her head, her hands lifted to her temples.

"Ellie, how can you say that? You know I love you. I want nothing more than to be married to you." He reached up and turned her back toward him, gripping her shoulders. "Marry me tonight! Send me to battle having known you." His ardor shone in his eyes as he slipped his left arm around her waist and drew her closer.

"Oh, Ted!" She started to tear up, her emotions rapidly alternating between anger and sorrow. "You know we cannot. There are plans made. Our mothers would…"

"This is about us, not our mothers," he stated quietly, his lips close to her cheek. He started to stroke her face with the back of his fingers. He ran his fingers down her face, neck and chest, slipping them into the top of her dress, searching her breasts within the confined area. When he felt her start to respond, he added, "I want you now, tonight. Marry me before I leave for Port Royal tomorrow."

She grabbed his hands, stopping him. "Tomorrow!"

"Yes, I have to report by tomorrow night. You see why it must be tonight. We have no time." There was urgency and desire in his voice and his touch.

"It is all too sudden," she protested, fighting the persuasion in his caress. She still did not trust his motives for joining the navy. She feared he was just running away from responsibility to play sailor. She feared he wanted to marry her purely to have sex and not for the partnership in life that she wanted from him.

"I know you want me, too. I know how your body reacts to me. Ellie, I have kept my promise to you. I need you." He bent his head to press a kiss between her breasts. Ellie felt her heart pounding and suspected that Ted did as well.

They heard a female voice, "You are so right; it is much cooler out here." Another couple had wandered out onto the veranda.

Ted and Ellie stopped their conversation and quietly slipped back into the ballroom unnoticed by the other couple. He whispered, "We will talk more of this later tonight." They joined back in with the other dancers, Ellie employing her fan to cool her emotions. She forced a smile onto her face and accepted the offer of a dance with another man.

Ellie danced and drank and danced some more. She did not have to think or make decisions. She enjoyed Ted's touch when they danced without feeling any threat; she laughed with him in the ways they had always laughed over the years. She sat close to him, whispering and flirting, between dances. As an engaged couple, their behavior was expected. She did not want this night to end.

Ellie and Ted held hands in the carriage, well hidden from others eyes by her voluminous skirt. It was late when the carriages pulled up to the Hamiltons' home. Ellie's Uncle Walker invited Ted in for a nightcap. She had mixed feelings, wanting to be with him and fearful that he would try taking more of her. Everyone excused themselves for the night with the exception of her two cousins.

W.S. pried Ted with questions about his naval assignment. Ellie couldn't help but notice Ted's enthusiasm when he talked about the new ships. She was sure he was looking for the excitement and an escape from the responsibility of looking out for the women in his life and the farm. Finally, she interrupted the discussion between the two men. "Will you be coming back tomorrow before you leave for Port Royal?"

"Since you would not marry me tonight and are forcing me to leave, I will come to say goodbye." He smiled and tried to sound as if he were teasing, but Ellie heard his annoyance.

"Good. I have something for you." She wanted to run out of the room right then, but was afraid she would anger him. "It is terribly late. When will you be back?"

Emmy and W.S. exchanged confused looks. Emmy did not understand why Ellie was attempting to dismiss Ted, but felt she should help her cousin. Before Ted could answer, she said, "You two gentlemen can spend the night drinking, but Ellie and I have to get our beauty sleep." She stood. "Come, Ellie."

Ellie kissed Ted on the cheek and stood. Ted grabbed her hand as if to restrain her from leaving. She laughed. "My cousin has always been bossy and I learned long ago not to go against her commands."

Ted kissed her hand, frowned, and let go.

As the two women climbed the stairs, Emmy asked, "I have always been bossy! What was that about?"

"Thank you, Emmy. I had to get away." She did not feel she needed to explain more; Emmy would figure out enough to understand.

The next morning, Ellie stayed home while the rest of the family went to church, fearful that Ted might show up when they were all out. She was still pacing when the family came home. When he did finally arrive, he looked as if he had not slept all night. She pulled him aside so they could have a brief moment alone.

"Ted, are you feeling well? You look terrible." She was suddenly filled with anxiety for his immediate health and safety.

"I would be feeling much better if you had married me last night," he growled, rubbing his temple.

"You went out drinking!" Ellie accused, realizing why he looked so worn.

"I told you before; I do not get drunk when I am with you. If you had let me into your bed, I would not have gone out." He glared at her accusingly.

"Ted, that is not fair. We are not married." Ellie drew back from his vitriol, stung by his words.

"If that is all that is stopping you, why did you refuse to marry me last night?" Ted's injured feelings and hangover seemed to be making him cruel.

"You know that was not possible," she reminded him.

"I am beginning to think you just want to tease me." He sneered the words at her.

"Please, Ted, that is not true. I want to be with you," she pleaded for him to believe her.

"Maybe next time you will prove that to me." He put his hand on her breast and squeezed it hard, a cruel smile on his lips.

"When will I see you again?" Her eyes squinted from the pain he was causing her and the shock of his cruelty. She had never seen this side of him. She forced herself not to react.

"I do not know, Ellie. My brother William will be coming into Savannah in the next couple of weeks. When you are ready, he will take you back to Beaufort." Then his anger seemed to subside. "Ellie, it is important that you do not travel without an escort. The waters are dangerous now. That also means no trips to Sheldon, either." When he saw her expression, he added, "Promise me!"

"Do you really feel it is necessary?" Her annoyance at his seemingly arbitrary limitations on her changed to genuine concern when she saw his sincerity.

"It is necessary."

"We will wait to hear from William," she promised him, and then hesitantly added, "You should say good-bye to everyone."

He pulled her tightly against his body, kissed her hard, pushed her away, and walked into the other room. After a brief interchange with Ellie's family, Ted headed for the front door. Ellie grabbed the small package on the sideboard and ran after him. "Open it once you get to your ship," she requested, holding the small bundle out to him.

He took the package. "Thank you. I will write and let you know where to write to me and when I will be in Beaufort."

Ellie felt terrible when he left and returned to her bad mood until William arrived two weeks later. He reported that the only thing he had heard from his brother was a letter demanding that he protect Ellie with his life. Ellie felt a weight being lifted from her; she had been upset about their last encounter ever since he left. The next week, Charlotte, Ellie, and Suzanne traveled by boat to Beaufort with William Campbell.

CHAPTER 45

Ellie was relieved to be out of Savannah, but she remained agitated and irritable. She hadn't heard from Ted and neither had his mother. Ellie vacillated as to whether she should be relieved, worried, or angry. It was the middle of September by the time she heard from him. His letter was filled with his excitement regarding the ship he was on and war news. He made no mention of their future or wanting her. If it hadn't been that his mother had received nothing from him at all, she would have been more upset.

Charlotte, Ellie, and Agnes had gotten into the habit of spending many an afternoon together. They wanted to have the invitations ready to mail by the first week in October. They had been mailed by the time Ellie received the next letter from Ted. She had been disappointed that he had not been able to get away to visit. However, this letter was much more personal and not one she was about to share with either Charlotte or Agnes. When they asked about it, she blushed and informed them he was doing well.

The Peters and Campbells had planned on leaving for Sheldon in the middle of November. The women had decided that two weeks before the wedding would give them plenty of time for whatever last minute preparations might be needed. However, on the twenty-ninth of October, Ted arrived in Beaufort. Charlotte and Ellie were visiting with Agnes when he walked in. He was insistent that both families leave immediately.

Charlotte was reluctant to leave early. "Ted, I just do not understand what you are so excited about. There is plenty of time to prepare for your wedding."

"Darling, I never expected you to be a nervous groom," his mother chimed in, not wanting her plans disrupted.

William looked at his brother strangely. "You think that now that you are an officer, you can order everyone around?"

"William, you need to take Mother and your wife to The Willows. I will escort Ellie and her mother and sister to Whispering Oaks."

"Ted, what is wrong?" Ellie knew him better than even his own family. She could see the fear.

"Beaufort is not safe. You must all leave by tomorrow."

"What has happened?" Ellie seemed to be the only one able to trust him.

"There is a fleet of Union ships coming. We do not know yet exactly where they will attack. We have information that they are well armed. It is supposed to be the largest fleet ever assembled. We may be the target." Ted was talking so quickly, he finally stopped to take a breath.

"Mother, we better go home and pack," Ellie urged, collecting her reticule and fan.

"But, Ellie…" Charlotte stammered, resisting any urgency.

"Mrs. Peters, your husband asked me to watch out for you and the girls before he left. You must go back to Sheldon." He turned his attention to Ellie, taking both of her hands in his. "I will be at your home tomorrow at ten in the morning." He kissed her cheek. "Do not leave anything of importance behind and do not talk to anyone about why you are leaving."

Ellie nodded, "I understand." She took her mother's hand, "Come, Mother, we have a lot of work to do." Charlotte reluctantly followed her daughter out.

The next morning, Ted arrived at nine. He directed the slaves and helped secure the wagons with the Peters' personal and some household items. Ellie watched him yelling orders, being abrupt, and impatient with everyone. She had never seen this side of him. He remained short even with Ellie until after they had disembarked at Bryan's ferry and were well on their way toward Sheldon. He finally started to relax, taking her hand in his and silently fondling it.

They still had a couple of hours ride home. Ellie leaned against Ted, feeling the comfort of his strong body. When they were in sight of the farm, she softly said, "Thank you for taking care of us."

"We may not be married yet, but you are mine, my little magnolia," he responded as quietly, smiling at her affectionately.

She realized how tense she had been since they had last been together in Savannah. It was finally starting to melt away.

When they arrived at the house, a number of surprised slaves came running out to greet them. Lottie came out. "Oh my! Miz Charlotte, Ah got nothin' ready fo' ya. Ah got no food ya'd eat."

"We have to eat!" Charlotte snapped. "Get something, anything ready immediately!" She flapped her hands at the cook, shooing her away imperiously.

"Lottie, just make some tea for now. I have a tin of butter cookies in my small trunk. Would you get them for us, Mattie?" Ellie patted her mother's arm. "A little tea and cookies, Mother, and we will all feel better. Lottie will figure out something for dinner." She was not about to let her mother ruin whatever time she would have with Ted.

Ted picked up on Ellie's need to sooth her mother and offered her his arm. "Come, Mother Peters. May I start calling you Mother Peters?" Before she could respond he continued on, "It would be such an honor. I confess, I already think of you as my second mother. If you were to say 'no,' that I have to wait another month... Well, I just do not know what I would do." He started walking her up the stairs to the house. "I may have to marry Ellie tonight, so I can call you 'Mother' right away."

Only Ellie guessed his true motivation and that he really did not want to wait.

"Oh, Ted!" Charlotte started laughing. "You may start calling me, 'Mother.' I would be delighted and honored."

He continued to tease and charm her until the tea and cookies were served. He motioned to Peter to add some brandy to Charlotte's tea, and then his own.

Ellie appreciated the way he handled her mother but, as it happened, she began to wonder if he handled her the same way.

Charlotte suddenly became serious. "Ted, will you be able to stay on now?"

"I am afraid not. I have to report in at Port Royal by the morning of the second. I will stay until the day after tomorrow."

"Oh, Ted, no! You cannot go back there. Not now!" Ellie was suddenly afraid for him.

"My captain has given me this time to make sure my family is safe and he has promised to give me leave in time for our wedding through the Christmas holidays. But I must go back." He laughed. "Unless you will marry me now. I am sure he would give me time for a short honeymoon." Taking Ellie's hand, he added, "You realize we have to postpone the trip to Paris until this is all behind us."

"Yes, we both have responsibilities here," she responded sadly. "Before you leave, will you meet with the overseer with me? There is something about that man I have never liked."

"Ellie, how can you say that about Mr. Barton?" Charlotte scolded.

"Has he been inappropriate with you?" Ted's anger started to rise.

"No, he seems to have a cruel streak, and Father is the only one who has ever been able to control him."

"Peter, send word to Mister Barton that Miss Peters and I will see him in Mister Peters' study first thing tomorrow morning." Ted's tone was sharp and obviously determined to take control. He turned to Ellie, "Are you up to a walk to the barn to check on Princess?" There was an underlying tone of authority.

"Yes, of course." She looked out the window at the setting sun. "It will be dark soon. We had better go now." She stood to leave.

"Do not stay long." Charlotte raised an eyebrow and seemed concerned.

Ellie realized her mother might have taken to Ted, but she had not forgotten his reputation. They had better not stay too long. Ted escorted Ellie out of the room, taking her hand as they went through the front door.

"We have had no time alone," he complained, pulling her closer to him.

"I have missed you terribly. You were so angry with me when you left Savannah." Ellie was feeling safe, knowing that it was feeding time in the barn and there would be a number of slaves working there.

"I could never stay angry with you for very long. I do not like being disappointed. I wanted you so passionately." He slipped his arm around her waist.

"It will not be long now." She allowed him to hold her that way until they reached the barn.

As they entered the barn, Ellie noticed Ted's frown when he saw the activity. She suppressed a chuckle. One of the grooms approached. "Miz Ellie, welcome back. Princess is in da end stall. We been keepin' up ya trainin'. Soon ya gonna be ridin' her."

Ellie walked into the stall with Ted right behind her. She started running her hands over the mare. "She seems thin," she commented with concern.

Ted pressed himself up against Ellie, reaching past her, placing both hands on the mare. "You are right; I can feel her ribs." He pressed his body against hers.

Ellie placed her hands on his and leaned back into him. She enjoyed the closeness of his body. He kissed her neck. "Tonight, Ellie. I cannot wait any longer."

"Ted, we will be married in one month." She felt the pleasure of the moment fleeing as Ted reconvened his pursuit.

"If we are married tomorrow, I will send word to my captain and be able to stay with you for a couple of weeks," he wheedled.

"Please, Ted. Everything is set for next month." She shook her head, sighing heavily.

"Then meet me tonight." He ran his hands seductively over her body.

"No! Besides, my mother suspects something. She will be on us like a hawk." She tried to push his hands away before she began to enjoy the contact too much.

"I will take care of your mother. You will beg me to bed you before I leave," he laughed wickedly into her ear as he clasped his hands on her breasts. Ellie felt his tongue licking at her ear.

"We better go back to the house," she stated, shivering and moving away from him, wondering what he meant by taking care of her mother.

"I know you want me," he purred into her ear, before he stepped back, grabbing her bottom, and then walking out of the stall. Ellie followed and they walked back to the house. When she tried taking his hand, he pulled it away and laughed.

Ellie had been right about Charlotte. If she was not present herself, Ellie found Suzanne on her heels. Ted realized he would not see Ellie later that night when Suzanne asked to sleep with Ellie, stating she was scared with the war so close; Charlotte supported her demand. Before Ellie started up to bed, Ted whispered, "We still have tomorrow."

CHAPTER 46

The next morning at breakfast, Ted appeared stern and formal. Ellie knew he was waiting for her to broach the subject of their wedding. She remained silent. They moved to the study as soon as they finished eating to wait for Philip Barton. Once the man arrived and greetings were exchanged, Ellie began asking questions. The overseer responded that there was nothing for her to worry herself with and that he was handling everything.

Finally, Ted interrupted. "You have not given Miss Peters one answer. Now, let us start over again and you will answer each question in detail." Ted sat down in John's chair.

The overseer frowned, and then provided the information that had been requested of him. Once the man finished, Ted got up and walked him to the office door. Ellie over heard Ted say, "If I hear you have treated my wife-to-be with anything but respect, it will be your last day on this farm."

Ellie smiled. She recognized that Ted had over-stepped his bounds, but she was pleased at his attempt to protect her. She did not recognize the authority, possessiveness, or control in his voice; she only saw his strength. Ted rejoined Ellie in the study and together they reviewed the books and discussed what the overseer had reported. They were interrupted by Peter announcing lunch.

Over the light meal, Ellie picked at her food. She was thinking about how nice the morning had been working with him. She did not want him to leave, but with the war going on, he would leave in two weeks anyway and her father would not be back until the end of November. Having her father at her wedding and giving her away was too important to her to give in to Ted's demands. They had already waited this long. One more month would not make any difference. She told herself the time would go by quickly. She excused herself from the table and slipped out of the house. She was feeling sad; she wanted him near and she wanted to make him happy. She headed to the barn and Princess. The barn was quiet. She started into Princess' stall, but noticed she had no hay. She pulled up her skirt, tucking it into her waistband and went up into the loft, planning to throw down hay. She was gathering loose hay when she heard the barn door open. "Ellie, are you in here?" Ted called.

"I am up in the loft," she yelled down.

She heard Ted climbing the ladder. "What are you doing up here?"

"Princess was out of hay." She shrugged, showing him the load she had forked up.

"That is what you have slaves for, my little magnolia. I do not want my wife to have calluses," he scolded her. Ellie suddenly felt like she was a mischievous child.

She did not like his attitude about work or the slaves, but chose to ignore it. They had been fighting so much that she did not want to make things worse; instead, she changed the subject. "I enjoyed working with you this morning. It was the first time we have ever worked together."

He smiled as he walked across the loft toward her. "We do make a good fit." He grabbed the pitchfork from her hand and tossed it aside. He pulled her close, wrapping one arm around her back. As he kissed her, he yanked her blouse up out of her skirt and slid his hand in. Feeling the corset, he broke the kiss. "I know other women wear these all the time, but once we are married, it will just be in my way." Seeing an expression of shock on her face, he laughed and pulled her close, lifting her into his arms. They kissed deeply as he carried her the few feet to a high mound of hay where he gently laid her down and stretched out next to her on his side. "Ellie, you have not given me an answer. If we are to marry now, I need to send out a messenger."

"Ted, I do not care about the celebration our mothers have planned. But my father...I want my father here when we marry. I do not even know where he is to send for him. It is only one month, we have waited this long."

He sat up and turned away from her. "There is no changing your mind, is there? I could have stayed with you." He sighed, and then mumbled, "You could have saved me from this battle if only you would marry me now."

"Oh, Ted, do not say such things! Stay anyway. Give them some other excuse." She felt a trickle of cold fear slide down her spine.

"There is no excuse in war," he responded, raising his voice.

She sat up and rubbed his back. "We do not even know if they will attack Port Royal." He turned and held her close. She realized for the first time that he was frightened. She wanted to make things right, to take away his fear. She started kissing his neck and whispered into his ear. "We will have a life together. I promise you."

He kissed her on the lips, slipping his tongue in as she opened her mouth to him. They slid down onto the hay side by side. He pulled her blouse up, running his hand over the corset, cupping her breast in his hand. He pushed her onto her back and kissed her chest above the corset, attempting to push her breast up and lick as much as he could reach with his tongue, pinching her nipples through the material with his fingers. She found herself responding to his caresses. She began to arch her back, offering her breasts up to him. He slid one hand down over her stomach and past the bottom of her corset. Her right arm was pinned under him and her fingers pulled at his shirt working their way under it trying to touch his skin, as her left hand pulled at the front of his shirt. She wanted to feel him. His hand slid down and grabbed her between her legs, squeezing; two thin layers of cotton were the only thing separating his fingers from her wet cavern. She could not let him go on; it was too frightening. She reached for his hand and tried pulling it away.

"I just want to touch you," he persisted.

"You will be angry when I stop you, and you will think me a tease."

He took her hand, pressing it firmly against the erection in his pants. "Feel me! It is already too late." She tried pulling her hand away, but he held it tight and rubbed it up and down his bulging pants. She felt it stiffen more. He smiled at her. "See what you do for me." He pinioned her hand with his arm and fumbled at the buttons of his pants, releasing himself from the confines of them. He wrapped her hand around his exposed penis. She had felt his engorged member pressing against her before, but not without clothing between them and not with her hand. She struggled with her fear and desire. "No, Ted! What if I got pregnant?"

"We will be married in a month. Do you think you would be the first woman to have an early baby?" He continued in his assault on her body, spreading her thighs with his knee, keeping her hands in place.

"Ted, no, please!" She hesitated to fight him physically, but she was becoming terrified by his behavior.

"I would never force you, Ellie. I will not penetrate you, but you will know what you are missing. You will moan for me every day until our wedding night, and then you will beg for me."

As he reached down to pull up her skirt, she let go of him and tried to grab his hand to stop him. He brought her hand back to his penis. "Hold it and do not let go! I am going to touch you." He pressed his fingers against her exposed mound, spreading her open.

"No..." she whimpered.

Removing his hand from her vagina, he said, "Then just hold me!" He then leaned over her, placing his mouth on hers. She responded to his kiss, holding his penis in her hand, not wanting to upset him, wanting him to forgive her for refusing him, and believing he had given up on touching her. When he felt her start to relax a little again, he slid his hand down over her belly and between her legs, slipping his fingers into the slit in her underwear. She stiffened at his touch and turned her head away from him. "You can say 'no' all you want, but I can feel how your body wants me. You cannot hide your wetness from me."

She held onto his penis, now in self-defense. He moved himself up and down in her hand. She felt his penis start to pulsate. It pumped out a thick white fluid. She saw his spent seed on her corset and dripping down on to her hand. He leaned back, letting go of her, satisfied. He licked his fingers, glaring into her eyes as he did so. She looked at her hand, not knowing what to do or where to wipe it. "It is wasted now. The one thing I wanted from you before going back to Port Royal, you denied me. But I am sure that now you will never want to deny me again." He pulled a handkerchief out of his pocket, wiped himself with it, and then handed it to her.

With a feeling of disgust and revulsion, she accepted the soiled cloth and gingerly wiped away the sticky mess. She wanted to cry, but she would never give him that satisfaction. Everything was wrong. She had refused the quick wedding. She had refused to let him take her. She felt frustrated; she felt dirty. Throughout all the years she had known him, she'd never felt she could not look at him, but now...and he was going back to fight a war the very next day.

After a few minutes, Ted stood and tucked in his limp member. He then offered Ellie a hand up. "Stand up. I will brush the hay off your back." She glanced at him briefly while he helped her up, seeing a satisfied smirk on his face. She tucked her blouse back into her skirt while Ted picked hay out of her hair. "Go on down. I will wait here until you give me an all clear."

Ellie climbed down the ladder and went into Princess' stall. No one seemed to be around; she walked back to the ladder. "You can throw down some hay for Princess and come down." She did not want to wait for him, but forced herself to stay. She felt as if she were in a fog. She scooped up the hay he had tossed down and put it in Princess' stall. "I have to go back to the house and change."

Taking her limp hand, he said, "I am glad we have had this time alone."

She looked at him with amazement and incredulity, realizing he had no idea how she was feeling. She was confused about who he really was. She sadly walked with him to the house. As she was walking up the stairs, she could hear Ted joking with Peter and ordering a scotch.

Ellie stayed in her room until dinner. By the time she came down, she had convinced herself that what had happened had been her own fault and was ashamed that she had led Ted to believe their behavior was fine before marriage. She hoped that, once they were married, their times in bed would be more pleasant. She decided it was her shame and fear that had made it so terrible. She would not let anyone know how upset she had been and she would make sure Suzanne slept in her room again. She would insure there would be no more opportunities to be alone with him until their wedding night.

Ted seemed to be in a particularly good mood. He continued drinking scotch and entertaining the women. Ellie had expected him to be disappointed in her for denying him his wishes. However, he remained gracious and complimentary to her all night. When they were about to turn in for the night, Ted grabbed her hand, and leaning in to kiss her cheek, whispered, "Do not think I am not disappointed. However, now I have a taste to hold me for the month."

Ellie refrained from cringing as she thought about him licking his fingers and forced a smile. She headed up to bed with Suzanne. She knew Ted would go back to the parlor for another scotch and, at the moment, she couldn't care less.

The next morning, breakfast was quiet. Everyone understood that Ted was leaving to protect their home and putting himself in danger. Charlotte made a couple of inane attempts to lighten the mood, but they went nowhere. She allowed the engaged couple the privacy of a good-bye. Ted kissed Ellie on the lips at the door, pinching her nipple hard. "Remember, you promised me a lifetime."

"I always keep my promises. Be careful Ted." Her sadness at his departure was genuine.

He ran down the stairs, jumped on his horse the groom had been patiently holding, and galloped down the drive and out of sight.

Ellie tried to push away the bad feeling she had once she could no longer see him. She did not understand what it was about. She still felt awful about what had happened the day before and was not sure if it was about disappointing him, misleading him, fear for him, or not being sure she wanted him. That last thought she quickly pushed aside.

When she walked back inside, Charlotte was waiting. She put her arm around her daughter. "He will be fine, Ellie." She squeezed her, not understanding the true source of her daughter's sadness. "Now, we do not want any worry lines on your face for your wedding. You are too young for that."

Ellie sighed, leaning her head on her mother's shoulder, wanting her support and wishing she could tell her the truth about her feelings and confusion. She decided to take a risk, "Mother, what was your wedding night like with Father?"

Charlotte laughed, "Is that what is bothering you?" She smiled as if remembering. "Your father was very gentle and gave me nearly a week before we.... Ted will know what to do. He has experience with... Well..." she wound down into an awkward silence.

Ellie could not imagine Ted being gentle or giving her any time at all. She tried keeping herself busy with Princess. The time dragged.

CHAPTER 47

On the fifth of November, Ellie and Suzanne took out a couple of horses. Ellie suggested they ride to the general store. Suzanne thought their mother would be angry, but she was excited about having an adventure. When they arrived, they were both surprised at how many of the townsfolk were gathered there and talking excitedly.

Word had come that Port Royal was to be the target of the Union fleet. There was talk of dozens of ships already anchored off the Sound. Ellie suddenly felt sick to her stomach. Suzanne, for the first time, showed Ellie compassion. She took her big sister's hand and led her out of the store to their horses, and then led them home. When Charlotte saw their faces, it was Suzanne who told her the news. Charlotte walked her oldest daughter to her bed and made her drink tea and brandy. She sat with her, pushing more tea down her daughter's throat until Ellie fell asleep.

The next three days, Ellie wandered the house unable to sit very long, unable to concentrate. The one thought going through her mind was, "I should have married him." On Sunday morning, the ninth of November, Charlotte insisted Ellie dress and join them in going to church. They'd had no word from the outside on what had happened and she could not let Ellie remain in a stupor any longer.

Everyone from the area was milling outside the church sharing the news. On the seventh, Port Royal had been taken by the Union. On the eighth, the Union troops walked into Beaufort unopposed, the inhabitants had fled, leaving behind a small contingent of unarmed slaves to guard their homes. Charlotte took Ellie by the arm after hearing the news and guided her to their seats. The priest led the congregation in prayers. He tried to help his parishioners through their shock and grief. He announced that the Confederacy had minimal losses considering the force they had faced. He asked all to pray for the lost souls. He had a list of the dead and wounded. He explained that it was too soon to know if it was complete, but he would read the list. Ellie hung on to her mother and listened intently. When Ted's name was not on the list, she squeezed her mother hard and tears of relief flowed.

On the seventeenth of November, the Campbells arrived as planned. John Peters had written that he would arrive on the twenty-ninth and James Peters was expected on the thirtieth. However, no one had heard anything from Ted. They had not been expecting Ted until the day before the wedding, but with no word, the tension was building. His family tried making jokes about how like Ted it was.

On the afternoon of the twentieth, as the Peters women and the Campbells were eating lunch, Peter came running in, "Miz Ellie! Miz Ellie, ya got a leddah from Marster Ted!" He handed it to her.

Ellie's hands were shaking as she opened the letter. A second page in a different hand fell out. She watched the paper flutter to the floor; confused, her heart sank. She only knew she had to read Ted's words to her. She struggle through the tears. The last lines read, "Your promise to me of a lifetime is the only thing holding me here now. You have never broken a promise to me yet. I will always love you. Ted."

Anderson Campbell was sitting next to Ellie. He had picked up the page that had fallen. He read the sheet silently as Ellie read the one to her from his brother. The family watched as Anderson's eyes filled up and understood that Ted was no longer. Anderson put his arm around the woman he had expected to become his sister-in-law. "I am sorry, Ellie. The first mate of his ship says he fought bravely, but was shot and knocked over board with the impact. They searched after the fighting stopped, but were not able to find his body."

Ellie looked into Anderson's eyes. "But I promised him a lifetime."

Agnes cried out, "No! Not my baby boy!" Thomas held his wife rocking her as she sobbed.

"It is my fault. If I had married him when he wanted me to, he would not have been there. I never gave him the one thing he wanted. It is my fault."

Anderson looked at his wife. He could no longer hold back his own tears, but held Ellie as she cried.

CHAPTER 48

"Jillian! Jillian, I've been looking all over for you." When Jillian did not respond, Joan tapped her shoulder. Jillian jumped, startled, and turned around on the bench where she was sitting. She looked blankly at Joan, confused, with no apparent recognition. Joan walked around the bench and sat down next to her. "Are you all right?"

Jillian shook her head as if to clear it. "I...I guess I must have.... Yes, I just feel a little dazed."

"Have you been crying?" Joan enquired with concern.

Jillian reached up and felt the tears on her cheeks. "I was thinking about..." she hesitated knowing Ted was the wrong name, "about Drake."

Joan's instincts told her Jillian was not just talking about being away from her husband. "We all go through difficult times in our marriages." She patted the younger woman's hand. "Come on, we need to get started for Savannah. We have a long day scheduled for tomorrow."

Jillian was still feeling confused, but stood and followed the other woman to the car. She fumbled with the door handle, and then got into the passenger seat. Joan did not push Jillian, but turned on the car radio for the drive back to Savannah. Once there, Jillian went straight to her hotel room and pulled the hand-mirror out of her carry-on bag. She sat on the bed, following the design with her fingers. Noticing the message light flashing on the phone, she reached over to retrieve it. She heard Drake's voice sounding mildly concerned, yet jovial. "I've been trying to reach your cell. Where are you, my little magnolia?" She mumbled to herself in shock, "Ted?" Then she pushed seven for the replay. After listening two more times, she saved the message and hung up. She looked at the magnolias engraved on the back of the mirror, tracing her finger over the pattern. *Am I keeping my promise after all? I'd better call him.*

Jillian took the cell phone out of her purse and only then realized she had forgotten to charge it. She plugged it in. After listening to one message from Drake, she held the four-button for home. The machine picked up. "Hi! I'm back at the hotel. My battery had gone dead, but it's on the charger now. Call me back!"

She wasn't surprised when he didn't call back and was actually relieved. She wasn't sure if she was ready to talk to him anyway.

Monday was a busy workday. She was happy to lose herself in something she understood. She missed his call Monday night, while she was out to dinner, and did not call back. Tuesday and Wednesday went by quickly with long hours. Drake and Jillian played phone tag, but never connected. Thursday morning, Mr. Johnson announced that if they worked straight through until 7:00 PM, they could make a 9:30 flight out and all be home by midnight. Friday would end up being a free day.

Jillian called home around 11:00 AM, planning to leave a message for Drake about the change in travel plans. Instead of reaching the machine, Drake groggily answered the phone. "Yeah?"

"Drake? I thought I'd get the machine! What are you doing home? No, don't tell me now. I'll be home around midnight tonight. We can talk then." Her stomach began churning with anxiety.

"Okay, Sweetie," he mumbled and hung up before she could say any more. Jillian sat listening to the dial tone for several seconds. She was fuming, but pushed her feelings down, determined to focus on completing the day's work.

A tired team boarded the plane for Cincinnati that evening. Jillian and Joan were seated together again. It was the first time Jillian allowed herself to feel anything since the earlier phone call. She was getting angrier with each passing moment, and confused by the odd experience she'd had. Her agitation was evident to anyone who cared to look.

"Would you like to talk about it?" Joan asked her.

"What?" Jillian asked, startled out of her reverie. "I'm sorry. I didn't hear your question." She tried to smile at Joan, but did a poor job of it.

"I couldn't help but notice you seem upset. I wondered if you'd like to talk about it," she explained. She tilted her head and waited to see if Jillian would take the opportunity to unburden herself.

Jillian shrugged and waved her hands helplessly. "It's nothing, really. I called home this morning to leave a message for my husband, telling him I'd be coming home early. It was the middle of the morning. He should have been at work, but he was in bed, sleeping."

"Oh. Well, I guess he was sick. I hope he's feeling better." Joan looked at Jillian, waiting to hear the rest of the story.

Jillian realized that she would have to explain further. There was no reason to be upset if Drake was only home with a cold. "I really don't think he's sick. I think he's lost his job. We didn't talk. I guess I didn't want to hear the bad news, so I told him we'd talk when I got home."

Joan's face showed her sympathy for her coworker. "That's rough. But you're making good money now. You should be okay until he can get another job."

Jillian nodded. "We'll be okay, financially. But I'm not so sure how we'll be emotionally. This isn't the first time he's lost a job, or even the fifth. Drake has a history of getting fired from jobs. He can't seem to hold on to them for longer than a few months at a time. Oh, he always finds another one, but they never last." Tears started in her eyes. "He always has some excuse. I used to believe him when he said his boss was a jerk or they were mistreating him in some way. But I don't believe that every boss in the world is a jerk or mistreats his employees. If he were a good worker, his boss would want to keep him happy. ...I don't know what to do about it. It just keeps happening." Her lip quivered with the need to cry out her frustration and helplessness.

Joan fished a tissue out of her pocket and offered it to Jillian. "I'm sorry you're going through this. You must be feeling so frustrated and lost. Have you sought some help, some professional counseling or pastoral counseling?"

Jillian shook her head. "Drake would never agree to that. Besides, it's always someone else's fault as far as he's concerned." She shrugged again.

"Well, maybe you should think about going to see someone for yourself. You could use the support. It could help you figure out what it is you want to do. At least, it's some place to go where you won't be judged whatever choice you make."

"I don't know. I'm not sure what I want or need to do right now. I just know I can't take much more of this." She dabbed at her eyes and wiped her nose with the tissue, and then wadded it up and stuffed it into her pocket.

"You have to do what feels comfortable for you, of course. But if you decide you would like to see someone, let me know. I have a list of therapists that take our insurance. I could give you a couple names of people near you." She smiled encouragingly and patted Jillian's hand.

"Thanks. I'll keep it in mind. And thank you for listening to me complain," she returned the smile. Joan seemed to understand that Jillian needed to think things over quietly and let her complete the flight undisturbed. When they had collected their luggage at the airport, Joan gave her a quick hug and wished her good luck at home.

CHAPTER 49

As she rode home in the shuttle, Jillian knew she should be exhausted, but she was still wound up, even after her talk with Joan. He'd obviously lost another job, probably due to his drinking. She started to blame herself. If only she had been there; then she reminded herself that he'd lost plenty of jobs, even when she was there to hold his hand. But he was alive. They would still have a chance.

She fumbled with her key in the front door, wondering what she would find. It was worse than she could have imagined. There were dirty dishes, empty beer cans, and dirty clothes all over the house. Drake was sprawled out on the couch with a beer can in his hand, watching Jay Leno on TV. "Sweetie, you're home! I've been waiting up for you."

"What happened here? It looks like a tornado hit!" Jillian started collecting dishes.

"That can wait. Come here and give me a kiss!" He leaned forward, opening his arms to embrace her without getting up from the couch.

Jillian ignored him and kept piling up dishes. When she carried them into the kitchen, she reacted. "Dear Lord in Heaven, Drake, what have you been doing?"

"It can wait until tomorrow. Come here!" Jillian could hear the impatience gathering in his voice.

Jillian walked back to the living room, too drained to face the mess and knowing there were more important things to deal with now. She sighed as she sat down on a chair facing him. "Drake, what happened to your job?"

"Those idiots tried cheating me. Can you believe it? I've made more money for them than anyone else there in the first month alone. And they had the nerve to tell me they were not going to give me a draw against future commissions anymore. So, I walked out." He gestured broadly with the beer can, sloshing beer on his lap and the couch. Jillian squeezed her eyes closed and prayed for patience.

"How much time did you miss?" she demanded quietly.

"Now you're sounding like them. Whose side are you on anyway?" He sat forward on the couch again, leaning toward her, challenging her.

"Drake, you've been drinking. Did you even go in to work while I was away?"

"Of course I did. This has nothing to do with drinking. Don't worry about it, Sweetie. I'll get another job. I always do, and the next one won't be for a bunch of crooks." He flashed his best smile at her. "I've missed you. You must be terribly tired. Let's go to bed. We can talk more tomorrow." He struggled to his feet, wobbling a bit as he waved her toward the bedroom.

Jillian was about to continue arguing, but she was tired and maybe she was meant to help him. "You're right. Let's get some sleep." She sighed and stood up.

Drake turned off the TV and she turned off the lights behind them. As she entered the bedroom, she saw more of the same kind of mess. When Drake grabbed her bottom, she said, "Not tonight!"

"Aw, come on, Sweetie. You've been gone so long. I need you, baby." He clutched at her, wrapping his arms around her from behind. She could smell the beer on his breath as he murmured in her ear, "You've been away for nearly two weeks. I know you want me, too." He reached up and squeezed her breast, humming appreciatively as he did so.

Jillian pushed him off of her, protesting, "Please, Drake, not tonight. I'm tired."

He came up behind her again and ripped her blouse out from her skirt. Pulling her against him, he reached up and grabbed her breast once more. He pinched her nipple hard, and when she flinched he said, "I know how your body reacts to me." She could feel him rubbing his incipient erection against her.

The memory of Ted in the barn came into her mind. She immediately felt the shame and anger of that assault once more. "Not again! Take your hands off of me," she demanded, struggling to get away from him.

"Fine!" He let go, turned, grabbed his keys, and stormed out of the apartment, slamming the front door behind him.

Jillian locked the bedroom door, stripped, and started the shower. She stood there crying, letting the water flow over her body until there was no more hot water and it was nearly ice cold. She crawled into bed, physically and emotionally exhausted, but unable to fall asleep. She needed to know he was safe. She finally heard the front door open and close, and then the TV went back on. She guessed he had bought more beer at the All Night Pony Keg and was probably sitting on the couch drinking it. She was relieved; he'd probably pass out and never even discover she had locked him out of the bedroom.

CHAPTER 50

Jillian woke with a start shortly after nine. She figured Drake would still be sleeping and she didn't want to talk to him until he'd had plenty of time to sleep off his beer and wake up. She dressed and slipped out of the house without even a cup of coffee. She headed for Starbucks. While waiting in a long line, she debated with herself where she was going to go. The place was packed with business people and friends meeting. She really wanted someplace quiet where she could think. She ordered a latte with two sugars in the raw and an iced lemon pound cake to go. By the time her drink was ready, she had decided on Eden Park. The drive would only be another fifteen minutes from the Starbucks. There was so much to sort out; she hadn't even begun to figure out what Ted had to do with Drake or what the whole thing had been about.

She had no difficulty finding a good parking space. Being a Friday morning in late October, it was not very crowded. She took her latte and lemon pound cake and found a peaceful spot to sit. It was chilly, but her heavy sweater kept her sufficiently warm. As she sat on the bench in Mt. Adams, looking down at the distant Ohio River, she found herself reviewing what she knew about Ellie and Ted. She wished Anna wasn't at work; she needed to talk to someone to help her figure it out. Was it a fantasy, a hallucination? Was she crazy or was Anna right about reincarnation? It was something she had never seriously considered before. She thought about what Charlotte had said about sex with John. She had implied that men could be gentle and patient; that certainly had not been her experience with Drake. She wondered what her own mother would say. Her girlfriends always talked as if sex was something they enjoyed. She had always believed something was wrong with her. The only parts she enjoyed were how engaging Drake could be before and knowing how happy it made him. She liked the way he used to touch her before they'd ever had sex, except when he hurt her nipples. She knew she could not talk to her mother. She didn't even know how to ask anything of Anna or Sally without giving away her secret. It was bad enough that they both knew about Drake's drinking. She was starting to regret she'd never gone all the way with anyone before him. She had no basis for comparison. Ted had treated her sexually the same way Drake had. At least, Drake hadn't chased women. She knew he'd had sex before they'd met, but certainly not since they'd been together. And other than the lottery or an occasional football game, he wasn't a big gambler. After all, everyone played the lottery, she rationalized. If she could get him to stop drinking, she could save him yet. When she realized it was already nearly one, she decided to go home and talk with her husband.

Drake was up and about when Jillian arrived home. He had made a pot of coffee and consumed most of it, leaving the nearly empty pot to scorch on the machine. There were the remnants of a new sandwich on the coffee table. As she looked around, she saw that he had done nothing to even start cleaning up his mess. She heard the sound of the shower in their bathroom. Sighing, she walked into the bedroom just as he turned off the shower. She sat on the bed, staring at the bathroom door, waiting for him to emerge.

He came out with one towel wrapped around his waist and another that he was rubbing through his hair to dry it. He didn't see her immediately and was startled when he did.

"Where've you been? I woke up and no one was here. I figured you went to work." He dropped the wet towels and began rummaging through the dresser looking for clean shorts and socks.

"I have the day off. It's a reward I got for hard work," Jillian told him.

"Is that supposed to be some kind of comment about my quitting my job?" Drake glared at her through bloodshot eyes.

"No. I wasn't being sarcastic. I want peace, Drake. I want us both to get along, to be happy." Jillian shook her head in frustration. This wasn't going as she wanted. She needed to break through Drake's defensiveness so they could work out the problem.

Drake pulled on his shorts and sat on a chair to put on his socks. She could see he was still brooding.

"We need to talk this out, Drake. You've...we've got a problem. You can't keep bouncing from job to job like this. I know you don't want to hear it, but your drinking is becoming a real problem. I'm really frightened about what's going to happen to you, to us, if you don't stop." She looked at him, pleading for him to listen and to understand.

"I can get another job. I always do. It'll be better this time. I don't have a drinking problem. So I drink a little. A man has a right to a couple of beers after a long day, especially when he puts up with so much crap in his life. Just stop worrying about it so much. Everything is under control," he told her, leaning forward with his elbows on his knees.

"It's not under control, Drake," Jillian responded, trying to keep her voice calm and reasonable. "You can't keep a job. You can't go even one day without drinking too much. And you and I are fighting all the time. Can't you see how out of control it all is?" She felt herself becoming more agitated, but couldn't stop it.

"You worry too much. You're always blaming me for the problems we have. If you didn't nag me all the time, there wouldn't be any problem. And it doesn't help that you're so damned frigid, either." He stood up and grabbed a pair of jeans, pulling them on.

"I'm not frigid!" she exclaimed, stung by the accusation.

"What do you call it when you won't go to bed with me? Or when you just lay there like a dead fish. You have no idea how to please a real man. I swear to God, I don't know why I stay with you. I could have any woman I wanted, but I always come home to sweet little Jillian, thinking this time she'll make me feel welcome, make me feel like a man instead of a bad little boy!" He pulled on a tee shirt and reached for a sweater, pulling that on too. He pushed his feet into his well-worn cowboy boots.

"Why would I make you feel welcome when you come home drunk in the middle of the night and begin pawing me? You don't make love to me! You just use me to masturbate with, and then pass out. You get yours and the hell with me! The question should be, why do I stay with you?" As soon as the words were out of her mouth, she wished she could call them back. She saw the quick flash of hurt on his face that was swiftly covered by anger. "Oh, God, Drake, I'm sorry!" She reached out to him, wanting to soothe the hurt she had inflicted.

"That's too damned bad. I'm out of here." He brushed past her, pushing her back onto the bed. Grabbing his coat and keys, he stormed out of the apartment.

"Oh, damn it!" she moaned as she watched him leave. "Why couldn't I keep my big mouth shut?" Retrieving the wet towels off the floor, she hung them in the bathroom while she berated herself for escalating the situation. It hadn't been what she wanted. She really wanted to make peace. But Drake had said some very hurtful things, and he didn't even have the excuse of being drunk at the time.

Jillian picked up a garbage bag and started collecting his garbage. *Once again, I'm left to clean up the mess while he goes off to soothe himself in a bar somewhere. ...What am I doing? He can clean it up himself. I'm getting out of here. Anna should be home from work soon.* Throwing down the garbage bag, she grabbed a jacket, her purse and keys, and left the house.

CHAPTER 51

She arrived at the Ward home before either Anna or John was back from work. She parked in the driveway and closed her eyes, trying to clear her head, but the afternoon's fight kept replaying in her head. After about fifteen minutes, a tap on the window startled her out of her reverie.

"You're back early. Come on in." Jillian got out of her car and followed Anna into the house. Anna understood something had to be wrong, but knew Jillian would share it in her own time. As they walked into the house, Anna said, "How about starting a salad while I change?"

"Sure!" Jillian went into her friend's kitchen and started pulling ingredients out of the refrigerator. She was still washing the vegetables when Anna joined her.

"Hey! I like the way you've fixed your hair. I've never seen you wear it that way before," Anna complimented her friend.

"Huh? I didn't do anything different." Jillian was confused by the comment and patted her hair with a wet hand.

Shrugging, Anna let it go. "When did you get back?" she asked as she set the temperature on the oven.

"Last night. ...Drake lost his job. Another one down the toilet." She bit her lip and tore a chunk of lettuce in half, dropping the pieces into the bowl.

"Oh, Jillian, I'm sorry to hear that. I was really hoping he'd show us all that he was finally starting to grow up. Do you know what happened?"

"He gave me the same song and dance, pouting about them not appreciating him, but…"

"Was he drinking while you were away?" Anna asked when her friend shrugged.

Jillian laughed humorlessly. "Anna, you wouldn't believe the apartment. It's a disaster area. And to answer your question, there are enough empty beer cans for an army to have been there."

John came in through the garage door. "Jilly, I didn't know you were coming for dinner. Is Drake here, too?"

Jillian snapped, "No!"

Anna explained, "Drake lost another job while Jillian was in Savannah."

"I'm sorry to hear that. I really like Drake; he's always a lot of fun. I wish I could tell a joke the way he does, but Jillian... well, let's just say, I wouldn't let him within ten feet of either of my sisters."

"Why not?" Jillian enquired. She was more confused than angered by his comment.

"You don't need to hear the list from me. You already know it. I just want you to know, we're both here for you, anytime." He started pulling off his tie. "I'm going to change."

The two women worked on dinner together, keeping the conversation on the food preparations. John returned just in time to help them carry the dishes into the dining room. Conversation throughout dinner remained light. Both Anna and John had questions about Savanna and her trip. Anna probed her for details of the historic district, adding that she'd always wanted to visit the place. When they finished eating, John volunteered to do clean up. "You two go ahead and visit. I'm just going to go on-line after I straighten out the kitchen." He started cleaning the table. Wanting to make Jillian feel somewhat better, he turned back to her, "Jilly, the new hair style looks good on you."

"Thanks, John." Again, Jillian was puzzled by the compliment. Anna stood, smiling, "Coffee in the pallor, Jillian?"

She joked back, "By all means, but if you'd excuse me for a moment?" Jillian went into the half-bath off the front hall. As she washed her hands, she looked up into the mirror, wondering what her friends had meant about her hair. She was shocked to see it was arranged the same way as Ellie wore her hair during the day.

Jillian was dazed as she walked into the living room to join Anna for coffee. As she sat down on the couch, she heard Anna say, "You look like you just saw a ghost."

"I guess you could say I did. ...Anna, I don't want you to think I'm crazy, but I have something to tell you, something that happened to me while I was in Savannah." Jillian hesitated.

Anna looked at her friend, immediately concerned. "My God, Jilly, what was it? You look so...freaked out!" She moved over to sit next to her friend on the couch.

"You and I talked on the phone about past lives and reincarnation. You were the one who put this in my head! Anna, I think I saw myself in a previous life; one that took place in South Carolina during the Civil War." She looked at her friend to see how she was responding to this news. When Anna didn't appear offended or ready to call for a straight jacket for her, Jillian proceeded to tell her about what she had "seen" in the past. She told her friend about the relationship with Ted and how she believed Drake had been Ted. The only part she left out was the sexual abuse. She was too ashamed of that to share it, and feared Anna's disapproval. "Ted promised that he would not sleep with any other women if I married him, and I promised to spend my life with him. I think that might be what I'm doing now, with Drake; trying to keep him alive, trying to save him from destroying himself again."

She paused to look at Anna again. "So, what do you think? Am I crazy?" She smiled weakly, fearing what might come next.

Anna sighed heavily, as if she had been holding her breath, and shook her head. "Oh no, Jilly, I don't think you're crazy. Not at all. It would explain a lot about your relationship with Drake. And it helps me to understand a bit more of why Drake is the way he is. You know I've believed in reincarnation for a long time. It must have been an unnerving experience for you, seeing all these things, getting so much of that life back all at once. Are you all right with it?" She reached over and took her friend's hand.

"I guess I am. It's an awful lot to take in all at once. I'm not sure how much of it is real. But it feels real. I was there. It was all happening to me. Even though I didn't look the same, I knew it was me and I know that Ted was Drake. I can't prove any of it, but I know with all my being that it's true. But how does that change the present?"

She looked so forlorn that Anna hugged her. "The knowledge doesn't change the present, it only helps to put it into better perspective. If you are trying to fix something in this life that happened in that one, you can decide whether you want or need to do so now. You didn't cause Ted's death and you could not have kept him alive when it was his time to die. And you can't keep Drake alive by staying with him. Ted said he didn't get drunk when you were around, but he did get drunk when you weren't around. Drake doesn't stop himself from getting drunk when you are around. It seems that his problem is getting worse in this life. He needs to find a way to change himself. You can't do that for him. We all have lessons to learn in each life; no one can do these things for us. So you need to understand what it is you're supposed to learn from that life and this one, and grow from that lesson."

"But what is the lesson?" Jillian asked, plaintively. "Am I supposed to be here to save Drake from dying? Do I owe him the life that Ted and I never had because I didn't marry him? Am I supposed to help Drake stop his drinking and self-destruction? Was that what I was supposed to do for Ted? ...I'm so confused by all of this." She scrubbed at her face with her hands.

"Drake has made a real mess of his life, and is steadily messing up yours. Whether you stay with him or go, you need to find ways to take care of you more. If you keep on rescuing him, he's never going to learn to do it for himself. He's never going to have to be an independent, functional adult, Jilly. You have to let him grow up or blow up, so that he is taking responsibility for his life even if he shares it with you." Anna grasped Jillian by the chin, turning her friend's face toward her. "You aren't doing him any favors by not allowing him to experience the consequences of his choices in life. Even, if you are the best choice he ever made." She smiled at her friend to take the sting out of her words.

Jillian smiled back with a bit more certainty. "I know you're right. I just want us to be happy together. I want a partner, not a child. I know he has it in him, if he'd just dig down for it instead of taking the easy way out and running away from responsibility all the time. Oh, well. I'd better get going. There's more than one mess waiting for me at home." She laughed at her predicament and hugged her friend. "Thanks for dinner and for listening. I'm glad you're here in this lifetime."

"My pleasure. Keep me posted, and we'll have to do lunch soon." She walked her friend to the front door and watched her walk to her car.

As Jillian was leaving, Anna called after her, "Don't clean up the house! He's got to start cleaning up his own messes sometime."

Jillian gave her friend a thumbs up. She was pleased when she pulled up at their apartment building and saw that Drake's pickup was there. For once, he was the one doing the waiting. She walked in feeling a little smug.

CHAPTER 52

"Where have you been? I was afraid you left. What kind of game do you think you're playing? You take off for nearly two weeks, and then you have the nerve to turn me out of our bed. Where did you take off to?" He had been drinking again.

Jillian found her brief moment of happiness fly rapidly out the door, replaced by the anger and resentment she had been fighting off. "How's it feel to wait? To wait and not know if I am ever coming back? That's what I go through with you all the time."

"You're not putting the blame for this on me. You could have called to tell me what you were doing. I came home and there was no dinner. The place is a pigsty, and you're off playing around who knows where. You nag me about being grown up and responsible. Were you being responsible taking off like that?" Drake got closer and closer to Jillian throughout his tirade. By the time he stopped ranting, he was standing nose to nose with her. Jillian felt frightened, but was determined not to back down from him.

"You were the one who took off first. And I don't think you were going out to a job interview in jeans and your ratty old cowboy boots, unless they're interviewing at the bars these days. You think I should sit around the house and make dinner for you? I'm the one paying for the dinner, unless you forgot that part. As for this place being a pigsty, what pig got it that way? It sure as hell wasn't me. So, if you're hungry, cook something. And if you don't like how dirty this place is, clean it up. But don't you dare tell me that I'm the irresponsible party in this relationship!" Jillian stood her ground and stared Drake down. She could hear her heart pounding fiercely in her chest as she watched her husband clench and unclench his fists. The thought crossed her mind that he was going to punch her, even though he had never engaged in that kind of abuse before.

"You think you're so damned high and mighty, don't you. Too good for me. You're nothing, bitch. Nothing! I keep coming home to you, even when you treat me like crap. But are you grateful? Do you appreciate me? Hell no! I'm warning you, Jillian. One of these days, I won't come home to you to be abused and criticized!"

"And I'm warning you. If things don't change around here soon, I won't be here for you to come home to. Then what will you do? Who's going to buy your groceries and cook them for you? Who's going to clean up your multiple messes while you go out and get drunk? I mean it, Drake. I can't take much more of this!" She turned away from him and kicked an empty beer can across the room.

"There's no point in talking to you. I'm going to bed." He stomped out of the room. Jillian grabbed a blanket and curled up on the couch.

CHAPTER 53

Jillian awoke to the smell of coffee brewing and the sound of water running in the kitchen. She stretched, feeling stiff from sleeping on the couch, and went into the bathroom. After brushing her teeth, she got out of the previous day's clothes, showered, and threw on a sweatshirt and clean jeans. By the time she made it to the kitchen, the coffee was waiting and the dishwasher was running. Drake was collecting the empty beer cans to add to the blue recycle bin. Jillian poured her coffee and sat at the table. She fumbled through two weeks of unopened newspapers looking for the most recent. She heard the front door, and then Drake showed up handing her Saturday morning's paper. "You don't want the old ones, do you?"

"No, there are too many to catch up on." She hid a smile, thinking, *He knows he's really in the dog house this time. He's even separating the recyclables. I'm not going to help him. Anna's right. Let him clean up his own mess.* She continued to ignore him and to read the paper, but was having difficulty concentrating. There just didn't seem to be anything of interest. She refilled her coffee cup and looked at the pile of dirty dishes; she hadn't realized that they owned so many dishes. It would take at least two more loads. She took the cordless phone off the charger, went into the living room, plopped down on the couch, and put her feet up on the cocktail table. Drake continued to clean. She was enjoying this. She called her mother. "Hi! I'm back, safe and sound." Her father had picked up the extension and she proceeded to tell them about Savannah and the business portion of her trip.

Once she got off the phone, Drake said, "I have to wait for the dishwasher to finish, so I thought I'd go to the market. I'm afraid there's no food left in the house."

Accepting his efforts at cleaning up the place as an implicit apology, Jillian decided to be gracious. "Why don't we go to I-HOP, and then go to the store together?"

Drake seemed relieved. "My treat."

She restrained herself from making a nasty comment and quickly made out a grocery list. He opened the passenger door of his pickup for her and bowed as she got in. She had a brief flash of Ted handling Charlotte. I-HOP was crowded, but they did not have to wait long for a table. Jillian found herself observing as Drake cajoled the waitress to get his special order. Jillian just went with her usual.

While they waited, Drake entertained Jillian with wild tales of the lives of the other customers. He kept her giggling until the food arrived. Drake picked up the check, and then they headed for Kroger's. He pushed the cart as she loaded it up. He made no comment when she by-passed the beer. Jillian used their ATM card at the checkout.

They stopped briefly at Blockbuster and picked up a couple of videos. Upon returning home, they maintained a sense of normality and laughter as they put the groceries away. No mention of the previous night's fight was made.

Jillian maintained her determination to let Drake finish cleaning up his mess. She informed him that she needed time to organize herself for Monday after having been away. She had a hard time not suggesting to him that he continue to wash and clean. Yet, she wanted to see if he would do it on his own. She went into the bedroom and started unpacking; she could hear him unloading the dishwasher. When she came out of the bedroom carrying the laundry basket, he grabbed it from her and started adding his own things that were strewn around the apartment. He started the wash, and then went back to re-load the dishwasher. It was late in the afternoon before he finished vacuuming. When she heard him in the kitchen starting dinner, she decided it was time to join him and offer to help.

She enjoyed it when they worked on something together. They seemed to have a rhythm that flowed. She liked the feel of being his partner. They seemed to be at their best as friends. It occurred to her that was when Ellie and Ted had been at their best: as friends. Their difficulties began when the relationship changed.

After dinner, they popped in a DVD and curled up on the couch together. Drake maintained a running monologue making fun of the acting. Jillian giggled in agreement. During the second movie, the two fell asleep, arms and legs intertwined. In the middle of the night, Jillian woke as Drake lifted her off the couch. She rested her head on his shoulder as he carried her into bed. They struggled out of their clothes and slipped under the covers. Drake wrapped himself around her and they slept.

CHAPTER 54

Sunday morning, Jillian made coffee and, as it finished brewing, Drake appeared in the kitchen. She poured two cups and placed one in front of him at the table. She sat with her coffee and the Sunday paper, sorting the sections. When she looked up to hand the sports section to Drake, she saw that his hands were shaking as he attempted to sip his coffee, nearly spilling it. Jillian felt as though she had been slapped in the face. While she had admitted that her husband drank too much, she had always defended him when friends or family called him alcoholic. The angry moods, the fights, the job losses, the money problems, the frequency and the amounts of alcohol that he consumed, and now the shakes: she could deny it no longer. "Drake, your hands are shaking," she said with concern.

"I just need some food. Didn't we buy a coffee cake yesterday?"

Jillian got up and cut him a piece, thinking how strange it was that he would ask for cake. He rarely ate sweets. As she handed him the plate, she watched it wobble until he put it on the table. She was going to cut a piece for herself, but suddenly lost her appetite. "You can't go on like this; we can't go on like this."

"What are you saying?" he asked, having trouble focusing on her words.

"The alcohol." Her voice became shaky. "It's going to kill you."

"Please, Jillian, don't start on that."

"I don't want to lose you. I'm afraid you'll die on me." In her mind, she added, *Again.*

"Don't be ridiculous. My drinking is not that bad," he denied, getting defensive.

"You've been lucky so far. How many times have you driven home drunk? Look at your hands! You've got to stop." She started crying.

"Jillian, I can stop anytime. If it means that much to you, I'll prove it to you."

"Oh, Drake, would you really stop for me?" She wiped her tears away, looking at him with so much fear and hope in her eyes.

"I don't like to see you so upset. I'll show you; it's no big deal." He leaned over to hug her.

Jillian thought, *Since when?* But she held her tongue. "If you want, I'll go to counseling or AA with you. Whatever will help!"

He released her, sitting back, rejecting her offer. "I don't need help. I told you it's no big deal."

"Are you sure? We have insurance. I could make an appointment." She reached toward him, willing him to accept the offer of help.

"I'm not going to counseling." He was starting to get annoyed, and then relaxed, reaching across the table to take her hand. "Don't worry, Jilly. I'll be fine."

She could feel his hands shaking as they held hers. She started crying again. Drake stood and walked behind her. He rubbed her shoulders and kissed the back of her neck. The chills it gave her stopped the crying. This was the good side of Drake, the side she loved, vulnerable, gentle, and caring about her feelings.

"Let's go dancing tonight!" he suggested, quickly changing the subject, hoping to influence her with his optimism.

"Are you sure you're feeling up to it," she asked, tentatively, wanting to believe that he was.

"I'll be fine," he reassured her again, squeezing her shoulders and kissing the top of her head.

"We will have to go early. I need to get up early tomorrow. I'm sure, after being away two weeks, there's a ton of paperwork and messages piled up for me," she stated, feeling more positive and excited about the idea.

"That's tomorrow. Let's enjoy today together." Drake sounded very excited by the plan as well. There was a new heartiness in his voice.

"Okay!" She took one of his hands and kissed it, leaning her head back against his body.

They went out early for a nice Thai food dinner, nothing fancy, but not fast food take out. Drake was entertaining and charming. Jillian couldn't help but think that the old Drake, the one she fell in love with, was still there. *If he just stays away from the booze, he's so great!* she thought, smiling at him. He kept her laughing through dinner and through the drive to the Tri-County Dance Club. They went through the movements of the quadrilles, reels, schottisches, and gallops. Jillian was breathless when Drake suggested they sit down for a while. He offered to get her a drink and walked away to the bar. Jillian tensed, waiting for him to return with a beer or something stronger in his hand, but he surprised her, returning with two diet sodas. She was so delighted that he hadn't chosen to drink alcohol that she kissed him a bit more passionately than he might have anticipated.

"What was that for? Not that I'm complaining," he asked her, surprised.

"Just because I love you so much and I'm having such a wonderful time with you tonight," she told him, leaning in to rub her nose against his. They sat in companionable silence, watching the other couples dancing. Drake put his arm around her and Jillian leaned her head against his shoulder.

When a waltz was announced, Drake stood, took Jillian's hand and bowed. "May I have the pleasure of this dance, my little magnolia?" he drawled.

"I would be delighted, sir," Jillian responded, rising from her seat. As they swirled around the floor, Jillian had the strangest experience for just a moment. She seemed to see Ted's face smiling at her, overlaid onto Drake's. The experience caused her to miss a step and Drake pulled her close to keep her from falling.

"Are you all right?" he asked. Jillian was usually very light on her feet.

"Just a little tired, I guess," she covered.

"Do you want to stop? We could go home," Drake offered, concerned for her.

"I want to finish this waltz with you, first," Jillian demurred, smiling.

"If you're sure," He stated, waiting for her to nod her readiness before whirling her around and continuing the dance. Jillian loved the feeling of floating as they moved around the room, swaying with the music. She thought this was the happiest moment she had had in a very long time and wished it could continue forever. But the dance ended, and so did the evening.

On the ride home Jillian found herself staring at Drake's profile, mentally comparing it to Ted's as she recalled it. She had to admit that they looked nothing alike, yet she had no doubt that Drake had been Ted. When they got inside the apartment, Drake asked her what had her in such a pensive mood.

"You'll think I'm crazy, and you might be right," she laughed weakly.

"I promise not to think you're crazy...well, not too crazy anyway. Tell me," he invited.

Jillian went into the bedroom and brought out the mirror she had bought at the auction. She told him about the dream of him as a redhead and explained that she felt drawn to the mirror. She thought it held some significance for her. Jillian hesitated to tell him her belief that they had been together in another life; however, she told him about her experience while sitting in the lobby of the bed and breakfast in Savannah.

"It was so real. I could see all these people wearing clothing from the nineteenth century. I could hear the music playing. It was real enough to touch it. And it felt like I had been there before," she told him.

"Sounds kind of weird, Jilly. You don't really think you were seeing the past, do you? I mean...are we talking ghosts or time travel?" he laughed, obviously thinking she was joking. "You must have seen the house in a movie or something. They're always using those old places to make movies. That kind of stuff just isn't real. Come on. Let's go to bed. You said yourself that you have to get up early tomorrow," he held out his hand to help pull her up off the couch. She took his hand and allowed him to pull her up. He put his arm around her shoulders and walked her into the bedroom.

Jillian was disappointed by his reaction. She had wanted to tell him about Ted and Ellie, but decided against it. There were things about Ted that might just have upset him. Maybe it was better if he didn't know. When he started kissing her neck and running his fingers around her neckline, slipping them into the top of her dress, she gave up talking and let the tingling take over. He followed the line drawn by his fingers with his tongue. He reached behind her and unzipped her dress, smoothly unhooking her bra with one hand. He reached up and pulled her dress and bra strap off one shoulder, exposing her breast. He began sucking on her nipple. She tensed, preparing herself for the pain, expecting him to bite down, but this time he did not. She relaxed again once he let go of her breast. He quickly stripped off his own clothes. She started pulling her dress up over her head. "No. Leave it on!" He pulled her panties and stockings off, pushing her down on the bed. He climbed onto her, pushing his way in. For the first time in a long time, it didn't hurt; she enjoyed the feeling of him. To her disappointment, he came quickly and collapsed on her. She held him and was grateful that he was not drunk and enjoyed the memory of dancing with him. Once she was sure he was asleep, she rolled out from under him and undressed, and then slipped back into bed. She smiled as she drifted off to sleep, believing that this was a new beginning.

CHAPTER 55

Monday morning, Drake got up and had coffee with her before she left for work. He opened the employment section of the paper and started marking possibilities. He indicated he would also be going on-line to search. Jillian left for work hopeful. Her day passed quickly. She returned home to the smells of dinner cooking.

Each day seemed to be going better to Jillian. She was enjoying her work and feeling she was concentrating better than she had in a long time. Drake was enthusiastic about a number of job possibilities. Jillian looked forward each night to getting home to be with him. She did not stop anywhere on her way home. By Thursday night, he had set an interview for Friday and three for the next week.

Friday morning, Jillian left for work looking forward to the weekend. It had been a week since Drake had any alcohol and he had job interviews lined up. As she drove in, she thought about how fortunate they were to find each other again. She felt satisfied with herself that she had done the right thing this time around. She was saving him, even if it was only from himself. She was making good on her promise. She hoped that, with his new attitude, he would feel differently about her family and be willing to go to her parents for Thanksgiving. However, if he was not ready, they would have their own Thanksgiving at home.

Jillian called Anna to see if she could meet for lunch; she was excited to share some good news about Drake for a change. She left the office early in order to have time to stop downstairs; she had been so anxious the night before to see Drake that she hadn't made her transfer of funds and gotten any cash. When she arrived at the lobby, she realized she did not have time to visit with the tellers. She pulled out her ATM card and inserted it into the machine. Her heart sank. She was unable to make even the smallest withdrawal from the account. The balance showed that there was barely enough money in it to keep the account open. She mumbled to herself, "No, he wouldn't have. Did I take it out? No…I know I didn't take it. It had to be Drake or a bank error." She rushed back upstairs to her office and pulled up her account on her computer. The check had been deposited into the joint account at 10:01 the previous day. And then this morning, all but ten dollars had been withdrawn. The transaction had occurred at the branch near their home. He had taken out the entire check, and then some. "Damn him!" She called his cell and was shocked when he actually answered. "Drake?"

"You bitch! You lied to me about your raise!" he screamed at her.

"I wanted to…" she stammered.

He hung up before she could finish. She rushed out of the office, not wanting to be seen by anyone. While he had destroyed her plans for a pleasant lunch, Anna was waiting for her and she needed more than ever to see her. Jillian rushed into the café and found Anna at a table waiting. "Oh, Anna, I've done it again."

"What happened? You sounded so happy this morning," her friend asked, very concerned.

"He must have found my check report and discovered I've been lying about my raise." Jillian was pale with anxiety and hurt. He drained our account!"

"He took all your money? Why?" Anna was shocked.

"I don't know! He withdrew three thousand from the account. Now, he's furious with me. He hung up on me before I could explain." Jillian sat rocking in her chair, her hand pressed to her mouth to stifle her desire to sob out loud.

"Jillian! What are you thinking? He's furious with you? Three thousand dollars! If John did that, I don't know what I'd do." Anna reached out toward her friend, wanting to comfort her and wanting to stop Jillian from blaming herself.

"I know, but we had such a good week. He hadn't had a drink since last Friday. He was doing it for me." She started wiping her eyes trying not to make a scene in the restaurant. She didn't want to say aloud that he was probably on a binge.

"I know you lied to him, but that's not an excuse to steal from you."

"He didn't steal from me. It was in our joint account; it's his money too," she started to defend her husband.

"Jillian, stop! Please, listen to yourself." Anna put her hand on her friend's arm. "You've told me he's taken money before, but has he ever taken this much?"

Jillian shook her head. "Oh God! Anna, do you think he's leaving?"

"Did he empty the account?" Anna asked, trying to be pragmatic.

"Almost." Jillian looked to her friend for reassurance.

"He'll be back." She smiled at the other woman, trying to comfort her.

"I hope you're right. I couldn't bear to be alone." Jillian's lip trembled at the thought and she began crying again.

"Jillian, I know you. You're much stronger than you think. I believe Drake will be back. He needs you far more than you need him, no matter what you believe. If you had to, and you don't, you could survive without him. He's just trying to punish you. Don't let him get you down. He can't possibly spend all that money on booze. He'll be home late, and probably drunk, but he will be home. Try to eat some lunch and don't worry so much." Anna squeezed Jillian's arm and offered her a tissue to wipe her eyes. Jillian accepted her friend's comfort and reassurance. She was able to eat some soup, knowing that she had to have something in her stomach so she could finish her workday. They ate in thoughtful silence and parted with Jillian promising to call Anna later to tell her how things went at home.

Jillian went straight home after work to wait for Drake. She left three messages on his cell phone apologizing and trying to explain her lie. He did not come home. She called Anna Saturday morning in a panic. It was the first time he had not shown up and spent the entire night out.

"I don't know what to do. What if something happened to him? I'll never forgive myself if he's injured or.... Oh, God! I can't bear to think about it." She began sobbing.

"Jilly, slow down. If he were in an accident, the police would have called you, or the hospital. He's all right. I'm sure of it. He's probably just sleeping it off somewhere. Have you tried calling his friends?" Anna asked.

"What friends? He doesn't have any friends any more. He hasn't kept in touch with his friends from school. Maybe the hospital doesn't know how to reach me. I need to go. I'm going to start calling them. I have to find out where he is." She was just about to hang up when there was a beep on the line. "Hold on, Anna. I've got another call. It might be Drake." She clicked the button and said, "Hello?"

"Jilly...don't be mad. I got arrested last night. I need you to come down to the jail and bail me out," Drake said, his voice sounding exhausted and panicked.

"In jail! Why? What happened? Are you all right?" Jillian felt relieved that he was alive, but terrified that something serious had happened to him.

"I'm fine. No one got hurt or anything like that. Don't worry about why; just get me out of here. I can't stay in here. Please, Jilly. Get me out!" he begged.

"All right. I'll have to get a bail bondsman to put up the bail. It may take a little while. I'll be there as soon as I can. Just hang on." She got the information from him as to where he was being held and hung up, switching back to Anna. She very quickly informed her friend of what had happened, and then hung up so that she could find someone to bail Drake out.

She managed to find someone downtown near the jail who agreed to meet her at his office. Driving there, Jillian couldn't help thinking about how Drake's behavior was really out of control now. She berated herself for dreaming that things were getting better for them both.

CHAPTER 56

It was in the bondsman's office that she learned the charges against Drake. He had been arrested for public drunkenness, resisting arrest, and soliciting a prostitute. Jillian felt her heart sink. *But he promised he'd never be with another woman if I agreed to marry him. How could he do this to me when I've been trying to save his life?* She felt the tears begin to run down her cheeks as she filled out the paperwork promising to pay back the full amount of the bail if Drake failed to show up for court. The bondsman offered to show her the way to the jail and where she had to go to pick up Drake. Jillian gratefully accepted his offer of assistance.

She sat in the lobby of the jail, waiting for them to bring Drake out. Hours went by while she sat there. Finally, an officer brought him out. She jumped up and ran over to him where he stood waiting for the return of his personal effects.

Drake turned to face her, his visage reflecting anger. "Don't start with me, Jilly. I don't want to talk about it." Jillian felt all her fears drain away and her rage rising. She walked out the door without looking to see if he followed her. She stood by the car waiting for him to catch up. When he did, he demanded the car keys, but she refused, climbing into the driver's seat and starting the engine. Drake had no option, but to get into the passenger seat. He slammed the door to demonstrate his anger with her.

Not wanting to get any angrier when she had to concentrate on driving, Jillian held her peace until they got into the apartment. Drake had barely closed the door when she turned on him, releasing the pent up ire she had been holding in for the entire drive.

"How dare you! How dare you do this to me; put me through all this agony, and then act like I'm the one who offended you? I can't believe that you'd go out and pick up a whore! You spent my money on a cheap slut! How can I ever trust you again?" She was pacing the living room, swearing.

"Don't put this on me! You were the one who lied to me; acting like you didn't have any money. Acting like we were broke. And all the time you were stashing away all that cash! You got just what you deserved. Yeah, I took 'your' money and spent it on a whore! At least she was hot and eager, not like your dead fish performances. I wouldn't have called you at all if I didn't need you to get me out of jail!" He stood directly in front of Jillian, throwing his insults back into her face, daring her to challenge him.

She stood there breathing heavily, trying to choose her words with some care. "How much money do you have left?" she demanded.

"I don't know. A few bucks. What the hell difference does it make? You're loaded now, miss big shot bank executive!" He pulled out his wallet and threw it across the room.

"A few bucks? What happened to all of it? You took three thousand out of the bank. What did you do with all of it?" she challenged, going to pick up the wallet and checking inside to see what it still held.

Drake headed into the kitchen, opened the refrigerator, and pulled out a bottle of beer. "I had a few drinks, and then went down to the casino boats on the river." He shrugged and drank down about half his beer.

"And the whore? That just seemed like a good idea?" she sneered at him. "You know you betrayed me. How could you do that to me, Drake? How could you just forget your promise to me?" she demanded, tears choking her voice.

"What promise would that be? The promise not to cheat on you? You cheated on me. You deliberately lied to me about how much you were making. Why, Jillian? You were the one who betrayed me. Did you think I wouldn't find out? Did you think I wouldn't care or feel humiliated? So, I went out looking for a little feminine comfort. It didn't take anything away from you and it was making me feel better, until the damned cops got involved." He drained the rest of the beer in the bottle and threw it into the sink in the kitchen. Jillian heard something break and cringed at the violence. "I don't want to argue with you about this anymore. I'm beat and I'm going to go crash. You can sit here and sulk all you want." Drake stalked out of the room, leaving Jillian impotently standing there.

She felt her tears drying up. He would never understand how he had hurt her. She couldn't stand the thought of staying in the same apartment with him. She needed to get out, to get away from him and from the mess their lives had become. She needed some time away from him to think about the situation and what she wanted to do.

Once she heard him snoring, Jillian crept into the bedroom. She retrieved her luggage and began filling her bags with some clothing and necessities for a few days or so away from home. She grabbed up her jewelry box and packed it, fearing that Drake might pawn the little bit of good jewelry she had. Going into the bathroom, she collected her toiletries. Once she had everything she thought she would need, she surveyed the darkened bedroom, and then pulled the door closed behind her and took her luggage down to the car. She didn't bother to leave a note for Drake. She'd call him in a few days to let him know where she was. For now, she just needed to be away from him.

Jillian thought about where she would go. She knew that Anna and John would welcome her, but she felt that she wanted to stay where she would be fiercely defended from Drake. Sally would do that for her. Anna would want to mediate between them. Sally would just want to lynch him and that was exactly what Jillian wanted to do herself. She headed for Sally's house, hoping they were home.

Jillian pulled into her friend's driveway. She took a deep breath and, leaving her bags in the car, went up to the front door and rang the bell. George opened the door. "Jillian, come in." Confused by her sudden unannounced appearance, he ushered her in. "Sally's upstairs putting the baby in bed."

"Thank you, George." She walked into the living room and, as soon as she sat down, started crying.

George was not sure what to say or do, so he went to the kitchen and put on the teakettle. He came back carrying a tray with an array of teas, milk, sugar, honey, mugs, and brownies. As he set it on the coffee table before Jillian, the whistle of the teakettle called him back to the kitchen. She looked up as he came back in with the hot water, a hotplate, and napkins. She couldn't imagine Drake ever having been so thoughtful or kind, especially with nothing to gain. He poured the water, set down the kettle, and handed the teas to her, still saying nothing. She chose a bag of chamomile and handed the teas back to George. She managed to choke out, "Thank you."

Sally came down at that moment. She plopped down on the couch next to Jillian. She patted her friend's knee and looked longingly at the brownies. "What did he do?"

"What didn't he do would be a better question! He caught me in a lie about my raise, so he took three thousand dollars yesterday morning. He went drinking, and then gambling, and then topped it all off by getting arrested with a whore." Jillian felt the bile rise in her throat at the thought of his betrayal.

Sally's response was, "That shit!"

George attempted to extricate himself from the room.

When Jillian spotted him, she said, "No, George, please stay. I want your opinion, too. Am I over reacting?"

"No, Jillian. Sally would have killed me if I'd pulled a stunt like that."

"He broke his promise to me." She looked back and forth from Sally to George. "What should I do?"

The couple thought she was talking about their marriage vows. Neither of them knew of Ted and Ellie's story. "Only you can answer that question," Sally responded. George just nodded, feeling uncomfortable and not wanting to be involved in this conversation.

"I don't know what I'm doing. I can't even look at him now. As soon as he fell asleep, I packed my bags and left." She sat wringing her hands and shaking her head, the tears coursing down her cheeks.

Sally pointed to Jillian's car keys on the table. "George, will you please get Jillian's things out of the car and bring them upstairs?"

George grabbed the keys, relieved to have an escape, and headed out the front door. He stayed upstairs while the two women talked. Eventually, they came up too. Jillian crawled into bed expecting to have difficulty sleeping, but she fell asleep quickly, feeling numb and emotionally exhausted.

CHAPTER 57

Sunday morning, Jillian slept in. After a long shower, she joined Sally and George in the kitchen. They'd been up for hours with the baby. Jillian helped herself to some coffee and watched the baby sleeping in the portable crib. The sight brought tears to her eyes. She was relieved that she'd never had Drake's baby, but sad that, now, they'd probably never have one. Then the panic began to set in. How could she go on alone? She expected to be with Drake forever and never have to be alone. She did her best to hide her fear from her friends and to put on a brave face.

Jillian offered to baby-sit while George and Sally went to church. They had already returned, when her cell phone started ringing. She tried to ignore the sound coming from her purse. After the third time it rang, she took it out of her purse and looked at the caller ID; they were all from Drake. She turned it off. Sally and George said nothing about the phone. George changed and took off for his brother's house to watch the football game. When Sally's phone rang, Jillian jumped. "Don't answer it!"

Looking at the caller ID, Sally said, "It's okay. It's Anna." She answered the phone. When she hung up, she announced, "She is coming over. Drake called her looking for you." The phone rang again; she looked at the number. "It's him. What should I tell him?"

"Don't answer it. I don't want him to know where I am." Jillian's eyes pleaded with her friend to protect her.

Sally let the machine pick it up.

It wasn't long before Anna arrived. "What happened? Drake is freaking out. He said your closet was half empty. I think he's calling everyone you know. He'd already called your parents before he called me."

"I better call them and let them know I'm all right." Jillian turned her cell phone back on. There were ten new messages; her mailbox was full. She called her parents without checking the messages and spoke to her mother. She told her she was at a friend's and that she would explain later.

"Let's move your car into Sally's garage, and then you can fill me in." Anna still didn't know what else Drake might have done; she was sure Jillian hadn't left over the money.

Jillian updated Anna. While she was sad for her friend, knowing how responsible Jillian felt for Drake's very existence, she hoped this would free her from a commitment made nearly one hundred fifty years ago. "Now that Drake has broken Ted's promise, what are you going to do?"

Before Jillian could respond, Sally interrupted. "Wait a minute! Who the hell is Ted?"

Anna explained to Sally about Jillian's trip to Savannah and Jillian's recognition that Drake was the reincarnation of Ted. Meanwhile, Jillian was pacing and inserting angry comments describing Ted's character flaws.

Sally shook her head while listening to Anna's explanation. Finally, she asked, "You two really believe this crap?"

Jillian swung around. "You weren't there; you didn't see what I saw. You'd better believe I believe, this 'crap!'"

Being startled by the vehemence of Jillian's response, Sally said, "Okay, if that's what it takes for you to get rid of that idiot, fine. What is the promise you're talking about?"

"Ted swore to me that he'd never be with another woman," Jillian explained.

"But before Drake...Ted...whoever, met you he was with other women and you never felt betrayed by that?" Sally challenged.

"When we married this time, he renewed that promise as I renewed my promise of a lifetime together with him." She stopped pacing. "What am I doing?" Her hand went to her mouth. "I'm breaking my promise to him."

"Jillian, no! By breaking his promise, he has released you from yours. Ted also told you he never got drunk when you were around; Drake has violated that commitment, too," Anna reminded her.

"It was bad enough having him die on me when I could have saved him, but now I have to abandon him intentionally?" Jillian dropped down on the couch, appalled at what she was contemplating.

"You're not abandoning him; he abandoned you a long time ago for the bottle," Anna protested.

"But what will happen to him? How can I hurt him this way? What if he dies again because I'm not there for him?" Jillian looked up at Anna, her terror written on her face.

"You don't have to make the decision now. Take some time away from him to think things out." Anna was afraid she would run back to Drake and apologize for leaving.

"You can stay here as long as you want," Sally offered.

"If he would just stop drinking, he wouldn't do any of this other stuff. He really cares about me. Maybe I can get him some help," Jillian rationalized, not willing to accept that she was powerless.

The phone started ringing again. After checking the caller ID, Sally didn't answer it, but turned up the volume on the answering machine. The three women could hear Drake yelling, "Sally, damn it! Pick up the damned phone! I know she's there! Let me talk to her...." The machine cut him off.

"What am I going to do? I've never heard him so angry." She started pacing. "I've got to get out of here." Jillian began moving toward the stairs, planning to get her luggage and escape.

"It's okay, you can stay here," Sally insisted, beginning to rise.

"I don't want him to scare the baby again with his yelling." She continued toward the stairs to gather her things.

The doorbell rang loudly and repeatedly. Jillian jumped and turned toward the front door. At that point, Drake started pounding on the door and yelling, "Jillian, open the door! I know you're in there! Open the damned door!"

Jillian stepped back and looked to her friends. The banging continued. She hesitantly stepped up to the door. "Go away. I'm not ready to talk to you," she yelled back through the closed door. She reached up to check the dead bolt.

Sally, fearing Jillian was about to open the door, yelled, "Don't let that man in. He's crazy!"

Jillian was startled by Sally's words, remembering having heard them before from Mattie. This time, she heeded the advice. "Go away, you're drunk!"

"I am not drunk!" he yelled back, pounding on the door with each word. "I just want to talk to you. You're my wife and you will come home right now!"

Sally said, "That's enough. I am calling the police." She started to dial 911.

"Drake, you'd better go. Please! Sally called the police. They're on their way," she pleaded with him, not wanting him arrested again, and desperately wanting him gone.

"This is not over!" he threatened, pounding the door again.

Anna looked out the window and informed Sally, "He's getting into the car. It's okay. He's leaving."

Jillian leaned against the door sobbing. Anna put her arm around her friend, leading her back to the couch. Sally informed the 911 operator, "It's okay. The man left."

CHAPTER 58

Jillian had given in to Sally and Anna and spent the night at Sally's. She dressed for work and came downstairs lugging her suitcases. Sally was in the kitchen nursing the baby and George was eating breakfast and reading the morning paper. Sally watched Jillian pour a cup of coffee, and then sit at the table. She continued watching as Jillian wiped her tears as she sipped the coffee.

"You are not going to work today," Sally commanded, amazed.

"I've never missed a day. I have to go." Jillian sniffled, looking stubborn.

"Jillian, you're not in any shape to go to work." Her friend was trying to be patient and reasonable.

"What will they think if I don't go? I have to go." She appeared to be on the verge of helpless tears again.

George reached across the table and patted Jillian's hand. "It will be worse if you go in. Trust me, Jillian, call in sick. Give yourself a day. You're allowed."

It was so rare for George to offer unsolicited advice that she heeded him. Jillian sighed and capitulated. "I'll call Jerry."

"Good. George, will you take Jillian's bags back upstairs?" Sally asked, raising the baby to her shoulder to burp her.

"No! I'll go to my parents," Jillian refused, speaking louder than she had planned. She realized that she sounded a bit ungrateful and went on to explain, "Drake might come back and you two have put up with me long enough. Thank you, both of you, for all your kindness and support, but I wouldn't feel right putting you through any more drama."

George looked at his wife who shrugged in agreement. "I'll put them in your car for you." He kissed Sally on the cheek and the baby on her forehead. "I need to leave now. Good luck, Jilly," he said as he crossed over to her where she sat and gave her a quick peck on the cheek as well. He took the suitcases to her car and left for work.

"Sally, what am I going to tell my parents?" Jillian asked hesitantly after George had gone.

"The truth!" her friend responded vehemently, not willing to protect Drake any longer.

"But, if I go back to him, they'll hate him." Jillian sighed heavily and sipped her coffee.

"You're not really thinking of going back, with all he's done?" Sally's voice was filled with scorn and incredulity.

"I don't know," she moaned. "But if he'd stop drinking..."

"He's not going to do it on his own," her friend told her firmly.

"Maybe I should go back." She shook her head in confusion, chewing her lip.

"He drank when you were there." Sally was getting annoyed with her friend. "You can help him best by refusing to go back. Tell him he has to get help, real help. You know, a rehab or something."

"You really think so?" Jillian was confused and uncertain. Sally seemed so sure of herself.

"If you don't believe me, go see a professional yourself," her friend suggested.

"You're right, a professional can tell me how to help him," Jillian muttered to herself. "But would they understand about Ted and Ellie?"

"I don't know about that stuff, but you'd better start dealing with today's reality. Call work, and then arrange for your next check to go into a new account." She rose and put the baby into her portable crib.

"I'll call Jerry, but I have to go in person to change the deposit and open a new account," Jillian explained, beginning to move away from the table.

"Good, now you're starting to use your head," Sally encouraged her.

Jillian left a message on Jerry's voice-mail at work, hugged Sally, and left for her parents' house. By the time she arrived in Springdale, her father and brother had already left for the day. She was relieved she would only have to face her mother.

When she walked in carrying her bags, Fran ran to her, throwing her arms around her daughter. "Oh, I've been so worried. Where have you been? What happened? Are you all right? Did he hurt you?"

"Please, Mom! One question at a time. Is it all right if I stay here for awhile?"

"Of course. Why are you even asking? Come, sit down. We'll get you settled later. Have you eaten anything?" Fran bustled around the kitchen trying to put together something for her daughter to eat.

"No, Mom, but I'm not really very hungry. But..." She started crying.

Fran held her daughter, rocking her, waiting until she would be ready to explain. Finally, she asked, "What did he do to you?"

"Mom, it's really my fault." She hesitated, seeing her mother did not believe her. "Well, at least, I started it. I lied to him about my raise. He found out, took the money, and went on a binge." She was reluctant to elaborate.

"Jillian, you have tried hiding it, but I know he's done this before. What makes this time different?" Fran asked, pushing her daughter away so that she could look into her face.

The tears began running down her face. She looked into her mother's eyes and mumbled, "He got arrested."

"I'm not surprised. All that drinking and driving! No one was hurt, were they?"

"It wasn't for that.... Oh, Mom, he was with a prostitute."

"Baby, that...." Fran did not know what to say.

"Mom, how could he? If he hadn't been drinking...." Her voice trailed away, knowing she couldn't really defend what he had done.

"That is no excuse. Oh, Jillian, are you sure this is the first time? Could you be...sick?" Fran ventured, hesitantly.

"Mom, no!" Jillian was shocked at the suggestion.

"You're going to the doctor, today!" Fran was all nurse at that moment, taking charge of the situation.

"Mother!" Suddenly, Jillian felt like a little child again.

"I'm calling right now, no arguing!" Fran stated, picking up the phone and dialing.

Jillian sighed, recognizing the tone. There was no point in arguing.

Her mother pleaded with the appointment secretary until she agreed to work Jillian in that afternoon. Jillian came home from the appointment, having been poked and prodded, her blood had been drawn and she had received a referral for a psychologist. She'd have to wait for the test results until the end of the week. She hoped her mother had called her father while she was gone; she didn't want to tell him herself. Her brother was already home from school.

"Hi, Sis," he greeted her, sitting in the kitchen calmly munching chips.

"No comment?" She expected Billy to be ranting.

"I overheard Mom telling Dad. I figure you don't need me harassing you, too," he shrugged, biting down with a crunch.

"Thanks." She went over and hugged him.

CHAPTER 59

The family kept dinner conversation away from Jillian's problems. The next morning, she headed in to work. She felt as though everyone was looking at her strangely. Jerry came in to find out if she was feeling all right, and then quickly exited. Joan Fitzgerald called and asked Jillian to come down to see her after lunch.

During lunch, Jillian went downstairs and opened a new checking account. She was relieved she'd get another check before their rent was due. There was barely anything left in the joint account to cover it and she didn't want to touch her savings. She was uncomfortable about going to Human Resources. She couldn't imagine being called in for missing one day of work. Joan greeted her warmly, offering a chair. "Joan, did I do something wrong?"

"No, Jillian, but your husband showed up here yesterday looking for you," the HR woman reported with a grimace.

Jillian paled at the thought of the scene that must have taken place. "I'm sorry. I had no idea. I'll talk to him," she apologized.

"You don't have to talk to him; security took care of it. I take it from what I heard about his drunken ranting, that you've moved out." Joan was obviously being very tactful.

"Yes...at least for now." Jillian sat with her fingers locked together, her knuckles white.

"I have some referrals for you," Joan explained, opening a folder and removing several sheets of paper. "I think it would be a good idea if you took advantage of our Employee Assistance Program. You're entitled to six free sessions and it's completely confidential."

"Am I required to do this?" Jillian was trying to hide her defensiveness.

"You don't have to go, but Jillian, it's been my experience that when people try doing this on their own, eventually...it does become a requirement." She handed her a brochure for the EAP and one for Alanon. "This explains our program and the other is for people who have friends or family with alcohol problems."

"I'll think about it." She took the materials, looking very uncomfortable.

"Jillian, any time you want to talk...off the record," Joan left the offer open.

"Thanks, Joan." Jillian stood to leave. "I might take you up on it."

She returned to her office, closing the door behind her. She filled out the paperwork changing the accounts for her deposit and sent it to payroll through the interoffice mail. She tried working, but couldn't concentrate. Finally, she picked up the EAP folder and called a psychologist requesting an appointment. By the end of the day, she was able to arrange one for Friday at lunch. At home that night, she finally listened to Drake's messages from Sunday. They ranged from crying and begging to cursing and blaming. She discovered he had continued to call her parents' house and her friends all day. She dialed their apartment from her cell phone.

"It's about time you called. Where are you?" he demanded, very hostile.

"Drake, I know we have to talk, but I'm not ready," she told him quietly.

"What do you mean you're not ready?" When are you coming home?" His voice was getting louder.

"I don't know, but you have to stop calling everyone and you can't go to my office. You're going to get me fired." She tried to be firm in the face of his growing ire.

"Sure, that's all you care about, your high falutin' job. You don't care anything about me!" Jillian heard the hurt buried inside of his anger.

"That's not true!" she responded defensively, stung by his accusation.

"You selfish bitch..." he shouted into the phone. Jillian winced at the words and held the phone away from her ear while he continued yelling. Her brother walked up behind her, grabbed the phone and pushed the end button.

"Billy, what are you doing?" she exclaimed, startled by his action.

"You don't need to listen to that shit." He turned the phone off when it started to ring again.

"You're just going to make him angrier," she warned, thinking of how Drake might react.

"So what! You're the only one here who has any right to be angry. He fucked up," Billy stated, waving the phone.

"You don't need to use that kind of language with me." Jillian's nerves were jangling already and she felt very sensitive to her brother's comments.

"I thought...." Billy stopped himself. "I'm sorry; it just makes me mad to see you worrying about him after what he's done." He sat down next to her and slipped his arm around her shoulders.

"I know, but if I can just get him to stop drinking...." Her lower lip quivered and her eyes glittered with more unshed tears.

"Jilly, you've been trying for years. It's time to start taking care of you." Billy squeezed her shoulders affectionately.

"So everybody says." She leaned her head against him briefly.

"Maybe we're right." He kissed his sister on the top of the head and, rising, left the room.

Thursday, she received a call from the doctor's office. She was informed that the test results for sexually transmitted diseases were all negative, but that did not mean her husband would also be negative. That night, Donna called from LA and was surprised by Jillian answering their parents' phone. She went through the entire story all over again for her sister.

Friday, Jillian left the office early enough to make her appointment with the EAP psychologist. By the time she arrived, she was very nervous and had no idea what to say or where to start. She finally settled on, "My husband has a problem...." By the end of the session, she had agreed to try Alanon. She had been told to try a few different meetings before making up her mind about it as she might relate better to one group of people rather than another. She was given a list of meetings and made a second appointment.

She turned on her cell phone when she got home that night. It was the first time since her brother turned it off. Her voice-mail was full of irate messages from Drake. Angrily, she called him. She left a message on the machine, "Go to rehab and stop drinking, and then maybe I'll come home." She called his cell and left the same message. Satisfied, she turned her phone off again.

CHAPTER 60

Saturday morning, Anna called to announce she would be picking her up at 11:30 and taking her out for lunch. Jillian needed the distraction and looked forward to seeing her friend. She hadn't told her family or the psychologist about Ted. Anna seemed to understand, as if she knew Ted herself. As they talked about the events since they had last been together, Jillian was struck by a sense of familiarity with Anna that had nothing to do with their long friendship. She found herself staring at her friend, seeing her in a different setting and a different time. Suddenly, she was sure; Anna was Ellie's cousin Emmy. They had known each other in that lifetime and Anna had known Ted as well. Jillian shared this information with her friend. Anna considered it carefully.

"I can't say I have any clear recognition of it, but it would certainly explain why we became such good friends so quickly. I felt I knew you well the first time I met you. It might also explain why I felt such concern about you and Drake developing a relationship," Anna conceded.

They talked about Jillian's memories of Emmy during the rest of their lunch. Jillian pulled out her list of Alanon meetings and asked Anna if she would go with her. There was a meeting at a nearby church in an hour. Anna agreed to go too.

They found the church and saw several people going in. Jillian asked one of them where the Alanon meeting was being held and the woman quickly assured her she was in the right place and welcomed them both. Anna and Jillian followed the other woman into the classroom in the basement of the church and found seats. Jillian was moved by what she heard there. It felt comforting to know she was not alone in what she was going through with Drake. She listened to the stories told by the older members of the group, but was a bit nervous when she was invited to share her story. No one pressured her to speak, which made it easier to do so. By the end of the meeting, Jillian had the phone numbers of several other people who all invited her to call if she felt she needed someone to talk to who understood what she was experiencing. It crossed her mind that this was just the thing that Drake needed as well, a group of people who were fighting their problem and learning a healthier way to live, while offering support to each other.

Sitting in the car after the meeting, Jillian listened to Drake's newest batch of messages. He sounded drunk and was angry that she thought he was an alcoholic.

The meeting had given her the resolve to continue to demand he get help before going back. With Anna by her side, she called him again.

"Where are you?" Drake demanded.

"Drake, I love you but…"

"Where are you?" He cut her off with his repeated demand.

"Please, just listen." She wanted to share her experience with him and the hope it had given her.

"Come home and I'll listen!" he countered.

"I can't come home unless you go to treatment and AA," she responded firmly.

"Fuck you!" He hung up on her.

Anna rubbed Jillian's back while she cried. "He's making it impossible," Jillian moaned.

"Maybe he just needs more time to understand you're serious," Anna suggested.

After receiving more drunken messages, Jillian went to another Alanon meeting on Tuesday night. She realized from listening to the others' stories that Drake probably was not taking her seriously. She needed to do something so that he would understand she meant it; he would have to stop drinking before she would come back. She went home and asked her father if he would meet her at her apartment Wednesday after work to get the rest of her clothes. She turned her cell phone on and waited for Drake to call again. He seemed surprised when she actually answered the phone.

"So, you finally decided to talk to me," he slurred.

"There are a lot of things we need to talk about. How did the arraignment go yesterday?" she enquired, trying to remain calm.

"Fine! When are you coming home?"

"Drake, I just don't know yet."

"You've made your point, but do you understand I was angry about your lying to me?"

He's still not taking responsibility for his actions, Jillian thought. "My lie did not warrant you cheating on me. You haven't even said you were sorry."

"Okay, I'm sorry. Now, come home." There was no regret in his voice, only command.

"It's not that simple. You have to stop drinking and go into treatment and to AA. Then we can talk about it," she stated.

"So, you must be staying at your parents'. Is this their idea?" She knew he was looking for anyone to blame but himself and his behavior.

"No, Drake. If you love me and want me back, you'll get help for your drinking," she reiterated.

"Don't give me this bull shit! Just get home tonight!" he raged.

"No!" Jillian was frightened by his anger and determined not to give in to it.

"No? You're my wife; stop playing games and get home!"

Jillian felt her anger take over. "You should have remembered you had a wife before you fucked a prostitute. You broke your promise," she accused.

"Maybe you should act more like a wife!" he snarled, his voice full of loathing.

"What's that supposed to mean? I do everything for you. When are you going to settle down and act like a husband and keep your promises to me?" she shouted back at him.

"You owe me!" he screamed at her.

"It's not going to work anymore. You blew it; I don't have to feel guilty anymore. You have to stop drinking!"

"Fuck you!" He slammed down the phone.

Jillian was furious, frustrated, and scared. She turned her phone off, her thoughts swirling in conflicting directions. She hoped he would not show up at her parents'. Yet, she couldn't imagine being without him and alone. She didn't know if she could ever trust or believe him again. She hoped that, if he stopped drinking and started behaving differently, she might be able to forgive him and to learn to trust him. She had never doubted his fidelity before; she realized that she had tested and learned to trust him as Ted. Even with his drinking, Ted had kept his promise. She wondered if he would have continued to keep it if they had been married, and what she would have done as Ellie if he hadn't. She couldn't imagine Ellie tolerating infidelity. What had happened to her since that day in November? How could she have come to put up with such treatment? But anything seemed better than being alone.

Jillian didn't understand the intensity of this fear. Ellie wanted a husband, but did not seem fearful of being without one. Jillian's head kept spinning. She was relieved she had already asked her father to meet her at the apartment or she might be tempted to back out of what her head told her was the right thing to do. She tossed and turned all night.

CHAPTER 61

She had difficulty concentrating at work, fearful of a confrontation with Drake when she went to pick up the rest of her things. The day dragged on. By five o'clock, she just wanted to get it over with as quickly as possible.

Jillian pulled up to the apartment and found her brother already there, waiting for her. She had not been expecting him, but was glad for the additional support. Their father pulled up just as they were unlocking the front door. Drake's truck was not in sight.

Jillian opened the door and gasped. It wasn't just the empty beer cans and dirty dishes with half eaten food. Their framed personal pictures had been smashed and were lying on the floor. There were scotch bottles and glasses that had been thrown against the wall and shattered on the floor. She gingerly stepped over shards of glass, heading toward the bedroom.

Trying to lighten things up, Billy stated, "Wow, Sis, I knew you were a rotten housekeeper, but this…"

Jillian gave her brother a dirty look.

"Leave her alone, Bill," their father interjected.

"Oh God! Daddy!" Jillian regressed, looking at her clothes that were strewn around the room. She picked up the dress she'd worn the last time they went dancing together to find he had torn it. "Billy, will you get some garbage bags from the kitchen?"

"You're not going to clean this up?" he asked her incredulously.

"No! I'm going to put everything I own in them and take them. I'll figure out what's worth keeping later."

Jillian and Bill Senior heard, "Gross!" coming from Billy when he entered the kitchen.

As she started picking up her things, she found the molded silver hand-mirror under a jacket. She gently picked it up, fingering the back of it, tears starting to gather in her eyes. When she turned it over, she saw that it was broken. As the tears flowed down her cheeks, she mumbled, "He broke it. He broke it just like everything else. Just like he broke his promise." She sighed wiping away the tears. "November was always a bad month for us. If only I had said 'no' the first time he asked me to marry him. I was right about him and everyone else was wrong."

"What are you talking about?" Her father asked.

"Nothing, nothing that I could ever explain. Never mind. Let's just get all this stuff into bags before Drake shows up." She began grabbing up articles of clothing.

She hadn't originally planned on taking the files. As she pulled out the top drawer of their filing cabinet, her brother saw what she was doing and told her to take the garbage bags, that he'd take care of the files. They were in the apartment for nearly two hours before Jillian was satisfied she'd taken everything she wanted. As they pulled away, she sighed in relief that Drake had not come home while they were in the apartment. Her father was leading the caravan, and pulled into an Applebee's on the way home. He used Jillian's cell to call Fran and let her know they were out of the apartment and had stopped to eat. He had already told her not to plan on them for dinner.

First thing Friday, Jillian checked to make sure her pay went into her new account. She went to her second EAP session at lunch. She started filling Dr. Pie, the psychologist, in about what she had done since their last session.

"...I was just going to take my clothes to make a point, but when I saw he had broken the mirror I had brought back from South Carolina, something snapped. I don't know; I just knew our time together was up...."

The psychologist encouraged her to continue going to Alanon and they set up another appointment. As she was about to walk out the door, she asked, "This might sound crazy, but do you believe in reincarnation?"

"That's not crazy, eighty percent of the world's population believes in reincarnation in some form or another. But it doesn't matter what I believe; what's important is what you believe," the therapist responded, not wanting to start a discussion that couldn't be finished.

"I'm going to be late. See ya next week." Jillian quickly exited.

The phone calls from Drake increased. He again called her friends, her parents, and even her sister Donna in California. He begged them to get her to come back. When they refused to get involved, he ranted that everyone was against him. No one reported to Jillian that he was accepting any responsibility for what had happened. Feeling stronger after the Tuesday night Alanon meeting, she answered her phone.

"Jillian," Drake whined drunkenly. "Please come home."

"Call me back when you're sober." She hung up on him this time. Initially, she felt a sense of satisfaction and pride. However, the sadness quickly drowned the moment. The hopes and expectations for their life together had been killed by his infidelity and drinking, as surely as they'd been killed before by a Union bullet. For the first time, she was beginning to understand that it had never been her fault. His life had not been her responsibility now or then. She had stopped trusting her own judgment regarding him the first time and had carried the false beliefs about who he could be into the present. She had maintained it against all evidence.

She wondered how much of his apparent panic about her leaving was from his time as Ted. She hoped he would stop drinking for himself. She would always care for him and truly wanted the best for him, but she could no longer sacrifice herself for him. She arrived at her parents, sad, but resolved in her decision.

Drake's harassing phone calls to family and friends continued. She called him on Thursday night after work to tell him to stop calling everyone.

"Drake, I need to talk to you," she began the conversation with him.

"It's about time. Come on home and we'll talk," he demanded.

"We can talk on the phone," she stated definitively.

"I haven't had anything to drink today. Come on over." Jillian realized he was trying to manipulate her.

"That's good, but I'm not coming over. Drake, you have to stop calling everyone I know. It's not going to fix anything between us. You're just upsetting people."

"I want to talk to you in person. Come over."

"I can't. Listen, stop calling everyone and I'll meet with you Saturday, but only if you're sober. I won't talk to you if you're drunk," she offered.

"You're holding all the cards right now," he conceded flatly.

"Saturday, I'll call you in the morning and let you know what time." She was about to hang up when he spoke again.

"Jillian, I know it hasn't been easy for you. But I really want you home." She could hear the deep longing in his voice and felt her heart twist in sympathy.

"We'll talk Saturday. Bye." She hung up quickly and turned off her phone.

CHAPTER 62

Friday, Jillian went to her appointment with Dr. Pie. "As you were leaving last week you dropped a question about reincarnation. Was there something you needed to discuss about it?"

"I believe I've known Drake before. Things ended badly that time, too. He had been my friend. I didn't want to marry him, but my family convinced me it would work. He died before we married. This time I did not listen to my friends and family and married him. I'm beginning to think we should have stayed friends. He really was my best friend until sex became involved. Is this crazy?" she asked, looking up to see how the therapist was responding to her words.

"Does it help you to understand your relationship with Drake now?" he asked.

"Yes." She nodded with certainty.

"Maybe that's what's important." The doctor tilted his head and raised an eyebrow.

"Yes, I guess it is…. I told him I would talk to him face to face tomorrow. I'm going to tell him it's over. I'm nervous about how he'll react." She licked her lips, feeling her mouth go dry.

"Are you afraid of him?" the doctor asked, concerned for her safety.

"A little," she conceded.

"Has he ever hurt you or threatened you?"

"Sometimes he has grabbed my arm hard when he's been angry," she acknowledged.

"If you feel you need to see him, maybe you need to meet him in a public place," the psychologist suggested. "Meet at a specific time; have somebody else who knows where you are and set a time for you to call them when the meeting should be over."

"I hadn't thought of that…" Jillian immediately felt safer at the thought.

Jillian left after making another appointment and promising to take safety measures. She called Drake in the morning to tell him she'd meet him at Chili's at noon. He attempted to convince her to come home. She stood firm. She called Anna and let her know what her plan was.

Jillian waited nervously. She fiddled with a manila envelope she had brought to the restaurant to give him. He arrived carrying a single flower, kissed her on the cheek, and handed the flower to her. She stiffened at his touch, but accepted both the kiss and the flower without comment. She noticed that he had cleaned himself up and did not smell of alcohol. "It's been so long; you seem to be even more beautiful. I've missed you terribly."

She realized his intent in this meeting was to get her to come back. "Drake, I'm glad to see you're not drinking. Are you going to get help?"

"If that's what you want, I will." He was trying so hard to convince her that he was sincere.

"No, you have to do it for you, not me." Jillian realized that he was still in denial of having any problem with drinking.

"I can stop; I have stopped," he argued.

"I hope you do, but it's not going to bring me back." She continued fiddling with the envelope.

"What's that?" He indicated the envelope. Things were not going the way he'd planned. He wanted to change the subject.

"When I was going through the filing cabinet, I found your truck papers, some old records of yours, and the apartment lease." She pushed the envelope across the table toward him.

"Jillian, what can I do to get you to come home?" he pleaded, reaching out to try to touch her hand. She pulled away from him before he could reach her.

"I'm not coming back, Drake. It's over. We have three months left on the lease. The last month we paid when we moved in. I'll pay December and January. If you want to stay in the apartment after February, you'll have to renegotiate the lease yourself."

"But what would my life be without my sweet magnolia?" Drake was starting to tear up, and then scowled.

Jillian reached out and touched his hand. "We should have just stayed friends." Tears came to her eyes, too. "We were always best as friends."

"Who is he? You've met someone. You've been different ever since you came back from Savannah," he accused.

Shaking her head, Jillian responded, "There's no one else."

"Don't lie to me again. I know you. You never could stand being alone." He was starting to get louder and angrier.

She swallowed hard. "Drake, I'm going to file for a divorce."

His face drained of color. "Jillian, give me a chance. If there isn't anyone else, you owe me that much. I'll do anything you want." He tried taking her hand again.

"I'm sorry. It's too late." She started to cry. She stood, kissed his forehead. "I'll call you." She put two twenties on the table for the check and quickly left. She got in her car, wiping the tears from her eyes and drove away. She had promised Anna she'd call, but drove directly to her house instead, rang the doorbell, and began sobbing. She felt the same sadness and loss as when she heard that Ted was dead. Anna attempted to comfort and reassure her that she was doing the right thing.

CHAPTER 63

The week passed slowly. She looked at ads for divorce attorneys, but could not bring herself to place a call. Friday, she went to see Dr. Pie again.

"...Everyone is telling me I should be happy, that my life will be so much better without Drake. But I'm miserable."

"You've said that he was your best friend, as Ted and as Drake. Maybe you need to mourn the loss of the friendship," he suggested to her.

Jillian's response was to cry. After a few minutes, she reached for a tissue, wiped her eyes, and blew her nose. "How do I do that?"

"In a way, you've already begun that work," he assured her.

Thanksgiving week was terrible for Jillian. She obsessed about how Drake would spend it and broke down, answering two of his calls. She nearly invited him to have dinner with her and her family. However, when he attacked her parents for not sending her home to her husband, she quickly set the thought aside.

The following week, she called an attorney and made an appointment for a consultation, wrote a letter to the management company of their apartment complex stating she had moved out, would not be renewing the lease and included December's rent check, and then made another appointment with Dr. Pie.

"Thanksgiving was awfully sad. I should have been relieved to have missed out on the drinking and the money problems and stuff." She laughed without humor.

"What's the stuff?" he asked her gently.

"Drake says I'm frigid. Maybe I am. I always wanted him to want me, but then, when we did it..." She trailed off and looked away.

"Go on," he encouraged her.

"It was terrible," she blurted out.

"Was it always that way for you?"

"It was with Drake." She didn't add, but realized it was terrible with Ted, too. "I'd never…gone all the way with anyone before Drake."

"What about the foreplay? How was that for you?" he questioned, trying to establish how prevalent the problem was.

When Jillian hesitated, he added, "With Drake or before him?"

"It never hurt before Drake. In the beginning, he said it was my inexperience, later that I was frigid. Is he right? Is there something wrong with me?" She looked to the psychologist for confirmation of her fears or reassurance.

"Jillian, sex with someone who loves you and cares about your feelings doesn't hurt. Some women can have a difficult time with penetration initially, but that usually passes. Sex should be pleasurable for both participants. If your partner takes the time to find out what you find stimulating and does that for you, his pleasure and satisfaction will be increased as well because you will be more responsive to him and will be more eager to participate in sex with him. Any man who doesn't take the time to arouse his partner is a selfish lover. It's that simple," he told her.

Jillian looked at the doctor, taking in his words, remembering how she had enjoyed the foreplay she had experienced with Ted, until he became violent and impatient. Drake had never been patient with her at all, never considering her needs or pleasure. She wondered what sex would be like with a man who was patient and generous. *If there ever will be another man*, she thought. She felt the fear rise in her, threatening to overwhelm her with tears.

She looked at the doctor and confessed. "I just don't want to be alone. I know I can survive by myself but…the thought is terrible….like I'm going to die."

CHAPTER 64

Christmas and New Year's Eve were difficult for Jillian. She reminisced about the good times that she'd had with Drake over the holidays and her times with him as Ted. She continued to mourn the loss of his friendship. She decided to have him served with the divorce papers after the first of the year.

Her anger and tension levels had subsided in the absence of Drake's behaviors and piercing criticisms. Since she had stopped smothering her anger with food and was consistently eating meals at regular times, she no longer had any desire to stuff herself. She had started losing weight over the last two months. She decided to join a gym. Although she was still living at her parents' house, she did not plan to stay there forever, so she joined one near work.

She'd never been to a gym before and found the sights and sounds of all the equipment and activity a bit daunting. She started with the treadmill three times per week because it was a machine she could readily understand. Soon, she noticed that she was starting to feel better physically. Eating, sleeping, and exercising had become more regular. Weekdays, she was busy at work; she had a long commute, and the times at the gym helped. She often read herself to sleep. But weekends were lonely. Everywhere she turned, people seemed to be coupled; activities of interest to her, she felt required a companion.

She decided to try some of the classes at the gym. She needed to fill more of her time and hoped to meet some single women with whom she could spend some time on the weekends. She couldn't remember when she'd last gone to a movie and going alone was unthinkable. All her friends were either married or involved in relationships. She'd met some of them for lunch, but she hadn't been out to dinner since she and Drake had last been together. She continued attending the Saturday Alanon meeting, but since leaving Drake, it was not as significant for her.

One Friday after work, she tried a yoga class at the gym. She was surprised to discover Joan Fitzgerald lying on a mat relaxing while she waited for the class to begin. Once Joan opened her eyes and sat up, Jillian greeted her. As the class began, it was apparent that Joan had been doing the postures for some time. She frequently interrupted one of her own stretches to assist Jillian. At the end of the class, Joan suggested that they go to the juice bar together.

"How are things going?" the older woman asked, smiling kindly.

"Things at the bank seem to be going well. I'm really enjoying my work there. It would be nice if some of the women on my floor were a little friendlier, but I guess that's the way it goes. How's the antiquing going?" Jillian asked, sipping from her juice.

"We tend to slow down on it a little over the winter, between the holidays and the weather. If you've caught the bug, you're welcome to join us in the spring." Joan laughed at her own foible.

"Right now, I'm trying to save as much money as I can. I want to buy a house. I'm hoping to get out of my parents' before summer. They've been good about it, but it's a long commute."

"Yeah, it's not easy moving back home. I stayed with my parents for a couple of months before George and I were married. No matter how old you are they keep asking, 'Where are you going?' or 'What time will you be home?'" She laughed. "How long have you been there?"

"Since the day Drake showed up at my office drunk, looking for me." Jillian felt a blush beginning to paint her face as she remembered how humiliated she had felt.

"I take it you two weren't able to work it out," she enquired gently.

"No...I guess too much had happened." Jillian looked down, sighing sadly

"How are you doing?" Joan asked with genuine concern.

"All right. The weekends are the hardest. I hate being alone. That's why I came to the Yoga class. At the least, it will fill my Friday nights." She shrugged and tried to smile bravely.

"Do you have any other hobbies?"

"No, everything was always about Drake." Jillian was struck by that thought. She really had spent most of her adult life taking care of her husband or cleaning up after his mistakes and neglecting her own needs. She shook her head sadly.

"Hmmm. Well, is there something you always wanted to do?" Joan probed.

Jillian cocked her head thinking. Then a smile spread over her face. "Horses! I've always wanted to go horseback riding, but never could afford it."

"Have you ever been on a horse?"

"Once, I was about five years old. I threw a temper tantrum when they took me off." She laughed at the memory, suddenly feeling excited.

"Well, I know you're saving money for your own place, but maybe it's also time you indulged yourself," Joan suggested, smiling encouragingly as she stood to leave.

"Thanks. I think I'll look into it," Jillian promised as her coworker left.

Jillian thought about how she had loved the horses in her life as Ellie. She was sure she'd feel the same way now. She wondered if the American Saddlebreds Ellie's family had bred were still around.

Jillian went home and invaded her brother's room. He was out; she turned on his computer and logged on. She began her search, looking for American Saddlebreds. She discovered that the breed was still flourishing and a very popular show horse. They were considered extremely versatile and showed both under saddle and in harness. She then narrowed her search to the greater Cincinnati area. She found a breeding farm and two show stables. Both stables offered lessons. Billy showed up as she was printing out the information.

"I'm glad you find my things useful," he commented sarcastically. He was obviously annoyed.

"I'm sorry, Bill. You weren't around to ask and I was excited to get this information." She smiled apologetically, and pointed to the printer.

He walked to the printer and looked at the print out. "Horses?"

"Yes, they're going to be my new hobby."

"You're nuts! Now get out of my room!" He waved the pages at her.

"Thanks for use of the computer." She grabbed the pages from his hand and skipped out of his room.

CHAPTER 65

First thing Saturday morning, Jillian called both stables and found out that they both had indoor riding rings. She asked about what they offered for a new rider and got the rates. They were even more expensive than what she had guessed, but she made an appointment for a half hour private lesson for the next weekend anyway.

The week seemed to drag as Jillian anxiously awaited her first horseback riding lesson. Friday, after yoga, she excitedly told Joan of her plan. The next day, she had no trouble finding Misty Glen Stable. She was there early and enjoyed watching the horses being taken through their paces by experienced riders. Most of them were children or adolescents; she was relieved to see another adult who did not seem to know what she was doing either. Although the lessons were all inside, she found herself bouncing in place to stay warm while she watched. Finally, her turn came. The instructor explained how to hold the reins and mount, and assisted her up onto an old chestnut gelding named Slatsy. As soon as she swung into the saddle, she forgot everything else in her life and could only hear the voice of her instructor, Josie. The half-hour flew by and she regretted not having scheduled a full hour, but her aching muscles told her she'd had enough for one day.

Once she had dismounted, she scheduled another appointment for the following weekend. She drove home feeling exhilarated, mentally and physically, by the experience and the promise of more to come. It occurred to her that she had not heard anything from Drake for the last couple of weeks, and she wasn't missing him. She hoped he was all right and starting to move on. However, she needed to find out if he was staying in the apartment or not. If he wasn't, she didn't trust him to leave it in good condition. She could be held financially responsible for his mess again.

When she walked into the house, her mother complained she smelled like a barn. She hadn't noticed. She grabbed a sandwich, and then went upstairs to change and shower. Feeling invigorated, she decided she could handle talking to Drake about the apartment and dialed their phone number.

"Hello?" a woman's voice responded.

Jillian was taken aback. "Uh…Is Drake there?"

"No, he isn't. What do you want?" The woman was obviously annoyed.

"Who are you?" Jillian questioned, feeling very confused.

"Tina. I'm Drake's fiancée," the woman responded.

"Drake's fiancée? ...Well, Drake's fiancée, tell Drake to call his wife." She quickly hung up. She was shaking. She was furious. She paced her small room. Gradually, she seemed to burn off her anger and started laughing. *Oh, Drake, I should have known you'd find someone to take care of you.*

A couple of hours later her phone rang. "What the hell are you doing? Haven't you caused me enough problems? You're still trying to ruin my life!" Drake yelled.

"Me? You're the one with a woman in our bed!" she yelled back.

"She wouldn't be there if you hadn't deserted me."

"I'm not so sure about that," she snapped back, and then sighed. "I'm sorry. I really don't want things to end like this."

"You're the one who ended it, but I should have, years ago." Drake was obviously trying to be hurtful. Jillian was determined to try to keep the peace between them.

"Drake, please. It was a bit of a shock. I just wish you had told me yourself," she said, trying to placate him.

"It's no longer any of your business. It stopped being your business when you left."

Jillian heard his pain under the anger. She felt the pull to make things better, to take the responsibility for his emotions. As soon as she realized what she wanted to do, she stopped herself.

"You're right. Drake, I really do want you to be happy. It's good that you're going on with your life."

"What'd you want anyway?" he asked suspiciously.

"I was wondering if you were going to stay in the apartment after the end of the month or not," she informed him.

"What difference does it make? No, don't tell me. You want half the security deposit back," he sneered.

"No, I don't care about it," she replied, calmly.

"I signed a new lease. They rolled it into my lease," Drake told her challengingly, bracing for a struggle.

"That's all I wanted to know." She was proud of herself for the matter-of-fact tone she was taking.

Drake seemed to be disarmed by her attitude. "I also signed the divorce papers."

"Thank you." She hesitated. "And, Drake, good luck."

"Thanks, Jillian. You, too." He hung up.

Jillian pushed the end button on her cell phone and sighed. It was really over. There was no turning back. She thought about the future, and the loneliness crept in.

CHAPTER 66

After Jillian's third riding lesson, she increased her schedule to a group lesson on Saturday mornings and a private lesson on Wednesday nights. The more she rode, the more she enjoyed it. Now, posting to the trot was a far less conscious action and her muscles were strengthening. Josie was encouraging, and she believed that she was making good progress. She started spending more time at the barn on Saturday. She felt a little out of place because most of the other riders had horses of their own and were either younger than she or had been riding for years. However, once they started inviting her to join them at lunch, she felt accepted anyway. She was disappointed to hear that the show season was starting up and that, most weekends, everyone would be on the road. There would be no Saturday lessons when Josie was at a show.

She had almost forgotten that she wasn't yet single, when she received a call from her attorney. The court date to finalize the divorce was set for the next week. He informed her that, since Drake had signed off on it, she would not have to make an appearance. Drake would be there since he didn't have an attorney to represent him. She wasn't sure what she wanted to do. She let the attorney know she probably would not go, but she'd call the day before court to confirm.

Jillian felt torn. A part of her wanted to show off to him. She'd lost fifteen pounds since he'd last seen her; she only had five to go to meet her own goal. Another part of her did not want him to have to go through the legal procedure alone. Yet, she did not know if she could get through it without crying. She did not want to give him the satisfaction. She could not let him know how afraid she was of being alone. She called Anna.

"Hi. Are you busy?" Jillian asked plaintively.

"No. What's up?" Anna replied, concerned.

"Oh, I'm just creating problems for myself, I guess. I can't decide whether I want to go to court for the divorce proceedings or not. On the one hand, I'd love to flaunt the new me in Drake's face so he'd know what he lost. On the other hand, I hate to think of him going through this alone. I'd really like to stay friends with him, if possible. ...I guess I should just stay away. It might be the smartest thing to do in the long run. And I don't want to make a public spectacle by crying in court. ...I just can't decide," she sighed.

"Jilly, do you really think he'll notice how fabulous you look? He never did before. It's always been about him, for you and for him. What would make you feel better? What would be best for you?" her friend questioned.

"I don't feel like I want to be in that courtroom, Anna. Once it's over, I know I'll feel so alone. I don't want Drake to see that. He'd feel so smug about it. He'd probably even tell me that I deserved the pain." Jillian thought that might even be true; it might be what she deserved.

"There's something else to consider. ...How will you feel if he shows up with that Tina person?" Anna asked quietly.

There was a long silence. "...Damn," Jillian responded. "I hadn't thought about that. Thanks for the wakeup call," she laughed without humor.

Her hopes of keeping his friendship sank; she knew she could not possibly face Drake and Tina together. It would only force her to accept that she was truly alone without a partner in the world. She did not go to court, but waited anxiously for her attorney to call.

"Jillian, this is Gavin Oft. You're a free woman, Ms. White."

"Thank you. How..." She began to ask about Drake, but stopped. She didn't feel as happy as her attorney sounded.

"You have your name back. You should have the papers by the end of next week. If you don't get them in the mail by then, give me a call."

"So, that's it?" she asked, weakly.

"Yes, but once you get them, you'll need to make copies and notify Social Security, motor vehicles, your bank, and any place else you want your name changed. You can even get a new diploma for a small fee," he explained to her.

"It's really over. I'm on my own now," Jillian mumbled, finding it difficult to grasp the reality of the situation.

Hearing the sadness in her voice and misunderstanding the source, he added, "Jillian, I don't normally say anything, but I could smell beer on him, and the new girlfriend looks like a real slut. You're better off rid of him."

"Thanks for your help, Mr. Oft." Jillian hung up feeling sad and alone. She needed to break the silence of her office. She picked up the phone and called HR. "This is Jillian Harris. Is Joan Fitzgerald in?"

"Jillian, how are you?" There was surprise in Joan's voice when she answered.

"Okay. I was wondering what I need to do to get my name changed. I'm going back to 'White.'"

"I can get things started from here and notify payroll, but you'll have to change the name on your accounts downstairs yourself. Usually, they want proof, but they know you. If they give you a hard time about it, just have them give me a call."

"Thanks for the help," Jillian replied, trying to sound normal.

"Anytime. ...I take it the divorce is final?" Joan asked.

"Yes." Jillian needed to keep the conversation brief and professional. She didn't want to break down and cry at work.

"Will I see you at yoga Friday?"

"I'll be there."

"Good, we'll go out afterward and catch a bite to eat. My treat. Let's just say we're celebrating a new life for Jillian White."

"I'd like that. See ya Friday." She forced a smile into her voice.

Jillian hung up and took the elevator to the first floor. After making the changes to her accounts, she went back upstairs to inform Jerry and to have Sue Ann order her new business cards and name plates.

Friday, after yoga, Joan and Jillian went to Mike Fink's down on the river for dinner. Before Jillian could say anything, Joan ordered two glasses of sparkling wine. Joan started them off with a toast, "To new beginnings!"

Jillian thanked her, and then asked if she was back on the antiques trail now that spring had arrived. Joan started sharing the plans she and George had made to go away weekends on their search for nineteenth century armoires for their bedroom. Eventually, the conversation turned to Jillian's horseback riding.

"I really love it. I wish I could afford to have my own horse and be able to ride whenever I wanted," Jillian related, enthusiastically.

"How often have you been riding?"

"Twice a week, but they'll be going to horse shows soon and I'll only be able to ride once a week." Jillian made a sad, wistful face.

"Will you be going to the shows?" Joan asked with interest.

"I don't ride well enough for that, at least not yet." She laughed, and then becoming more serious, she added, "I guess the weekends will continue to be tough."

"Why don't you go to some of the shows to watch?" the older woman suggested.

"I don't know. It would seem strange going alone to something like that. Maybe, if there was one close by. But these people travel all over the country with their horses." She shrugged, indicating that there was nothing she could do on her own.

"Well, maybe if you start going, you'll get to know someone to go with."

"Maybe. But I should start spending weekends looking for my own place now that the divorce is behind me," she said, taking a sip of the sparkling wine.

"Are you still at your parents?" Joan inquired, fiddling with her napkin.

"Yes," Jillian responded, "and they assure me I can stay as long as I want. A lot depends on what I want to buy."

Joan nodded. "What did you have in mind?"

"I want something that would be a good investment and thought a house would be best. But then, I'd have to stay longer at my parents to save more for a down payment, and it would make my monthly payments higher." She frowned with frustration.

Joan looked at her new friend. "You don't sound very enthusiastic. I thought you wanted your own house for a long time."

"I do, or rather, I did; but I never expected to be alone." She sighed and shook her head. "My head tells me it's the right thing to do."

Joan pursed her lips and cocked her head. "What's your heart tell you?"

"You'll think this is foolish." She paused and looked at the other woman. "My heart tells me to buy a small condo and spend my money on a horse."

"Jillian, you're young and, for now, you're free to do whatever you want. Indulge yourself while you can." Joan punctuated her words with nods of her head.

"You don't think it would be irresponsible?" She looked skeptically at her companion.

"You're still talking about buying, not renting. I doubt you could be irresponsible if you tried." Joan laughed.

Jillian looked down at her lap, contemplating her options. "I still couldn't afford my own horse, at least not one fully trained, and training costs a lot."

"Find yourself a place to live. The rest will come. Trust yourself."

It seemed to Jillian that when she had trusted herself things went wrong or, at least, they had with Drake. Or was it that she had learned as Ellie not to trust her own judgment about Ted? She wondered what the rest of her life had been like after Ted died. "I'm not sure I do trust myself anymore."

"It will come back to you," Joan reassured her.

As the food was served, the conversation shifted again to the restaurant and the service. By the time Jillian left for her parents, her spirits had been lifted and she felt more hopeful about her future.

CHAPTER 67

Jillian had been hesitant to buy either a condo or a house before her divorce was completely processed. She didn't want Drake to have any claim on anything she purchased. She had decided that her best option would be a previously owned condo. It might reduce the potential resale value later on, but it would be affordable and she could look for a three-bedroom instead of settling for a two-bedroom new place. That would also leave her money to furnish the place since she had left all the furniture and other necessities of housekeeping with Drake. After much assessment and heart searching, she decided on a price range that would reduce how much money she had to save for the closing and for the down payment. She got herself pre-approved by the bank for a mortgage and began checking the classifieds to get an idea of what condos were selling for in some decent neighborhoods. At last, she decided it was time to move forward with her plan. She really felt the need to get out of her parents' house and into her own place.

As soon as the divorce papers arrived in the mail, Jillian called a realtor to begin her search. The first three weekends, she saw a lot of places that she hated. She was starting to think she should start working with another realtor, but then the woman told her she thought she finally knew what she wanted. She convinced Jillian to go out looking one more day.

Much to the realtor's relief, Jillian fell in love with the next property the woman showed. It was a three-bedroom condo in Hyde Park, an older building with a balcony that overlooked a little park with lots of trees. Jillian was charmed by the open layout of the kitchen, living room, and dining room area. The master bedroom had a large walk-in closet with two rows of bars to hang clothes, and shelves at the top for storage. The appliances in the kitchen were fairly new and there was a washer and dryer in a small utility room. She was delighted by the idea of not having to lug heavy laundry baskets downstairs to a common laundry room. She thought that the place would need very little work to be ideal for her. The asking price was at the high end of her price range, but she hoped the owners would come down on their price. She made an offer immediately, giving the realtor a check to hold the place.

The owners were out of town and she had three days of waiting. They were anxious to sell, however, and accepted her lower offer. Both she and her realtor were surprised, having expected a counter offer. Jillian wondered if she should have offered even less, but both her father and the realtor assured her she had done very well and probably would have ended up paying the same amount. Once she realized her monthly housing cost would be about the same as she and Drake had been paying for their apartment, but with the added tax benefits, she was thrilled. A closing date was set for the end of June.

Jillian had been keeping up her Wednesday night riding, going to the gym during the week, and Friday night yoga. She knew she was starting over and would have to buy everything new, from the furniture down to the pots and pans, but she wanted more time with the horses. After another weekend of nothing, she decided to brave attending a horse show by herself. A number of riders from Misty Glen would be showing. She left early Saturday morning, following the directions Josie had given her. It was a pleasant two-hour drive out into the countryside. She searched out the area to find where the Misty Glen group was stabled.

At the stable area, everyone seemed rushed. Riders made last minute touch ups to makeup and hair, while grooms wiped down horses with mineral oil rags before saddling them. Josie was checking on the grooms work, picking a tail here or there. No one seemed to notice Jillian watching the preparations. Three of their riders were competing in the next class. As soon as they mounted, everyone followed them to the warm up area. Jillian trailed along, feeling awkward and alone. Some of the other riders, friends, and family members of the competitors headed to the grandstand to await the call of the Junior Three Gaited Class. Someone finally recognized Jillian and invited her to sit with the group. The woman explained to her the event would be judged on the horses who would be ridden by riders seventeen years of age or younger. They would be asked to walk, trot, and canter in each direction of the ring, and then stand their horses for the judge to examine their confirmation. Jillian appreciated the explanation and felt comfortable asking an occasional question about the class. Ribbons were awarded to the top six horses. A small, engraved, silver platter accompanied the blue ribbon and was won by a member of her stable. She was surprised that she was already thinking of Misty Glen as her stable. The next event was for jumpers. The show hands started dragging out the jumps to set up. Everyone from her stable quickly left. Jillian followed.

Jillian went with the group back and forth from the stable area to the ring and back to the stable all day. When the five-gaited horses entered the ring, Jillian became spell bound. The flowing manes and tails sailed gracefully by the rail, around and around the ring. One chestnut mare reminded her of Ellie's Princess. She found herself mesmerized by the addition of the slow gait and rack to the three other gaits. She was exhausted by the time they broke for dinner. When they invited her to join them, she declined and started her drive home.

Wednesday night, she greeted Josie, "I want to learn to ride five-gaited horses."

Josie laughed. When she saw the frown on Jillian's face in response, she explained, "You've got the bug. First, let's get you riding three-gaited, and then we can look at getting you on a five-gaited horse."

"I need to ride more than once a week if I'm ever going to get there." Jillian felt her frustration building.

"We'll work it out. Now, let's get started; mount up!" Josie ordered.

Jillian spent her free time going to the gym, riding, and preparing to move into her new place. Anna dragged her through one furniture store after another, trying to help her spend the money she had allotted. Yet, something held her back. She finally bought a queen-size bed and arranged for it to be delivered the Saturday after the closing. She couldn't decide on anything else. The last Sunday before the closing on the condo, Jillian called Anna and asked her to go to Bed, Bath, and Beyond with her. Jillian needed all new linens and everything for the kitchen. She knew Anna would have fun helping.

Jillian's father offered to go with her on her walk-through and for the closing. She turned him down; it was a difficult choice. If she had believed that he only wanted to go with her to share her excitement, she would have accepted. However, she felt that he wanted to go to take care of his little girl, as if she were not capable of signing the papers on her own. It was something that she would have expected to do with her husband and did not really want to do it by herself. However, she saw it as the adult thing to do. If she were going to be alone, she needed to try to get used to it. Everything went smoothly. The next morning, Jillian and her brother loaded her car, his SUV, their mother's station wagon, and their father's sedan with all her belongings, new and old. Fran insisted no one leave until they'd all eaten breakfast. She also packed a cooler with drinks and sandwiches.

Everyone bustled about the condo, carrying in boxes and dropping them in the rooms Jillian had designated for them. Fran took charge of the kitchen immediately, opening the bags and boxes of new utensils, dishes, pots, and pans, washing them, and then putting them were she thought they should go. Jillian looked in on her labors, and her mother took the opportunity to fuss about the total lack of furnishings.

"There's not even any place to sit down to eat!" Fran exclaimed. "How are you going to get breakfast down in the morning or watch TV? You have got to get some furniture, Jilly! This is just ridiculous. You're not a college freshman anymore."

"It'll be all right, Mom. Don't worry about it so much. I want to find the right pieces for this place. I don't want to settle for just anything. Meanwhile, I'll make do. I promise to have furniture before you come over again." She hugged her mother to reassure and pacify her. Fran harrumphed in discontent, but held her peace. They all took a break around noon and 'picnicked' in the middle of the living room floor. By the middle of the afternoon, everything had been put in place as much as possible. Jillian's clothing was hung in her closet or was still sitting in suitcases waiting for a dresser to arrive. There were old, vertical blinds on all the windows, so she'd have privacy. Her bathroom had towels, soap, paper, and her toiletries all in place so she could get ready for work on Monday. The bed was made up with new sheets and a quilt. She had a lamp on a large, overturned box next to her bed. There was another lamp in the living room, sitting on the floor, but at least it was plugged in so that she wouldn't have to try to find her way through the condo in the dark. Looking around the place uncertainly, her family hugged her and departed, her mother reminding her that she could always come home if she wanted company, or a place to sit down.

While Jillian was glad for their help, she also would have liked to enter her own place for the first time alone. She felt she needed to become accustomed to the concept. It had only just occurred to her that she had never before lived alone. She had lived with her parents, with Anna and Sally, and with Drake, but never by herself. She wasn't fearful of living by herself; she had become quite efficient at handling everything that might need to be done while living with Drake. Her fear was of the loneliness, of never having someone to love or share her life.

CHAPTER 68

The silence was disturbing. She had told herself she needed to wait to buy furnishings until she had a feel for the place. The reality was that the only things she had seen that appealed to her were nineteenth century antiques or quality reproductions. She had not wanted to give in to the past of being Ellie mourning Ted or, for that matter, Drake. She realized that she didn't even have a radio much less a sound system, TV, or computer. The cable was on, the phone line was connected, but she had no way of using either of them. She found herself walking from room to room, trying to feel at home. At last, she walked out on her balcony and looked at the view of the park nearby. As she stood there thinking about her new home and the emptiness inside it, she felt a chill that she wasn't certain could be attributed only to the breeze blowing over the balcony. Rubbing her arms and chiding herself for feeling sad, she turned and went back inside.

She tried reading; when that didn't help, she made a list. Then, she went to a nearby CVS pharmacy and purchased a radio-alarm clock. Then she entered Kroger's. She perused each isle slowly. She picked up a quart of mayonnaise; she stopped before putting it into the cart. Looking at the jar, she held back the tears and returned it to the shelf, exchanging it for a pint size jar. She was alone now. Two hours later, she loaded the groceries into her car and drove to her new home. She set up the radio and, as she put away the food, began reorganizing her mother's organization of her kitchen.

Jillian had managed to putter away the evening. She finally turned in, tired. She tossed all night; her dreams were mixed with visions of Ted, Drake, and Princess. She rose early to the sound of coffee beans grinding. She'd been putting off going through her clothes to see what could be taken in to fit. By noon she'd run out of things to do. She drove to Best Buy, having already done her research. She picked out a cordless phone with an answering machine for the kitchen and a simple one for her bedroom. When she got to the TVs, it suddenly occurred to her that for the first time in her life she could afford to buy nearly anything she wanted; she didn't have to settle or answer to anyone. She smiled. *HDTV, DVD, surround sound, CD player, tuner, receiver.* She turned on her cell, ignored the two new messages, and called her brother. He wasn't home, but answered his cell. "I need your SUV," she told him.

"When?" Billy asked, somewhat hesitantly.

"Now!" Jillian asserted emphatically.

"Well, I can meet you in about an hour," he offered, and then added, "What if I hadn't answered?"

"But you did. Please?" Jillian wheedled.

"Oh…Okay," her brother conceded, a bit annoyed at her haste.

She told him where she was, adding, "I love you, Billy. Kisses!"

While she waited, she started looking at the computers. She found herself drawn to the laptops. She'd always wanted one, but…the cost. She also picked out a small color printer. Her brother found her in the store looking at DVDs. They went to the checkout with her cart and the slips from the salesperson. She'd spent most of her furniture budget and she didn't care. Billy helped her take everything into the condo and out of the boxes, setting them on the floor. She turned the box for the 32-inch TV upside down and placed the laptop on it, stood back, and smiled.

Bill started laughing, "You could use the printer box as a stool and the surround sound box as a dining room table."

"Hey, that's not a bad idea." She knew her brother was joking, but she was serious.

"You've got to be kidding!" he exclaimed, shaking his head.

"I just spent most of my furniture budget," she explained, shrugging.

"What are you going to tell Mom?" her brother asked her, cringing at the thought.

"Nothing, and neither are you!" She poked him in the chest with her finger, very much the big sister.

Billy just shook his head, "Come on. Let's move the TV into place, and then I'm out of here."

Jillian spent the rest of the day playing with her new toys. Over the next few weeks, she kept herself busy with work, the gym, and riding. She tried to stay out late, only going home to eat dinner on the floor in front of the TV. She'd then get on-line, trying to find lost friends to e-mail and go to bed blurry eyed. Weekends remained the most difficult. She'd ride when possible and went to another show that wasn't too far away. By the end of July, she was tired of sitting on the floor and putting off her friends who wanted to see her new place. She bought a faux suede couch and a complementary chair. It wasn't the style she'd been thinking of, but the colors were muted to blend with whatever else she decided on and, most importantly, they were comfortable. She continued gradually, over the remainder of the summer, to buy a piece of furniture here and there.

By Labor Day weekend, the condo was furnished sufficiently for Jillian to feel comfortable allowing people to come to see it. However, she greeted each one with, "It's not finished yet." At the annual family get-together, she found it easier to face her relatives than she had expected. All were supportive. She realized for the first time how pleasant and relaxed it was without having to worry about Drake's behavior.

CHAPTER 69

As the fall progressed, Jillian continued to keep herself busy. She had been in her new position for a year. She was anxious about what kind of performance review she would receive. She was enjoying the job more. Jerry Green had given her more accounts and she had brought in a couple of her own. He also had expanded her responsibilities. The work was challenging and she loved the opportunity to learn new things. She looked forward each morning to getting to work. While she had not made any friends at the office, the secretaries were much friendlier than they had been and she was frequently invited to join the junior executives for lunch. She stopped planning parties, but made a point of acknowledging everyone's birthday with a card and occasionally brought in donuts or a cake. She would leave them in the coffee room, never mentioning it to anyone, yet everyone knew who was responsible.

The morning of her review, she arrived earlier than usual. She believed she had been doing good work, especially the last six months, but her stomach was still doing flips. She was concerned that she might have missed a critical management expectation. Jerry didn't call her into his office until nearly eleven. She sat on the edge of the chair he had indicated across from his desk; her annual merit raise would be related to this review. Jerry pushed a paper across the desk and told Jillian to read it, and then they would talk about it. She picked up the evaluation with some trepidation. As she began reading the numerical scores, she felt the tension start to melt away. When she reached the narrative at the end, a smile came across her face.

"Do you have any objections?" Jerry asked, smiling himself.

"No objections, none at all!" she exclaimed enthusiastically.

"I'd like you to add your goals for yourself for the next year," he instructed her.

Jillian thought for a moment. "I'm not sure how to quantify it, but I'd like to bring in more accounts myself. Also, I'd like to have more varied responsibilities."

Jerry helped her to objectify her goals and added them to the bottom of the review. They both signed and dated it. "Human Resources will send you a copy," he informed her, putting the review into a folder and closing it.

Jillian started to stand. "Thank you, Jerry. I'm really flattered by your evaluation."

"There is one more thing that you might be interested in before you go back to your office." He took another sheet of paper out and handed it to her.

It was her raise, another twelve percent, on top of last year's raise for her promotion. "Oh...uh...thank you." She almost added, "This is too much," but stopped herself.

"No, thank you. You've been doing a great job. You deserve it." He took the paper back. "You'll receive a copy of this, too. It won't be in your next check, but you'll see it in the one after that."

Jillian continued thanking her supervisor as she left his office. She was excited and wanted to share her news with someone. But no matter whom she thought of calling, it didn't seem right. While her friends would be happy for her, it would feel like bragging. Her mother would worry that her employers might be expecting more of her than she could deliver and her father would lecture about saving it for a rainy day. It reminded her that she was alone without a partner to share her life, not that Drake had ever really been a partner. However, she was no longer able to delude herself. She pushed the thought away, smiling as she entered her own office. She sat at her desk and wrote down personal goals. "Believe in myself. Trust my own judgment. Have confidence."

Jillian still did not want to become a CEO or CFO, but she was beginning to see herself in a new light. She was beginning to understand why her peers, her supervisors, and the secretaries perceived that her intense striving for excellence meant that was her goal. For the first time, she wondered if she could do it. However, she knew she would never trade career and financial success for love. When she thought of being alone, waves of sadness washed over her. Her best defense was not to think. She dove into her work with a new resolve.

Jerry Green, the vice-president of Contracts, Mergers and Acquisitions, had called a meeting with the other vice-presidents and several staff members, including Jillian, to resolve the difficult question of which of two well qualified firms, Heinlein, McCaffrey, and Weiss or Southland, would get their company's southeastern states advertising and marketing business for the next year. As Jerry's assistant, it was Jillian's task to develop the detailed summary evaluations of their proposals, carefully comparing their strengths and weaknesses to the pre-set evaluation criteria she had been given. She concluded her report by recommending the newer upstart Southland, much to the consternation of most of the vice-presidents who favored Heinlein, McCaffrey, and Weiss because of their past relationship and lower cost.

Jerry opened by reading Jeff Jacobson's strong and dismissive rebuttal of Jillian's recommendation; she wished she could have disappeared under the table in embarrassment as the marketing vice-president's disdainful critique hit her ears. *Why was Jerry doing this to her?* Then Jerry announced, "I have only two points to make. First, I want to bring a consensus recommendation from this group to our president; I have to bring in a consensus recommendation! The reason I have to do that is to show that all of us are committed to expanding and developing our business in the southeastern United States so that we are the dominant financial firm within five years. The economy is expanding so rapidly there and much faster than our experts predicted; if we do not grow with it, we will lose this market. Jillian has pointed the way to our almost certain success. She recommended contracting with Southland because they are affiliated with many of the medium-sized and faster growing businesses; Heinlein, McCaffrey, and Weiss is linked with older, larger, and more stable firms. In her appendix, she recommended acquiring Southland in anticipation of implementing our southeastern strategy over the next few years. With Southland's dedicated expertise, we can reduce the risk and move now."

Silence. Then Phil Grey stood up, "Jillian, you saw a wonderful opportunity we all missed. Well done!" Her face reddened at the sound of approval from her peers.

With her raise, she had become more excited about the possibility of being able to afford her own horse. She opened another savings account as a horse fund. She wasn't sure how much she would need. She didn't want an untrained horse that she'd have to wait years to ride. She also realized she would need to wait until she was a better rider. She wanted a five-gaited horse with a bit of spirit. She was still only riding the three-gaited ones. She was frustrated with her progress. She remembered how confident Ellie had felt on a horse and wanted to experience that feeling again. Yet, she was able to honestly tell herself she was doing well, considering the amount of time she'd ridden.

CHAPTER 70

It seemed that every weekend Josie was off to another show with the stables. Jillian rode during the week and complained about not having enough time to ride. Josie encouraged her to come to more shows, saying she could also learn from watching critically. Jillian wasn't sure how much she could learn, but she had enjoyed the couple of shows she did attend. However, each time she drove home from a show with an increased longing.

"We're going to Indianapolis the weekend after next. It will expose you to some of the best competition. There aren't many shows left in the season," Josie suggested the next time they met.

"But that's too far. I'd have to stay overnight." Jillian felt inexplicably anxious at the thought of driving so far by herself and staying alone in a hotel room.

"Yes. Is that a problem?" She looked at Jillian questioningly. "We really have a good time. They have a wonderful exhibitors' party with a buffet, open bar, and live music. I have some extra passes that will get you into the show and the party."

"It sounds like fun…but I don't know." Jillian chewed her lip, pulled in two directions.

"We have a block of rooms reserved. Tell me you have something better to do?" Josie challenged her student.

"No…" she admitted reluctantly, shrugging and trying to find an excuse for not going.

"Good, it's settled then." Josie turned her back and began checking the cinch on   the   horse's   saddle.
Jillian felt cornered. She couldn't bring herself to say "no" to Josie. She realized she wanted to please her just as she did Jerry, and just as she wanted to please everyone else in her life. She wasn't sure if she should try to find a way out.

Jillian planned on looking for new window treatments on Saturday. She hated the old, verticals blinds and Anna had volunteered to go with her. It would be a good opportunity to talk it out with someone. She was unsure if she should stand firm and refuse to go to the show or not.

As they were debating the merits of blinds versus shades or drapes, Jillian brought up the horse show trip. "It would be a long drive, and I'd have to stay overnight. I love the shows, but I'd have to go alone. And I don't really know anyone who's going to be there. I really think I should pass on it, but Josie is so insistent. It's really hard to say 'no' to her." Jillian sighed, thinking that she was doomed to lose either way.

"I can understand your reluctance to drive so far alone, but it would still be daylight and it's mostly interstate driving. It's not likely you'd get lost. And you've stayed alone in a hotel room before when you went to Savannah. Besides, Jilly, you love these horse shows. It's almost all you talk about now." Anna laughed to reassure her friend that she wasn't being critical.

"I know you're right, but I feel so awkward just trailing after these people. If I had made any friends, or even a friendly acquaintance with any one of them, but..." she shrugged helplessly.

"Jilly, you can't make friends with them if you don't spend time with them. They all love horses and riding. That certainly gives you something to talk to them about. It takes time to make friends. And they've never done anything to make you feel unwelcome, have they?" Anna asked, cocking her head.

"Well, no. They've always been very pleasant. But preparing for the classes and riding takes all their time and attention. Most of them don't have the time to chat with me." Jillian realized she was sounding rather petulant and childish, but she really did feel uncomfortable.

"Granted, they don't have time during the show, but that's why everyone gets together afterwards to socialize. If you spend the night, you'll have a chance to get to know them better. More importantly, they'll have the chance to get to know you. And that will guarantee that they will want to be your friend. You're a lot of fun to be with...when you're not moping!" She punched her friend gently on the shoulder and smiled.

Sighing, Jillian realized that Anna was right. If she wanted to make friends with these people, she would have to spend more time with them. She decided that she would go to the show after all.

Wednesday night, Jillian confirmed with Josie that she would go to the show, but that she wouldn't get to the hotel until Friday night around nine. She put her suitcase in the car before leaving for work so that she could leave right from the office. She took off at four o'clock, heading northwest. When she checked in, there was a message to join the group in the cocktail lounge. She dropped her bag off in her room and went back downstairs.

She was surprised to see so many people from the stable. There was a large table of teenagers drinking soda and munching on snack foods. The adults had pulled together a few small tables and were talking and laughing loudly. She noticed that the beverages ranged from coffee and soda to wine, beer, and liquor. It had been a long time since she'd had any alcohol, but decided on a glass of white wine since she would not have to drive. Someone ordered a platter of cheeses. It was apparent that exhibitors from other stables were staying at the same hotel. Occasionally, someone from another barn would stop at their table to chat on their way back or forth from the bar. Although everyone was friendly, Jillian felt somewhat out of place. She listened to the conversation as it moved from the idiosyncrasies of the judges, to who had recently acquired a new horse, to who from another stable was getting a divorce. She realized she had much to learn about the people involved in this sport and about its nuances. She didn't think it was what Josie had in mind when she'd told her she could learn by watching.

When the group started to break up, Jillian was surprised to see that it was already nearly midnight. The evening had flown by and she had actually forgotten that she was there alone. By the time she retired to her room, she was too tired to remember.

She discovered that this show was much bigger than the others she had attended. There were two rings and a separate hunt course. The first class she watched was an equitation class for fourteen to seventeen year old riders. It was judged on the riders' skills. There were so many entrants she did not know how the judge could keep track. After going through all three gaits in each direction, the riders were required to trot their horse three-fourths of the way down the ring, stop, make a figure eight by cantering a circle to the left, stop, change leads and cantering a circle to the right, stop, and then trot to the judge, stop again, stretch their horse, and then back four steps. Jillian was amazed by the ability demonstrated in controlling the horses and that the riders could remember it all. She also saw how the exercise separated the abilities of the riders and the training of the horses.

The day went by quickly; Jillian closely followed the Saddlebred classes. She checked the numbers on riders' backs with the names in the program. She felt a need to learn who was who. She picked out the horses she liked the best in each class and waited anxiously to see if the judges would pick the same horses. Although she did not always pick the winner, she was pleased to discover that her choices consistently left the ring with ribbons. After the last class, she headed back to the hotel to shower and change for the party. She had asked what most people wore to exhibitors' parties, and was told that it varied, but this one was casual dressy. It was being held in the ballroom of the hotel where she was staying and was scheduled to begin at seven.

Jillian fussed, dressing carefully; she was pleased with the return of her figure. She took the elevator to the mezzanine, arriving at the ballroom at a quarter after seven. She had been concerned about being late, but found that people were just starting to stroll into the room. She didn't see anyone she knew; however, some faces seemed familiar. She guessed that she had seen them around the show grounds. A line started to develop at the bar and, rather than stand alone, she waited for a glass of wine. The two women standing in front of her were discussing the winners of the day, the merits of their riding, and the salient points of the horses they had been riding. Jillian listened quietly while they talked, and then interrupted with a question about one of the horses. This generated a discussion about the relative merits of one breed over another and what level of training would be good in a horse for someone who was just beginning to ride. The women invited Jillian to sit with them at their table and introduced themselves and their friends to her. When she recognized one of the women at the table as one of the riders who had won a ribbon during the show, Jillian congratulated her on her win and complimented her form. Jillian found she was really enjoying herself. She thanked the people she had been chatting with and excused herself when she saw Josie and some of the others from Misty Glen come into the room.

"Well, how'd you like the show?" Josie asked her.

"It was wonderful!" Jillian exclaimed. "I doubt I'll ever be good enough to compete like they do, but it was lovely just watching them."

"So you're glad you came?" Josie asked.

Jillian laughed, thinking about her reluctance. "Yes, Josie, you were right," she intoned, like a little child. "I'm glad I came. It really is fun." They sat down at the table to eat with several others from the stable. Jillian was gratified to find that they all welcomed her and treated her as if she belonged there with them.

After dinner, a DJ began playing music and inviting the crowd to come up and dance. Jillian sat at the emptied table, swaying to the music and watching as couples formed up on the dance floor. She was startled out of her reverie when an attractive man approached her and asked her to dance. Jillian almost refused, feeling suddenly shy, but then reminded herself that she was single and loved to dance. Her partner turned out to be light on his feet and fairly graceful. When the dance ended, he escorted her back to her table and thanked her. She didn't sit alone long before another man came over, introduced himself, and began chatting with her. He talked about riding and about buying his first horse. They were soon joined by others returning from the dance floor or the bar. Jillian found herself enjoying the babble of friendly conversation and competitive teasing that was going on at the table. As she watched the younger members of the party, teenagers from her stable and others, flirting with each other, it occurred to her that she might be able to meet a man who shared her interests in horses, someone she could go to shows with so that she wouldn't have to be alone. She looked around the room, noticing that there were several good looking, nicely dressed, well-toned men there, and not all of them seemed to be attached. One or two in particular caught her eye and smiled at her. She pushed herself to smile back without blushing or acting embarrassed. However, Jillian also noticed that there was a lot of drinking going on and some of the men seemed to be consuming more than their share, but most seemed to be drinking socially, not in excess. She definitely did not want another problem drinker in her life. Thinking it over, Jillian decided that it would be nice to get to know more of these men, and she added rapidly, the women, too, of course.

The next day, she woke late, checked out, and rushed to the show. She stayed close to the rings, even watching an open jumper class. She was surprised to see a Saddlebred as one of the top contenders. She found herself watching the handsome rider more than the horse; she did not understand the blush she felt rushing to her face. She drove home, proud of herself for going and determined to go to more events.

CHAPTER 71

Jillian walked into her dark condo and was struck by the emptiness. She quickly started turning on lights and the TV, attempting to fill the void with light and sound. She checked for messages; there was one from her mother wanting her to call to let her know she was home safely. She felt let down; she laughed to herself, it wasn't as though she was expecting anyone to call. There was no one. She returned her mother's call.

Jillian was enjoying the lifestyle she had set up for herself: work, riding, the gym, and yoga. There were occasional dinners at her parents' house, lunches with Anna, and visiting with Sally and the baby. The horse show season was starting to wind down, but she did make it to another one before it ended. As Thanksgiving approached, she realized it had been a year since she and Drake had separated. It was a surprise to her when she reviewed the year and realized how much she had accomplished.

Thanksgiving weekend, she began her Christmas shopping. Although she needed to set a budget for herself, it was the first year she felt she could buy for the people in her life and not have to worry that she'd have trouble paying her bills as a result.

The first Christmas party of the season was for the executives at the bank. It was a dressy affair for all the corporate departments and was to be held at the Omni Netherland Plaza. Jillian struggled over what type of outfit to wear. She bought a black cocktail dress made of stretch jersey. She decided that her new, trim figure could stand up to scrutiny even in a clingy dress. It had a scoop neck and back trimmed with shiny satin and long fitted sleeves made of chiffon. Smiling at her image in the mirror, Jillian thought that Ellie would have been very satisfied with the neckline, but both mothers might have been a bit scandalized.

The first person Jillian spotted that she knew when she entered the banquet hall was Joan Fitzgerald. She was delighted to see her. It meant she wouldn't have to dive right in meeting and greeting people she didn't know well. After checking her coat, she joined the woman and her husband, George, at their table.

"Do we have assigned seats or may I join you?" Jillian asked them after saying hello and being introduced to George.

"I think it's open seating," Joan responded. "Grab a chair."

George stood to pull out a chair for Jillian. They proceeded to exchange compliments on dresses and comments on the decorations the hotel had arranged. Jillian was impressed with the setting. There were enough tables for at least a hundred people, and it was to be a sit-down dinner. There was an open bar and a DJ for dancing later. A lectern had been set up so that the top executives could offer Christmas greetings. Each table had a candle and floral centerpiece. The tables were laid with crisp, white linen tablecloths and napkins. Even the china was festive with a Christmas pattern of holly around the borders. They were soon joined by other employees, some of whom Jillian had not met. John and Michelle Daggett sat next to Jillian at the table. John introduced his wife to the others. She was an attractive and pleasant woman, easy to talk to, and Jillian quickly decided she liked her very much. The men offered to get drinks for the women and left. The women continued to get to know each other.

While they waited for dinner to be served, the department heads circulated, greeting their employees and offering holiday wishes to all. Jillian was flattered when Phil Grey stopped at their table specifically to introduce his wife, Margaret, to her. Waiters began circulating with trays of appetizers while the guests mingled. Before long, the first course was being served and the noise level settled down some. When Michelle Daggett found out that Jillian was single again, she immediately wanted to fix her up with a single friend of theirs.

"John, don't you think she and Peter would get along? He's divorced, too. A doctor! Has his own practice. Very cute and very funny. I think you'd really hit it off with him. What do you think?" She was eagerly leaning across her husband to persuade Jillian.

Jillian hesitated, a forkful of roast beef halfway to her mouth. "Well, I don't know, Michelle. I'm not much for blind dates."

"Peter really is a nice guy, Jillian," John added. "I've known him for years. And I think he'd like you, too."

Jillian took a deep breath, and then shrugged. "Okay. You can give him my number." She watched as Michelle pulled pen and paper out of her evening bag and wrote down the number Jillian dictated to her. Jillian gulped and reached for her drink, sipping down some liquid courage. *Well, I have to start somewhere, and this guy's a doctor. That's a plus,* she thought to herself. Jillian danced with several of the men at the party, but didn't offer any of them her phone number. At last, she headed home, glad to be getting into bed.

CHAPTER 72

Christmas Eve, Jillian went to her parents. Donna surprised the family and flew in with her fiancé for three days. The house was alive with laughter and good humor. Billy slipped in and out of the White home to his girlfriend's, much to Fran's consternation. Jillian, however, stayed with the family throughout Donna's visit.

Jillian had RSVPed to the holiday party at Misty Glen for the Sunday afternoon between Christmas and New Years' Eve. She had learned with this crowd to arrive late for social events. This was a sharp contrast to anything involving the horses, when everyone seemed ready to go ten minutes early. She laughed to herself, thinking Ellie would have appreciated their attitude. She was surprised by the number of cars. The party was in Josie's old, sprawling house on the farm. She had never been inside of it before. She noticed the door leading in from the sun porch was open and headed in that direction. As soon as she crossed the threshold, Josie seemed to appear out of nowhere to greet her.

Josie showed her around, leading her to the eggnog set up near the Christmas tree. There were many new faces and Josie started introducing her. The front room led off to a foyer, and then into a large parlor with a pianoforte. Her hostess explained that the main part of the house had been built around 1830 and the piano had been part of the original furnishings. She had decorated the entire house from that period. The double sliding doors were fully opened, leading into another room with settees, chairs, and a big roll-top desk. A side door led back to the room with the tree. They turned right into the dining room where a buffet was laid out on the table. Josie continued making introductions as she led the way. They ended up in a country kitchen with a table that could easily seat twenty people. This was apparently the group Josie had been looking for. They appeared to be in their late twenties and early thirties; Josie introduced her and disappeared. One of the women invited her to join them. It became apparent to Jillian that the group had essentially grown up together riding horses. However, Jillian wasn't the only outsider. There were two spouses and a girlfriend. As a result, they explained situations to include Jillian and the others. A few of them were still riding, but only two still participated in competition regularly.

When the party started breaking up, most of them decided to continue their own party at a local bar and burger place; Jillian agreed to go along. She enjoyed the openness between them and how they readily accepted a newcomer. They seemed genuinely interested in her as well, once the old stories slowed down. Jillian excused herself, going to the ladies room. Mary and Lana, two of the women she had just met, followed along. As soon as the door closed, Lana blurted out, "Ed really likes you, Jillian."

"What? He's hardly talked to me." Jillian was surprised.

"He's been staring at you all night," Mary pointed out, nudging Jillian. "I know he's kind of goofy, but he really has a good heart." Mary added.

"I don't think he has one bad habit," offered Lana sincerely.

"Except maybe hanging out with Bill," Mary interjected, making a disgusted face.

"How's that a bad habit?" Jillian was confused. Bill seemed charming and was certainly better looking than Ed.

"They've been doing the same thing since high school. They meet a new woman, like you; Bill wines and dines her, flies her around for exotic weekends, and then disappears for six months," Mary explained, gesticulating to punctuate her tale.

"In the meantime, Ed has been designated the good friend," Lana added, shaking her head. "Poor guy. He gets left out because Bill steals his thunder."

"Thanks for the warning," Jillian offered, smiling.

"Ed's too shy to ask, but I'm sure he wants your phone number," Lana finished.

The three women rejoined the rest of the group. Things started to breakup around eleven. Mary and Lana asked Jillian for her number. She was sure it was an attempt to help Ed out, but gave them each a business card, jotting down her cell on the back. Ed had been standing awkwardly by. She turned and handed him one, too, adding, "Next time you're in town, give me a call if you want to go out to dinner or something." She purposely said nothing to Bill, but ran ahead to her car. She did not want to lead Ed on, but she also wanted to make a point. She'd had enough of charming, selfish men. Ed lived in Pennsylvania, so she'd probably never hear from him anyway.

She walked into her condo, pleased that men seemed to be noticing her. However, her longing to be held increased as the emptiness enveloped her. She grabbed the remote, but stopped herself from turning on the TV, setting it back down on the couch. She couldn't understand this loneliness and was determined to beat it.

New Year's Eve, Anna and John were having a house party. Jillian went over early to help decorate and cook. They had invited all their old college friends who were still in the area, friends from both Anna's and John's work, and some of their neighbors. It was supposed to be an open house from nine to whenever. Anna was unusually nervous about it. She confessed to Jillian that she was afraid everyone would show up at once and there wouldn't be enough room. Jillian reassured her friend that it was unlikely and that, even if they did, everyone would have fun.

Everything was in place by the time the guests began showing up. John had set up a bar so that people could serve themselves. Anna had trays of appetizers and bowls of snack foods set out around the living room and covering the dining room table. Jillian had to remind herself that she was living a healthier lifestyle now when she looked at all the offerings available. She quickly poured herself a diet soda and began mingling. It was fun catching up with old college friends she hadn't seen in some time. She even found herself enjoying meeting those guests she didn't know.

She had just returned to the bar for a refill of her soda, when Kurt, a short, balding, pudgy friend from college, approached Jillian. "Hi, Jilly. It's been a while since I've seen you. You're looking good, girl! Where's that trouble maker of yours?" He laughed, looking around for Drake.

"We're divorced," she explained, realizing that she didn't feel any pang of hurt with the statement.

"Sure, now that I'm married. I always had the hots for you, but you could never see anyone but Drake," he informed her conspiratorially.

"Kurt, I never suspected." She laughed, leaning away from him just a bit, smelling alcohol on his breath.

"I never could figure out what you saw in that guy," he stated, shaking his head.

"I guess I didn't understand it myself until recently. But that's a long story. Who'd you marry? Where is she?" Jillian asked, looking around to see if she could guess which of the women would have married him.

"I met Jan at work. I'll introduce you. She's around here somewhere." He took her arm and began leading her about the room, searching for his wife. When they finally found her, Jillian was surprised to see a tall, strawberry blonde, casually dressed. She thought that Kurt had done well for himself, marrying such an attractive woman.

"So you're the Jillian that Kurt mooned over in college. It's really nice to finally get to meet you. He's told me so many stories about all the fun your crowd had. Drake really sounds like quite a character. Is he here tonight? I'd love to meet...." She trailed off when she saw her husband making a face at her and shaking his head. "Did I say something wrong?" Jan asked, blushing.

"No," Jillian reassured her. "Drake and I are divorced. That's all. It's really a good thing. You didn't say anything wrong." She smiled to show that it wasn't a problem. They chatted a bit longer, and then Jillian saw Anna heading toward the kitchen with several empty trays. She excused herself to see if she could be of any help to their hostess.

"It's going well, don't you think?" Anna asked her, bustling about the kitchen, trying to refill the trays.

"It's a great success! There's a good mixture of people; they're all mingling. No one seems to be a wallflower. And the food is wonderful!" She hugged her friend reassuringly, then took one of the empty trays and began filling it.

"Are you having a good time?" Anna asked, concerned for her friend.

"Fabulous! I haven't seen some of these people in years! And you have some great neighbors and other friends." She smiled broadly at Anna.

Anna looked intently at Jillian to be sure she wasn't covering up her feelings. Satisfied, she handed her friend another filled tray and pushed her back toward the crowd.

People came and went, but a steady group was maintained right up until midnight. As they all counted down the seconds until the New Year, a glass of champagne in their hands, Jillian felt her first hint of unhappiness. She wished there was someone she could give a New Year's kiss to at midnight. Then she quickly chided herself and shouted, "Happy New Year!" along with everyone else. Outside there was the sound of firecrackers and even a gunshot. Jillian thought it had been a good year overall, and the new one would be even better, she promised herself.

CHAPTER 73

Jillian decided it was time to commit herself to completing her condo. She still had not bought a desk, there was nothing up on the walls, nor had she done anything with the third bedroom. Over the next couple of weekends, when she wasn't at the stable, she would try to make her place feel more like a home.

Sally invited Anna and Jillian over on Super Bowl Sunday to celebrate the end of football season. George was going to be at his brother's watching the game. Jillian made a walnut and coffee cream torte that she knew both her friends loved, but that she rarely made. Anna picked up a DVD. Sally made lasagna and salad.

The women settled themselves in the family room with the desert and coffee after eating the salad and lasagna. No one bothered to start the movie. There was plenty of time for that. They wanted to enjoy the absence of men and get in some much needed girl talk. The baby and her progress toward the major milestones of life took up much of their conversation. Sally showed off the most recent pictures of her daughter doing terribly cute baby things. Jillian smiled at her antics and felt a small pang of desire for a child of her own. But she had other things to take care of first, she reminded herself. Next, Anna brought out pictures from the New Year's Eve party and they all laughed about the adult antics.

"Do you remember David from John's work?" Anna asked Jillian, collecting the pictures as her friends finished with them.

"Vaguely. Skinny, dark hair?" Jillian's brow creased trying to recall the man's face.

"Yes, that's the one." She found a picture of him from the party and shoved it toward her friend. "He wants your phone number." Anna cocked an eyebrow at her friend, smiling knowingly.

"What for?" Jillian asked, leaning back against the cushions of the couch, her face wrinkled into a mask of confusion and surprise.

"You really have been out of circulation too long. To ask you out!" Sally chimed in, shaking her head at her obtuse friend.

"Oh…He's really not my type." Her face showed her distaste for the idea.

"So what. It's a date, not a marriage proposal," Sally exclaimed, pushing her friend's shoulder.

"You hardly know him. How do you know he's not your type?" Anna added.

"You have to get your feet wet sometime," Sally wheedled.

"I gave Ed my number," Jillian moaned defensively.

"That doesn't count. He lives in Pennsylvania and you did it just to put down his friend," Sally refuted that argument mercilessly.

Jillian sighed and made a conciliatory shrug. "True. I don't know what I'd do if he did call." She pulled her legs up onto the couch protectively.

"Go out with him?" Anna asked, tentatively, widening her eyes and wobbling her head as she looked at Jillian.

"Besides, you have to have a rebound affair," Sally pronounced, picking up her walnut torte and stabbing it with her fork.

"That's not funny." Jillian gave Sally a haughtily disapproving frown.

"You have everything going for you, and you whine about being alone. Now, you have men interested in you, and you're not interested." Sally shook her head in despair over her friend's attitude.

"I don't want to be alone, but..." Jillian trailed off, hugging a pillow for comfort.

"That's it. I'm telling John to give your number to David," Anna stated definitively.

"Anna, please...." Jillian turned to her friend, her eyes wide with anxiety.

"You're dating. I'm going to ask George if there's anyone at his work, too." Sally added.

"I don't want to go out on a blind date." Jillian looked back and forth at her two friends, pleading, "Isn't there any other way I can do this?" Seeing the determined expressions on both their faces, Jillian groaned and covered her face with the pillow.

Later in the week, Jillian received a call from David. She agreed to meet him at Starbucks for coffee late Saturday afternoon. She dressed in jeans and was surprised that she was not feeling the slightest bit nervous. She attributed it to the fact that she really was not interested in him, but was going to get Anna and Sally off her back. David was sitting at a table facing the door; he quickly jumped to his feet to greet her and escorted her to the order line. Conversation was awkward as they searched for some area of commonality. In the process, she discovered he was allergic to cats, dogs, horses, dust, and birds. He couldn't dance, but loved scrabble and computer games. The only thing they both enjoyed was chamber music. They couldn't even find a movie on which they agreed. After an hour, Jillian excused herself.

Jillian's workweek schedule continued to be full. Saturday mornings, she spent at the stable. She watched others riding in addition to her own lesson. Occasionally, she'd join some of the other riders for lunch, but usually she'd head home to get cleaned up. She felt she was riding much better and had started harassing Josie about putting her on a five-gaited horse.

One Saturday, as Jillian was dismounting after the group lesson, Josie approached her, "Are you in a rush today?"

"No, I don't have anything going on today," she responded, her curiosity piqued.

"Good. Do you want to ride an old five-gaited horse?" Josie asked, a small smirk tugging at her lips.

"Yes!" Jillian was so excited she grabbed her instructor by the shoulders and gently shook her.

"We'll tack her up for you about two." Josie went back into the ring to teach the next lesson.

Jillian went up to the lounge that overlooked the ring to have some coffee and watch the next class. As she started to pour the coffee, a familiar voice said, "It's stale."

"Ed! What are you doing here?" Jillian exclaimed in surprise as she turned toward the speaker.

"I came to look at a horse Josie wants to sell. I was watching you ride; you're really doing well." He smiled shyly at her.

"Thank you." Jillian blushed. "Josie's going to let me ride a five-gaited horse this afternoon."

"That's great. So you'll be hanging around for awhile?" he asked tentatively.

"Yes. She said about two." Jillian nodded and smiled.

"What are you doing for lunch?" he ventured, feeling a bit brave.

"I hadn't thought about it." She shrugged.

"Come on, let's get something to eat." He extended his hand to her.

"Uh...Okay." Jillian put the coffee pot down and took his hand.

The two went off to a local diner in Ed's SUV. Jillian was concerned that it would be uncomfortable, but she discovered that Ed was a good conversationalist. When it came to the horses, shows, and riders, he was very knowledgeable. She also enjoyed his quirky sense of humor. She could see how women would see him as a good friend. It was easy to be with him. Their two-hour lunch passed quickly. She realized she enjoyed spending time with him, but he was such a nice guy, she'd hate to mislead him.

They arrived back at the stable just in time for Jillian to mount a bay mare. Josie lengthened her stirrups, lowered her hands, and increased the separation between the snaffle and curb reins. She then had her walk and trot the mare for a while, loosening up the old horse and giving Jillian a chance to accustom herself to the changes in leg and hand positions. She then had her first experience of the slow gait, rack, and loping canter. She felt as though she were floating in the clouds. She became more determined than ever to buy her own five-gaited horse.

That night she tried to explain to Anna about the experience. While Anna indicated that she was happy for her, it was apparent to Jillian that her friend just didn't understand.

The very next day, Jillian received a call from Peter Burke. "Jillian? This is Peter Burke; I'm a friend of Michelle and John Daggett." He had a warm baritone voice.

"Uh...Oh, yes." Jillian felt her pulse quicken.

"This is kind of awkward, but Michelle has been insistent that I call you. ...I'm sorry. That must have sounded terrible. It's just that I've never been on a blind date before." Jillian could hear his discomfort.

"That's okay, neither have I, but..." She was trying to think of an excuse to avoid meeting him.

"Could we meet for coffee or something? You'll get Michelle off my back and, who knows, maybe she's right that we'd really hit it off." He laughed trying to ease the tension.

Jillian laughed, too. "Well, when you put it that way, how could I refuse?" She thought about getting Anna and Sally off her back. And she had to admit that she was a bit intrigued.

They finally settled on meeting at Starbucks the next Saturday afternoon. This time, Jillian was anxious about looking just right. She wanted to make a good impression; Michelle might have been right and, even if she were wrong, she didn't want Peter to give the Daggetts a bad report.

CHAPTER 74

Jillian hesitated as she walked through the doorway at Starbucks, looking around in an attempt to figure out who might be the doctor. A dark haired man in faded blue jeans and a long sleeved, light blue polo shirt approached, extending his hand. "Jillian?"

"Peter?" She stopped herself from immediately checking him out. What she could take in was very attractive, and he had a great smile.

They both started laughing. Jillian noticed a twinkle in his blue eyes as he laughed. She couldn't imagine why this man would need a blind date. She thought there must be nurses chasing him constantly. She instantly became wary and on alert for the flaw. However, after trying to find something objectionable about the man for two hours, all Jillian could conclude was that he was a real catch. They both enjoyed the same types of movies. Even if he wasn't totally enamored of romantic comedies, he liked a good "chick flick" once in a while, especially when with a woman he liked. They were both crazy about Asian cuisine and good Italian food. They shared the same taste in music, generally, and agreed on the best singers and musicians. Peter even liked dancing, although he stated he was not much on ballroom dancing. He reported that he had no pets of any kind at this point in his life, but he loved dogs and cats. He had thought about buying a ferret at one time, but his wife wouldn't have one in the house. He preferred furry pets to feathered or scaled, but he was open to other options as well. The main drawback to having pets for him was the number of hours he spent working. He felt it wasn't fair to an animal to be left alone for so long. While he had no great interest in horses, he said they were certainly beautiful and he was sure that riding was good exercise. Still, he added, he preferred a gym to the smell of a stable. She found that he was a good listener, as well.

"I can't imagine anyone letting you go," Peter stated, wanting to hear what her story was.

Jillian told him the basics of her history, ending with, "I finally accepted that I was not the one responsible for my husband's drinking. He was on self-destruct and he was taking me with him. I guess self-preservation finally kicked in." Jillian shrugged and sipped her third half-caf, double latte. "And you?"

"Time! I have very little of it. I guess my wife thought once med school was over I would, but it only got worse during my residency. I still don't have any." He shook his head and sighed, looking a bit sad.

"That's good." Jillian laughed when she saw the look of confusion on Peter's face and realized how it must have sounded. "It's just that I don't have a lot of free time either. Between work and the horses, and now I'm thinking about going for my MBA part-time, if I can get the bank to pay for it."

Peter started nodding. "That's great. I appreciate ambition." He looked at his watch and appeared amazed at the amount of time that had passed. "Wow! We've been talking for over two hours. It seems like we just sat down, except my legs are going to sleep. May I call you again?"

"I'd like that," Jillian agreed readily, collecting her things and rising. They said good-bye at her car. She was surprised to find herself singing along with the radio on the way home and laughed at herself. She hoped Peter would find the time to call soon.

Two weeks later, they were able to agree on an evening they both had free. They had a relaxing dinner at a downtown restaurant. Jillian was happy to see that Peter drank only one glass of wine with dinner and didn't seem compelled to empty the carafe before they left. After dinner, they went to a popular club in northern Kentucky to go dancing. Peter was light on his feet and had a sense of rhythm. His movements were masculine, but graceful. Jillian enjoyed watching him dance. When a slow song was played, she liked the feel of his arms around her and his body moving against her. It was all very pleasant, but she had to admit, there was no electricity there. They had no problem with long awkward pauses in their conversation. Peter was very bright and knew how to ask questions about her work that encouraged her to respond in depth. He was very willing to talk about his work as well. They both had fun laughing and joking throughout the evening. When it was finally time to go, Jillian felt comfortable with Peter taking her arm when they left the club.

Peter walked Jillian to her door. After having slow danced, it seemed natural when he took her in his arms. The kiss was slow and gentle. As Jillian closed the door, she smiled happily. There were no chills, no tingling, but a warm pleasant contentment filled her. She reflected how it might be better if there were no chills, at least for now. Her visceral responses to Drake had interfered with her judgment from the beginning. She had mistaken the chills, the tingling, and the sense of familiarity for passion when, in reality, it had only been recognition and recall. It was nice to have someone she felt comfortable with in her life again, but not taking over her life. It was pleasant to converse, knowing that her words as well as her body were appreciated.

Still smiling and humming one of the slow songs from the evening, she turned off the lights and headed to bed. It had been only a first date, but it gave her hope that someone could chase the loneliness away, someone who could stand on his own two feet and love her standing on her own two feet. She knew that she was now ready to face the future that would find her and that she would shape. She didn't need to rescue anyone any longer. At last, she was free to be herself and to grow as a person. She had an interesting new man in her life and a promising career that she really loved. Life looked very appealing to Jillian for the first time in many years. As she curled up in bed, snuggling against her pillows, she sighed with contentment and with a sense of happiness that had been long delayed. *Yes, life is good,* she muttered as she drifted off into sleep with a smile still on her face.

AUTHOR'S NOTE

The authors have attempted to present an accurate account of life in nineteenth century America. Descriptions of food, clothing, furnishings, transportation, and entertainment are representative of the time. Specific descriptions of the churches, businesses, streets, and homes in Beaufort are correct.

The names of some of the characters are actual historical persons; however, their lives as presented are largely, if not completely fictitious. None of the other characters in this book is a real person. The political events of the time have been presented with as much accuracy as possible. The language used within dialogs approximates that used at the time and was gathered from published diaries, "Journal of a Residence on a Georgian Plantation in 1838-1839" by Frances Anne Kemble, edited by John A. Scott, 1984, by Brown Thrasher Books, The University of Georgia Press, Athens, and "Mary Chestnut's Civil War" by Mary Chestnut, edited by C. Vann Woodward, 1981, by Yale University Press. While Gullah would have been spoken by the African-Americans of the South amongst themselves at that time, it was felt attempts at reproducing it would have been more distracting than beneficial to the reader's understanding of the period.

Join Jillian on her continuing adventure in "Whispers in the Tall Grasses."

CHAPTER 1

As spring came to Cincinnati, 29 year old Jillian White seemed to have it all. She was extremely busy at Midwest Bank where her work was becoming more and more engrossing. She was building connections and confidence, and finally felt that she deserved the salary she was making.

Since her divorce, she had tried to fill her time with things she enjoyed. For the first time since she'd met her ex-husband, she was taking care of herself. Jillian was 5'6'', with long dark brown hair and emerald green eyes. She was pleased that she had not only maintained her trim figure, after losing weight following her divorce, but had also toned her muscles with her activities. Weeknights, she went to the gym to work out or attend yoga classes.

Jillian had been dating the handsome and extremely eligible Dr. Peter Burke for nearly two months. This delighted Jillian's mother, but was not exactly an ideal situation for Jillian. Peter was busy building his practice and had little free time. This suited Jillian in that she had developed a lifestyle that left her little time for dating or for a relationship. Initially, the schedule was an attempt to avoid the loneliness, but she had come to enjoy her schedule of activities. Although Jillian was willing to occasionally miss a night at the gym for a special occasion, she refused to change her Wednesday night riding lesson and Peter couldn't understand what he called her "obsession." Still, they had fun together and shared many of the same interests.

Yet, while everything was going so well in her life, she was still lonely. She had told no one, not even her best friends, Sally and Anna; she didn't believe they would understand. Since meeting in college, they'd been there for her through her loss of self throughout her caring for her ex-husband, Drake, her painful marriage, and divorce.

It would be easy to adapt her schedule and lifestyle to spend more time with Peter. She had contemplated doing just that in the hope he would drive away the loneliness. However, it wasn't just that Peter wanted nothing to do with the horses and could not understand her love of them--he would not object or interfere with her riding--but rather that she could not see herself with him forever. Their relationship had not chased away her fear of being alone; the fear was too deep. She could not understand where it came from, but she knew that it had paralyzed her in the past and that it kept her running in the present.

As the horse show season started up, her excitement about attending more shows overcame her disappointment about not being able to ride many Saturdays when her instructor, Josie, would be away. She was not interested in competing herself, but she enjoyed watching the process and was proud of the riders from Misty Glen when they did well. Jillian wondered how Peter would react to her going away for a weekend by herself. She enjoyed his company and hoped he would be tolerant; but she knew she'd go whether he was or not. It was part of the reason she knew she and Peter would not last. The fact of the matter was she would rather spend a day at a horse show than be with him and was willing to lose him over it.

She fought down the fear. What if no one else came along? What if she ended up alone? She didn't believe she could bear such a fate, and wondered if she was making up her mind about Peter too quickly. She liked him, but how could she have strong feelings for him when she hardly knew him? She only wished she could understand and heal the intense sadness that arose whenever she felt alone. It made no sense to her; she only knew she feared and dreaded it.

Jillian casually mentioned to Peter that she would be away the weekend after next to go to a horse show, and was relieved when Peter did not seem concerned. She was not ready for a confrontation and not sure she was strong enough to let go of the relationship. When she tried to bring up the confusion she was experiencing to Sally, the advice she received ignored her feelings, suggesting she forget about the horses and the past, but hang on to Peter.

Well, she consoled herself, *Sally was always the pragmatic, cut to the chase type. She focused on practical matters.* Jillian knew that her feelings were not something she could be pragmatic about. She refused to get into another long-term relationship that wasn't right for her, one that would make her forget her own needs and desires, and was angry that Sally couldn't understand after what she had been through with Drake. If she wanted someone to empathize with her, it would have to be Anna. She called her friend and arranged to meet for lunch with her.

The two friends made small talk until they had placed their orders, and then, picking up her iced coffee, Anna looked at Jillian and said, "Okay, what's eating you? You look like a month of rainy Mondays."

Jillian laughed humorlessly. "I didn't realize it was that apparent. It's really kind of silly, I guess. I've got what almost anyone would say is a great life. I even think it's a great life, but I'm still not happy. And I don't know why." She sighed and reached for her coffee.

"Have you got any idea what you're unhappy about?" her friend probed.

"I have this...irrational is the only word for it...this irrational fear of being alone. It's ridiculous. I'm almost never alone. Most of my time is filled with doing things I love. It's as if I'm looking for something I've lost, something I had, but don't have now," she explained, waving her hand at the nebulous thoughts that plagued her.

"Do you think this is still about your past life as Ellie?" Anna asked, referring to Jillian's recovered memories of a life lived during the Civil War. They had talked a lot about Jillian's previous incarnation as Ellie and her relationship with her fiancé, Ted. Jillian had realized it was that life that had held her in her unhappy marriage to Drake.

"No,...it's not that. At least, it's not about Ted and Ellie. But that's as much as I can say for certain. It has the feel of that kind of loss, however, only much worse. I just can't put my finger on it. I just fear that I will live out my life alone and die alone. And the feeling creeps up on me when I'm least expecting it." She looked up at Anna, hoping her friend would be able to give her some direction or suggestion.

Anna looked down at the table in contemplation, fiddling with her knife. "I wonder what happened to Ellie after Ted died. We don't know what happened to the family during the war. We don't know if Ellie ever married or how she ended up. I think that might be important information to find out, don't you?" Anna cocked her head and looked up at her friend.

Jillian nodded, feeling as if she finally had some way to deal with her problematic emotions. "It might be worth looking into. Heaven knows, there's nothing in this life that should be making me feel this way." She found she was able to smile at Anna. "Thanks for the suggestion. I knew there was a reason I kept you around." Both friends laughed with some relief and proceeded to enjoy their lunch, talking and eating.

12770891R00182

Made in the USA
Charleston, SC
26 May 2012